The Ghosts of Paris

The Ghosts of Paris

A Novel

Tara Moss

DUTTON

DUTTON
An imprint of Penguin Random House LLC
penguinrandomhouse.com

LIBRARY OF CONGRESS CATALOGING-IN-PUBLICATION DATA
has been applied for.

ISBN 9780593182680 (hardcover)
ISBN 9780593182697 (ebook)

Printed in the United States of America
1st Printing

BOOK DESIGN BY ELKE SIGAL

For Janni, always remembered

The Ghosts of Paris

Prologue

—⁂—

He pressed back against brick and stone, arms over his head, shielding himself as the buildings shook and the earth beneath him rumbled.

When the blast subsided and he opened his eyes, the square was shrouded in white dust and ash, a sight both curiously beautiful and chilling, as tiny fragments of the town and the people in it spread like unearthly snow all round. This was not destruction from a single grenade, that comparatively tiny, violent salvo of resistance, nor was this from the Nazis' devastating Goliath tracked mines. For days the west of the city had been raided and torched, residents shot on the spot or tortured for information, and so he knew this ash was not only the remains of building and concrete, but also the remains of those who had perished within the village square during days of tireless massacre. The *Verbrennungskommando*, the burning detachment, was destroying evidence of the massacre here, and so his photographs, if he could smuggle them out, would matter all the more. He tried not to breathe in the deathly smoke, tried not to let it inside him. Over the past two days he had not eaten, had barely found a sip of water, and he was almost glad somehow, as the stench in the air would surely have made him retch.

There had been shouting and movement, a grenade explosion, and now the noises stopped, a kind of respite to match the eerie, slowly falling ash. He wiped his face, raised his camera.

Crouching, he moved forward on one knee. It was not safe. None of this was safe. Just a few more shots and he would retreat to the makeshift shelter inside the bombed-out building behind him, the building that for now obscured his presence, and that of his ever-present camera. But he would have to find a safer place before the dogs were let loose to see out survivors to be killed. Already half his focus was on escaping with his photographs. He had been in tight situations before, smuggling film out in empty toothpaste tubes, but this, he feared, was yet more serious. How would he do it? The conflict had quickly revealed itself to be a homegrown uprising of Polish rebels against a well-planned and -resourced Nazi mission of outright extermination. The German soldiers were killing all citizens, all witnesses. If they found him, they would not let him live. That, he knew.

Makeshift barricades constructed of torn-up and shattered flagstones had been manned by several young Polish boys with rifles and homemade grenades and bombs—one of which, no doubt, had caused the latest blast—but as the dust cleared, he noticed that the brave boys were nowhere to be seen, their modest supply against the Wehrmacht, Dirlewanger Brigade "Black Hunters," and SS Police Battalions doubtless spent. He seemed alone in the bloody square, though he doubted that was the case. Had the resistance—such as they were after five years of occupation and days of nonstop fighting—retreated to where they had a better stronghold, the square now ceded? The dusty air that moments before had been alive with bullets, boots, and ash had now settled, it seemed, to make way for something greater, something slow and menacing. He heard the heavy crunch of tracks moving over the ground and knew instantly what it was. There was shouting in German, but he could not make out the words. From somewhere came a woman's screams, disturbingly urgent and clear in the temporary quiet. A new rumbling grew louder.

Something was coming.

A German tank moved into the square, gun first. It was a mighty Tiger II, weighing nearly seventy tons, moving right into the line of sight of his Argus camera. The massive machine, with its brutal gun turret, thundered steadily into the square, toward the makeshift barricades, lumbering inelegantly over each bump like a great impenetrable beast, crushing everything in its path. No barricade would be equal to it. He pushed his back into the dusty building again and his shutter clicked, clicked again. He brought the camera down from his face.

No, he was not mistaken. There was something hanging on the front of the tank. Something tied there.

Not something, *someone*.

A woman.

It was her screams he had heard—a woman in civilian dress, tethered by the wrists to the huge gun, her body dwarfed by its size and stretched out, legs pulled back and secured by the ankles to either side of the front of the tank. Her dress was dirty and torn, her white face twisted in horror and framed by lank brown hair. Petite and terrified, she might have been fourteen or forty, a mother or a child. All he saw was primal terror in her large, dark eyes. Again, her screams filled the square, far above the din of the tank's infernal rumbling.

The sound proved too much.

Before he'd even begun to comprehend his actions, begun to form a plan, he foolishly rushed forward, hands outstretched, his Argus swinging awkwardly at his side, momentarily forgotten. He crossed the square in seconds and leaped onto the front of the massive, slow-moving monolith, which would not pause for him, not for anyone save its master at the helm. Caught in a kind of temporary madness, he tore at the ropes that bound the struggling woman with a singular focus. Once he had freed her left ankle, she twisted in place and gestured to her other ankle. *"Tamten!"* she shouted in Polish. *That one!* He had to get the other next or she could fall face-first before the tank and be crushed under it. He tore at the binds and heard the great hull opening, a soldier shouting.

There was no time; the soldier was climbing out and reaching for his pistol.

From the corner of his eye, he caught the movement as the woman—she was indeed an adult woman, perhaps in her twenties, he realized—swung herself nimbly upward onto the mammoth gun with a grunt of effort and locked her dirt-streaked legs around it. She was hanging upside down beneath the gun, and, despite his own dangerous position, he watched as if mesmerized as she inched herself forward with surprising speed and a survivor's will, as nimble as any acrobatic performer, until her secured wrists slipped off the end of the giant gun and she fell backward, swimming in the air, dress and hair hanging, suspended by her legs, the ropes now loose and no longer binding her. With a mechanical grinding the gun turret moved to the left, taking her with it, and she let go, throwing herself from the giant tank, then disappearing from view.

There was a pistol shot, then another, and reality came back to him with a crash as he realized how exposed he was, the precariousness of his position on the enemy tank. He turned to jump but was not fast enough; the Nazi soldier was faster, and as he hurled himself off the tank's side he was caught across the neck, body jerking back and upward, killing all breath, a sick, gurgling sound in his ears. He hung like a rag doll from the side of the tank by his own leather camera strap, and the mighty Tiger II continued through the square, gun roving, the great beast not halting, not even slowing.

Desperately, he clutched the strap at his neck, frantic for air, and saw blood on his fingers, his hands. It was his own, he realized. The strap of his camera was cutting in, his neck opening up. There was shouting in German, another pistol shot, and the world went black.

One

—⚏—

On May Day, the client walked into the offices of B. Walker Private Inquiries, announced by a faint buzzer. Billie Walker heard this from her position at her small sixth-floor balcony, where she'd been smoking a Lucky Strike and regarding, with a well-honed emotional detachment, the safety bridge that connected Daking House to Station House. She heard the door, heard the little buzzer, heard her secretary-cum-assistant welcome the stranger, their voices muffled by the closed connecting door, and took a long drag. On the slow exhale, smoke floated from Billie's red lips, creating a temporary haze across her view of the city streets.

Cigarette dangling, Billie turned, closed the balcony doors behind her, and walked to the oval mirror on the wall inside her office. She checked her emerald tilt hat and red lipstick in one quick and practiced movement, regarded the steady blue-green eyes staring back at her in the reflection, and, satisfied, made for the corner of her wide wooden desk and stubbed out the last of her fag. Smoke drifted upward, settling in the air. The Bakelite clock above her door informed her that this potential client was right on time. This one had made an appointment, though Billie had not been furnished with any information regarding the nature of her query, complaint, or troubles, only a surname. Things having improved at Billie's humble agency in recent months, Ms. Walker—the B. of B. Walker Private Inquiries and the principal agent—no longer had to wait out long days for the phone to ring or a knock at the door, and, for the moment at least, did not need to contemplate the empty walnut chairs in the small waiting room and find odd jobs for her secretary to do. Business was booming for Sydney's most famous—or was it infamous?—female inquiry agent.

Billie smoothed down her skirt suit, opened the connecting door, and leaned against the open doorframe to take in the stranger who had entered her waiting room. She did so hope this wasn't another divorce job.

"Ah, here she is now. May I present Ms. Billie Walker," Samuel Baker, her tall secretary, announced, right on cue. "Ms. Walker, this is Mrs. Richard Montgomery."

She still had no first name of her own, Billie thought. Shame.

Amusingly, the woman's gaze was fixed on Billie's secretary in his lightly pin-striped suit and flattering tie of burgundy and sky blue that brought out his baby blues. A flirtatious smile played on the older woman's painted lips as she regarded him. To be true, Sam was a pleasing sight. He was a strapping Australian lad whose experience of the war had left him changed, most notably his injured left hand, which was always covered in a leather glove, lending him a touch of mystery. That hand had come up against an Italian thermos bomb and was now missing a few fingers, replaced by wooden prosthetics. Sam had already proved himself invaluable on numerous occasions, so if Billie had his injury to thank for the fact that he was happy to work for her, well, the army's loss was her gain. He didn't mind taking orders from a woman—far too rare a trait, in her opinion—and his trigger hand was as whole and steady as you could ask for. It was a bonus that he was something like Alan Ladd in appearance, though far taller, and built several ax handles across, as the saying went.

As Sam provided a handsome distraction, Billie took in the woman's appearance quickly and efficiently, observing cues drilled into her from work as an inquiry agent and before that as a war reporter, and a childhood spent listening to her father, Barry Walker, the policeman turned private investigator who had inhabited these very offices, sitting at that wide wooden desk and smoking on that same small balcony where his only child now spent her moments of contemplation. *Always look at the shoes,* he would say. *The fit and quality of the suit. The timepiece. The hat. Look at the eyes. Each detail tells a story.* Indeed it did.

At a trained glance, this woman's story appeared to be one of style and apparent luxury—not something one saw in great abundance since the war. The suede burgundy shoes were new and well crafted, the stockings nylon and without flaw. (Billie suspected this woman had never had to stoop to painting her legs with gravy and drawing a line up the back with eye pencil to create the illusion of stockings, as so many had.) The Akoya pearl set she wore was delicate and quite real, Billie was sure, that particularly desirable luster not being possible in the new fakes. Her navy skirt suit was notable for being of the latest style, echoing the scandalously feminine silhouette of Christian Dior's "New Look" that had taken the fashion world by storm months before: softly rounded shoulders, nipped waist, a slightly fuller skirt falling to mid-calf—not quite full enough to cause outrage on the streets of Sydney, rationing still being in place, but enough to set this woman apart as a specimen of fashion, a local doyenne of the Parisian trend. Yes, it set her apart, as did the genuine high-quality glass-eyed fox stole she wore around her shoulders. This was no prewar throwback.

Mrs. Montgomery somehow had her finger on the pulse of international fashion trends and had money and the tailors to pull it off for her. Billie rather wanted to get a name. One thing was for certain: This was a woman of means, and that impression was confirmed by the crowning glory of her engagement ring, which was more than a carat, Billie's trained eye told her, and completely overshadowed the comparatively simple wedding ring worn with it.

"Pleased to make your acquaintance, Mrs. Montgomery," Billie said, and meant it, satisfied that she was attracting the kind of clientele whose checks were unlikely to bounce like rubber. She lifted her shoulder off the doorframe and smiled, locking eyes with the Joan Crawford–esque beauty. Mrs. Montgomery had large eyes in a strong, rectangular face, her gaze direct and framed by dyed red hair worn short across the forehead and swept back in a center part beneath a flat, tilted navy hat. It was the face of a strong-willed woman of high standards.

"Won't you come into my office?" Billie said, and turned on her stacked Oxford heel. She disappeared inside and the woman followed in the investigator's wake, her posture erect and proud, eyes flicking back to Sam, who was trailing just behind. If he was bothered by the woman's flirtatious gaze, he didn't let on.

The office Billie Walker welcomed this fashionable stranger into was not the kind of surrounds where Mrs. Montgomery would seem, under normal circumstances, to belong. Though Billie was not exactly unglamorous herself, with the striking contrast of her dark hair and pale skin, and her Tussy's Fighting Red lipstick, the utilitarian office suited her like a battered trench coat or well-traveled uniform. It was a place of action, with Billie herself a devotee of action, as the war years and more recent events as an inquiry agent attested.

Fashion was something she enjoyed and employed in her profession to gain entry to all echelons of society, but her office had very few frills about it. Her aristocratic mother, if she ever again deigned to lower herself enough to grace those four walls with her presence, would complain the place "lacked a woman's touch," despite the space now being occupied by Billie and her so far exclusively female clientele. Billie had left it much the same as when her late father had operated his agency. The carpets were rust red, the filing cabinets a fading hunter green, the wooden desk appropriately scarred, all of it imbued with the sense of his presence, now further layered by this new generation of Walker investigator. The only concessions to its new occupant were the placement of the handy mirror, a small bottle of Bandit perfume on a shelf, some personal photographs, and the addition of a few of the more fashionable women's journals in the waiting room. The place suited Billie well, as if her late father had lovingly worn it in for her.

Sam plugged the doorway to the office, waiting, knowing the next part of this client ritual well.

"Would you care for tea, Mrs. Montgomery?" Billie asked, once the woman was comfortably seated across the desk in the chair she reserved for clients.

"Thank you kindly," she replied, and broad-shouldered Sam disappeared, gently closing the door behind him with a barely audible click. Billie had seen him throw full-grown men across an alley with his good hand, but he played down his physical size and strength in situations such as this, his strategic invisibility well practiced.

Mrs. Montgomery—who had taken the time to watch Sam go—was now surveying the space around her. Although such roughly finished spaces did not seem her natural habitat, she showed no signs of disappointment. Perhaps, if she'd been living as a bird in the proverbial gilded cage—as was one theory Billie was forming—more salubrious surrounds would not be comforting in this moment. Something had brought her out of her natural habitat and into Billie's.

"Are you the only woman investigator in Sydney?" Mrs. Montgomery asked.

"Sometimes," Billie said, and leaned one elbow on the wooden desk. One of her competitors was currently in jail for some petty matter, nothing to do with Billie, of course. Her main competition came from male investigators, however. They dominated the trade, and always had. In fact, much of her post still arrived for Mr. B. Walker, as if the fact of her obvious femininity was not quite enough to overcome the assumption that the principal at a private inquiry agency would be a grizzled gentleman gumshoe.

"How may I be of assistance today?" Billie asked.

"You assisted a friend of mine, Nettie Brown, you may recall," the woman began.

Billie did recall. That had been in late 1946, almost six eventful months before, and had begun as a seemingly routine missing person case, a search for Nettie's seventeen-year-old son, and evolved into something far larger and more sinister. She resisted looking again toward her smoking balcony, even while a vivid image of the Nazi who had flung himself over it flashed through her memory. Yes, she did indeed recall the case. A fair bit of Sydney did, also.

"Nettie was quite impressed by you. She recommended you rather highly," the woman went on.

"That is pleasing to hear."

Billie's gaze moved to the glass-eyed fox around Mrs. Montgomery's shoulders, as if it could tell her that it had been purchased at the Brown family's fur shop at the Strand Arcade. Her muscles had tensed at the memory of the case. There had been a good outcome, but not without shots fired, and lives altered and lost. But then, she and trouble knew each other rather intimately. No reason the end of the war would stop such a seemingly natural pairing, she supposed.

"I understand you spoke with her a few months ago?" Mrs. Montgomery continued.

"Yes," Billie replied.

She had, in fact, run into Mrs. Nettie Brown, in the literal sense, under quite the most extraordinary circumstances on New Year's Day. It had been a frightfully humid day, and just as Billie was having her semi-regular afternoon tea with her informant Shyla at the Central Railway Refreshment Room, a freak hailstorm had hit, assaulting Sydney from the skies with considerable violence. The clock face above the station was smashed, and the skylight along the entire main assembly platform had been decimated, raining shards of glass on those below. To Billie it had sounded like a squadron of bombers, and those who had been there could be forgiven for thinking it the return of the Blitz. Fortunately, most of the waiting commuters had only recently been whisked away on their various journeys.

In the midst of this maelstrom, Billie had sprinted from the refreshment room to determine the cause of the thunderous crashing—always the type to run toward chaos and not away from it—and Nettie Brown had run straight into her, head on. After a moment of shocked recognition, the women had sheltered together by the central concourse until the storm passed. Their somewhat bruising meeting had felt peculiarly like foreshadowing at the time. The case for the Brown family was officially closed, but loose ends niggled at Billie, never quite letting her go despite the passing months, and it seemed the powers that be weren't keen on releasing her, either. She only hoped those loose ends weren't weaving themselves into a noose, for her or for someone else.

The year 1947 had announced itself with a bang. Billie had almost been waiting for this follow-up.

"The case quickly faded from the headlines, which was a small miracle," Mrs. Montgomery continued when Billie offered nothing more. The Browns would not have liked the publicity. And the case had faded from the headlines, but not before making a considerable impression.

"Yes, though I'm afraid I can't claim responsibility for such miracles. I'm not that powerful," Billie remarked of the press eventually moving on.

Mrs. Montgomery frowned. "Nettie assured me you can be discreet."

"Discretion I *can* guarantee, Mrs. Montgomery. Discretion is an important aspect of my work. Had I had it my way, the Browns' case never would have made the papers at all, but once a Nazi war criminal is involved, there's no holding the papers back."

"He's the one who . . ." Mrs. Montgomery trailed off, lifting a manicured hand toward the now-closed balcony doors, one finger extended for a moment, before curling back, as if broaching the subject might have been too vulgar.

Billie nodded, pushing away the rather too vivid memory.

The Bakelite clock above the doorway ticked. Billie's prospective client shifted in her chair and seemed for a moment to sink into the embrace of the deceased fox wrapped around her shoulders, as if it could comfort her.

"The public's appetite for a grisly story is always ripe," Billie said, offering that morsel of truth to ease an uncomfortable silence. "But they move on. There's always something else to catch their attention. I can't claim any credit for steering them away." The case had steered new cases to Billie's agency, however. The women of Sydney had come knocking, and now here she was, gainfully employed for the first time since the war. For many women, the war had been a time that had first provided the independence of a proper wage, modest or otherwise. That Billie's agency was doing a roaring trade now, after so many women were again out of work, was a stroke of luck for Billie, but that winning streak was not guaranteed to continue. Billie was becoming rather concerned that she would soon run out of disgruntled wives, having aided so many through her offices. How many more could there be in one city?

Not that it appeared Mrs. Montgomery would be able to relate to the financial worries of single workingwomen.

"I am at your service, Mrs. Montgomery, and you have my discretion. Nothing you tell me will leave this room without your blessing," she said, hoping to move things along.

"It gives me no pleasure to be here, you understand," Mrs. Montgomery admitted. "Oh, no offense."

"None taken. Like dentists, perhaps, few revel in our professional presence, but we are a necessary evil, you could say." *If you don't want the rotting tooth to fester—or the rotten marriage—and eventually take the whole patient with it.*

There was a gentle knock at the door, and Sam appeared with a tray, upon which two teacups and the necessary accoutrements were neatly assembled. This felt like good timing. The woman had still not given a single clue as to the reason for her appointment, and Billie was starting to become impatient. In her experience there were two types of clients: the kind who came in with a rush of tears and stories rolling off the tongue, and this type, reticent or hard to read. Anything might be on Mrs. Richard Montgomery's mind, though the impression of the bird in the gilded cage still clung to this woman. What had made her fly the coop, if that's what this was?

Was there a job on offer, or not? Billie had been busy, but there was a worrying hole in her calendar coming up. She could use a touch more security from well-heeled clients such as this one.

"Sugar?" Billie offered, and the woman nodded. She prepared a cup and pushed it across. "Now, if you will, how may I be of service?"

The Joan Crawford jaw flexed, relaxed. The woman took a sip of her tea, decided something, and those bright, glinting eyes fell on Billie with a different intensity. "It's a delicate matter. You see, my husband is a very wealthy man, and he . . . well, he likes his little adventures."

"I see." *A divorce case, then.*

Some part of Billie shrank, but then again she was the one who had decided to reopen her father's inquiry agency. Divorce work came with the turf.

"You are perhaps wondering where his adventures have led him?" Billie suggested gently. This was a frequent complaint for the clients who entered Billie's office. "Another woman?"

"Undoubtedly," Mrs. Montgomery replied. "Perhaps several. Or I believe there was."

"Was?" *Past tense.*

"Miss Walker, my husband hasn't been heard from in almost two years. That is an awfully long time."

"Indeed it is," Billie agreed.

"You see, he's an advertising man, quite successful, and some government department—what do they call it again?—the Bureau of Information, well, they got him to help them out with their war efforts and so on."

Billie had heard of the department, though she didn't know a great deal about it. From what she did know, its bureaucrats were responsible for the promotion and advertisement of war bonds, government propaganda, and censorship of information.

"There was this *Australia in Peace and War* exposition in Paris, you see, just a couple of months after Victory in Europe Day, and nothing would have it but to send him all the way over for that. It was the jewel in the crown of the department, this exposition, and he was—or is—one of their top men. He flew to London—he hails from there—and then arrived in Paris a week or two later with the rest of the men. He wrote to me from the hotel there—the Ritz Paris, a very fine hotel. He seems to have done his work for them and then just . . . vanished. After that letter nothing else came, and there was no word of his return. I was not alarmed at first, but it is unlike him to not send *any* letters at all, so when there was no second letter, and time stretched on, I became worried. I have contacts in Paris"—Billie had guessed this, and now she nodded—"but they tell me they haven't heard from him. Naturally, I contacted the Bureau of Information, which wasn't altogether as easy as I'd expected, and they said he didn't work for them. I mean, *really*," she said, aghast. "It was quite galling. The advertising firm he works for said he was working for the department, and round and round it went."

"The Bureau of Information denied that he worked for them?" Billie asked, intrigued.

"They told me my Richard had completed his employment and he no longer worked for them. Yet the advertising firm said he'd left them to work for the department."

"I see. And how long ago was this?"

"A few months after the exposition, toward the end of '45. At first I thought he was . . . well, just being Richard. But I did become concerned."

"Of course."

Mrs. Montgomery watched Billie's face carefully. "You mustn't judge me, Miss Walker," she said. "My Richard is a good man of sterling reputation. He works hard, and naturally a man of his status and demanding workload deserves a certain amount of . . . freedom. He's very . . . masculine, a leader. So, you see, although some may find my attitude shocking, it's the only way to ensure harmony in our marriage. We had an understanding."

Billie nodded and leaned forward, meeting the woman's large eyes. "You do not need to defend yourself, or your marriage, to me, I can assure you of that." If there was one thing Billie had learned in life, and certainly in the course of her work, it was that marriages took many different forms. "Judgment is not my job, and I don't trouble myself with it. My job is to find your husband, if you choose to employ my services for the purpose."

Mrs. Montgomery's shoulders dropped beneath the rounded contour of her tailored suit. "Thank you," she said simply.

Billie leaned back and thought for a moment. "How much did your husband discuss the scope of his employment with you? The aim of his work at the exposition, his day-to-day, and that sort of thing?"

"We never discussed work or financial matters," Mrs. Montgomery replied, shaking her head adamantly, as if this non-communication on issues of finance was a wifely virtue. "Richard was the man of the house. That was his role. His work was his own affair. He was a good provider, Miss Walker."

Billie had no reason to disbelieve her. "Have you any employment, Mrs. Montgomery? Any—"

"Certainly not," she shot back before Billie could finish. The very idea seemed to aggrieve her.

"Of course," Billie replied, keeping her expression even. This view was commonplace; if a woman like this worked, it was thought it was because her husband was not an adequate provider, not for reasons of human need, independence, or personal fulfillment.

Mrs. Montgomery paused, perhaps realizing the implication of her views. "No offense," she added again, looking around Billie's office. "Some women are *forced* to work, I understand."

Billie held her tongue. After all, she couldn't claim she didn't have to work, but it hadn't always been simply for necessity. Puzzles enlivened her, and the work she did during the war as a reporter . . . Well, she was proud of what she'd achieved. In truth, she didn't much savor the idea of a life without some mystery to solve. Not for her was the bliss of ignorance. Billie wanted to know what was happening below the surface—and there always was something.

"If your husband returned to Australia, as seemed to originally be the plan, in your opinion is there any possibility he could have entered the country without your being aware?" Billie did her best to read this potential client, who she hoped would not be insulted by this suggestion. "Please understand this question is one of logistics," she decided to add. "I am not casting aspersions on your relationship with your husband."

Mrs. Montgomery appeared to consider this. "I think I understand what you mean." She took a sip of her tea, frowning, and contemplated something. "The fact is, my Richard never liked to keep a low profile, so I'd say yes, I would simply have known if he was in Australia this whole time. Yes, absolutely." The Crawford jaw flexed as she considered her errant husband. "I don't believe my Richard could return to Australia without my knowing, certainly not for this long, and certainly not to Sydney. And he wouldn't have any reason to. I never kept him on a tight leash. It just wasn't like that." She shook her head for good measure. "No, he simply doesn't know how to keep a low profile, even if he were motivated to."

Was he motivated to? Billie wondered. Many men had returned from the war in secret, to live out solitary lives in the Australian bush, too psychologically damaged by war to face society or the lives they had once known, or unwilling or unable to endure the uncomfortable stares of neighbors and pointing of children at scars and war wounds they could not hide. But this woman's husband had gone missing in Paris just *after* the end of the war in Europe. He wasn't involved in combat that they were aware of, and there was unlikely to be a great deal of danger in his particular line of work. It didn't fit.

"And what have you done in the intervening years?" Billie asked gently.

"I won't mince words, Miss Walker. I have been fairly comfortable, though bothered by the mystery of it." She paused, and Billie wondered if this woman's pride was somewhat more injured than her heart, but then, after so long, one had to find ways to cope. Billie knew that more intimately than she'd like to.

"It did me no favors socially, I can say. It seemed to others at first that I was a deserted wife," Mrs. Montgomery added. "However, in time most assumed he had passed on. It became accepted that I might be a widow. After all, there are so many widows nowadays. I guess part of me accepted that, too."

"Is that what you believe?" Billie asked.

"Well, I don't quite know what to believe," she replied, and at face value Billie sensed she was being honest about that. "After a time I went to the usual agencies, naturally, the constabulary, the Red Cross, but I'm afraid it hasn't been much help. Well, it hasn't been any help at all, frankly, and the whole thing is such a frustration, especially now." She swallowed, and Billie wondered if she detected a flicker of guilt. "Without some evidence of his adultery, or a certificate of death . . ."

"You will remain married, and unable to move on. Should you wish to," Billie added.

Mrs. Montgomery nodded. She seemed a determined woman who knew what she wanted, and often got it, Billie wagered. Forced to remain married while abandoned would be an unsuitable status quo for such a woman, particularly one who considered a wage beneath her, or a sign of failure. That gilded cage may have been fine for a while, but it had surely tarnished with time. It would be getting lonely in there.

Billie leaned back and quite inconveniently cast her eyes over one of the photographs on her wooden desk. It was *that* photograph—the one in the small frame. It had been an unconscious impulse to look at it, the image she had taken of Jack in Vienna. In the image Jack was smiling, and his smile was intoxicating, eyes alive with the irresistible chemistry that had erupted between them like a bright flame. This was the weekend they'd fallen in love, before the war had begun, before the world had been irretrievably altered, and long before their makeshift wedding and her father's sudden passing that followed, taking her far from him and their work together. Her husband was just as he looked in those flashes that haunted her each time she closed her eyes. That smile. Those hazel eyes. That lean, tanned face. And those lips she had kissed for untold stolen hours, locked in embraces in bombed-out buildings, hearing shells in the distance.

Jack Rake. Sitting up, Billie averted her eyes and swallowed. It was only the tiniest movement of her throat, a subtle sign that this conversation was a touch close to home. Someone who knew her well might have caught it—her mother would have—but not this stranger, who was quite understandably caught in her own thoughts about her marital troubles. Billie's bread and butter was missing husbands, and cheating husbands. That Billie's own husband was missing was something she hardly needed reminding of. With all the war had done, there was rather an increase in missing men. Professionally, she was adept at looking for missing husbands, but in time she'd all but given up on her own.

Mrs. Montgomery was still talking, oblivious to the gooseflesh that had crept up Billie's legs, and her words returned suddenly to Billie's ears, like a radio turned back on. ". . . and between us, I can't access more finances unless he, well, unless there is some resolution . . ." She paused. "You see, I can't remarry unless I divorce Richard."

"Indeed. I see your predicament," Billie replied smoothly. The money—which must have been substantial—was running lower than was comfortable, along with this woman's patience for answers. This was understandable. After two years, she needed a divorce settlement or the proceeds of probate. But even in the event that finances were not a pressing concern, and that was indeed rare, the social suspicions cast upon unmarried women were not something widows were spared, particularly not if they appeared eligible, as this well-turned-out woman did. It was assumed that such a woman wanted a man, and there were certainly fewer going around these days. Single women had long been considered threatening—one reason daughters were routinely married off while still barely children—and a woman who was not attached to a man was viewed with suspicion by many, with no male hand to guide her, rein her in, and keep her from seducing the unsuspecting husbands of others. Billie was all too aware of these notions.

"It must be terribly hard for you, not knowing."

Mrs. Montgomery nodded, her eyes glistening. Finally, a hint of emotion, a hint of vulnerability.

"Sadly, I see these sorts of cases far too often," Billie continued. She understood there were millions of missing persons recorded by the International Red Cross Missing Persons Bureau in Geneva. Just how many of those stories would have happy endings was increasingly few as the years wore on. "You have my sympathies, but I'll be frank, Mrs. Montgomery: If you are sure your husband is not in the Antipodes, I fear I can't be of much help."

With this, the arms crossed, and Billie caught a better look at the glittering engagement ring—a central large solitaire diamond surrounded by two cascading swirling tiers of round brilliant-cut diamonds and glittering baguette diamonds. It was well and good to have clients from the high end of town walking into Billie's office, but not if she couldn't help them. It seemed a shame to turn Mrs. Montgomery away.

"Nettie said you were the one to come to, that for missing persons you are second to none. What is your rate for this kind of case?" Mrs. Montgomery pressed, ignoring Billie's observation as if it hadn't been raised.

"It's the same as it is for all of my work," Billie explained calmly, having already decided this was going nowhere. "We charge fourteen pounds a day plus expenses." Her rate had gone up recently, with her higher profile after the complicated Brown family case. "We dedicate ourselves entirely to our clients for the duration. There is no guarantee of how long any individual case may take. Some are resolved in just a couple of days and some take far longer. I have found many a husband," Billie said without false modesty. "However, as I mentioned, I fear we are not suitable for your particular needs, given the likelihood your husband did not return to this country. We can certainly explore any local connections, but it does seem you likely need an inquiry agent in Paris, and possibly London as well. Sadly, I don't believe I have contacts on hand to offer you, though I could look into it for you, if that would help."

She tried her professional smile, hoping to ease the woman's disappointment.

"But you do have contacts," Mrs. Montgomery replied, to Billie's surprise. "Did you not work there yourself during the war? You will go to Paris for me on the next available flight and you will find out what happened to my Richard."

Billie was caught without words for a moment. Since returning in '44 and reopening her late father's agency, she'd worked in Sydney and surrounds, as he had before her. The possibility of traveling for the work had not occurred to her.

"Oh, I had you checked out, naturally," Mrs. Montgomery added, while Billie searched for a response. "I wanted to know who I was hiring. You were a reporter, weren't you?"

Billie nodded. She missed that work, though not the war. The newsrooms of Sydney had not been so keen on women reporters once the men returned.

"You must understand, you couldn't get me on one of those beastly deathtraps . . . airplanes . . . for all the tea in China," Mrs. Montgomery continued. "My aunt died in one of those cursed machines and Richard never could convince me to get in one. No, I am not going over there, and I am quite determined to have you do it. I will pay handsomely."

Billie could certainly see that determination was real. There was no doubting it. But though she was not the type to dissuade a clearly well-heeled client from hiring her, she wasn't prepared for this idea, and it set off a series of conflicting thoughts and feelings.

"I'll admit it's an intriguing idea," she replied cautiously, "but it would come with some considerable expenses, you understand." She watched the woman's response, but her warning did not seem to faze her. Could she be the only woman in Sydney not to feel the pinch of the war years? "I can't guarantee my assistant will be available," Billie continued. "I'll have to consult with him on that, and look into our calendar."

Billie must have appeared uncertain, because what Mrs. Montgomery said next sealed the deal.

"Naturally, Miss Walker. I'll pay double your usual rate."

Billie Walker had seen a fair bit in her years, particularly since

'39, so it was rare for anyone or anything to raise her brow, but Mrs. Montgomery had succeeded.

"So it's a day rate, yes?" Mrs. Montgomery added. "I'll double your fourteen-pound day rate when you are outside the country, all expenses paid. Reasonable expenses, of course," she specified. Those eyes focused on Billie with an unusual directness. "I want this done, Miss Walker. I've waited quite long enough and I won't take no for an answer." The square jaw was set.

And with that the woman slid two hundred pounds across the battered wooden desk and handed Billie a formal card, embellished tastefully with an illustrated spray of flowers.

MRS VERA MONTGOMERY

Vera. She had her own name after all.

Two

—⚹—

Once Mrs. Vera Montgomery had swept out of the offices of B. Walker Private Inquiries, leaving the unmistakable scent of good French perfume in her stylish wake, Billie closed the office door and looked to Samuel Baker, guessing instantly that her assistant had indeed caught some of the relevant details of their discussion. The communicating door of her offices was not very thick, and frankly it saved everyone a lot of time when her assistant eavesdropped just a *little*. After all, most women who came to her found it easier to open up without a man in the room, but it was understood that every relevant detail would be brought to bear in meeting their particular needs. Sam was discreet.

He was standing in front of his desk, those baby blues of his wide and excited. "Twenty-eight pounds a day? Crikey!" he exclaimed. "Does it mean . . . ?"

"Indeed, you did hear correctly, Sam. Indeed you did," Billie replied, shaking her head. She couldn't deny that the prospect of returning to Europe was both unexpected and compelling. Was it too good to be true, though? Already she was wondering if the money for such a journey could really be available.

She squinted and sat down on the edge of Sam's desk, deep in thought.

"Did we accept the case?" he asked.

Though he was understandably expectant, there was a great deal to be settled, to her mind, even if that deposit went a long way to nudging her in the direction of Vera Montgomery's demands. "I must say, Sam, I think Mrs. Montgomery is a fan of yours," she teased, not giving him what he wanted. She crossed one leg over the other and raised a brow suggestively. "Look out, she may not be Mrs. Montgomery for long, if we do our job well," she joked.

Sam's eyes widened again. "She is quite an impressive woman, Ms. Walker," he said diplomatically. "Another divorce number, then? A wayward husband? Did you agree to the trip? Did she say *Paris?*"

"Perhaps," she replied. "Let's just say that regardless of how her husband has been spending his time the past two years, she appears keen to extract herself, and someone will have to do the work. It may as well be us, I suppose, though there is a lot of detail to work out if we are to do it." Again, she ruminated on the possibilities. Could she close the office for a few weeks once she was finished with her latest caseload? If she was to start turning down cases, she would have to possess some rock-solid assurances in the form of cash and contract.

"Aah," Sam said. "Two years he's been missing. You think her husband's been lounging in a pine overcoat?"

Billie smiled at his turn of phrase, and a chuckle escaped her red lips. "Possibly he's in a coffin somewhere, but it's hard to say." She waited a beat. "Yes, you heard it right. Double, Sam. She offered double our day rate if or when we're out of the country, to find her husband and acquire either proof of desertion or death."

He whistled. "Golly."

"It's an attractive proposition, *if* she's good for it."

"Did you see that ring?" he remarked, now well practiced at looking for such details.

"I did."

"Is her husband a baron or something?"

"No. He's an ad man, and was working for the government."

Sam looked surprised.

"I'm thinking inheritance," she said. "Besides, not everyone with a title has money to back it up." Her mother, a baroness, was a fairly good example of that principle. She'd lost most of her money in the Depression, as so many others had. It spoke well of her resourcefulness and resilience that she still had a glamorous flat to live in, even if she'd had to sell the palatial house in Potts Point where Billie had grown up, not to mention several antiques and family heirlooms.

Billie looked at the time. "This is all very intriguing. However, we do have some immediate paid work on our plate. Are you ready for tonight?"

At this, Sam straightened and nodded, seemingly standing at attention, ever the dutiful soldier to Billie's backstreet general.

"Let's hope we can wrap up this case before we get too excited about our potential new client and that pretty payment she's dangling." The prospect of Paris, and that fee, was quite enough to distract Billie from the work at hand, and she couldn't afford that.

Using the little oval mirror in her office, Billie carefully removed her tilt hat and hatpins and grabbed her dark trench coat, cap, and gloves. "All right. It's time to close up, Sam. We've got a nasty night ahead."

—⚬—

The York Motors sign on Bayswater Road went black with a buzz and a faint pop.

Billie stopped to look up at the extinguished neon sign and the starry sky beyond. She frowned, cinched her deep navy trench coat tight, and squinted against the cool wind on which was carried the faint scent of tobacco, meat pies, male sweat, and something more exotic she could not place. Tonight she had pulled on a dark blue cap and matching gloves, as much to avoid touching her surrounds as for any standard of fashion. As the sun had fled the area, these garments were almost like a cloak of nocturnal invisibility, strategically blending her into the shadows. Only her stocking-clad calves and ankles were exposed, and her trusty stacked-heel Oxfords—shoes she could wear in most acceptable establishments, and could run in. One never knew when such qualities might matter.

Billie's assistant stood next to her, silent and ready. They were in Kings Cross, which had earned a reputation as Australia's Montmartre. Without looking at the time, she knew that it would be eight fifteen in the evening, the time the big advertisement was shut off each night. Kings Cross and bright neon signage went hand in hand, but there had been a protest by neighbors about this advertisement in particular, and the daily death of the sign was their compromise. In fact, she noticed many of the district's famous big neon lights were in darkness, still waiting for their postwar resurrection, though this York Motors sign and the Capstan cigarettes one had started up again at some hours—literal and metaphorical signs that the city was doing its best to move on after the deprivations of the war.

She dug her gloved hands into her pockets, and Mrs. Montgomery drifted into her mind—that chic Parisian suit and square, determined jaw. Had a woman like her ever spent an evening skulking around like this? It seemed doubtful. Billie adjusted the leather satchel slung over her shoulder, inside which resided a photographic camera.

"Where's our boy headed now?" Sam pondered aloud, voicing Billie's very question.

The bars had closed after the infamous six o'clock swill—the frenzied speed-drinking session that preceded early closing of the bars at six each evening, thanks to a law dating back to the first war in an attempt to improve "public morality"—and many of the visitors to this district were now looking for other, more intimate pleasures. Tonight it was Billie and Sam's business to tail one such visitor for a client. Less than a block ahead, their prey was in a yellow knit vest, plaid sports coat, and cream trousers, hands in pockets, walking languidly. After closing up the office they'd followed him from his workplace to a pub, and later a modest restaurant, and now they shadowed him as he moved quietly through streets alive with establishments selling takeaway food and cigars, and darkened doorways that offered secret temptations. On nights like this, having a male assistant was particularly useful, Billie had found. She could handle herself, but it was easier this way, easier if it appeared she had a lover at her side and was not open to the eyes of others. A glance from one of the hungry single men who roamed this area and she could thread her arm through Sam's, and then be clearly not on the evening's menu, thank you very much. When they were together like this, neither Sam nor Billie was an obvious object of scrutiny, the illusion of being a couple allowing them to fade from view in a scene that was increasingly charged with propositions and enticements as the evening wore on.

As she moved in her dark apparel, Billie felt almost like a shadow herself, experiencing a rare moment of near invisibility the night and her chosen attire offered her. Their prey, however, was turning heads in his yellow vest as touts and spruikers in doorways cajoled him to cross the threshold into their establishments. So far, he did not seem swayed, and he walked on, seemingly oblivious to the shadows at his back.

Their target's name was Mr. Robert Charles, and this was another night of divorce work, Billie's least favorite aspect of the trade.

It was, however, certainly one of the most consistent ones, as long as the tumultuous marriages of Sydney continued to need escaping from, and as long as the stiff-lipped men of the law required tangible proof of adultery to enable the escape. It was the business of a private inquiry agent to provide such proof. Tailing lascivious men was distasteful, perhaps, but it was bread-and-butter work to an agent like Billie, as it had been for her father before her. At times she longed to turn down these jobs, wondering if this was what her life had come to, but for now she was still turning up for this work, and in truth it was paying better than ever. Someone had to do it, she supposed. She had shifted from tailing Nazis in France to tailing walking libidos in the Cross. Was this really her future?

Paris . . .

Jack smiling, holding her hand, pulling her into an abandoned cottage in the French countryside just a day's travel from the city. Jack kissing her, his mouth wet and soft and eager, their bodies locking together, intertwined and falling to the floor willingly, hungrily, the threat of German patrols becoming a distant threat in his arms, if only for a while . . .

"You seem elsewhere," Sam observed softly, and Billie snapped back to the moment, guilty as charged, the sights, sounds, and smells of the Kings Cross streets flooding back in from all directions—tobacco and baked rabbit, hungry male, the scent of urine on the pavements. For a moment she'd been distracted by the carrot Mrs. Montgomery had dangled in front of her, pulled in by the prospect of Paris and the puzzle of Jack Rake.

"I'm sorry, Sam. I'm here now." She shivered, her painted lips set in a line. "But just where our man is headed next is another question," she added. He was taking them farther off the beaten track, away from the lights and action. Tonight might bring a breakthrough. She could sense it, like a hunter on the prowl.

This was the domain of Sydney's darker side—or rather, the part of Sydney's underbelly that advertised somewhat openly. Since the 1930s this notorious suburb had developed into its own international neighborhood, a settlement of sorts for foreigners of all descriptions. Their delicatessens and pie shops offered a slice of Europe and one could buy good frankfurters, rissoles, or some pies or steaks from Wolfe's, Dunbars, or Booths. But as many knew—and certainly any private inquiry agent worth their salt knew—this was also where one came for sexual dalliances. It was said that during the day you came to Kings Cross to feed your belly with the European grocers, take-away, and cafés; in the evening to feed your mind with entertainment and bohemian society; and at night to feed your vices. This was the home of forbidden liaisons and the call of lust. This place shared neon signs and takeaway vendors with the women of the night; with Rosaleen Norton, the "Witch of Kings Cross"; with artists and moon worshippers; the underworld and narcotics peddlers of all varieties. If you wanted something taboo, unconventional, or downright shady, this was where you came for it, and the farther from the bright lights of the takeaway operators, the more Billie was convinced it was the call of some vice that animated her prey tonight.

Mr. Charles walked on with that curious languor, up the block and back, and then the next. It was peculiar to Billie that he did not appear to be trying to lose a tail—he was moving far too slowly for that. His wife, should she have wished to, could have followed him almost as easily as Billie and Sam. Was he biding his time? Waiting for someone? Deciding something? More than an hour passed this way before he eventually paused next to one of the food stalls and spoke with a man serving food, evidently having decided he was peckish.

"Come on . . ." Sam muttered under his breath.

"Patience, dear Sam," Billie soothed. One required a good deal of patience in this line. Mr. Charles might wander like this for hours yet, as far as they knew, and while this was already their fifth such night, and plenty of cases were resolved by this time, there might be many more nights spent like this before there was a result. Still, she sensed something would break soon. The little woman in her gut felt it—the little woman who knew things, informed by a thousand cues and signals, deductions and fragments of knowledge, sensed that something was coming. Yes, Mr. Charles would reveal himself.

"Ms. Walker," Sam whispered.

"You can call me Billie, Sam. You know that."

"Billie, do you think you'll go to Paris, like Mrs. Montgomery wants you to?"

Paris.

There it was again. When she thought, even fleetingly, about the possibility of returning to Paris, the need to be there—the place where she'd last seen Jack—felt so urgent, so necessary, it frightened her. What if she went back across the seas to the place that had changed her life so completely? What would she find? Surely there could be no happy endings to be found there, not after so long.

"I don't know for certain, Sam, but the prospect is intriguing . . . Are you hungry?" she asked suddenly, watching Mr. Charles across the road with new interest, her head cocked.

"Pardon?"

They'd already eaten, though it wasn't much, and she'd witnessed Sam's appetite before. He could eat like a sheep shearer. Sam shrugged. "You know me. I could have a bite."

"Good. Go ahead and order something, then," Billie suggested. "You never know, you might strike up a conversation with our man. In fact, if you see an opening, that's exactly what I'd like you to do. Don't push anything, mind, but if the opportunity arises, feel out what he's up to, will you?"

"I could do that?" He looked uncertain.

"It wouldn't hurt, I think," she said.

Perhaps impatience was making her take risks, but Mr. Charles seemed unaware that he was being watched, and that slow walk of his was driving her a bit mad, truth be told. Was he waiting for a friend? Or working himself up to something? If so, what? Or was this man just dead set against getting home until his wife was safely asleep? Sam was still fairly new to the trade, though he'd learned a lot under Billie and was a quick study. He'd do fine if a conversation opened up with the man. He wasn't one to grandstand or make a show of himself. Yes, he'd do fine, and he could use the practice, she decided.

"Go on. Order some food, be friendly if the moment strikes, but don't worry if it doesn't. Have a bite, and I'll be watching. Just whatever you do, don't look my way. Copacetic?" she added, adopting the slang she'd picked up from American soldiers.

"Um, copacetic, Ms. Walker. Err, Billie."

She slipped her charge a few shillings for his order and he left her for the opposite side of the street and bright lights of the food stall.

Billie slid back into the shadows in her strategically dark ensemble and pulled a Lucky Strike from the case in her handbag. Soon the end of her fag glowed like a single red eye from the darkened doorway, as she leaned against the wall and thought of Paris, the occasional headlamp of a passing car lighting up nothing more than a stocking-clad ankle.

Three

—⚞—

It's kind of gruesome, isn't it?" Billie Walker remarked, looking eyeball to eye socket with a human skull.

The lighting was dim, the ceilings low in this strange place, but Billie could see well enough, perhaps too well. The empty skull before her appeared to be slowly disintegrating, a slice of forehead missing—or perhaps that missing piece had been what spelled the end for its former owner. The centuries-old head was balanced upon another more intact one, with yet another beneath that, mandibles nowhere to be seen. Together the skulls formed a kind of morbid totem pole of the dead, their curved heads protruding like strange bricks of yellowing ivory, greening at the edges, set among the stack of femurs and humerus bones. This surreal sight stretched in both directions, interspersed with barred-off side tunnels, trailing into low, shadowy paths. Each wall of bones was set with its own design, skulls turned inward to show occipital bones and outward again to show empty craniums through wide eye sockets, lines of skulls rising and falling, or set into diagonal patterns.

Femur.

Skull.

Femur.

Up ahead, Billie could see limbs stacked in a circle like a giant barrel placed in the center of the underground pathway, rows of skulls providing grim centerpieces, a forceful memento mori. Perhaps that was what drew them all here, the tourists like herself: to remember they, too, would die one day. Billie wrapped her coat more tightly around her, feeling the dampness of the old quarries and their long-deceased inhabitants.

Death came for everyone.

"Do the bones bother you?" her companion asked. He was a good-looking man, she reflected—lean and tanned, with bright hazel eyes. In his slacks and collared shirt worn open and casually beneath his sweater, he looked practically at home in this curious environment, like an archeologist or adventurer. She wondered if he even owned a tie. Somehow, it seemed less likely than his owning a pith helmet.

Billie registered his concerned face in the half-light and then turned her attention back to the bones. "No, they don't bother me," she replied simply.

They were standing in the Paris Municipal Ossuary—known to many as the catacombs of Paris—and Billie barely knew this fascinating British man she was with. He went by the name of Jack Rake and worked as a photographer and correspondent. One day prior, some of her Parisian friends had introduced him to her at the Café de Flore, over glasses of red wine and grand tales of his recent heroic triumphs, which had involved surviving a light-airplane crash and smuggling film past German officers. As the story went, he was driven to expose the Third Reich and Adolf Hitler's plans for Europe, including Britain, which he felt was in imminent danger despite Prime Minister Chamberlain's recent signing of the Munich Agreement, and Hitler's so-called bloodless expansion of Germany's borders. The agreement, designed to appease Hitler, was a disaster and wouldn't hold back war for long, and it seemed Jack was dedicating his life to spreading the news about Hitler's true plans and the abuses of the Third Reich against German, Austrian, and now Czech citizens. To that aim, he was evidently willing to risk that life of his with some regularity, too, or at least that was how Billie's friends had described him. Jack himself had remained rather quiet throughout this excited storytelling, wine in hand, shirt open a touch, blushing lightly beneath his tan, making him seem enigmatic and perhaps a touch embarrassed by his friends' boastful stories about his daring exploits. This, of course, had only made him more fascinating to Billie.

It seemed the interest was mutual. The two had locked eyes several times, and as the group dispersed they had spoken, and now here they were, the next afternoon, a Brit and an Australian, near strangers, touristing below the streets of Paris, walking the pathways of the Empire of the Dead.

"Are you sure?" Jack asked, checking to see if she was indeed genuine.

"No, I'm not bothered by the bones," Billie replied, and blinked at the assortment before her, drawn again to the empty faces that had once been part of living, breathing, and loved people, long since forgotten. People who had names. People who had walked on the streets above.

"I thought perhaps I shouldn't have suggested we come here," he added, evidently unconvinced.

She shook her head. "It's actually very interesting to me, Jack, so I'm pleased you did. I've always been curious about this place. It is fascinating to finally see it for myself. How odd the arrangements are." Billie shifted on her feet and tilted her head. "I do realize we've only just met, but you should know now that if you believe me to have a weak stomach you are quite mistaken."

"Oh?" At this challenge he grinned. "Tell me."

Billie pulled her gaze from the bones and looked squarely at him. In the half-light she could see that he hadn't shaved since the day before. She was unused to it, and it was a touch shocking, but somehow it made her want to run her fingers across his jaw, which was peppered with light stubble. She noted her odd impulse and ignored it. "My father is a private inquiry agent," she explained, and slid her hands into the pockets of her battered beige trench coat, her elbows pointing outward in a subtle gesture of strength. She was no frightened little girl, if that's what this man thought, nor was she about to swoon over him just because their friends had told some tall tales about his exploits.

"Is that so?" Jack replied.

"It is so. He was a detective before that, working at Central Police in Sydney. Dinner-table conversation has always been colorful, to say the least. I've seen a fair bit myself," she added, though that was only partially true. Through her father, she was more familiar than most with Sydney's underworld, con men, hustlers, and crooked cops. She'd never shied away from anything taboo, not when there was something new to learn and discover, and her dad had not seemed keen to discourage her interest. What good was it pulling the wool over your own eyes? she figured. Billie wanted truth. She wanted experience, and she had come to Europe—to Paris—for precisely that, and to see more of the world, to be in the thick of it. Perhaps this was what drew her to this stranger she knew so little about. He seemed to have seen so much, but still, she was determined not to be dazzled by it.

"It must be an interesting trade, PI work," Jack remarked.

"It is," she answered, and began slowly walking again, moving along the uneven pathway of bones.

"And you are a reporter. I read your interview with Churchill, actually," he said, catching up with her.

"Oh?" She had not known he was familiar with her work.

British politician Winston Churchill had recently visited Paris and met with Paul Reynaud and Georges Mandel, members of the French cabinet who wanted to resist Germany's Führer. Billie had secured an interview with Churchill, and he'd spent hours with her, scotch in hand, freely giving his views. He was an elegant speaker, though very set and forceful in his views, a statesman of the old-school tradition. A couple of weeks later, he had made a rather stunning and incendiary speech damning Chamberlain's appeasement of Hitler and the Munich Agreement. His views on the matter had been one of the topics they had covered, and she had to admit his argument was compelling. Among other issues, the agreement had given over areas of key military defense to Hitler, meaning that if he did want war, he would be in a stronger position than before.

"It was a very fine interview," Jack said. "You've got moxie, as the Yanks say. He must have loved you."

Churchill had been generous with his time, and she had been generous with the scotch. "I guess you may as well know that I agree. About the Munich Agreement being a mistake, I mean. I'd thought so even before."

Billie appreciated that Prime Minister Chamberlain wasn't blood-thirsty, or a warmonger—both qualities to recommend him—but Adolf Hitler was, by all accounts, and she'd seen no evidence to convince her otherwise. A man like that would not be easily pacified, and if anything, the tacit approval from these democratic countries would only stroke the ego and sense of entitlement of a totalitarian leader like him. He already had Austria, and now France, Italy, and Great Britain had given him the lands and people in northern Czechoslovakia, on a platter. This may well have averted an immediate war, but for how long? It had been interesting to hear precisely the same argument up for debate at the café. It seemed this question was on everyone's minds—what would Hitler demand next? Could he be stopped?

"Signing over the Sudetenland gave Hitler's regime and expansionist ideas an air of legitimacy, in my view," Billie said. "And the people now trapped under the regime of the Third Reich didn't get much choice in the matter. I think Chamberlain is wrong about Hitler only wanting the Sudetenland. I don't know what their discussions were like behind those closed doors, but it seems like wishful thinking, if you ask me."

Jack stopped and looked her in the eye with real affection then. "You are a woman after my own heart, Walker."

She smiled.

Their eyes held and it seemed then that anything they had wanted to say next about Chamberlain or Churchill or Hitler or the threat of war evaporated on their tongues. After a moment the silence became awkward, and Jack laughed softly to himself, vocalizing an acknowledgment of a chemistry that was all too obvious to them both.

"Come, Billie . . ." he added, offering his hand. "There's something I want you to see."

She accepted his extended hand. It felt large and warm, even here far below the streets of Paris, where the bones and limestone had a damp, permeating chill. She was aware of a curious electricity about his skin that was both delightful and alarming. The pair of them had gone quiet, an intimacy building between them that for now didn't require words. She allowed him to lead her along the dark, bone-lined pathways, past the great barrel of limbs, and onward through the cavernous ossuary. Yes, she liked the feel of his hand, she decided. It was an odd stab at courtship, coming to this place, if that's what this date was, but she was certain of one thing: Jack Rake was not boring. And "not boring" was exactly what Billie liked. In many ways, it was just what she'd come to Paris for, though she had not expected him.

"These were mines before, is that right?" Billie said after a spell, still holding his hand as they walked. "They dug up the stone here to build the city?"

"*Oui* . . . Yes," he said. "Lutetian limestone deposits ran under much of the Left Bank. They mined so much of it the city began to collapse."

That wasn't all. Billie had heard the infamous tales of the terrible stench of Paris as dead bodies built up, the city's cemeteries overrun with corpses. "It's so strange, the history of this place. I heard that long ago . . . in the late 1700s, I think, a part of a property adjoining Les Innocents Cemetery collapsed under the weight of the mass grave behind it," she said. Paris had been literally collapsing with bodies and broken earth, and what resulted was this place, the Empire of the Dead, where six million or more bodies now resided, arranged in these strange designs. "Napoleon decided this place should be a tourist attraction, I believe. I wonder if they would have created these designs if he hadn't. Perhaps not. Perhaps they simply would have piled the bodies in and sealed it up."

"For a girl from the Antipodes, you know your Paris history," he observed.

"Some of it. Not at all as much as I would like. Though I am a woman, of course, not a girl," she added unapologetically.

Again, her companion stopped and gave her an affectionate look. "Right you are, Miss Walker. Right you are, again. A woman, indeed. I shall not make the mistake twice." He smiled, and she could see she had not offended him.

He led her farther along the paths and presently they came to the entrance of a small room. They stepped into the darkness, Jack stooping to fit through the doorway, and he pulled out a battered Rayovac torch and switched it on. Billie brought a hand to her face, looking around her with awe. A miniature city was carved into the rock, far below Paris. She gaped.

"Remarkable, isn't it?" Jack said.

"It is. It's incredible. What is this doing here? It's not part of the ossuary, is it?"

"No. This was already here before the bodies were moved in. It's called the Sculptures de Décure. Legend has it a former soldier and lone quarryman, Décure, carved all of this himself in secret, back when these were just quarries. This was his passion, his obsession."

The space was filled with three exquisitely carved sculptures, like a small city hiding away from the rest of the world—or three different cities, she noted. Part of the carving showed grand pillars, above which was written "Quartier de Cazerne." It looked like a miniature model of sorts, and she could almost imagine people moving over the steps and through the doorways. How on earth had someone carved this by themselves, with the simple tools available to a quarryman centuries ago?

"Sadly, the poor chap died here during one of the quarry cave-ins. He was carving stairs to these sculptures, it is said, and died right here, somewhere near this spot, I imagine."

Billie stifled a shiver.

"We can go, if you'd like," Jack said.

"No," she replied. "I want to stay awhile longer. Décure created something hauntingly beautiful. Such fine craftsmanship. He must have spent so many hours here. Why here, underground, I wonder. He could have been an artist."

"This was the canvas he had at his disposal, I suppose. The conditions were frightful down here, they say. Perhaps this creation gave him a sense of purpose, even freedom. It is said that he did it all from memory, and the sculptures tell a story about his life. He'd been a soldier, and a prisoner, before working here in the quarries."

Billie squatted down in place, sitting on the heels of her Oxfords, and took in the strange beauty of Décure's legacy.

"Is this where he was detained, when he was a prisoner?" she asked, pointing to one of the structures that looked like a fortress of some kind.

"I don't rightly know, but yes, I think so. I can't imagine what it must be like to be a prisoner," Jack remarked. "To be without my freedom . . ."

In time Billie stood, smoothed down her coat, and joined Jack at the entrance to the little room. He switched off his torch and they walked together in reverent silence, moving slowly down the long pathways of the ossuary, passing thousands of bones. This time they did not touch. They walked quietly for some time, perhaps a quarter of an hour, before they reached a spot where the rogue skull of some long-dead soul had fallen across the path.

Billie bent down for it.

"The bones don't bother me," she reiterated as she picked up the skull gently, as if to prove her point. No, death did not scare her, nor did its signs, totems, and remains. She marveled at the skull, and how it just sat there within reach of the strangers who passed through. So odd, she thought. She placed it softly on the head of another of its kind, skull upon skull, bone upon bone, once arranged by someone with an eye for morbid symmetry, now long since dead themselves.

Jack watched her with interest.

"The mortality they represent doesn't bother me either," she added, letting go of the skull and checking that it was balanced in place, stable. "It's not even the public display of the dead, nor the way it became an attraction. It's morbid, of course, but . . ." She shrugged. "No, it's the way they are displayed, Jack, each femur, each skull removed from its part of a whole, and made into something else. This ossuary . . . it's not like a grave . . . not even a mass grave. Where once these people's remains were whole, their ancestors able to visit their graves, the collective dead of Paris have been rendered nameless and without identities here, without individual histories. I think that is what I find unsettling."

Something in what she said had moved Jack Rake, his mood having shifted, she could see. He took a step toward her and took both of her cold hands in his. In the low light of the electric lamps, she caught a look in his bright hazel eyes. They had turned dark somehow, troubled by something. Was it anger in his eyes?

"Billie, that's what they're doing at the camps. The Third Reich."

"What do you mean?" she said.

She'd heard horrifying things about the Third Reich and their Gestapo, rounding up Jewish people and those they accused of "asocial" behaviors—women who stepped out of line, "gypsies," as the Romani people were often called, homosexuals, disabled people. She'd heard rumors about the camps—of Dachau, Sachsenhausen, and Buchenwald—and she knew there were certainly others, but she'd not seen them herself.

"At the German camps they take the clothes and belongings of the Jews and political prisoners—anything they have with them when they arrive—and then, once they're dead, they take their teeth, everything they can use. They separate the people from their identities, not to"—he looked around them at the strange array of bones—"make room like this. They separate each person from their humanity to commodify their bodies and remains. First, they commodify their victims through their possessions and forced labor, and then, when they perish, they commodify what's left of their starved bodies. They even use the hair."

Billie stepped back, pulling her hands away. At first she couldn't speak. She felt sickened, and now their surroundings were too much, the bones, the death. Her stomach churned and flipped.

Jack must have seen her pale. "I'm sorry. I hadn't intended to talk about all that today," he said. "I wanted to leave politics alone, for once."

She cast her mind back to the café. Improbably, it had been just the day before when she'd first set eyes on this quiet, attractive figure, though it felt like she'd known him longer. As a photojournalist, he had covered the annexation of Austria earlier in the year, and the recent Nazi march into the Sudetenland. What else had he seen? she now wondered.

"How do you know all this?" she asked. "Where is this happening, exactly? Are you saying they're profiting from the bodies of their prisoners?"

"I haven't seen it myself. Not yet. But I have a friend in British intelligence. We grew up together in Sutton. I . . . I trust my sources," he said, leaving it there. "You must understand, the purpose of the German camps isn't only to hold political prisoners so they can't be a threat to the regime, and to deter people against resistance. No. These camps are set up to *eliminate* opponents. And they fuel the regime itself, strengthening the German position through slave labor."

She had heard about the terrifying SS Death's Head Units, SS-Totenkopfverbände, in the concentration camps. They wore death heads—the skull and crossbones, or *Totenkopf*, as the Germans called it—on their uniforms not simply as a reminder of death but as a threat, a personification of Death's power.

Jack took off his hat and ran a hand over his hair. "The prisoners are building, always building, expanding the capabilities of these giant camps. When they can no longer build, their bodies having given out, the prisoners die or are killed. They make them dig their own graves, Billie."

She was shocked by Jack's blunt words, and yet not completely surprised. During the Olympic Games in Berlin, where Hitler had showcased his power, she'd heard many terrible rumors about his methods and his plans. By now the world knew much more about Hitler's regime, but many still seemed to accept it as a problem for someone else, something self-contained, something that would go away. It was the foreign athletes who spoke in whispers about what they saw, the things that unsettled them. Hitler already had enormous power then, and he wielded it with violence. Billie was not convinced that Hitler would stop wielding that power out of choice, and Jack evidently felt the same.

"Tensions are building in Austria, I've heard. There are reports of Gestapo raids, attacks on citizens in the street. Next weekend I'm going to Vienna to see what I can find for myself. Perhaps I can even get close to Mauthausen," he said. "The world has to see what they're doing."

"An assignment?" Billie's heart sped up. Mauthausen was a camp that had been built shortly after the annexation of Austria. It was built by the prisoners from the camp at Dachau. She didn't know much about it, except that it housed many Austrian citizens believed to be a threat to the Nazi regime—intellectuals, politicians, socialists, communists, homosexuals, and Romani people.

"Maybe you'd like to come with me? You write a good piece, and you clearly have a strong stomach," he said, indicating their morbid surrounds.

Billie smiled, avoiding giving him an answer. In truth her stomach didn't feel so strong in that moment. She turned and began walking casually along the grim pathways of the ossuary, toward the exit, Jack at her heels.

"Will you consider it?"

Would she? She hardly knew this man, but she'd been trying to get closer to the action, away from local reporting and interviews, and into more in-depth investigative reporting. It was an exciting prospect.

"Is it true what they said last night?" she asked as Jack caught up with her. "About you smuggling film past Nazi guards in shaving cream?"

He nodded. "And tubes of toothpaste, yes. Will you come with me?" he asked, reaching for her hand again. "I know we've just met, but I think we'd make a good team."

Four

—∞—

A cool wind whipped at Billie Walker's collar as she watched her target in his yellow vest finish his pie, exchange a few words with her assistant, and stroll away down Darlinghurst Road again. Samuel Baker turned his head to watch him go, then looked searchingly in Billie's direction, though it seemed he could not see her nestled into her dark hiding place across the street.

It had already been five days and nights of tailing this seemingly hapless character whose wife was quite convinced he was cheating. Was she right? The little woman in Billie's gut was not yet sure. Night after night they watched him leave from work, buy packets of cigarettes, take trams, and drink alone. Civil and social enough, but alone. As yet there had been no sign of a lover. The man appeared courteous and not taken to particularly odd habits, though he certainly was guilty of spending less time at home than he could—and there was something else, something she couldn't yet place. Considering his wife had come to Billie, it was easy to imagine some tensions brewing at home, so it was not unheard of to avoid being there, and, after all, enjoying a drink was not a crime nor was it grounds for divorce. This Mr. Charles still came home at night, if later than his wife liked. According to her, he didn't lay a hand on her, not even in ways a wife might hope for. A cold bed, among other complaints, tended to make for trips to Billie's office. Instead of warming the marital bed, he was here in the Cross on a Thursday night, avoiding it. Billie inhaled deeply and let out a puff of smoke. Something would break.

Something.

Sam had reached her side of the road and now he walked on the footpath in her direction, head swiveling from side to side as if lost. Billie flicked her glowing cigarette on the ground, put it out with her heel, and stepped out of the shadows of the doorway.

"Jeepers, there you are," he said, and sidled up. They performed one of their faux greetings for anyone watching—a quick embrace and polite pecks on the cheek, European style. "I don't know how you do that, Ms. Walker. You just disappear," he said under his breath, marveling at her skill.

Billie grinned. "Remember, you can call me Billie, okay?"

He nodded. "I know, I know." He looked down at his shoes.

"So?" she prompted. "I noticed you two talked. Was it fruitful?"

"Well, I don't know. Mr. Charles seems like a nice fellow," Sam said, sounding almost disappointed by the fact.

"Nice fellows can end up in unhappy marriages, Sam. I don't judge." *Much*, she thought. Sometimes there was reason.

"Hey, are you all right?" he asked, bending to look her in the eye with concern, just as Jack had done down in the catacombs.

"I'm fine, and I do wish you'd stop asking that. My stomach is just a bit off, that's all," she lied, stepping back out of the light of the streetlamp, wishing he wasn't quite so perceptive.

Though bereaved after Jack's disappearance, she hadn't thought of herself as particularly down in the mouth until Mrs. Montgomery came sashaying into her office, swathed in the New Look and dangling the possibility of Paris—and, perhaps, the possibility of answers. After '44, with the loss of her father and disappearance of her husband, Billie had got on with things in Sydney as best she could. Like so many others, she lived with what she'd been forced to accept. But what had been Jack's fate, really? Was his body in some unidentified grave in Warsaw, like everyone believed? Would knowing for certain free her heart and put his ghost to rest?

"Something we ate before?" Sam asked.

Billie shrugged, not wanting to get into the real reason for her queasiness. It was like the Paris ossuary was still around her, in the chill of the Sydney air—the bones, the anonymous death. Perhaps something on the wind had triggered the memory, some scent, now that thoughts of Jack had risen so close to the surface. "What is our Mr. Charles like? Come on," she prompted. "I'm not here for a medical."

Sam tilted his head, jaw flexing. "Sorry, Billie. Well, like I said, he was just real nice. He seemed a pleasant sort of fellow."

She made a face, brows raised. "Sam, you'll have to do far better than that if you desire to stay in this trade. So, our Mr. Charles is a lamb. What else?"

Her words may have sounded harsher than intended, she realized.

"Sorry." Sam stood up straighter, as if asked by his commander to present himself. "Robert Charles is clean-shaven and neatly dressed. Nice duds. He seemed like he'd had a few drinks, as we saw, but he wasn't sauced. He seemed maybe . . . nervous?"

"That's an interesting observation. What makes you say that?"

Sam looked down again. "Well, I don't know, exactly," he reflected. "He just . . . there was high color in his cheeks or something . . . or like an excitement in his voice, like he might be nervous."

She contemplated that. "Do you think he's onto us?"

If so, he was a good actor. He hadn't been showing any of the telltale signs that he knew he was being observed, but even if her instincts in that regard tended to serve her well, she could always make a mistake. Perhaps he intended to simply wander around each night, driving them to distraction while his wife racked up a bill.

"No, nothing like that," Sam assured her.

"Are you quite sure?"

He shrugged. "I really don't think so, or he wouldn't have been so nice. Maybe it wasn't nervousness, exactly. I'm sorry, Billie, I can't quite place it. He didn't appear suspicious of me, more interested in a bit of chitchat, you know? Maybe it was the drink, after all."

"Well, he's on the move, so we better get tailing," she said, noting he was partway up Darlinghurst Road in that vest, broadcasting his location like a beacon. "If, goddess forbid, he spots us and makes an approach, introduce me as . . . Mae, okay?"

"I told him my name was John."

"Very good," Billie said, and smiled to herself. Perhaps Sam was unaware that by using that particular name he might have implied he was "a john," looking for a woman of the night. That certainly was what a lot of men came to Kings Cross for. "What did Mr. Charles think of that?"

"What do you mean?" he asked, a touch confused.

"Nothing. Come on, he's on the move."

If she was worried about losing their target, she needn't have been. He had assumed his frustratingly slow saunter again, hands in pockets, head down. They hung well back from the man and, shadowing at a good distance, observed their quarry in window reflections and casual glances, pretending to be a couple taking in the sights of Kings Cross. Billie did enjoy the hunt, even if she found nights like this morally uncomfortable.

A taxi honked as the pair slid past, the finer automobiles having all but given over the suburb to the night. She took a deep breath and caught the scent of cigars drifting from the open window of a café. A group of men in navy blue service uniforms emerged from around a corner, passing Mr. Charles on the sidewalk as if he weren't there. The men talked among themselves in elevated voices, pushing and shoving and taking up space in the way such men did when they were feeling free and boastful, and had a gut full of liquor to exaggerate their movements. She guessed, given it was May Day, tonight for them marked the start of a long weekend onshore, to blow off steam and chase the kind of action they dreamed of in their bunks at night. They would only become rowdier as the weekend progressed. The sight of the men made Sam stiffen. Their accents, and jauntily worn neckerchiefs and white naval caps, gave them away as visiting US sailors from nearby Garden Island—a naval base joined to the mainland in 1942. It was only a short walk away, and the evolution of the forbidden trades here in Kings Cross was no coincidence. As they passed Billie and Sam, a couple of the young men looked up to take in Billie's profile and trench-coat-clad figure, though it covered just past the knee. One handsome sailor whistled softly and gave Sam the kind of look you might give a lottery winner.

"Look at the pegs on her . . ."

Billie leaned into Sam's collar to dissuade the sailor's attentions, and in turn Sam threaded an arm protectively around her slender waist. He smelled faintly of a pleasant cologne. "You know, Sam, I had my doubts that Mr. Charles was up to something these past few days," she whispered. "A few more days and I might have even let him off the hook. Now I'm not so sure. Look at where he's headed."

Sam nodded his chin. "Aye."

Something would break soon, and she could feel it. And it had to break, or Billie would have little to report to her client except that her husband seemed a nice man who liked the odd tipple and lived a rather lonely existence outside the home. Perhaps his mates had died in the war, like so many. Perhaps he was battling internal demons his wife could not understand. Or perhaps tonight was to be the breakthrough they were waiting for, and his desires would reveal themselves. Was it women of the night? Opium?

They continued their slow pursuit, Billie hanging on tightly to Sam in case another group of sailors emerged—they did tend to roam in packs—and their target started down toward Woolloomooloo. He slowed, looked guiltily over his shoulder for the first time, and, seeming not to have noticed them, picked up his pace.

"Finally," Sam remarked. "He's hunting for, uh . . ." He hesitated. "He's looking for a sheila."

The change of mood was unmistakable, and the possibility quickened her heartbeat. Though there was something satisfying about informing a client that her husband was on the straight and narrow, she'd soon learned it would be something she'd seldom report. The thing of it was, by the time a client came to Billie, there appeared to be strong odds their suspicions were correct, and though Billie did so hate proving them right, her proof would mean resolution, and perhaps the much-needed escape her client sought—escape from unhappiness, from abandonment, or from violence.

"He's fishing all right, but this could take some time," Sam muttered under his breath. "There aren't a lot of, uh, ladies here yet."

Billie could see her assistant was right. A man in a colorful collared shirt and jacket appeared and was now talking with Mr. Charles. It seemed they knew each other. She cocked her head, having a notion.

"I think we'd better hang back," she said, holding on to her assistant and bringing him to a stop. The little woman in her gut told her this was it.

A question was on her assistant's lips.

"Trust me," she said in a low voice.

The man Mr. Charles was talking to had his hands in his pockets—they both did—and he wore khaki trousers and sneakers, his jacket slung over one shoulder despite the chill. They looked both ways, again giving Billie the familiar thrill up her spine that came with knowing she was catching something of interest, and with that Billie did her best to slide farther into the shadows with Sam. She put her arms around Sam's neck as if they were about to kiss, lest they be spotted by the men. He stiffened under her touch, she noticed, though he was used to this by now. It was part of the job.

The two men continued talking in low tones, and together they turned down Brougham Lane, a narrow pathway between two tall buildings creating a natural amphitheater so that anyone could hear even the most intimate of conversations.

"Get the camera ready, Sam," Billie whispered, and pressed it into his hands.

"Now?" he asked, and at her nod in the darkness he obeyed her instruction. He took the camera from her, steadied it on her shoulder, and pointed.

Mr. Charles took the other man by the hand, a sensual movement, and in a flash he was pushed against a building, the slightly shorter man straining his entire body against him in a deeply erotic gesture. The men kissed passionately in the shadows, the silhouette of their heads haloed by a streetlamp.

"Well, I'll be a monkey's uncle," she heard Sam say under his breath. The camera's shutter clicked.

"Is there enough light?" Billie asked, inclining her head. If they had to use the flash, the game would be up.

She could feel Sam nod, and she turned her head again to look. Yes. At the right angle, the streetlight at the far end silhouetted the men's figures. It would be enough.

"That'll do, if you think you got it," Billie said, a lump in her throat. She felt a touch sick, but not because the sight of the two men upset her. This would successfully resolve the case for her client, but it did, for Billie, complicate things. Mr. Charles had tastes that set him at odds not only with his wife but with the law. "If you've got it, let's go," she said, troubled, and then turned back the way they'd come, back toward Bayswater Road, pulling a dazed Sam along with her.

"He seemed so nice," he said under his breath, working it through in his mind, before stumbling as his foot connected with a piece of metal junk lying on the ground.

It had been loud, louder than was wise, and the next part happened as if in slow motion.

There was a gasp from one of the men, a shout, and Mr. Charles shot out of the alley toward them, catching Billie by the right sleeve of her dark trench coat. She could feel her heart throbbing in her throat, her fight-or-flight response kicking in, and the gun on her thigh seemed almost to tingle. Sam was there, camera dangling around his neck and hands balled into fists, ready to make Mr. Charles back off at her cue. Violence almost had them in its grip, but the man's expression gave Billie pause. She raised her gloved left hand as if to freeze the moment, and Sam waited, tense.

"You . . . you've been following me, haven't you?" Mr. Charles said, looking from Billie to Sam. He gasped when he recognized the man he had spoken with over the pie, his face distorted with the pain of the betrayal.

"Don't let's all get excited," Billie warned in an even voice, body still, tensed in waiting.

"Please . . . Please, you can't do this," he begged.

She willed her heart to slow, and soon it found its rhythm again. "Mr. Charles, you may as well know that I have been employed by your wife to acquire proof of your adultery so she might secure a divorce," she managed. "She has grounds and is well within her rights." The script was well rehearsed. This was not her first rodeo, as she was fond of saying.

The man swallowed, his eyes instantly welling up. Those eyes looked to the dark pavement, then into the middle distance, seeing something that was not physically present—perhaps his wife and her painful disapproval. His romantic friend, whoever he'd been, had already vanished, having fled down the alley and out to the connecting street below.

These kinds of confrontations were deeply uncomfortable, but Billie was prepared. This was the part where they insulted her character, insulted her line of work, swung a fist, or tried to. She braced herself for what was to come, but Mr. Charles just stood there, motionless, and brought a hand to his face.

"Fair enough," he eventually decided aloud, speaking in a sad, resigned tone. "She does have reason to be unhappy. I know that. That's between us." He hesitated. "I can't blame her, really. But no one needs to see those photographs. You can't. Please. I'll be ruined."

That was true, and Billie knew it. She was already wondering if she really could release these photographs to her client, knowing they would likely make it to court. She disagreed strenuously with the law, but this man could be put away if it was shown that he had committed homosexual acts, or "buggery," as the courts called it. They'd only caught the pair kissing, but it was proof enough that her client's husband sought the company of the same sex. They would not let him off easy, not with the politicians and police so keen to show how righteous they were, so soon after a war that had forced

THE GHOSTS OF PARIS

many men into intense and intimate bonds with other men, some discovering tastes they had not previously known and would be shamed for and worse if they were revealed.

"My loyalty is to my client," Billie explained stiffly, not yet quite knowing what to say on that point of law, though her mind was working hard on solutions. She wondered fleetingly if her client had already known.

"Please, I beg you. We can work something out," Mr. Charles pleaded. He still hadn't let go of Billie's sleeve, and when she looked down at it, then up at his face, he withdrew his arm immediately. Sam visibly relaxed.

"There's no need for begging here," Billie replied, having formed the steps of a plan in her mind. "Give me your card, and I will be in touch tomorrow afternoon, when we've all recovered our senses and can think clearly. Yes? In the meantime, your secret will be your own."

"Thank you," he panted. "Do you promise?"

"My word is good. Until we speak tomorrow, Mr. Charles. Rest well," she said, knowing that were she in his position, there would be no peace tonight.

Five

—⁓—

On Friday morning, Billie was striding up to Daking House, feeling invigorated despite a restless sleep, when she spotted a familiar figure outside the entrance. It was not the distraught Mr. Charles, having tracked her down to her office, as men in his type of predicament were sometimes wont to do, instead of waiting for her call. No, it was someone Billie was rather pleased to see.

Outside the door stood a dark, small-statured young woman with tightly curled, near-black hair, wearing a heavy coat and a delicate gold crucifix. She held a small handbag in her gloved hands. Her head was held high, and even from a block away her distinctive pose was unmistakable. Billie's heart lifted at the sight, a smile spreading across her face. This was her friend and sometime informant, Shyla Davis. Her timing could not have been better. The office and the morning papers could wait.

"Shyla," Billie said, walking up briskly and slightly breathless. "Would you care for some tea? Perhaps a wee bite?" She adjusted her coat collar, which had caught in the wind, rising up against her ears.

"Billie." Shyla nodded, her intense amber eyes locking with her friend's, and the two women turned away from Daking House and crossed the road toward the large sandstone structure of Central Railway Station.

The Central Railway Refreshment Rooms were not busy at this hour, and, as usual, Billie and Shyla seated themselves at a table far from the entrance, in one of Billie's preferred spots, where the private inquiry agent could observe the comings and goings of the clientele and passersby and the movement of the waitresses. Before them was a crisp white tablecloth, and silverware stamped with the railway's distinctive insignia. Metal fans whirred softly above them. The space was well-appointed, hemmed with pillars and carved wooden partitions, fresh flowers adorning many of the tables. All in all, Billie found this was a convenient meeting place and an excellent spot to watch the flow of regular commuters and out-of-towners coming in on the interstate trains. The space filled and emptied like the tides.

"Scones and tea?"

"Thank you," Shyla replied with her usual reserve, staring at the white tablecloth as she spoke.

Despite her seemingly quiet disposition, Billie had once seen Shyla take down a barricaded window with an ax. Not a sight she would soon forget. She keenly wanted Shyla to work for her in an official capacity because she knew she'd make a first-rate investigator, but the younger woman wouldn't have it.

This type of rendezvous was their usual routine, if it could be called a routine when Billie could not, in fact, set the dates and times for these meetings. Shyla was a Wiradjuri woman, the people of three rivers, and despite the growing camaraderie between the two women, she did not have a calling card or address she was willing to share with Billie, and had only recently furnished Billie with her surname, Davis—though it was unlikely to be a family birth name; more likely it had been bestowed on her by the missionaries at the Bomaderry Aboriginal Children's Home. Shyla was cagey about personal information, and perhaps not unreasonably so. Having escaped the Aborigines Welfare Board and the family she had been put to work for, she likely did not savor the prospect of being tracked down by authorities of any kind again. She had her own system of contacts with her mob, as she often called the girls and young women still working in domestic service. The information gleaned from them was sometimes valuable to Billie in her work. Wealthy families often chose to overlook what their domestic staff were privy to. And so Shyla's contacts learned things they were happy to pass on to Shyla, who in turn would be an informant for Billie—if and when she chose. There'd been many a time she wanted to call up Shyla to ask for her assistance, but Shyla was available when Shyla was available, and that was that.

"How are your brothers?" Billie asked her.

A waitress arrived with their tea, looking at Billie and avoiding eye contact with her companion. Some of the women who worked here whispered about them, finding the Black-and-white pairing odd, even after the many meetings they had witnessed between the two women.

"My brothers are better, thank you," Shyla said softly of her recently reunited family members. Helping to track down Shyla's brothers had been more difficult than Billie had expected.

When the waitress returned, she placed the scones near Billie, and Billie pushed them across to the middle of the table. "They're for both of us, me and my friend," she said, annoyed.

"Of course, miss." The waitress walked off.

"I'm glad you came to see me today. I have someone I would like you to discreetly ask around about, if you are happy to. A Mr. Richard Montgomery. An ad man. He is, or was, very wealthy and had house staff during the war."

At this Shyla sat up and nodded. This was a common request from Billie, and part of their trade in information and services. Like Billie, Shyla rather liked a puzzle, and some of her contacts were domestic staff used by Sydney's elite, or "upper four hundred," as Sydney's most wealthy were known. The girls trusted Shyla, and Shyla in turn trusted Billie—even if she didn't quite trust Billie's relationship with the cops.

Billie wrote down Richard Montgomery's name and her client's address in Potts Point.

"His wife, Vera Montgomery, is a new client. She has been try- ing to find her husband for two years, she tells me, so he is either hiding out in Sydney somewhere, living a double life with unusual success, or he is overseas living it up, or dead."

Shyla secreted the piece of paper in a pocket. "I'll ask around."

"Thank you. It's somewhat pressing, so if you could get back to me soon, I would appreciate it." Meanwhile, Billie and Sam would have to ask around about Montgomery at the advertising agency he used to work for. The advertising world in Sydney was small enough. They all tended to know one another—and compete.

Shyla nodded. "I'll find you if I have something."

"I also have a job proposition for you, Shyla, if you're interested in more paying work at the moment." Shyla's expression did not change, and her full lips stayed sealed shut.

"I know I already asked you about the possibility of joining the agency in an official capacity, and you said that isn't something you want. I respect that," Billie said. "However, if you are interested in something casual, just for a few weeks, a month or so, then I would love to have your help."

"What is it you need?"

"This new case for Mrs. Montgomery may be taking me back to Europe for a while, it looks like. Should be confirmed either way in the next day or so. I don't know how long it will take to get a result, but I will need someone to look after the office while I'm away, just checking the post that comes in, making sure everything is in order, and taking any urgent messages that may come in."

"You already have a secretary," Shyla pointed out.

"Sam would come with me to assist on the case," she said. "I'm still working out the details—it's early days—but I would dearly love your help. If it goes ahead, I'll close up the office for a while, once I wrap up the case I'm on. But, Shyla, I could really use someone to keep an eye out for any telegrams or important mail, in case I need to be reached. I trust you, and there aren't too many people I trust in this city at the moment."

Having made her case, Billie sat back and enjoyed a scone while Shyla considered her request.

"No gunjies?" she asked.

Gunjies. Cops.

"No cops," Billie confirmed.

This was a sore spot between the women. Shyla was suspicious of the police. For Billie, whose father had been a cop before getting into the private inquiry business, cops were part of her world. She had friends in the police, and enemies, too, perhaps, but more often than not she was on pretty equal footing with them. She could bend the law a little here and there and get away with it. For Shyla, and those in Aboriginal communities, cops were an entirely different matter. Contacting the authorities about anything might lead to being arrested for something else entirely, or men in the community being taken away, or the Aborigines Welfare Board removing children from their families "for their own good," as had happened to Shyla and her siblings. She had been taken by police when she was just four years old, placed with the Aborigines Welfare Board, and raised by Christian missionaries, later to be trained into domestic service. A person did not just forgive and forget that. It wasn't surprising then that when a lot of Aboriginal folks saw a police officer, they ran the other way, even when they'd done nothing wrong. Billie had seen it with her own eyes and, through Shyla, knew some of the deeply troubling history.

"You won't need to deal with any police," Billie assured her. "This is just for me, I promise you. As I see it, you shouldn't have to deal with anyone but me and the odd telegram service. The office will be closed, after all."

Her friend considered this. "But you are still talking with that big cop?"

Detective Inspector Cooper. Billie nodded. "I am seeing him today, yes," she admitted. "He's one of the good ones, Shyla." Billie had something of a soft spot for Cooper, that was true, not that he ever really let her in. But her fondness for the stoic cop aside, if there was one local policeman she trusted, who also had enough power to get things done, it was him.

Shyla's eyes narrowed, and a deep line appeared between her brows. There was a painful history there, involving the frustrating release of a Nazi war criminal they had caught the year before at considerable personal risk. Not only had he been trading in goods stolen from concentration camp victims in Europe during the war, but he had also cruelly exploited and abused several young Aboriginal women—and girls. It hadn't been Hank Cooper who'd been involved in Hessmann's release, but he hadn't been able to stop it either. But Billie's proposed travels had nothing to do with Detective Inspector Cooper or the New South Wales Police. Her assignment was to find Mrs. Montgomery's missing husband, and perhaps even her own, if she could uncover any information about what had happened to Jack. If she did find time to dig around into the colleagues of the Nazi who had come all the way to Australia and wronged Shyla's mob, all the better.

"This would just be a favor for me, Shyla," Billie reiterated. "You would have pay, of course, and you could work it in with your other commitments, I imagine. No cops." Billie spread out her palms, as if to illustrate the lack of hidden details.

Shyla looked down into her cup, as if the tea leaves could give her answers. "It would be a favor for you?"

Billie nodded. "Yes. It would be a favor for me, Shyla. Only if this trip goes ahead, mind you, and I'll confirm that soon."

After some thought, Shyla nodded. "If it goes ahead, I'll help."

Billie exhaled. "Thank you, Shyla. I owe you one."

The two finished their drinks and made small talk about the state of the world; the politics of the new NSW premier, McGirr; and the ongoing fallout of the war on their respective lives. As usual, Shyla kept a lot to herself, even the current neighborhood she called home.

"You'd make a good spy. Perhaps I will get you pulled into the profession yet," Billie added cheekily as she went to stand up. Billie had to head to Central Police soon, somewhere Shyla would not want to go.

"*Billie!*" Shyla chided.

She laughed out loud as her friend slapped her wrist.

Six

—⁓—

That afternoon Billie entered Central Street on foot, just a short walk from Daking House, and arrived at a place that was almost as familiar to her as the old von Hooft Walker family home in Potts Point.

Central Police.

Her father, Barry Walker, had quit his job in policing in favor of private inquiry work by the time Billie was born—had in fact met her mother while helping her acquire her divorce—but this three-story building and the maze of holding cells beneath it had been the setting for many of her father's stories at the dinner table. And once Billie had returned from Europe and made the decision to reopen her late father's inquiry agency, professional life kept bringing her back. It had almost become an extension of home, in a way—a connection usually peculiar to career cops and criminals.

Pausing under the grand arch at the entrance of the station, Billie removed a cigarette from her case and was almost immediately offered a light from one of the plainclothes detectives loitering nearby. She reflected once more on the odd location of this place, hidden as it was down what was essentially an alley, despite its name.

Central was just wide enough for the automobiles that brought in prisoners and the police motorcars that came and went through the day and night—a private world of crime, tucked back from the more palatable goings-on of the Sydney streets outside.

Billie absentmindedly thanked the officer and went through a mental checklist of her day. She had made arrangements by telephone to meet the worried Mr. Charles, sent Sam off to do some valuable background work on Mr. Montgomery and confirmed that he was more than willing to accompany her on the investigation, received further assurances from her potential client that arrangements would be made and costs covered for their travel to London and Paris, and even secured Shyla's services for caretaking the office in her absence. At this rate she'd be able to solve all of Sydney's problems by sundown, and a few of her own besides.

Should she tell Cooper about her plans?

Squinting in thought, and fag smoldering, Billie entered the police station and made her way to the reception desk, where she recognized the bouncing, curly locks of the blonde who was bent over her work. A smile crept over her face.

"Boo," Billie said to the part in the hair.

"Cripes!" Constable Primrose exclaimed. "You gave me a fright, Billie. How do you do that?"

Constable Annabelle Primrose was a resourceful and athletic young woman of about twenty-three, hailing from the country. No matter how long she had lived in the city, working at this desk job, she still looked like she rode horses in the sunshine all day. The police force was wasting her considerable talents, Billie thought. She fancied that Primrose, who was stocky and strong, could wrestle bank robbers with one arm and clobber narcotics peddlers with the other if only her employers would let her. But such excitement was rare for the few women they allowed on the force. The rules stated that women officers had to quit if they married or, heaven forbid, became pregnant, and the constabulary seemed to keep them in a sort of preemptive holding pattern until they did, evidently using the prospect of them dropping out as a reason to all but compel them to do so. Women officers like Primrose were not given pensions or superannuation, weren't allowed to join the Police Association due to their sex, were rarely permitted to carry sidearms, and weren't given uniforms. These rules, written as they were by men, all amounted to one more compelling reason Billie was happy to remain her own boss, thank you very much.

"It is mighty fine to see you, Constable," Billie said, grinning mischievously. "What's new? Anything exciting going on around here?" She leaned in conspiratorially, her elbows on the desk.

"Billie, it's a crime wave," Primrose whispered with wide eyes. "There's been bashings and stabbings and brawls."

"Naturally," she said coolly. That was Sydney for you. It certainly wasn't the safe haven she'd dreamed about when she was in Europe during the war. Billie's rose-colored glasses had well and truly been discarded. "Are those visiting sailors involved?"

"Beg your pardon, Billie?"

"Never mind." The boisterous sailors she had seen in the Cross had probably been blameless good-time boys, adding some shillings to the economy, underground though some of it might be, and who was Billie to judge that?

"Have you been following the developments in that Bronia Armstrong murder?" Primrose asked. "They convicted the poor woman's boss," she went on, shaking her head. "Her boss! Now they say he's hanged himself in the jail cell, and left a note proclaiming his innocence."

"An awful business, isn't it?" Billie agreed. The fifty-year-old accountant in Brisbane looked to have strangled his secretary and was sentenced to life with hard labor for the crime, though some thought the local police had rushed the conviction through. The poor girl had been only nineteen. It was a shameful affair, and now two people were dead. It was perhaps because of the changing times that the nation was caught up in the tragedy of one girl's life taken horribly, when only a few years before, mass death had seemed omnipresent and unstoppable, a force so all-encompassing it almost could not be remarked upon.

"What about you? Any exciting new cases?" Primrose asked, keen for gossip.

"Just the usual marital work," Billie said, leaving out the details about the not-so-usual case of Mr. Charles the night before. "But I do appear to possibly be heading back to Europe for a spell, on a job."

"Oh!" The constable's blue eyes widened. "Really? Gosh, I'll miss you, Billie. Tell me you're still socking it to those Nazi bastards."

"When possible," Billie responded, grinning again.

Constable Primrose looked up and Billie turned, following her gaze to the tall figure of Detective Inspector Hank Cooper, the lift closing behind him.

"I should go. I've a date with the DI," Billie whispered to her friend, and turned to face the detective. She greeted him with a smile and leaned back with her arms on the desk.

Cooper had doffed his hat for her, holding the welt edge in elegant hands, and as she stood up and walked toward him, she had a flash of their first meeting outside the locked door of her flat at Cliffside. She'd woken to find a dead man had been planted in her bedroom, had known a stitch-up well enough when she saw it. It had been a rough and memorable weekend, that one, but among the unpleasantness and the stench of corruption had been this man, Hank Cooper, with his honest face and rangy physique, and his willingness to do what he could. A good egg among a questionable batch, to her mind. Just like this, he'd doffed his hat at her that morning as she'd approached, a gentlemanly type right down to his toes, while his partner, the detestable Constable Dennison, huffed and puffed.

"Pleasure to see you, always," she said, and slid into the small lift with him. As it ascended, she looked him up and down and settled on his neck, which was around her eyeline. "Nice tie."

"Thank you," he replied, poker-faced, and not looking in her direction, nor remarking on her little tête-à-tête with Primrose. Billie didn't bother looking away, instead doing her best to read his profile, and finally settling her gaze on his pale eyelashes. She considered saying something about them but decided it would be a step too far in their little game.

The pair reached the third floor and he invited her to step out first, then led her down the hall as the lift closed behind them. She felt eyes leering at her—the usual boys, restlessly holding papers or cigarettes and raring to get out onto the streets for the action they'd signed up for. Arriving at the room he used for his office, Hank opened the door and invited her in, whisking her away from his colleagues. They had a way of making her skirt suit feel like a slip. Closing the door on them was like switching off a spotlight.

"Thank you kindly," Billie said.

This was not her first time in the small room, which smelled strongly of cigarettes and men. Each time she entered the cramped space, Cooper courteously opened the window, despite the season. It was presently ajar in anticipation of her presence, a small, cool breeze moving through the room. Like many public buildings in Sydney, Central Police was bursting at its seams, having been built when the population was somewhat smaller, and crime arguably less sophisticated. Much had changed since 1892, when the new building and the connected cells and court complex must have seemed more than adequate. Now there was barely space to turn around.

The detective inspector pulled out a wooden chair for Billie. He took his place on the other side of the battered desk.

"Thank you for the invite, Cooper," she said, settling into the chair and contemplating the auspicious timing of his call. How much should she tell him about Europe? She crossed her legs and leaned back. "Is this about Moretti?" She went straight to the point.

He closed his eyes, took a long, irritated breath. "It's good to see you, too, Ms. Walker."

Oh dear. Formal names. Perhaps I should have gone a bit easier, she thought.

"I called you here to discuss another matter," he said.

Billie cocked her head. "And Moretti is . . . ?"

PI Vincenzo Moretti was the proverbial thorn in Billie's side, a nasty piece of work if ever there was one, and someone she was convinced was involved in a recent matter of some interest—the same matter that saw Billie and Shyla face-to-face with a Nazi war criminal who was peddling his wares through an auction house right here in Sydney. Capturing him had been a very dangerous exercise, and yet he walked free from the jail he'd been held in, released by someone apparently unaware of his importance. Or at least that was what Billie was meant to believe. What a slap in the face that was.

"We can't get Moretti on anything. At this stage."

Billie held back a bitter laugh. "Oh, I see. By the way, I saw my friend Shyla today. She asked how things are going."

Cooper opened his mouth to speak, then closed it again. His look told her all she needed to know.

"So things are going nowhere."

"I'm trying."

At least he's using the present tense. Plenty of men in his position would already be claiming they'd "tried," they'd "done what they could." Story over. Billie tilted her head. "Sorry, Hank. I do appreciate what you've tried to do, but I'd hoped you'd brought me here to give me some good news."

"If you're willing to let me do some of the talking, I do have something that may be of interest, though it's not as much as I would wish."

Billie leaned forward, interested if not quite chastened.

"It's something you may well already be aware of."

"And if not, I didn't find out from you," she replied softly, warming again. "Do go on. Please. I mean it."

Cooper cleared his throat. "I called you, in fact, because I got a tip-off on some hot jewelry. Earrings."

"My mother's sapphire earrings?" Billie asked immediately, eyes widening. There was only one pair of earrings he could mean. If so, he really was coming through with something. This jewelry was of particular significance, having been swiped from her bedside table— when she was in her bed, asleep.

"A young woman was seen wearing them, or something very similar, at The Dancers."

The Dancers? Why is it always The Dancers? she thought. Sydney could sometimes be a terrifically small town for a "big city," as so many Australians thought of it. Everything seemed interconnected. In fact, her private inquiry work had only proved that was the case.

"There aren't many similar pairs about, and considering their value, well, my mother will be very pleased to say the least," Billie said. The drop earrings held ten little square sapphires in a vertical line, surrounded by small diamonds in an Art Deco style.

"This is why my informant found it of interest. I gather your mother's earrings have not been returned?"

"You gather correctly," Billie replied. "Do you have them, or details of this young woman? My mother has the matching necklace still and can prove ownership."

"I have no doubt. No, I don't have them, but if the woman is seen with them again, I'll have them bring her in for questioning. I'm sorry I don't have more for you."

Billie frowned. "That's all you have?"

He nodded, looking a tad sheepish.

This could have been a telephone call, she realized. The information he had for her wasn't particularly shocking or hush-hush. Cooper had wanted to see her, she thought . . . she hoped. "I'd feel better about it if you had a drink with me," she said.

Cooper's mouth opened, and something passed behind his eyes. He looked ready to turn her down.

"Come on, Hank. It's a Friday, and a helluva week, and you know I don't drink alone. You don't want me to drink alone, do you?"

He sighed, laughing softly to himself, and after a moment he opened the top drawer of his desk, where she knew he kept a good, medicinal tipple, as so many cops did. "You are a persuasive woman, Ms. Walker. Just one." His pale eyes went to the clock.

She smiled as he poured out two small glasses of whisky, neat, and placed them unceremoniously on the desk. "Here's to you getting my mother's earrings back," she said. "Thank you for that, and more, I hope. I'm sorry if I was a bit harsh earlier in that regard."

"Not at all. I can imagine your frustration."

"Oh, I have something I need to ask you, actually," she added. "What's the police department's view . . . well, I should say, what is the department doing these days with reports of homosexuality?"

His eyebrows shot up.

"Men loving men," she specified.

"Thank you. I am aware of what it means," he said.

"Are men like that likely to be charged for their particular proclivities?" she ventured. "In 1947?" Surely there were more important matters to focus on than what consenting adults got up to behind closed doors.

"For buggery? I believe so," Cooper said, frowning.

Billie flinched.

"Don't look at me like that," he said, taken aback by her displeasure. "I don't make the rules. It's section 79 of the Crimes Act. 'Kamp' men, as they sometimes call themselves . . . well, they take a hell of a risk."

"Kamp." Billie was familiar with the acronym, said to have come from the police lingo "Known Associate of Male Prostitutes."

"Why are you asking about this, anyway?" Cooper asked.

"No reason." She folded her arms. Her concerns about Mr. Charles's fate were well-founded, then.

"No reason?" he repeated back to her, sounding unconvinced. "Your assistant, Sam . . . ?"

"Samuel? No, but if he did enjoy the company of other men, I don't see why it would be my business," she said pointedly. "Who would that harm, exactly? So, they still charge people for such things. I see. I was just curious whether anything had changed while I was abroad."

Cooper watched her carefully as she downed her glass, then cleared her throat.

"Speaking of abroad, I have some news for you," she added.

"Is that so?"

"Yes. It seems likely I may be heading to London for a while, and Paris." She thought she detected a slight change in his expression. Was it disappointment? Would he miss her?

Billie pushed her small, empty glass forward.

"Oh?" he said after a moment. "Back to reporting?" He looked down at her glass, and then to her.

"Yes, I will have another, thank you," she said. "And no. It's for a case. A missing husband."

"Do you know how long you'll be gone?"

"As long as the job takes, I suppose," she said.

"Europe? Isn't that a touch outside your usual jurisdiction, so to speak?"

She'd said the same words to him once, she recalled, as they stood on the edge of a precipice in the Blue Mountains, hours outside Sydney, following a harrowing and ultimately fatal car chase. Neither of them seemed keen to be strictly confined to the requirements of their profession. They were motivated by far more than clocking on, clocking off, and gathering the necessary paycheck.

Billie watched Cooper for a moment, considering how much information to divulge. In the end she didn't see the harm in it. Cooper could be helpful—when they weren't busy arguing. "It's a missing man, a Sydneysider from a British family. His last correspondence was from Paris in '45."

His pale eyebrows rose. "I see. A soldier, then."

She shook her head. "An ad man, actually."

His mouth turned down a touch.

"Too old to serve, though he was working for the government," she added in Montgomery's defense. She realized that like many men who had served, Cooper would have little time for those who could be seen as having shirked their responsibility to their country.

He frowned. "It's a long way to go for a divorce case, Billie."

"She's a paying client, Inspector. A well-paying client, I might add," she said. "And it may not be a divorce case, exactly. If I don't find him alive."

"I see. Now, I'm not going to try to tell you how to do your job—"

"Well, that's a relief," she shot back. "I might stick around for a bit in Europe, off the clock, and see if there are any leads on Hess-mann's gang."

Something flashed across Cooper's face at the mention of Hessmann—the Nazi they had discovered living in their midst the year before, who had tried to enact revenge on Billie for breaking his cover and bringing his horrible postwar schemes to ruin. It had been a close call, that day. Too close. Cooper frowned again, then pulled out the whisky once more and poured another two drinks.

"What is it?" she asked, holding her refilled glass. "There's been movement? Some leads on who was aiding him here, and how he got to Australia?"

Billie knew Cooper had served in the 2/8th Battalion in North Africa and New Guinea before being recruited to Z Special Unit, from what she had gleaned. That was military intelligence. It had taken some quiet digging, but she was pretty sure he remained con-nected, though he had never confirmed the fact.

His mouth opened and closed again. "I'm not at liberty to tell you that," he finally said.

Billie raised her arched brows incredulously and blew out her breath, not hiding her disappointment. "Intelligence, is it?" she guessed. "Well now, it's not very intelligent to keep it from those who might be able to help, is it?"

Cooper laughed. "You may be surprised to hear this, Ms. Walker, but you aren't actually in the employ of the intelligence services, here or abroad."

That made her smile. Cooper was growing a sense of humor, slowly but surely. Billie rather liked it, even if this whole routine was becoming a well-worn track for them—she pushed, he pulled back, he extended the olive branch, then whipped it away again just when she thought she had it in hand. Billie picked her cigarette up from where it smoldered in the ashtray on Cooper's desk, seeming to send up cryptic smoke signals, took a drag, and then exhaled, letting the smoke spiral upward.

"Billie, I know you," he said, and met her eyes. "I want you to reconsider poking around in Europe after Hessmann," he continued in a low voice. "It could be very dangerous for you. These Nazis . . . and these Nazi sympathizers, the fascists who aided them, the ones at the top . . . they have access to a great deal of money and resources. I'm quite sure Hessmann wasn't acting alone. These war criminals . . . their movements appear *organized*, and with some big players on their side. Only a mere handful have been brought to the trials."

The executions from the latest round of war-crimes trials had been happening all month, but she knew those convicted represented only the smallest fraction of those who had intentionally murdered civilians, en masse. Yes, Hessmann, who had reigned over women's lives at Ravensbrück, must have been helped getting to Australia. She was aware that there were high-ranking Nazis still evading capture—Adolf Eichmann, for example, the SS-*Obersturmbannführer* who was one of the major architects of the Final Solution, and Martin Bormann, Hitler's deputy, rumored to be dead by some, but spotted alive by others. They were both sentenced to death in absentia at the recent trials, but what justice was that? What lives were they living out, and where? The more she heard about Auschwitz, the more urgent it seemed that they find the likes of Josef Mengele, a doctor who worked there and was known by survivors as "the Angel of Death." Many more were also unaccounted for. How many deaths were they responsible for between them? And who was helping them?

She frowned. "So you're sure now that Hessmann got here through an organized group of some kind, is that right?" she asked, ignoring his warning.

"Undoubtedly. Yes. He was furnished with false papers some-where, perhaps in more than one place, and given the go-ahead to ship large amounts of war loot across, perhaps to sell here and send money back . . ."

Hessmann's remote house had been stuffed with rare artifacts and items of value, as Billie had discovered—and barrels full of gold fillings, their owners long since murdered in the camps. It was far more than what he alone might need to live well in his comfortable exile. And then there was the auction house. His connection with the owner seemed established. Just how many goods had he been selling through Sydney? Why would he have so much if he wasn't holding it for others?

"Well, if that's the case, the international authorities need to know about it."

He shrugged. "They do, to an extent. But it's not that simple. What you happened upon with Hessmann is just the tip of the ice-berg, I fear." He looked at her earnestly. "You know I'll worry about you over in Europe. I realize I can't stop you from looking into Hess-mann's associates from Ravensbrück, if that is what you have your mind set on, and I confess I'd do the same if I were the one getting on that plane, but please consider my warning."

"Consider me warned," she said evenly.

He frowned and exhaled. "Perhaps keep an ear out for the word 'Odessa.'"

"What's it about? Nazi smugglers?" she asked, leaning forward.

"Yes and no. It's unclear what they're doing, but 'Odessa' seems to be a type of code for Nazis to access aid or transportation, at the very least. Something to do with a ratline. Most importantly, though, I want you to have this." He pushed a card into her hand. "This is an associate of mine, a man I trust. He's a good man, from Sutton. He knows London, and also Paris a fair bit."

Sutton. Now that the possibility of returning to London and Paris was dangling in front of her, Jack—who was born in Sutton—was everywhere, in every thought. She had to try to untangle thoughts of him from this trip, or it could be disastrous. She had to keep a clear head, make the right decisions for the agency and for her client.

"Intelligence?" she guessed, looking at the card. It simply said *Harrison,* and had a series of numbers written on it in pen—a telephone number, she could see, followed by a four-digit code. She slipped it into her purse.

Hank didn't reply, but his eyes indicated she was correct. "Promise me that if you start digging around over there, if you catch a trail, hear about Odessa, promise me you won't try to go it alone. Promise me you will reach out to him on that number. He may be able to help you if things get . . . serious."

Billie considered his warnings for a beat, then picked up her glass and tilted her chin back, finishing the last of the bracing liquid inside. She pressed her red lips together and placed the empty glass on his desk.

"I promise," she said.

—⌘—

Billie said good-bye to Constable Primrose on her way out, after the detective inspector had escorted her down to the ground floor. "Thank you again for my Fighting Red," she added, speaking of her final tube of Tussy lipstick, which the constable had gifted her recently. It was her favorite color, had been for some years now, yet it had been discontinued, which was a damn shame if you asked Billie. Presumably someone in marketing thought women no longer had to fight. Billie, for one, had not found that the case.

Seven

—⚭—

The woman who went by the name of Ginger was preparing for her workday much as any other woman would.

Seated straight backed and proud before her mirror—the vanity in front of her set up with her tools of lipstick, rouge, cream mascara, loose powder, puffs, brushes, and pins—Ginger went through her daily beauty routine with the precision of someone who had gone through the same motions many hundreds of times before. She wore a slip beneath an open silk robe, and a long fur stole around her shoulders, providing some warmth. Her favorite fabric-soled shoes were on her feet, along with a good pair of stockings clipped neatly to her garter. Ignoring all but her face for now, she leaned into her mirrored reflection, examining her skin, powdering it, and applying a generous amount of rouge to the apples of her cheeks. Satisfied, she picked up her mascara brush and, wetting it lightly, dabbed it in the cake of mascara. She applied the dark mixture to her long eyelashes, exaggerating them even more. Turning one way, then the other, she assessed her reflection through squinting eyes, as an artist does their canvas, and, evidently pleased with the effect of her work, was happy to pause her preparations to speak to the woman visiting her.

"So, this fella we're talking about, what's his story again?" she asked.

What was different from most women's routines was that this was late on a Friday afternoon, Ginger had just woken up, and what she was wearing was as close to a uniform as she needed for her profession. In truth, Ginger was not like many other women. Every inch of her was sex—lips pert and red; skin like butter, smooth and expensive, and scented with Egyptian Musk, no doubt a gift from a well-traveled suitor. She wore her hair in pin curls and dyed as pale as that of her famous namesake, Ginger Rogers, and she held her petite body almost as a ballerina might if she had no boss, no rules, no *premier maître de ballet* breathing down her neck. Ginger was at the height of her physical prowess and hyperaware of her physical form—its limitations, powers, and possibilities—and how to make the most of the latter two.

"I can't tell you his story, precisely," Billie Walker told her in response. "But I can assure you he seems a decent fellow."

At this, Ginger laughed. "And he knows he'll be photographed?" She paused again from her preparations to look at Billie through the reflection in her vanity mirror.

She was about ten years younger than Billie, though painted as she was, it was hard to pick her age. The stole around her slim shoulders was created from the fur of water rats, fashioned to look like mink. It was pretty good in the right light, and Billie recalled the impressive glass-eyed stole on Mrs. Montgomery's shoulders and reflected once more on how such accoutrements told a tale of social status and Lady Luck. But if anyone knew how to dazzle, subtly or not-so-subtly manipulating the minds of others to bend to her will, it was Ginger. Her specialty was the minds—and bodies—of men. If she willed it, the fur was mink, she was a Hollywood movie star, and any man she was with was, for a short time, the most important man on earth. That was what she was paid for.

"Yes," Billie confirmed. "The gentleman will know he is being photographed."

"And he has agreed to this?" Ginger turned on her vanity stool to shoot Billie another questioning look. "That's what you expect me to believe?"

Billie nodded. "Yes." Well, that was a white lie. He hadn't agreed to it yet, but Billie had her own powers of persuasion, different though they might be. He would agree.

"I must say that's a first," said Ginger, and rose from her stool to sweep back her robe and place her hands provocatively on her slim hips. She fixed her gaze on Billie again and then shifted it to Billie's male companion, whom she had not previously met. She rocked back on her heels, and her expression changed.

Her shoes were beautiful, Billie noticed, if awfully high by her own reckoning. Red and velvety. Ginger's stance—her changed posture—had transformed her somehow. Yes, it was Sam who had caused it. Consciously or unconsciously, she had switched into performance mode in the presence of male company.

"That is not usually how this caper goes," Ginger pointed out. "The poor lambs are generally quite unaware." Her long-lashed gaze had fallen on Sam, as if he were the proverbial lamb to the slaughter, and she the lion.

Billie knew that Ginger did some work for some of Sydney's other private inquiry agencies. As a rule, she didn't hire women to lure cheating men into setups—that wasn't how she chose to operate. Ginger had the odd bit of valuable information, however, so although this was their first setup, it wasn't their first piece of business.

Billie knew Ginger was perfect for this role. She would be believable, professional, fast.

It would work. At least, she hoped it would.

"And I just have to kiss the gentleman; that's it?"

"That's as far as it will go. Yes," Billie assured her. "Though let me be clear. It needs to look good. You get my meaning. There can't be any way to explain the encounter away as platonic."

Ginger shifted her gaze back to Billie from Sam, and he exhaled. "When I kiss a man, he knows it's not platonic," she said.

Billie smiled. "I imagine so."

"And you said no cops, right?" Ginger asked, her powdered brow creasing.

"No cops," Billie said for the second time that day.

The younger woman cleared her throat, scuffed a red heel on the ground. "Okay, it's a deal, even if I still don't get it. Two pounds, one kiss. Just one. I'll make it good, you know I will. You'd just better be there to capture it, 'cause it's double if I have to do it again."

"That's fair," Billie said. "We have a deal. We'll be there, and I'll give the signal to confirm, then you do your thing. It should only take a few minutes of your night."

"I'll have to redo my lipstick," she pointed out.

Billie grinned. Ginger was good, wily, but she was not going to pay her more. Two pounds was a lot for a few minutes. But it was fair. It was work.

"Anything else . . . your man gets handsy or anything . . . and our deal is off. It'll cost more, right?" Ginger said.

"Understood, though I don't think you have to worry about that. What do you do, anyway, in instances when one of these gentlemen wants something that's not agreed?"

Ginger looked back to Sam, who had remained near the door, appearing distinctly stiff and uncomfortable in her company. "What about *him*? He'd get a long way for free," she teased, giving him a playful look as she appraised him from his head to his shoes and up again.

Amused, Billie waited for Sam's response to this, but he seemed to have temporarily lost his power of speech.

"Well, gentlemen do have a way of causing trouble from time to time," Ginger agreed, having moved back to the conversation at hand. "But I'm no Dulcie. I don't know if I could even swing an ax."

Billie laughed aloud. Dulcie Markham, or "Pretty Dulcie," had been booked for prostitution dozens of times and was rumored to have used an ax on a client or two she didn't like. She was notorious for her gangland lovers, but she could hold her own without their muscle—and even against them. In fact, if the rumors Billie had heard were true, Dulcie was every bit as lethal as the standover men she frequently kept company with.

"But don't you worry about me, Billie," Ginger told her. "I've got a few boys happy to help me out," she said, and winked. "I'll be all right."

Billie hoped so.

—◊—

Around quarter past six, Billie recognized the figure of Mr. Charles enter the Grand Concourse of Central Railway Station from the northern side. He wore a neat fedora and crisp suit, and he made his way toward her through the after-work crowd, his head bowed. He looked over his shoulder from time to time, as if he might still be under surveillance. This was an altogether different person from the one who had walked leisurely through Kings Cross. The poor man seemed to be quite affected by recent events. She couldn't blame him for that, especially after Cooper's confirmation of what Billie already suspected—in Australia, even in 1947, homosexuality continued to be prosecuted as a serious crime.

Mr. Charles came to stand a yard to Billie's left, took a cigarette from his case, tapped it, and held it near his mouth. "Miss Walker," he said, a touch unsteadily.

"Mr. Charles," Billie replied softly, and inclined her head in his direction. "Thank you for meeting me here. I did not wish to meet you in my office in case your wife unexpectedly graced us with her presence, however unlikely that might be." She took a Lucky Strike from the case in her handbag, brought it up to her face, and he made a gesture to light it for her. "Are you happy to meet with me in the refreshment room?" she asked him as he leaned in. She gestured toward the entrance. "One of the corner tables is available. It should be comfortable and private enough for our purposes, if that is suitable for you."

"Okay," Mr. Charles replied nervously. He lit her fag with a hand that lightly shook, and then retreated to light his own.

She leaned against the sandstone wall behind them as they smoked, her keen gaze taking in the moving crowd. "I'll meet you at the corner table in, say, five minutes?" she said after a breath.

Mr. Charles looked up at the large railway clock that hung beneath the vaulted ceiling of the concourse and nodded. Cigarette dangling from her lips, Billie turned and left him, and entered the Railway Refreshment Rooms for the second time that day. She took one of her usual corner tables and ordered herself some black tea. She needed it after her afternoon drink with Cooper. Her lips turned up at the corners with the memory.

Mr. Charles entered precisely five minutes later, as instructed. That bode well for the proposition ahead. To get through this, she needed him comfortable with taking and following instructions. He folded himself into the chair opposite Billie and held up a menu as much to shield himself from her as to actually order anything.

"Coffee? Tea?" Billie suggested.

Behind the menu he shook his head.

"We can make this quick if you like. We find ourselves in a pickle, as they say. As I mentioned on the telephone, my client has the right to her resolution," she said, as delicately as she could. "Further, I'm sure you agree I can't keep charging your wife for a job I completed last night. I'm being paid a daily rate."

"Oh yes," he said, staring intently at the menu, which he now had laid flat on the tabletop, and blushing the color of beetroot. "Miss Walker, I . . . I guess you know I will never work in this town again if . . . And if it goes to court . . ." He could not quite form the words, and he didn't need to. Billie was aware of his difficult predicament. And hers. "My wife is a good woman, you understand, but she will be very cross. You can't let me be put away."

"No, I cannot," she conceded. "And it's Ms."

"Pardon?"

"It's Ms. Never mind." She was quite used to mistakenly being called "Miss," as wrong as that felt in her bones. It was like admitting her makeshift wartime wedding was no wedding at all—at least not so far as many were concerned. Barely any witnesses—at least few that she'd seen since. No rings. No husband. "The point is," Billie continued, barely missing a beat despite the tightness in her chest, "I can't guarantee what your wife will do with these photographs, or how angry she may be, as you rightly point out. However, if you agree that she is determined to divorce you, and we should not stop her, she will require proof of your adultery to do so."

Private inquiry agents were often considered a necessary evil, thanks to Australia's marital laws. Grounds for divorce were slim, and proof had to be black-and-white—usually of the photographic variety. It was true that society was hostile to divorced women, but if these women really could not remain in their marriages— and they were best placed to make that decision themselves, Billie felt—she was compelled to help them out of them. As a rule, she believed her clients deserved the truth, nothing more, nothing less. But cheating spouses did not deserve jail.

"What do you propose?" Mr. Charles asked nervously.

"I propose we give her the proof she requires."

At this, the poor man's blushing face seemed to drain entirely of color. He opened his mouth, but she cut him off, raising a palm.

"Tonight, in the very same location where you went last night," she said, and noted him cringe at the mention, "you will find a woman. You will kiss that woman, and then you will go on your way. And you will pay one day's standard rates for the services of my agency, to be paid discreetly in notes so as not to show up in your checkbook. Do you agree to these terms?"

He blinked. "Well, of course I would agree to that, but—"

"Please understand, Mr. Charles, this is entirely against my ethics. Your wife deserves the truth, but the risk to you is greater than I am willing to take professional or personal responsibility for. I will expect to see you tonight, as discussed, ten o'clock sharp, and to find fourteen pounds in an envelope with my name on it, given to John, the lift operator at Daking House, no later than Monday. You will recognize him. He is a war vet, and he will be expecting you. I do hope things with your wife resolve smoothly in the best interests of all parties. I mean that," she said. "All going well, we won't speak again."

His jaw was slack. She took the opportunity to finish her cup of black tea while he absorbed the plan laid out for him. The hot liquid felt invigorating, which was a good thing with another late night ahead of her. Perhaps this could all be put to bed by ten thirty or so, and she could focus entirely on Montgomery.

"Do this and I will present the photographs from tonight to my client. The ones from yesterday will be destroyed. You have my word."

He looked hopeful. "You mean it?"

"I'm no blackmailer, Mr. Charles. Your secret is safe with me, and I consider it none of my business, beyond providing my client with what she needs to get on with her life."

He swallowed then, and she fancied there was some pain there at the thought of losing the woman he had married, and perhaps even loved still.

"Do you agree to these terms?" she pressed.

"I will find it uncomfortable, of course, but I do agree." He looked sick with relief. "I owe you one, Miss Walker."

"You'll be paying for my services, Mr. Charles, and should feel no debt," she assured him. "Justice would not have been served by the clear alternative to this arrangement."

Eight

—⌇—

Again, I'm so sorry to have to give you this news about your husband,
Mrs. Charles."

Winnie Charles, handkerchief dabbing her eyes, and dressed in
dark clothes almost as if in mourning, sloped out of Billie Walker's
office at quarter to five on Saturday afternoon. Samuel Baker stood
up from behind his desk, offering condolences with a solemn nod.

"I knew. I just knew . . ." she said through sniffles, then blew her
nose loudly in the reception area as Billie and Sam watched silently,
heads bowed. She patted her lambskin purse, wherein an envelope
of stark, freshly developed photographs told the necessary story.
Ginger had done her part, as had poor Mr. Robert Charles, despite
how he might have felt about the setup. Now Mrs. Charles's purse
had furnished B. Walker Private Inquiries with something just shy
of a week's wages, her husband having provided the rest without her
knowing. The unhappy woman had had her suspicions confirmed,
and they were mostly correct. It was done. An unsatisfactory conclusion that was better than the alternative.

Sam opened the door.

"If there is anything else we can do to assist, do let us know, won't you?" Billie said gently. "We wish you the very best during this difficult time."

Child-free, and soon to be divorced, Winnie Charles doubtless had more tears to shed before all was through, but she had possibilities ahead of her. It would not be easy for her as a divorcée, but although the war had cut men down like a scythe at harvesttime, maybe, just maybe, she would find the kind of love she had always hoped for. Sam courteously held the door open for her, and she disappeared down the hall toward the lift.

"There goes another happy customer," Billie remarked, deadpan. *Marital work.* They often celebrated after a successful case, but this resolution had not brought on one of her more celebratory moods. She did hate being compromised, her ethics in conflict, but, more to the point, her mind was quite caught up in further pressing business.

"She got what she needed," Sam pointed out, and Billie hoped he was correct. "Look at what I was reading," he said, pointing out a newspaper article spread across his desk. "It mentions one of those camps."

The smile having dropped from her face, Billie rested a hip on the reception desk and swiveled around to read the bold headline:

THREE HORROR CAMP WOMEN HANGED

May 3, 1947. Australian Associated Press, LONDON, Sun.—Retribution has caught up with more Nazi war criminals. Three women were among a number hanged on Friday for camp atrocities.

HAMBURG report states that Dorothea Binz (26), Elizabeth Marshall (60), and Reta Boesel (25), members of the staff of Ravensbrück concentration camp, have been hanged. It is reported from Berlin that Johann Schwarz-huber, Ludwig Ramdour, Gustav Binder, Gerhard Schid-lausky, and Rolf Rosenthal, sentenced to death by a British Military Tribunal for their part in the Ravensbrück con-centration camp war crimes, were hanged at Hamelin, in addition to five other war criminals hanged on Friday.

"A nasty business," Billie said, her stomach uneasy. She looked at the clock. More work called. "I must head out now, Sam. I think I'll handle this one alone."

"Are you sure?" he asked, folding up the paper.

She was sure. Though it had only been two days since they made the acquaintance of Mrs. Vera Montgomery, it felt like longer. Already Billie found herself questioning her business, questioning her response to Jack's disappearance, questioning just where she would be by the end of the month or even the next week. She needed an-other one-on-one with this new client if they were to move forward. Samuel could clearly prove a good distraction for the woman, if their first in-person meeting was anything to go by, but that wasn't what Billie needed right now. What she needed, in short, was certainty— a much better feel for the woman's material circumstances—before the prospect of overseas travel played on her mind and with her plans any further.

"Close up if you will, Sam." The phone service could take the rest of the weekend calls, if there were any. "We had a big night last night, and you did a fine job with those photographs. You deserve a bit of weekend time off." That was something that had become a rare commodity lately, weekends being prime time for many of the unsa-vory things the pair were paid to document. They knew that week-ends in Sydney weren't all family picnics and church services.

THE GHOSTS OF PARIS

She could only carry out this overseas investigation and close her office to other clients for a spell if her pocketbook agreed. And there was the other thing, the thing that had been on her mind since that first meeting two days before: How did she really feel about returning to Europe, after all that had unfolded there? It was all tied up with Jack. She couldn't jeopardize all she had painstakingly built with her inquiry agency for a trip down memory lane. It had to make business sense.

"You drew up the contract for Mrs. Montgomery, Sam? Twenty-eight-pounds-per-day rate when out of the country, and the larger deposit for expenses to be discussed?"

"I sure did." He handed the paperwork to her. "Gosh, that's some day rate," he remarked. "Pennies from heaven."

"We're going up in the world, dear Sam," she said, sincerely hoping that was the case.

—◦—

Waiting for her on Rawson Street, just outside Daking House, was a sight that never failed to delight Billie Walker—her '33 Willys Roadster, black paint shining in the sunlight. This particular model had a red leather interior, a trusty engine that roared at her command, and a silver ornament depicting Winged Victory taking pride of place on the bonnet, head tilted back in pleasure.

Her beloved wheels.

On her twenty-first birthday, her mother, Baroness Ella von Hooft, had gifted her this fine automobile, and in a way it was a throwback to more prosperous times for the von Hooft Walkers, Billie thought as she walked toward it. A reminder of prewar times. Times when their fortunes were not quite so strained. Billie's keen mind was firmly on her mission of improving her mother's finances as she slid inside her sleek machine, shut the door, and retrieved her leather driving gloves from the glove box. She started up the engine, felt it warm to her touch, and pulled out from the curb into the traffic.

The address Mrs. Montgomery had provided was in a desirable part of Potts Point, but Billie had not counted on just how close it would be to the old von Hooft Walker home. She allowed her eyes to drift up the block, to the mansion in which she had grown up, the home her mother had owned before the Depression, before the family money had run low and they'd been forced to move to the smaller, more humble arrangement at Cliffside Flats. Her former home seemed impossibly large now, part of another lifetime, another world. Two stories of luxury it had been, with gatherings often spilling into the back garden under the blazing Sydney sun, and with parties on summer evenings amid the songs of cicadas and local musicians happy to play for a good drink or two and appreciative company. How much the world could change in just fifteen years, or indeed in just three, with her father now gone, and Billie a widow, or whatever the case might be.

Her gaze returned to Vera's home, a narrow, well-tended Victorian terrace, its off-white paint mostly unchipped by the weather, attractive plants cascading from the wrought-iron balconies. Billie parked near the entrance, her motorcar's satisfying roar quitting on command.

Barely two blocks away from this genteel strip, where Victoria Street connected with Darlinghurst Road and William Street under the giant Capstan clock and the Penfolds sign, trams and traffic would be coming and going and the infamous six o'clock swill would be under way, men drinking their troubles away, for a couple of hours at least. Perhaps Mr. Charles would be among them. A different world just up the road.

With a steadying breath, Billie stepped up to the door of the

Montgomery residence and found it opened promptly by an older woman in plain, somewhat matronly clothing—a housemaid, it would appear.

"I'm Ms. Billie Walker. I believe Mrs. Montgomery is expecting me," Billie told the woman and was led inside without delay, her eyes sweeping around the entrance and lounge area. Vases from China set with fresh flowers. Photographs in gilded frames on the tables and walls. Polished hardwood floors. Persian rugs.

"This way, please," the woman said, her face unreadable, and led Billie up a wooden staircase, where the sweet scent of flowers wafted from the next floor.

Billie's intriguing new client stood to greet her, making no less an impression than she had the first day. Vera Montgomery was resplendent in a luxurious soft-pink silk number with an empire waist, the hem grazing her ankles, and a fur-lined shawl draped around her shoulders. Her vibrant red hair was curled, and she wore a matching silk turban, secured with a round, glittering brooch. She held a cocktail glass, and it appeared she had been enjoying an early-evening aperitif by the balcony, much as Billie's mother liked to do. If she had dressed to make an impression, she had succeeded.

"Join me, won't you?" she invited Billie warmly.

Billie followed her into the room, which had been decorated with a sensuous, Art Nouveau flare—gilt-edged paintings of flowers and plants, the real thing adorning polished tables. Vera and her maid kept the place well—it was spotless—though Billie detected an emptiness in the corners, where furniture may have once been. Could it be that Mrs. Montgomery had visited the auction houses to keep things afloat, perhaps the same ones Billie's own mother had?

"Take a seat, won't you, Miss Walker?" Vera pointed toward a stuffed armchair and settled herself on the plush lounge next to a pampered-looking snow-white cat, which tracked Billie with yellow

eyes. Vera's glowing complexion was lit golden by the lowering sun, filtered through the windows of the terrace.

"It's Ms., actually. My husband is . . . missing in action, as it were," Billie explained.

"Oh, I'm sorry to hear that. Mrs. . . . ?"

"I go by Ms. It's an old title, coined at the turn of the century as a more neutral honorific for women." Billie had seen it mentioned in a *New York Times* article some years previous, at the time unaware it would later suit her so well. "It suits my circumstances, one could say. But perhaps you'll agree we are on a first-name basis now? You may call me Billie, if you like."

"Oh, certainly. And you may call me Vera. It seems we may have more in common than I knew, us both with missing husbands," she said. "Your husband was a soldier, I take it?"

"He was a war correspondent. We weren't married for very long, I'm afraid. We used to work together when I was a reporter, actually. That's how we met. We were both in Paris, just before the war."

"Ah, Paris. You see? You are the right man for this job," Vera declared, raising her glass victoriously. "I knew it."

"I do hope so," Billie cautiously agreed. "I may even be the right woman."

At that moment, the maid appeared with a matching crystal glass for Billie. It was a gimlet.

"Let's drink to your journey and success in this task," Vera declared, holding hers aloft.

The two women raised their glasses and sipped. The gin slid down smoothly, anesthetizing Billie's throat. It was a London Dry with an orange, herbal twist, she detected. A nice drop. Her hostess barely touched hers, instead leaning forward excitedly.

"You were a reporter? How terrifically exciting!"

"It was, at times. Yes," Billie agreed, and put down her glass. "May I ask how you and your husband met?"

"Oh yes." Vera leaned back into the cushions on her lounge, eyes unfocused as they gazed into the past. "Well, we met at work, too, you could say. I was a mannequin at the time, you see. It was just a bit of money on the side." She tilted her head at an attractive angle. "It was a bit scandalous, really. My parents certainly did not approve."

"I see. This is you?" Billie asked, and gestured to a framed black-and-white portrait on the wall to her left. It showed a fresh-faced, dark-haired young woman, pictured in profile. She was wearing a soft Peter Pan collar, her hair styled in perfect sweeping pin curls, the light hitting each one like sunlight on cresting waves.

At this Vera beamed. "I was so young at the time. Just sixteen in that photograph. Richard took it."

"He has a good eye," Billie remarked.

"He's a natural-born photographer, my Richard. We married just a few years later. He was quite insistent and kept asking for my hand after that shoot."

"That sounds very romantic." Billie gave her a smile, waited for a beat, and pushed the necessary contract across to her. "As discussed, we can begin right away with a full inquiry into his whereabouts, and you'll benefit from our full attention. It has been rather busy for the past few months, but we have an opening now to take on this new work, including the planned travel, as discussed."

"That's partially because of the case with Nettie's boy, isn't it?" Vera observed.

"How busy we've been?" Billie nodded. "In part, yes." That case had spilled into the papers, along with Billie's photograph and agency's name. A successful resolution to a missing person case was always good for business, but when it was advertised for you on the front page of the paper? Well, that was something else entirely. The press was not something she'd asked for, but she couldn't deny it had been a boon.

"And you didn't mind working for a Jew?"

Vera's choice of words gave Billie pause. She had been about to take another sip of her drink, but instead she put it back on the table and looked at her hostess intently. If Vera knew about the case with Nettie Brown's son, she would well know that it ended up involving a notorious Nazi war criminal. The papers had made much of that connection, even calling a Billie a "Nazi Hunter."

"Is that a real question, Mrs. Montgomery? No, I don't mind working for Jewish clients. Is that a problem for you?"

"You misunderstand. I ask because of my own background. Montgomery is a great surname for these times, to be sure, but it wasn't mine until I married Richard. I was an Aronowitz. My parents didn't approve of my marrying outside the faith, but they couldn't stop me." She smiled and looked up at that portrait of her younger self. "I was born in Australia, but like Nettie, I have relatives in Europe, many of whom are currently missing, I'm afraid," she added.

"I'm so sorry to hear that, Vera," Billie offered sincerely.

Anti-Semitism was not limited to the Nazis, Billie knew. Australia was a relatively safe place, but the papers had not been without their anti-Semitic cartoons, particularly in the previous few years—cartoons that, as always, reflected and emboldened prejudices in the communities. These sorts of sentiments may have influenced political responses to Jewish refugees during the war, like the Kimberley Plan to resettle persecuted Jewish refugees in Australia, which had been rejected in '44. And there was the MS St. Louis, a ship carrying nearly one thousand Jews, many of them children, which had been turned away by a range of Allied countries, including the United States of America and Canada, as recently as 1939. The St. Louis had been forced eventually to return the refugees to Europe, where, it was rumored, many of the Jews onboard had ended up in the deadly Auschwitz camp, a rumor Billie unfortunately found quite credible. To have been so close to safe haven, only to be turned away again and again, was a truly cruel fate. Anti-Semitic sentiments doubtless encouraged the international community to turn away from Hitler's abuses until it was far too late. Jewish people could hardly have failed to notice the response, wherever they were in the world. Yes, Billie quite understood Mrs. Montgomery's need to know where she stood with her.

"So, perhaps you can see why I came to you," Vera explained. "You are sympathetic, and, as I said, Nettie recommended you quite highly. And as you already know Paris, and have worked there, I am quite certain, as I said, that you are the right man for the job."

She wondered if Vera's vibrant red hair served a purpose beyond fashion, evoking a somewhat different beauty than that of the young Aronowitz she had once been. Billie had not picked her as Jewish, and certainly her home did not advertise the fact in any noticeable way—no Star of David, menorah, or other common Judaica was visible. "How do you and Nettie know each other, exactly?" she asked.

"Not from the synagogue, that's for certain," Vera said, and laughed. At length, she produced a cigarette case and offered Billie one, which she turned down. Vera lit hers with what appeared to be a golden lighter, smiling to herself. "I first met Nettie in her fur shop, and in time we developed a kind of friendship. We are not close, you understand, but we are friendly. I'm a client of hers. It was quite good for the Browns before the war. I think they did well for a while there," she remarked. "Well, we recognized each other as Jews, the way one sometimes does, but I'd married out of it, as much as one can, really, and that was not without some small scandal. Nettie, on the other hand, had changed the family name. We each had our way of dealing with things as they currently are, and we both have relatives back in Europe, and so we bonded over that." Vera shook her head sadly, and a bitterness came over her strong features. "I have come to accept what I cannot control."

"I am deeply sorry," Billie said, finding she was liking the woman more and more. That strength of hers was well earned. "I gather you have tried the NSW Police Missing Persons Bureau in relation to your husband's absence?"

Vera nodded and took another deep, medicinal drag of her cigarette. Her cat stood and moved away from the smoke, then curled into a fluffy ball at the other end of the lounge. "The NSW Police Missing Persons Bureau was of little help, I can tell you," Vera said, with a hint of injustice, "though I understand they are rather snowed under. I also wrote to the Missing Persons Bureau at Scotland Yard, Red Cross, the usual agencies."

"I see. The International Red Cross?" Billie asked.

Vera nodded, that Joan Crawford jaw set determinedly. After a moment she took a small sip of her gimlet, holding the glass and her cigarette as one might hold the essential tools of a mission. "Please understand, Ms. Billie, I'm a survivor. I've given a great deal of thought to this, and while I have come to accept Richard's absence, as you put it, I can no longer accept the circumstances it leaves me in. I am fortunate to have all of this," she said, looking around. "Don't think I don't know it. In order to keep it, though, I need a resolution."

"I understand," Billie said, and nodded. "Your husband has a will, I take it?"

She nodded. "Naturally. I've had my lawyer look at it. I am entitled to the estate, should Richard pass on. While he is absent, however, I am only given access to what he had provided me for housekeeping and my fripperies, as he liked to call them. You may think it a lot, but this house will not maintain itself forever."

It was clear enough. Vera had sold goods that were unimportant to her, to keep herself in the style to which she was accustomed, but now that she was more sure her husband would not be returning, and the end point on her security was in sight, she could no longer play the waiting game. That was enough of a reason for Vera to seek out Billie's services, but there was more to it, Billie suspected. The little woman in her gut—as relentlessly accurate as insurance man Barton Keyes's little man in *Double Indemnity*—knew that there was something else, another layer of pressure animating this woman, and that gut feeling was never wrong. "Are any other beneficiaries named in your husband's will?" she asked.

Vera shook her head. "He had a falling-out with his parents, years ago, and doesn't have siblings," she said. "As you may have guessed, we were not blessed with . . . children." There was a hesitancy there.

"I see. You say he had a falling-out with his family?" Billie said, sitting up straighter. "Can you tell me why?"

Vera shrugged. "His father passed away, and Richard was over here in Sydney. That may have created some bad blood with his mother." She crossed one leg over the other and took another delicate sip of her gimlet. "I never met his parents and stayed out of his family affairs. Best thing for it, really."

"And his mother lives there still? In London? May I have an address?"

Vera shook her head. "I've never met her, and don't have an address. Richard kept that sort of thing in his address book and he traveled with that. He hails from Surrey and I think she's still in the family home. She is terrifically difficult, I understand."

"No Christmas cards, then? That sort of thing?"

"Heavens, no."

How disappointing, Billie thought. She'd find a way. "Was there any particular reason Richard—an only child—came out here to live, so far away from his parents?"

"Not that he ever told me. He wanted to spread his wings, I suppose, instead of having the Montgomery patriarch standing over him. Or his mother. She's very religious apparently."

"And do you know if his mother has searched for him?"

"They've been estranged for years. I can't trust Richard's mother to sort any of this out. No doubt she'd rather I languish here in Sydney on the last shillings I can get hold of, on the paltry allowance Richard arranged, until it runs out, instead of getting rightful access to the estate. She has no interest in Richard, alive or dead, and she certainly has none in me."

Did Richard Montgomery go into the advertising business out of necessity? Billie wondered. The Antipodes were sometimes where upper-class families sent their difficult cases. Better to have them notorious in Sydney than in London, causing embarrassment. Or perhaps he simply was an independent type, or sun lover, dissatisfied with the offerings of smoggy old London Town.

"Vera, I must ask you about your finances. Did your husband have difficulties with money? Any debts, that sort of thing?"

"Heavens, no," Vera said, placing her cocktail on the table, her open mouth contorted with offense. "My husband has always been very good with money. Can you not see?" She waved her hand to indicate their surrounds.

"Indeed, your home is very impressive, and I'm sorry to have to ask these questions, but I'm afraid it's necessary, if I'm to help you find your husband's whereabouts. Looking over his books and documents may bring some insights, if you will permit me."

Vera shrugged. "He has a den downstairs. You're welcome to it.

Listen, Ms. Billie, I want you and your assistant in London as soon as possible, and then Paris as well. My Richard is there, somewhere, for whatever reason, and I shan't wait any longer for something to be done about it. If he has passed on, heaven forbid, his body must be brought back here. Whatever he's been up to, he deserves that. And if he is alive . . ." She paused, as if uncertain what that would mean for her.

"You require a divorce and proper financial settlement, or for his will to be enacted in the unfortunate case of his having passed. I quite understand," Billie assured her, thinking of how very hard it would be to contemplate such a betrayal. Vera nodded, and Billie gave her a moment.

"To that end, we've looked into some options," she continued after a pause. "There's a flight leaving in ten days, which may be our most sensible option. There's another that leaves in three weeks, and then there is the ship, of course." Each option was arduous in its way, some quicker than others, and though traveling by ship would be most delightful, she didn't think it likely this woman would accept months of waiting—paying each day—for them to arrive in London.

"There's nothing sooner?"

"There is a departure on Tuesday, as it happens, but—"

"Then you will be on that service."

That was less than three days away. Billie thought about what needed to be arranged. That didn't leave a lot of time, but if Shyla was willing to watch the office and Sam was as keen as he appeared to be to join her, she supposed it might be possible to make the flight. She felt a thrill course through her body at the thought.

"As you wish." She slid the relevant papers across to her new client. "These papers lay out the available schedules and prices. You can let us know what option you would prefer. Now, if you could sign this contract, agreeing to our terms . . ."

"Naturally," Vera said, leaning forward and signing with a flourish. "What's next?" she asked, satisfied. "I want things started immediately."

"Very good, Mrs. Montgomery. Now, as the contract states, we'll need a larger deposit, accounting for the travel. And please do furnish me with the complete address and details of Richard's employment, a full physical description, list of known associates, friends, family members, and any other particulars you feel may be important. I'll need a clear and recent photograph of your husband—as recent as is possible before his disappearance. If you have more than one, that would be ideal."

Vera nodded and rose. The contract seemed to have sobered her, or perhaps it was that they'd moved past the more general discussions, and it had all become very real for her. "Here's a recent photograph, and two more," Vera said, returning with them in hand. "I also have his last letter." She placed the items, stamped envelope and all, on the tabletop.

Billie sat forward and inspected the photographs. Richard was a somewhat heavyset man with a receding hairline, neatly dressed in the uniform of an ad man—upscale suit and tie. Even in the one-dimensional images he seemed to possess an outgoing quality, a certain spark. "Yes, these are good. Thank you. This may prove helpful, also," Billie said, noting that the letter stationery was from the Ritz Paris. "I'll return these to you as soon as I'm able," she assured her client. "Have you been to Paris yourself lately?"

"Oh, I have never left these shores," Vera explained, perhaps a touch sheepishly. "Richard was the one always traveling about, not me. But one of my dearest friends lives in Paris. She spent some time here in Australia before moving back there. She was a quite sensational mannequin in her day," she said proudly, and Billie thought again of that marvelous suit Mrs. Montgomery had worn on her first meeting in Billie's office. She did seem well-connected in Paris fashion, somewhere along the line. "Madame Josephine Laurent can help you in Paris. I don't know how much help she'll be, but you should get a good room and she could show you around if you like."

"A good room?"

"At the Ritz Paris, where Richard stayed. She knows some people there. She's very well-connected."

"How serendipitous. Did she help Richard and his colleagues when they were in town?"

"I believe so. The bureau paid for it all, owing to the exposition. I understand it was showing close to the hotel."

"Very good. Yes, that is helpful. And in London we'd ideally like to arrange accommodation wherever your husband stayed, or near to it. If you give us as much of his itinerary from the trip as possible, we'll give you a rundown on possibilities and costs. Leave it in our hands," Billie assured her.

Vera nodded. "Oh, and yesterday I sent off a telegram to the Caversham-Smithe family in London," she said, clearly expecting the name to impress. "The Caversham-Smithes are very dear."

Caversham-Smithe. Billie recognized the name as that of a prominent British family. "How are you acquainted with them?"

Vera took another sip of her gimlet, which appeared as if it had barely been touched. "The Caversham-Smithes sent their daughter, Jane, to live with us for a summer quite a few years back. Darling thing she is, and she simply *adored* Richard. Nice girl. I think she was interested in photography. They are a very important family."

"I see. Did he photograph her?" Billie asked.

"Oh yes. I remember he took some lovely shots."

"I'd be interested to see the pictures," Billie said, pleased that Vera had already put some thought into contacting the family. "In fact, any pictures of connections who might be of help in London or in Paris would be most advantageous. The more we know about Richard's circle and history, the better chance we'll have of delivering you your resolution."

Billie looked over the photographs Vera brought her, putting some aside to take with her. Suddenly her heart quickened. "Wait, can you tell me about this photograph?" What she held in her hand was a group image, men grinning in suits inside a ballroom or another type of lavish setting. Richard Montgomery was front and center, but she could see someone she recognized just behind him, someone who was also in advertising. It was Mr. Charles.

"That one?" Vera asked. "Oh, it's some business thing. They were always having conventions and things. Men talking shop. I didn't like to go." She leaned back and shivered slightly.

"And what's this?" Under the photograph was an unmarked white envelope. It had been sitting beneath everything else.

"Oh yes, I wanted to show you that," Vera said as Billie opened the envelope to pull out a single folded sheet of writing paper. "It's nothing really, but I got it a couple of years ago, a few months after Richard went missing."

WE'LL FIND HIM.

"How interesting," Billie remarked, looking at the three rather ominous words. Or were they encouraging? There was no signature, no address. "Who is 'we'?"

"I think perhaps it was one of the neighbors, secretly showing their support. They knew I'd been abandoned by him, you see. Or at least it seems that way."

Billie cocked her head. Her client had paled.

"Vera, are you okay?"

"I . . . I'm fine," she said haltingly, not at all the confident woman who had appeared in Billie's office. And then she made the slightest movement, a gesture, touching the stomach below that flowing empire waistline, and Billie felt a question surface.

"Forgive my directness, but is there perhaps another reason for your need to move on now? A . . . sensitive reason?"

Vera seemed to freeze.

"I observe, that is all," Billie explained. The first day, Vera had been wearing the cinched corsetry of the New Look. Today, at home, she did not have her full armor on but wore a more comfortable shape for a woman who was expecting. That glow. The delicate sips of her drink. She was perhaps experiencing the sickness of early pregnancy.

"What must you think of me," Vera said in a soft, sad voice, confirming Billie's suspicions.

"I do not judge, and if I ever do it is with the experience of someone who has seen a lot for her years and has been witness to the poor circumstances women are frequently left in," Billie said. Vera's husband was gone, whatever the reason, and life went on, whether she wanted it to or not. Like so many after the war, she had to find her happiness, despite the grief and uncertainty that stalked her.

"I've always wanted a family," she admitted, and though it seemed to Billie that Vera was still holding back, there was deep emotion there, sorrow. "But not like this. If I have this child . . ." A rogue tear rolled down her cheek as she spoke, hand at her belly, and she wiped the tear away swiftly with her other hand. "If I have this child while still married to Richard, the child and I will be disgraced. Everyone knows he is gone and can't be the father."

If society could be unkind to widows, that was nothing compared to how unkind they were to pregnant widows, especially when their husbands had been gone too long to be the father.

"Richard's mother will make sure I lose everything, too. Even though she has had nothing to do with Richard for many years, she'll be furious that I've tarnished the family name. She'll cut me out of Richard's will. And if he's still alive, I need him to divorce me." She turned and looked Billie square in the eye. "I want this baby, Billie. The father . . . he's a good man," she said. "I need a resolution, fast, or I'll lose everything."

"I understand," Billie said, comprehending the impossible position Vera was in. The baby she'd always wanted. The missing husband and no explanation. The waning finances. The new love.

"And no one can know about . . ." She looked down.

"You mustn't worry," Billie reassured her. "I'm a professional keeper of secrets. It comes with the territory. I will say no more on the matter. Don't fear, I will get you your resolution. There are never guarantees in this life, but I haven't let a client down yet. I will get you answers, even though you may not like them." Yes, she would crack this case. Richard was out there somewhere—or his corpse was.

She took a moment to allow Vera to gather herself. Her eyes had dried, but there was high color in her cheeks.

"Am I to understand that you don't have access to any bank accounts, or an account of your own?"

Vera shook her head. "Heavens, no. Nothing like that. Only the allowance I mentioned."

It was as Billie suspected. She came across this often in her work but found these kinds of arrangements infuriating. These adult women were kept on a leash whether they realized it at first or not. Their material security was conditional, and in time it became perfectly clear that they needed to make nice with the husbands who kept them. Financial institutions encouraged this inequality, not even letting women open accounts of their own without the explicit permission of their husbands. Would Vera have felt differently about her husband's "little adventures" with other women had they been on more equal footing? By the time wives in these situations walked into Billie's office, their financial situation was frequently desperate. One woman had been rationing at half the usual foodstuffs for months before summoning the courage to see Billie about her absent husband. She'd been skin and bones when she arrived, all to save up enough to get out of her situation.

"I have no choice but to ask this, Vera. How are you intending to fund our investigation?"

Her client didn't appreciate the question; that was clear. "I have my ways," she replied.

Billie waited for more, but Vera was not forthcoming. "Please understand, you have my confidence, in *all* matters, but I must know. We'll be taking some risk, business-wise, traveling overseas. Your second deposit will keep us going for a while, that is true, but should the funds run out, particularly while we're in Europe, it would spell disaster for my agency."

Billie had worked too hard to roll the dice like that.

"I signed the contract and you have my word," Vera said, seeming embarrassed at Billie's inquiries into her financial situation.

"Times have been hard for many of us, Vera. I know that as well as anyone. I don't mind saying that we had to sell some family heirlooms over the years, furniture, jewelry . . ." she prompted, watching the woman's face closely. "Needs must. There is no shame in it. But I need you to help me to understand how you can afford this."

Vera's face had dropped. She found this conversation deeply uncomfortable. Now that the carefully constructed glamour had fallen away, she seemed smaller somehow.

"Woman to woman here," Billie said. "We, too, must find ways to eat, to live, to pay for the things we need."

Vera sighed. "Yes. I have been . . . Well, I had to sell some of our things, here and there, particularly in the past year. It's not a crime, is it?"

Billie shook her head. "No, it isn't. Your husband may have been in charge of the finances at one time, but he didn't provide for these circumstances. It has been two years now, and no one would blame you, Vera. Please understand, your secrets are safe with me and our agency."

The maid returned to offer more aperitifs, and the women fell silent. Billie shook her head. "No. Thank you kindly. I should be going soon."

When the maid left, a sober-looking Vera stood up and walked off without a word, leaving her cigarette to smolder in its tray. She was gone for several minutes, and when she returned, she was holding a piece of folded dark velvet cloth in both hands. She sat down on the lounge and without a word laid it across the table and gently unfolded it. Sparkling gems were wrapped within—earrings in ruby and garnet, and an awe-inspiring three-tiered diamond necklace and matching earrings. The setting sun hit the jewels, sending rainbow prisms around the room. Even the cat turned its head to gape at the shimmering array.

"I have sold off a few pieces of furniture, as I think you guessed," Vera said, looking around at the room. "That and some of the jewelry I don't much wear these days. These pieces that I have left were gifts from Richard over the years. They're precious to me but more precious now is my freedom to move on. I think these should be more than enough to find out what happened to him."

Billie had to agree. Even with diamond values being diminished, with all the desperate people trying to sell off jewels to survive, these would fetch Vera Montgomery plenty of pounds.

"You'll have your money, Ms. Walker," she said. "You just find out what happened to my Richard. And I beg you, do it fast."

Nine

—ᄴ—

The wealthy pregnant widow . . .

On Sunday afternoon, Billie knocked at the front door and then walked into the flat at Cliffside almost in a single motion, having arrived straight from her second visit that weekend to Vera's place in Potts Point. As the details came together, she was excited at the prospect of the challenging and lucrative puzzle ahead of her—her favorite type of puzzle. It wasn't her own flat she burst into. It was one upstairs from hers, one that she knew almost as well.

"Billie!" Alma McGuire emerged from the kitchen with open arms, her eyes crinkling kindly in the corners. Her strawberry-and-silver hair was curled tightly, apron flour-splattered. "You look wonderful."

"Thank you, dear Alma." Billie grinned and paused to enjoy Alma's affectionate embrace—a hug from Alma was a comfort like few others, a Rock of Gibraltar in a changing world—and she glanced around the flat to see where her mother was. She didn't need to look far. As usual, Baroness Ella von Hooft was reclining on her lounge in the front room overlooking the waters of Double Bay far below, sherry in hand, her hair set in perfect, black-dyed marcel waves. It was Sunday, which meant sequins. The baroness was a creature of habit. Her daughter knew she was most relaxed at this time of day, and the sherry might help the conversation go more successfully. Billie's timing was quite intentional.

"You're going, aren't you?" Alma whispered, knowing something of the possibility of Billie's travel.

Billie nodded and smiled.

Being a widowed only child, with no children, her mother and Alma were all the family Billie had, or was likely to have, and though this would not be the first time she was leaving them for foreign shores, it would be the first time since the shocking passing of her father, Barry Walker. Alma—officially Ella's lady's maid but better described as her constant companion—was something like a wise auntie to Billie. She'd been employed initially to help raise baby Billie, back when they lived in their grand terrace in Potts Point and had the kind of staff appropriate to a house of its kind and to Ella's title, and even after everyone else was let go, Alma remained. Since the death of Billie's father in '44, Ella and Alma had been inseparable, but there was a loneliness—a deep sense of loss—there that Billie was reluctant to leave untended. She'd arrived back from Europe to it three years earlier and wondered if it would ever shift.

"No whispering, you two. Now, what would you like, darling?" Ella asked Billie loudly from her position on the lounge, raising a manicured hand in something like the young Queen Elizabeth's imperious wave. Billie's mother was, after all, the queen of her domain.

As the third of five children of the late Baron von Hooft, a former mayor of Arnhem, Holland, Ella had aristocratic blood, though she now led a somewhat less upper-class lifestyle, after two marriages, two world wars, a child, and the ravages of the Depression. She was not quite maternal but no less loving than Alma, in her way. She would do anything for her only child, Billie knew, but Ella was her own woman and did not bow to ideas of how a mother ought to behave.

"A drop of sherry will be fine," Billie told Alma softly, putting a hand on one of her soft, sturdy shoulders. "Thank you. Only a drop." She indicated the requested amount with her fingers. "But Ella may require another," she added with a sly grin, and both women laughed.

Billie walked over and settled near her mother, arranging the luxurious cushions to best suit her. "It's good to see you, Mum . . . *Ella*," she said, and turned to take in her mother's pale, porcelain face.

"And you also, my girl. I must say, you look radiant, though you know I do dislike it when you call me 'Mum.' You know it makes me feel old. Now, what's happening? I can see you have news. What were you two whispering about?"

"I'm sorry I wasn't able to join you for lunch today. I do have some news, actually," Billie began. Sunday lunch was their usual routine, and Billie tried her best to carve out time for it each week, but today she'd been to Vera's house again, working through what papers she could find in Richard's den, and earlier she had been busy packing. "Good goddess, the sunset is lovely this evening . . ." she remarked, stalling until Alma brought her a glass from which she could take a medicinal swig.

Ella watched her, shrewd eyes narrowed, until Alma came over, dainty crystal glass of sherry in hand, and passed it to Billie.

"Are you having one as well?" Billie asked her, and Alma shook her head, retreating with a gentle smile, likely knowing there would be fireworks.

"Out with it, darling," Ella urged impatiently from Billie's side.

Billie smiled and took a moment to take a swig of the sherry— the dry taste and the slightly sweet, nutty flavor moving over her tongue and stinging her throat on the way down. She took a breath, now suitably braced for the conversation, and looked out over the treetops. "Indeed, I do have news, and good news at that. I'm leaving for London, on the case I mentioned to you briefly on the phone. We're securing tickets on the Qantas Lancastrian service for Tuesday. It's quite a coup, actually. I thought it might take weeks to get a takeoff, if at all."

"Tuesday? So soon? And on a war plane?" Her mother sat up and frowned. "Honestly, darling, how *ghastly*," she said. "If this client is so well-heeled, as you claim, why on *earth* isn't she sending you over first-class, by ship, like other civilized people?"

Billie groaned and closed her eyes.

She had been rather hoping her mother would wish her luck, or perhaps even say something about the prospect of missing her daughter terribly while she was away. She might even congratulate her on her employment, something they were all increasingly reliant on these days, truth be told. Most people felt damn lucky to be employed at the moment, and Billie was no exception.

"My client is paying us by the day," she explained to Ella as patiently as she could. "Six weeks' passage with pay for every day I luxuriate in the first-class cabin of a ship, enjoying the sights, isn't what most clients have in mind when they engage me, you'll be surprised to hear." Particularly at the day rate she agreed to, Billie thought. "Besides, the Lancaster bombers have been converted for the service."

Somewhat. She had heard they were terrifically cramped and noisy planes, but it was the fastest way to London. In this case it really would be all about the destination and not the journey.

"Good goddess, you are *serious*, aren't you? Couldn't she stretch for the Hythe flying-boat service, at the very least?" Ella continued, evidently aghast.

Billie laughed to herself. The Hythe flying boats took longer than travel on the converted Lancastrian planes, with the next departure being weeks away, and there was only one class of travel available on the Hythe—first. Her little agency was moving up in the world, perhaps even rising faster than it had under her father when he'd first opened its doors years before, but you wouldn't know it to speak with Ella. The Lancastrian would be just fine, and Billie was rather pleased with her negotiations, actually. At only three days, travel on the Qantas service was blessedly fast and quite safe now that the Axis powers were no longer shooting these planes out of the skies. Billie and Sam would get to the other side of the world in one piece, if a touch rattled. She'd factored in a couple of days of rest on their arrival in London, which seemed sensible given the conditions and their travel through several time zones.

Ella was still shaking her head, evidently set on being difficult. It was as if she had entirely forgotten their financial circumstances. This wasn't 1925.

"We won't be dropping any bombs along the way, I assure you. If you must know, I'm quite pleased with the arrangements," Billie said. "I've made up a copy of the itinerary for you both, so you shall know where we are." She offered the papers and Ella snatched them up, reading aloud. Alma reappeared in the doorway of the kitchen to listen, curious, but wisely keeping her distance.

"Tuesday, nine p.m., depart Sydney," Ella began. "Wednesday, five a.m., arrive Darwin; seven a.m., depart Darwin; two thirty p.m., arrive Singapore; four thirty p.m., depart Singapore; eleven p.m., arrive Calcutta."

"Yes, I know it's—"

"Thursday, one a.m., depart Calcutta. One in the morning!" Ella cried. "Seven forty-five a.m., arrive Karachi; one thirty p.m., depart Karachi; eight p.m., arrive Lydda; ten p.m., depart Lydda. Friday, two a.m., arrive Castel Benito; four twenty a.m., depart Castel Benito; and, thank the heavens, eleven twenty p.m., arrive London." Ella put the papers down again, indignant that a daughter of hers would sign up for such a trip.

Billie took a breath. "Granted, by all accounts we'll be mostly deaf by the time we arrive in London," she remarked, only half joking. "But we'll get there."

"And did I hear you say 'we'?"

Billie took a sip from the dainty glass, now wishing she'd asked for more sherry, anticipating what was to come. "You did indeed hear a 'we.' Naturally I will be working, and traveling, with my assistant, Mr. Baker," she said evenly, making it sound like it was never a question of whether or not he would join her.

"Oh, now, that *is* good news." Ella grabbed Billie's wrist so suddenly Billie nearly spilled her drink. "He is one young man worth spending time with," she told her daughter, rather too forcefully making her usual point.

Billie looked down at the hand that gripped her. It was adorned with the remaining glittering von Hooft family gems, fingernails immaculately polished a deep cherry red. "We've been through this. Samuel is my employee," she said, gently pulling her arm away.

Ella and her judo moves.

"As I've told you, darling, there isn't a thing wrong with the man, including being your employee. It worked just fine for me."

"My dear father was not your employee, exactly," Billie pointed out.

"Well, I hired him," Ella shot back. In her periphery, Billie saw Alma slide back into the kitchen.

This was a well-worn track for mother and daughter, and an unhelpful one. It was true that Ella had rather cleverly managed to get out of one marriage and into another by hiring Barry Walker, private inquiry agent, who had successfully proved her husband's infidelity and won Ella's heart with impressive speed. But that little slice of family history was hardly the same thing as the working relationship between Billie and Sam. He was her assistant. Her secretary.

"Perhaps you will come back with a new husband," Ella remarked.

Billie narrowed her eyes, refusing to dignify the comment with a response.

"Haven't you seen the way that boy looks at you, Billie my dear? No wonder he will follow you on a rattling old bomber over the Indian Ocean. He'd follow you to perdition if you asked him."

Billie suppressed a laugh. Her mother did have a flair for the dramatic. "London isn't much described as hell these days, though they did have an awfully tough winter," she shot back.

It had been the coldest on record. Coal and petrol were terrifically scarce and families had frozen in their own homes, from the reports Billie had seen. The Victory Gardens planted during the war had been snow covered; animals had frozen or starved to death; and roofs had collapsed under feet of heavy snow. *Were there to be no fruits of victory?* had been the lament. The toll of war would likely be felt for years, for victor and vanquished alike, and Billie knew that London wouldn't have recovered, not by half, nor Paris for that matter, but going back was still an exciting, if daunting, prospect for her.

Billie had been pulled into her mother's baiting quite enough for one evening, thank you very much. "I did want to ask you if you have any contacts in London that might assist with my case. Do you know the Caversham-Smithe family by chance?" she said, steering the conversation away from her lack of a love life.

Ella's eyes flashed with interest. "Why, yes, I know of the

Caversham-Smithes, of course, but I haven't had reason to meet them, darling. Didn't they send their daughter down here some years back? The usual learning experience down under. She spent a while in Sydney, I understand."

Blast. No direct connection there. "Yes, I had heard that about the daughter," Billie said, and thought again of Richard and his tendency to photograph young women. Perhaps it was just the bias of Billie's profession—seeing as she did the worst of human behavior, including predatory men—but it made her question if his motives had been strictly professional.

"What will you do with your flat? Alma can look after it while you're away, can't you, Alma?" Ella suggested.

"Oh no, I don't need you to do that, Alma," Billie responded. "Thank you, but no. I am perfectly happy to brush away the cobwebs myself when I return."

"I won't hear of it. Alma, you must—"

Billie cut her mother off. "No, Ella. I mean it."

Billie didn't want anyone in her flat, and she certainly didn't need the very lovely Alma dusting her bookshelves or drinks cabinet. For what purpose? Had she a more normal life, she might possess houseplants for someone to look after, or a pet, or even a husband or child, but alas, strange fates and the demands of Billie's unusual profession did not encourage domestic routine or responsibilities.

"My colleague Shyla—you remember Shyla—she'll be picking up the mail at the office, and so on. There shouldn't be anything else to do. You have my contact details here," she said, again indicating the itinerary she had prepared. "Sam and I will be at the Strand Palace, London, and then at the Ritz Paris, if all goes well. If we stray elsewhere for the case, or for anything else, I will inform you by telegram at my earliest opportunity."

"Well, I'm relieved to hear you will be looked after when you land, at least. The Strand Palace and the Ritz are fine hotels. Good reputations, both. I do hope this woman has organized you a decent room."

"This isn't a holiday." The hotels were not likely to be quite the luxury establishments Ella imagined, the war having done damage to Paris, and to London in particular, and not the sort of damage one simply bounced back from. "These hotels are where Mr. Montgomery stayed before his disappearance," Billie explained. "I'm rather pleased his wife insisted we stay there. She certainly didn't have to. There are adequate hotels nearby, available at lower rates."

"You undersell yourself, Billie, my dear."

"Perhaps you overestimate the profession," Billie countered. "Or the market. There isn't a lot of money about these days, in this trade or otherwise. *You* ought to know that, of all people."

Ella looked down, a stab of shame in her features, and Billie immediately regretted how pointed her remark had been. She gazed at the ruby liquid of her sherry, frowning, then cast her eyes to the baby grand piano that sat, pride of place, in the middle of her mother's front room. It was undeniably spectacular, and she was rather proud to see it there, though its presence made her comment all the more insensitive. The piano had been in the family for some time and had been quietly sold by Ella in '46 out of financial necessity. When the money started coming in from the agency after the Brown family case, Billie had tracked down the buyer and got it back for her mother, paying slightly more than it had been sold for. Her mother was a proud woman, but she had teared up a little when the piano had been brought back into the flat. It was not so much an instrument of music to her, but a piece of personal history, having once taken center stage at their Potts Point mansion, played by artists and musicians at parties that had set Sydney aflame in the 1920s. It hurt Billie to see her mother's world slowly sold off, piece by piece, to keep them afloat, and she was determined to stem the losses if and when she could.

"Sorry, Ella. My point is that we are all doing the best we can," she said quietly, and the two women sipped at their drinks, Alma watching from the wings. After a time, she emerged with homemade pastries to sweeten the mood. Billie took one and ate it in small bites, looking out past the bay to the illuminated windows of the hundreds of apartments on the hill beyond. She knew that many of the residents of those were probably not as lucky as she and her mother and Alma. Australia had been less severely impacted than many Allied countries, but the deprivations of war had still been felt, the changed fortunes and the deaths, the losses. Plenty of families had lost whole generations of men.

"You seem elsewhere, my girl."

"Yes. Sorry. Sam said the same."

"Out with it, then."

Billie turned to look at her mother. "You'll stop badgering me about the travel and hotels? And my assistant?"

Her mother nodded. It was a truce.

"What puzzles me somewhat is just where this man Richard—the man I am tasked to find—got his money from. His family must have been quite wealthy, as he can't have made such a good salary as an ad man that he could afford that house he owns in Potts Point." Or those jewels Vera had shown her.

"But his wife can afford to pay for the investigation to go ahead?"

She is selling off jewels so she can pay to get answers, Billie was tempted to say, knowing Ella had done the same to be able to hold on to her lifestyle. She had gone through what she could of Richard's books that day, and while they could use more investigation, it seemed he had been receiving regular personal payments of various amounts, which must have helped them live lavishly for a time. Probably a family allowance, handled through a local lawyer. In that case, perhaps the Montgomery matriarch had been sending funds to her son. They had stopped around the time he disappeared.

"The money is there," Billie said. "And Vera Montgomery needs my help. I'm going."

"We're happy for you, Billie, and remember, Sydney will still be here when you get back," Alma chimed in, ever supportive as she walked over to offer them more of her delectable pastries. Billie shook her head.

"Yes, you should go on your trip, darling," her mother concluded, as if her say was the deciding factor. "I am pleased for you. I know you enjoy this work, like your father did."

"Thank you, Mum . . . Ella. And yes, before you say anything, naturally I will make a few inquiries about Jack with our mutual acquaintances from my reporting days, though I daresay we can't expect much after all this time."

Ella's penciled brows pulled together. "Are you sure you want to know?"

"Yes," Billie answered instantly, the word sounding urgent somehow, guttural. She wanted to know. There were no pretty answers waiting for her, and whatever she found would hurt, she was sure of it, but she could take it. And even if she found nothing after all that, perhaps she would be a touch more at peace somehow. Perhaps she could move on, Jack's ghost put to rest.

She put a hand on her mother's knee, regretting how irritable she had been. They both had a way of getting tangled in their words.

"You will take care, won't you, dear?" Ella said gently.

This time she allowed her only child to embrace her tightly, not even complaining when Billie crushed her perfect hair.

Ten

—✲—

Her dress was borrowed. There was no ring.

Billie was back in Donzenac, a French medieval town of charming old houses with gray slate roofs overlooking the river Maumont. It was the summer of 1944, and Jack Rake had shaved for the occasion of their wedding, and even borrowed a necktie from a local Donzenacois—it was one of his peculiarities that he never wore neckties unless forced. Holding hands and grinning, they had emerged from the Hôtel de Ville—the mayor having married them inside, Jack's lips reddened by Billie's Fighting Red lipstick—to be met with the whistling and shouting of locals and the shooting of guns by the assembled French resistance fighters, the Maquis du Limousin, a significant cell of which operated in the walled village.

They were less than two hours from Limoges, where the Germans had stationed themselves. Mere weeks before, a Gestapo Commando composed of Algerians had looted Donzenac, torturing a thirteen-year-old boy and killing another. The locals of Donzenac were used to invasions, dating back centuries, and many had shelters to hold whole families, crops, and provisions. It was from the provisions in some of these shelters that a wedding cake had been made for Billie and Jack.

Clouds had moved into the valley on the day of their makeshift wedding, and had risen during their short, informal service, making the village appear as if it were floating in mist, and for a moment the clouds licked the cobblestones outside the hotel, enveloping their shoes and Billie's dress, and making her wonder if finally, after so much war, so many battles, the mists would simply take them away, lifting them up . . .

"Go on, Jack, tell them . . ."

Now Billie was back at the Café de Flore, and Jack was on the other side of the table, too far away to reach. Her colleague, the war reporter Simone Chapelle, was there, in her trousers and shirt, and she prompted this man, this Jack Rake, to speak of his recent adventures. But as the stories were told, Jack's lips were not moving. She could hear his voice, but it was disembodied. She could still see him, his shirt open a touch, glass of wine in hand, but his mouth was closed. It was still. And he began to fade, like an old photograph, and Simone was saying, "Do you see, Billie? It's Paris. Do you see . . . ?"

Billie woke with a start, alarm pealing.

It was time to go.

Eleven

—⁓—

The three-day trip by air from Sydney to Darwin, on to Singapore, Calcutta, Karachi, Lydda, Castel Benito, and finally London felt somewhat more taxing than Billie Walker had anticipated, notwithstanding the times Billie had spent in bombed-out farmhouses, cramped safe houses, and bomb shelters during the war. Perhaps it was her relative safety as a paying passenger, confined for days in the unpressurised former war plane, that magnified the discomfort. After all, she was not cramped into this curious space under life-threatening circumstances. The half dozen passengers on the booked-out Lancastrian service, Billie and Sam among them, were positioned sideways in tight quarters to make way for the large volume of international mail that was the main purpose of the airplane's travel. It was pure economy.

Like the bomb raids of years earlier, the roaring engines of the Avro Lancastrian were deafening and continuous, hour upon hour, day and night. What made the rumbling worse was the sense of being right inside the vibrations themselves. The sensation was new to her and gave her a sense of what airmen had lived with, carrying bombs long distances to their strategic destinations, in uncertain and perilous conditions. The seating felt especially peculiar during the seven takeoffs and landings—Billie felt as if she was constantly about to fall into the lap of her stoic assistant, Sam, and Sam into a Mrs. Gavin, who apparently did not much like the flying experience and was overly vocal about it with her husband, and therefore the whole cabin, before blessedly reaching her destination in Calcutta.

Fortunately, the sideways seating converted cleverly into modest sleeping berths, in which Billie could stretch her long legs at night and dream of being on the ground again and able to breathe freely. Some small passenger windows had also been installed in front of each of the six seats, so that instead of staring at the internal hull of the converted bomber, she could enjoy the vantage point of the goddesses, over land and sea. It was a true privilege to see the world from such an angle; however, as time stretched on, sometimes in a tight oxygen mask that was hell on her delicate skin, often flying within a blanket of claustrophobic misty cloud and accompanied by the thundering and vibration of the war plane, conditions began to grate on Billie.

By the third day, thoroughly deafened and weakened by broken sleep and the high altitude, she almost wondered—*almost*—if her mother had been right after all. Perhaps she should have pushed for the Hythe flying boat departing weeks later.

The considerable noise of the Lancaster engines, and the need to wear oxygen masks at altitudes over ten thousand feet and during takeoff and landing, reduced Billie and Sam to largely nonverbal communication over the three-day journey. They passed the waking hours sharing newspapers and playing gin rummy, using books balanced on their laps to form a makeshift card table to play on. The arrangement forced the pair into rather close proximity, honing the improvised hand signals they had started to use in their work together. Fortunately, Sam knew when to use his impressive physical assets and when not to, and somehow, he managed to tread lightly even in these cramped conditions. That boded well for the travel ahead, Billie thought. There weren't many men she would be happy to face at odd hours, hair askew, with a splitting headache, but it seemed Sam was one.

"Look!" he mouthed, and pointed.

After a seventh thundering takeoff from Castel Benito and a gratifying trip across a brilliantly azure Mediterranean Sea, they finally were making their way over the island of Great Britain and the places they had longed to see: London Town and the river Thames. Somewhere below their airplane seats, the comfortable beds of the Strand Palace Hotel were waiting for them. As the Lancaster neared their destination and banked to the left, they leaned forward in their seats to catch glimpses of London. Her aerial view of the sweeping destruction that the Blitz had wreaked made Billie gasp. Riveted to the sight of the patchwork of dark, flattened city blocks, both she and Sam were speechless beneath their oxygen masks as the noisy Lancaster came in to land.

Poor London Town. Seeing it like this brought home the devastation more than any news article could. There would be much rebuilding for decades to come, Billie realized.

—⁓—

It was the early hours of Saturday morning when Billie Walker opened the door of a British taxicab and took a deep breath of the London night air.

She placed one heeled Oxford on the solid, blissfully stationary ground of the footpath outside the Strand Palace Hotel and sighed audibly—or at least it would have been audible to her had her ears been working. Her travel papers were in order, none of their baggage was apparently forgotten or lost, and her trusty Colt was back in place in her thigh holster, having been returned to her by the airline purser upon landing. They'd survived the remarkably threadbare facilities at London Airport, which consisted only of huts and ex-military marquees forming a tented village along the Bath Road, where they had waited until a taxicab was available. Although it was frightfully late now, they had arrived in London in one piece—rattled and bone weary but in one piece.

"This looks a dream," Sam remarked, having beaten the driver in coming around the side of the cab to open her door. "What a place."

Looking up, Billie read her assistant's lips more than heard him. Her ears were still ringing and she had a splitting headache, and she desperately needed modern amenities and a great deal of horizontal sleep before setting her focus on the mysteries ahead. With its promise of plush, flat, non-swinging beds, the Strand Palace did indeed seem a dream in that moment. It was a popular hotel and meeting place, not as dear as the Savoy across the road, but reputable and well-appointed. A rather large establishment, it was comprised of several floors situated in an Edwardian-era corner building on the north side of the Strand, not far from Covent Garden, Aldwych, Trafalgar Square, and the river Thames. The hotel had been redone in a luxuriously modern Art Deco style in the late twenties and had many hundreds of rooms. The street level featured awnings and delightful displays, some still visible despite the hour.

Two well-dressed couples in dinner jackets and gowns swept past the taxicab and entered the hotel via a revolving door, chatting and linking arms, evidently returning from a pleasurable Friday night of entertainment on the town. Their jovial mood encouraged Billie's own, and she felt that the sight of them boded well, considering all she'd read about what the city was still going through. Yes, this would do nicely, she hoped, as she cast her eyes upward, wondering which floor Richard Montgomery had stayed on. Maybe, just maybe, staff would recall him and his colleagues from the Bureau of Information.

The friendly cab driver appeared and extended a hand to Billie, insisting on helping her out of the automobile, against Sam's protestations. She was quite capable of standing on her own but was in no mood to refuse the help. He was a jovial chap, salt-and-pepper haired and kind faced, and through her partial deafness and between fits of involuntary sleep on the cab journey, she had heard him helpfully confirm that the hotel was still standing—a point that she hoped wasn't really in doubt—and, having picked up their accents, he had explained that the Strand was a popular destination for Australians, thanks in part to its proximity to Australia House. Billie had known this. Its position was an asset. Now to get inside, be shown to their rooms, and then close her eyes.

Billie paid and tipped him, apparently to his surprise, judging by the way his bushy eyebrows shot up as she revealed her purse—he had expected payment from the male of the pair—and she stood on the footpath grinning with exhausted relief, taking in the comparatively fresh air of the street. London's notoriously smoggy air seemed positively wholesome after being far too long strapped in the stale air of their flying machine. While Sam and the driver grappled with their luggage, Billie stood straight as an arrow, stretching her slender arms upward, not caring who saw her do her calisthenics as she leaned one way and then the other, feeling her ribs expand. Within moments, Sam came to her, a bag under each arm, and asked if she required assistance with her hatbox. She did not.

The hotel staff had spotted their arrival, and a neatly uniformed porter rushed out to them with a trolley, smiling politely and saying something to Billie that she could not rightly make out.

"Good evening . . . morning, I guess," she said in response, perhaps too loudly. "We have reservations. Walker and Baker. Sorry, my ears are ringing. The flights, you see."

She was answered with more ringing, though his lips moved. He took her hatbox and placed it on the wheeled trolley. As the driver pulled away with a wave, Samuel, being unused to such hotels, or perhaps simply exhausted and similarly deafened by three days of the roaring engines, walked straight to the entrance of the hotel with both of their large bags, carrying them as if they weighed nothing, while the porter followed at his heels with the trolley, trying to assist. For her part, Billie carried her handbag and followed the pair, amused. She watched as Sam, realizing he couldn't fit through the central revolving door at the entrance owing to their luggage, opted instead for what Billie took as the service entrance.

"Don't worry about Mr. Baker. He's strong as an ox," she said to the porter, who was perhaps expecting he might get in trouble for not doing his job.

"This way, miss."

He held out an arm to direct her and she walked through the revolving door, emerging into the hotel's beautiful foyer, which truly felt like a dream. Adorned with paneled marble walls, mirrored glass, chrome balustrades, and dramatic, lighted panels in exciting Art Deco curves and lines stretching along the walls and down the stairs, the effect of it was quite dazzling—Billie had not seen so much indoor lighting since before the war. To her right was a clothing shop selling attractive overcoats and hats, currently closed for the day. To her left, the well-dressed guests mingled before retiring for the evening. A floor-to-ceiling column glowed next to her. How far away Cliffside Flats seemed right now.

After catching her breath, she walked toward Sam, who seemed to be searching for her, and still clutched their suitcases tightly. Certainly he had not so much as broken a sweat carrying them. His injured left hand perhaps gave him trouble, she noted, as he preferred to carry the whole case under his arm rather than use the handle. The porter gestured again toward her companion and the trolley, and Billie shrugged. She simply didn't have the energy to worry about what he thought of not having to do his job. She tried to tip the frustrated man but he refused her and eventually walked away, having placed her hatbox at the front desk with a hurried bow.

"I must say, it has held up well," Billie remarked, stepping up to Sam and taking him by the arm.

"What?" he replied, but she didn't bother answering, instead guiding him to the desk and her waiting hatbox. Behind it, a desk clerk watched them and looked to Sam to speak for the pair.

"Welcome, sir—" he began.

"Yes, good evening, sir," Billie interrupted, with perhaps less patience than usual. "There should be reservations, for Walker and for Baker," she explained. She did so hope their rooms were ready and there wouldn't be a wait. Her eyes would soon close and she wasn't confident she could negotiate them open again. "I apologize as our hearing is a bit affected by the flights," she added, and gestured to her ringing ears.

From the clerk's expression, Billie might have been speaking with a touch too much volume, or perhaps he simply found her forthright manner jarring. He examined her over his glasses, doing a sweep of her somewhat crumpled apparel and that of her baggage-carrying companion with his leather-gloved hand, and he seemed to have some thoughts about what he saw, not all of them good. For the moment she could not muster embarrassment about the state of her well-traveled wardrobe or her hair—which needed washing and resetting, and was probably tangled into knots under her hat. The tiny mirror in the bomber's humble lavatory had not been adequate for her grooming requirements, but no matter.

"Mrs. Walker. Or is it Mrs. Baker?" he replied. She detected a tone of suspicion.

"My name is Ms. Walker—"

"That will be two single beds or one double?" the man asked as he looked away from the pair and down at some mysterious paperwork, out of view behind Billie's hatbox.

She blinked. "There should be two rooms. Walker and Baker." Had she heard that correctly? "Doubles are fine, but two different rooms, yes?"

"You don't wish to stay with your husband?"

Billie frowned. "Excuse me, sir, but Mr. Baker is not my husband—"

"If you are not married, I'm afraid you can't stay together. This is not that sort of hotel."

Sam, who had been quiet up to this point, took a tentative step forward to assist, catching on that something was not right. "Ms. Walker, would you like me to—"

Billie shooed Sam back, irritated by the man at the desk and keen to take care of this issue herself. She stood up very straight, leaned over the desk, and fixed the uniformed man with a red-eyed look that would make Medusa proud. "Sir, forgive my forthright manner, which you are perhaps not accustomed to, but needs must. I am, frankly, exhausted, and so is my colleague. I am Ms. Billie Walker. Ms. You may write that down. Walker, with a W. This is my assistant, Mr. Samuel Baker, who works for me. Baker is his name, like the bread-making trade, yes? We have traveled some distance and we would like to check in now, thank you kindly. There should be a reservation for *two* rooms." She held up the correct number of fingers, rather pleased she could presently muster the energy to count that high. "Decent rooms, I should hope. Check it now, please."

Something in her expression made the man's face drop, or perhaps it was her cold and even voice. For a moment he did not move. It was a moment too long.

Billie lifted one hand and brought her index finger down to the desk as one might to force a faulty call button. "Check it *now*, sir," she said slowly and firmly.

At this the man animated, nervously touching the knot of his tie. "Certainly, miss. I will do so now. Oh, look . . . here you are."

Her shoulders dropped. *Thank the stars.* It was not wise to mess with a Walker or von Hooft with a headache. She turned and leaned back against the desk, giving Sam a look. He was still holding their bags as if they were filled with nothing so heavy as feather down. She raised a brow, looked at their luggage, and he lowered the suitcases slowly. There, that was better. In minutes they were registered and walking down the patterned carpet of the fourth floor of the hotel, the doors blurring in Billie's peripheral vision as they passed, following a porter with a trolley. It really was a beautifully appointed hotel, from what little Billie could take in as her eyelids struggled to stay open.

"Your room, miss," the porter finally announced.

"Thank you."

A door was opened for her, luggage ushered inside, and a key placed in her hand.

"You must be sick of having your boss a handspan away from you day and night," she said to Sam from the threshold, using her last dregs of energy to stay upright. Gosh, she hoped they could still stand each other after this trip, however many weeks it might take.

"What?" he replied, cupping his ear.

"You must be sick of me," she repeated, this time louder.

Sam pointed a finger at her, making a face. "You? No, Ms. Walker. I can't get sick of a lady like you. Now go and rest."

She offered a tired grin. "Rest. Yes, but first . . ." She passed him a sealed envelope of local currency. "This is your per diem," she explained. "Spend it as you like. I shall be sleeping for a long while. On Monday morning we get to work on finding our Mr. Montgomery, okay?"

"Let me know if you need anything, won't you?" Sam offered.

"Thank you, dear Sam. I shall be fine. By Monday anyway." She placed a hand on his hulking shoulder. "Good night," she said, and slipped inside her room, shutting the door behind her.

Once she was inside, the dimly lit room began to spin. It was time to rest. She didn't investigate the room, only the lock on the door and the bed—a large, blissfully flat and stable double bed that did not move or groan or creak, and was completely without engine or pilot. There was only blissful darkness.

Billie's lids closed and she was out.

Twelve

—⁓—

Shyla Davis turned the key, heard the lock give, and stepped inside the offices of B. Walker Private Inquiries. It was a strange thing, she thought, this quiet space of neatly stacked papers and filing cabinets that hid the real business that went on here—the workings of broken hearts, betrayals, and jealousies.

All was as Billie had shown her before she'd hastened away on her journey, with the exception of the jumble of post spread across the floor. Already there was a small collection of mail for the agency, each envelope having finished up where it had landed on the rust-colored carpet after coming through the mail slot. Shyla would pick them up and sort through them for Billie, as promised, but first the place needed some air. It was depressingly claustrophobic.

The young woman stepped around the mail and moved to the communicating door. When she opened it, she found herself in Billie's office, a place she had studiously avoided so many times, except when Billie and her assistant had given her the tour to explain what needed doing while they were away. Shyla didn't want to work for a white woman, not even the likes of Ms. Walker. This arrangement was a compromise, she supposed, and she would do her bit, but there was something uncomfortable about being at the heart of where her friend did her work. It felt a touch close, and Shyla didn't want to be drawn in, not any further than she already was.

There was a small balcony in the corner and Shyla drew the curtains open and unlatched the doors, letting a breeze through. There, that was better.

With a bit of fresh air and light brought into the office, she found it less oppressive, though Shyla did not understand how Billie, with all her vitality and verve, could wish to spend time in so barren an environment. There was a map of Sydney on the wall and a few photographs of loved ones, but otherwise it was all business, hard and masculine. There was not even a single potted plant to bring life into the air.

Shyla circled back to the front door, gathered up the mail, and sat at the assistant's desk, looking at the inscriptions on the envelopes. One appeared to have been delivered in person, and it caught her attention. It was an unstamped envelope with *Miss Billie Walker* written neatly across the front in cursive. No address. It said "Miss," and so Shyla knew it was from someone who didn't know Billie well enough to realize she did not care for the title. Would Billie want her to open it? Yes. She had been instructed to, though it felt wrong. She had been assured that personal correspondence did not come here.

Shyla leaned back in Big Sam's chair, making herself comfortable. She removed her dark navy gloves and opened the envelope with a brass letter opener. It was as sharp as a bush knife, and it felt strange to use, especially after the years of being taught not to open correspondence in her domestic work, the work she had been pleased to escape. In those houses this would have been forbidden and would have come with a penalty to keep her in line. Against those learned instincts, Shyla removed the two pages contained in the plain envelope and flattened them on the desk, preparing to read.

The pages contained a phone number, she noted, and words she could mostly make out, though they were not written clearly.

Miss Walker, I know we were not to speak again, but one good turn deserves another. I have heard you are looking into the affairs of a man named Richard Montgomery, who worked at George Patterson advertising agency. A friend of mine is acquainted with him and has some vital information to impart to you . . .

Thirteen

—⚬—

On Monday morning in London, Billie Walker applied her favored Fighting Red to her lips, leaning into the mirror in her hotel room and studying her reflection.

Nearly a week after departing Sydney, Billie could hear again, and now, reasonably well rested, her eyes were no longer bloodshot, the irises bright blue-green against clear white. Most important, those sharp eyes of hers were quite willing and able to stay open again, and to focus on the task ahead.

Over the weekend she had telegrammed her mother with a short note for Mother's Day—a gesture that would no doubt be met by Ella with the usual combination of irritation at being called "Mum" and genuine pleasure at being remembered—and she had taken the time to detangle and wash her dark hair in the basin in her hotel room and wet set it for the week ahead. Visiting one of the doubtlessly delight-ful professional hair salons in the hotel would hardly be a reasonable business expense, after all. Billie could do a lot with a basin, running water, and her Savon de Marseille. She always traveled with a bar of it wrapped in a handkerchief among her underthings. It could be terrifically hard to hunt down good soap. To all the world, Billie was restored and would no longer be raising the eyebrows of any judgmental staff or guests, at least not on account of her grooming.

Before heading down for breakfast with Sam, she used her in-room telephone—one of the more practical luxuries of the hotel—and called the number she had for the Caversham-Smithe family, leaving a message with the staff explaining her presence and re-questing a meeting. She was assured the message would be passed on. She laced her stocking-clad feet into her trusty Oxfords, now shining after she'd made use of the hotel's electric boot polishers, and headed down to the foyer in one of the hotel's electric express elevators.

As Billie made her way to the hotel's vast dining room, she mulled over when the most opportune time might be to visit Aus-tralia House. Early in the day? Late? Some black tea would help her form a plan of action, no doubt. She did so hope she had missed the queue for breakfast, which had been quite fierce on Sunday, the guests of all 980 rooms apparently having regrettably woken at a similar hour. Thankfully, Billie arrived to find only two couples ahead of her, the rest of the guests having evidently been seated earlier on this Monday morning. The dining room was buzzing with chatter, and waiters rushing back and forth. A few tables were left. She would be seated soon, the maître d' told her.

Perhaps a visit to Australia House just before closing, when everyone is relaxed and ready to leave, she thought. By now her contact would have received her telegram, letting them know she would be in town, but she wanted to try to make it social, and hopefully forge some connections that might aid in her search for Mr. Montgomery.

In the meantime, she could work on tracking down Richard's "difficult" mother, and think about contacting the Caversham-Smithe family again. Hopefully they would return her call before she rang again, but she was reluctant to wait too long.

"Ms. Walker. Billie!"

Billie turned on her Oxford heel and found Sam several yards away at a table against a wall. He was dining alone and appeared to have consumed a startling number of fresh boiled eggs, given the cemetery of shells littering his plate. He stood up and waved her over, and the busy maître d' nodded for her to go on.

"Oh, Ms. Walker! You are a sight for sore eyes," Sam proclaimed, pulling out a chair for her. "You look pretty as a rose and twice as fresh."

"What a way with words you have, dear Sam. It's a delight to see you. Have you rested well over the weekend?" She sat, crossed one stocking-clad leg over the other, and took him in. Bright eyes. Ready smile. Pressed clothes. "You look ready to take on London."

"Thank you, Ms. Walker. I rested quite well," he replied. That was apparent. "Beaut hotel. It really is."

The Strand Palace had remained busy through the war and had become an official US rest-and-recuperation residence at one point, so she supposed it had never quite had the chance to fall into disrepair. She and Sam were seated next to a large panel of marble marked with hairline cracks that ran the length of it like spiderwebs. Cracks in the ceiling plaster above them were more evident, doubtless thanks to the enthusiastic bombing by the Nazis that had leveled buildings not far away. But the hotel was in better shape than she had anticipated and she could see barely any evidence of the bombing that had hit the hotel in 1940. The Strand had kept calm and carried on, as the motto went, even as so much of London disintegrated around it.

"You managed to rustle up some fresh eggs, I see," Billie remarked, impressed and somewhat surprised. "Someone here must like you."

Billie had been served powdered scrambled eggs over the weekend, and soybean "sawdust" sausages, though she'd also been provided with some rather nice fresh mushrooms. For her part, she hadn't seen a fresh egg in some time. It looked like Sam had consumed no fewer than four.

"I'll see if they have any more," he suggested, and started to stand.

Billie put a hand on his arm, keeping him in his chair. "Now, now, I think you've likely eaten the kitchen's entire supply. I don't need any fresh eggs; it's quite fine."

He reddened.

"And I can't think of a better place for them," she added, smiling. "You need your strength, good sir. Tell me, is your room adequate?"

"Oh, it's fine, Ms. Walker. Mighty fine. I've even got a view over the Thames."

"Delightful. I think we're facing the same side."

"Miss, what can I get you?" An attractive young woman in uniform had arrived at the table to take Billie's order. She was rosy-cheeked and plump, with curly red hair tied up under a cap, and her eyes flitted to Sam, long lashes batting, before turning her attention back to Billie.

The Strand Palace breakfast menu was emblazoned with a red crest in the logo of the hotel, a stylized SPH in Deco font. It informed her that iced fruit juices were available, and porridge, wheat-flakes, or baked beans on toast.

"Can my friend here have some of your eggs?" Sam inquired.

The girl smiled, her hand lingering around her clavicle. "We're almost out. But I'll see what I can do . . . for you."

Watching the young woman, Billie now understood perfectly how Sam had secured the coveted eggs. "Honestly, just one is fine if

THE GHOSTS OF PARIS

you think you can manage it," Billie said. "Don't put yourself out, okay? You've looked after my colleague here so well. Oh, may I have some black tea and toast?"

She perked up at Billie's confirmation of their professional relationship. "I'll bring a rack and a pot of tea over for you right away," she said, and scooped up Sam's plate, looking around almost guiltily before discreetly covering the eggshells with his used napkin. "I hope you liked them," she whispered, bending into his ear.

"Oh, they were a delight. Thank you so much," he told her. "You're a beaut."

The young woman blushed.

Billie gave the waitress her room number, and again it seemed to please the girl that it was different from Sam's, which she no doubt would have remembered. When she disappeared, Billie turned to Sam.

"Well, I know what your first job is," she said.

"What's that?"

"You are going to find out that girl's name, if you haven't already, and you're going to see if she was working here a couple of years ago when Montgomery and his colleagues were staying, and if she remembers them. That may be a stretch, considering the number of rooms and all, but as they were a visiting group, it's possible," she said, but even as the words left her mouth, she considered the chances slim. Perhaps in Paris the Australian delegates would have had more chance of standing out, rather than here, so close to Australia House. "If she wasn't here or doesn't recall, see if you can get her to introduce you to someone who was here and might recall the group who arrived."

"If Mr. Montgomery had a way with the ladies, she might recall him."

"Precisely. It's worth a shot. She's a good-looking lass. Perhaps he even tried to get her to pose for him, given he was such a keen photographer."

His eyes widened. "Got it," he said. "Do you think she's . . . fond of me?"

Billie gave him a look. "I suspect the whole kitchen could tell you that."

The young woman returned presently with a rack of toast for Billie with margarine, a pot of black tea, and two real boiled eggs. And bliss they were. She and Sam were informed in low tones that the kitchen had just started getting eggs in again, though it was irregular, and Billie noted theirs was the only table with evidence of any. The pair of them heaped praise on the girl and Sam managed to elicit a name: Betty.

"We are most grateful, Betty," Billie said. "We've traveled a long way, and my colleague here, Samuel, had to suffer through very uncomfortable seating on one of the Lancaster bomber planes, for three whole days. I'm not sure if he told you?"

Betty shook her head, wide-eyed.

"He's one of the Rats of Tobruk," Billie added.

"What's that?"

"He's a war hero. He'll have to tell you all about it when we finish our meeting," Billie said slyly, and Sam blushed. Betty was called over to another table, so had to leave them, but looked back shyly at Sam as she moved—or floated, it seemed—away.

Now alone again, Billie and Sam began their work over black tea.

"So, what is our strategy? After two years, where do you think our man might be?" Sam asked.

Billie always had a strategy, though this case posed particular problems. "We do have a challenge on our hands, to be sure," she admitted. "Two years is a lot of time to make up, but I am heartened by something Vera said about her husband—that he is not good at keeping a low profile. It wasn't in his nature, apparently. So, we do our best to retrace his steps and see just what kind of an impression he made, and with whom. The man comes here to London, stays in this hotel, meets with some colleagues at Australia House, and then they go to Paris. That's what we know. We need to find anyone who might have met with him, and go wherever he might have gone, just as we would with any other case. And where the trail goes cold . . ."

"We search the death house," Sam finished.

"Precisely." She took a sip of her tea. It was hot and invigorating. "The time that has passed won't aid us, but we're a fine team, Sam. We'll crack this. Betty can help you here at the hotel, perhaps, and later today we will make ourselves known at Australia House and see who might remember him there. I did get a couple of names from Mrs. Montgomery, but there wasn't time to hear back, so I can't say if they're expecting us, exactly."

Her experience and instincts told her she'd get further in person, with charm, than she would by the telegram she had sent—or by using that telephone in her room.

Sam saw that Billie had downed her first cup, and without a word he poured her another.

"So, Montgomery does his work with the exposition, yes?" She sipped her tea. "Nothing out of the ordinary so far, though, as we know he's a bit of a ladies' man," she mused. "He sends his wife a letter from the Ritz in Paris, and then stays on, and either doesn't want to come home, or can't. So, there is our first question. Why stay on? What has happened? Not sightseeing, and probably not any hob-nobbing with some new business contacts, though he does seem ambitious, so that can't be ruled out."

"A woman," Sam guessed.

"It's our most obvious avenue. Perhaps someone he meets in Paris."

"Perhaps a mannequin at the exposition," Sam chimed in. "A French girl steals his heart."

"Yes, perhaps a mannequin, or on that note even a woman from Australia House. A hostess at the Boomerang Club?" It was a club for the staff and Australian Services in the basement of Australia House. "We'll have to look into that. If she is connected to Australia House or the exposition, someone will have seen something, we can hope. I can't imagine he is worried about flirting openly, within reason . . . not while overseas and knowing his wife is . . . tolerant. Or at least he wouldn't worry about it until he knew he was going to steal away, if that's what he did. She did seem to feel it likely she'd been abandoned."

She took a last bite of her toast. Ah, the margarine was lovely. Not quite butter, but lovely nonetheless. Dry, stale toast dipped in weak tea had sustained her on many a morning in the field. Sustained her and Jack . . .

"But did he come back to London?" Sam asked. "You say it could have been a hostess at Australia House. I thought he didn't come back from Paris?"

"Of his movements after the Ritz in Paris, we just don't know yet. We only know that he didn't contact his wife again. He could be in Milan or Zurich for all we know. But he did not return with his colleagues. So perhaps he comes back in his own time, with his own agenda. It's a simple enough trip from the Continent, yes, or at least it was before the war." She wasn't sure how or when they would get across to Paris yet themselves. "He could have done it without advertising his movements. We have to assume the money Vera is living on isn't all that he had access to."

Montgomery's mother interested Billie. Just how bad was their falling-out? Could she be involved in his disappearance in some way?

"He does sound ambitious," she continued as Sam watched her

intently. "If it's business that kept him on, rather than something personal, perhaps he was working on something and . . ."

"A deal gone wrong?" Sam suggested.

"He got in over his head with something, or someone, perhaps. Or the hostess has a jealous lover." She drew her finger across her white throat.

Even more precise than the supposed "seven deadly sins," in Billie's experience there were less than a handful of human motivations behind most mysteries, murders, and, likewise, disappearances. "Love, lust, loot, and loathing," as her father used to put it.

Lust. Greed. Wrath . . .

Which of these loomed large in Richard Montgomery's disappearance?

Fourteen

—∿—

Shyla Davis chose a private corner table at the Central Railway Refreshment Room, farthest from the entry and the kitchen, and with her back to the wall watched the doorway, just as Billie Walker always did. She ignored the stares of the two waitresses who always seemed to be on shift when she visited and always looked at her as if she did not belong, and kept her eyes on the door.

After about five minutes, a sharply dressed white man with dark hair entered. He was a man of about forty years of age, and he cast his eyes from one side of the room to the other. She caught his eye and there was a question at first, then a flash of recognition.

"Miss Smith?" the man said in a low voice, still a touch uncertain. It was the name she had given him.

Shyla nodded, and the man slid nervously into the chair opposite her. "Would you like a tea? Some coffee, perhaps?" she said, and pushed a menu across to him. Just as Billie always did, she studied the man's appearance as he looked the menu over. His nails were neat and clean, and he had a square, masculine jaw, closely shaved. His hair parting was ruler straight, and, if she was not mistaken, his hair was dyed. The suit was of a high-quality lightweight wool. A typical rich whitefella, Shyla deduced. What would he have to say that was so important?

"I'll have a black tea," the stranger said, and folded his hands in his lap restlessly. There was a slight tremor in his voice, and his pale eyes were always moving—to the menu, and the table, and Shyla's hands, and the floor, and to the other tables—checking to see who was looking.

Anyone who was looking their way, Shyla thought, seemed more interested in her. She glanced toward the kitchen at the two wait-resses who were loitering there and with a wave indicated she was ready to order. After a whispered exchange, one came to the table and looked to the man seated there. Shyla then ordered two black teas, and the waitress turned on her heel without a word.

"We have some privacy," Shyla said, once they were alone again.

"Bobby . . . um, Mr. Charles told me you and your colleague were to be trusted. I expected the other woman, Billie, but when you called . . ." He trailed off, uncertain.

"Billie Walker sent me," she said.

He seemed to accept this as fact, and leaned forward. "I work at George Patterson, the advertising agency, and . . . You are looking into Richard Montgomery, right?"

Shyla nodded calmly, not betraying the fact that she really didn't know who the man was, only that it was a Montgomery who Billie was off to find in London. Billie hadn't got into the details, and she hadn't mentioned any Bobby Charles. Doubtless they had been making inquiries at the George Patterson agency and this man was involved. All those types of men knew each other. Shyla dearly hoped this excursion was worth it for her friend, though it meant she was going outside her own rules about getting more involved in the affairs of Billie's agency than she already was. From the day they'd met, nearly three years before, it had been a slow, inexorable pull, first working as an informant and now this . . .

Maybe Billie was right, and Shyla was suited to the work?

The stony-faced waitress returned with their tea, avoiding Shyla's eyes. As soon as she left them, Shyla took a sip of her hot drink. It was good tea. She liked the tea there. Her companion did not touch his.

"When I heard you were looking into his disappearance, I . . . Well, it brought some things back. Charles thought it might be helpful for me to speak to you," the man said, and swallowed, clearly uncomfortable. Shyla wondered what was on his mind. She tried to make a reassuring listening face, like Billie did, and this seemed to ease the way. "We are . . . *were* with the same firm, and on one of our business trips Richard . . . well, he caught me in a *situation*," he said, and swallowed again, his mouth seeming to go dry. "I realize now that it . . . well, it doesn't really matter, but he set it up, I think, and he managed to wheedle quite a bit more out of me than I care to admit. He threatened me with photographs, you understand."

"Threatened?" Shyla whispered.

"He said he'd go to our boss, and to the police, with the photographs, if I didn't pay him," he said in a low voice.

At the mention of police, Shyla frowned. "Blackmail?" That was a dirty business.

He nodded, and his face twisted with anger at the memory. "He told me he needed the money for one reason or another, and he had to do it. I paid him, of course. I had no choice, you understand."

She nodded, though she didn't quite understand. What situation had he been in? The police did not tend to threaten whitefellas like him, in Shyla's experience, though she did not doubt the man. She noticed his hands trembling slightly as he recounted what had happened.

"Well, he got a lot of money out of me for two years before his little disappearance," the man said bitterly. "I had nothing to do with his going away, mind you, but I can't say I'm sad about it."

That would be understandable, Shyla thought. Well, well, the people Billie got caught up with.

"He had photographs of you?" she asked.

"He told me he did. I never saw them, but I didn't have to. He always had that camera with him when he traveled, and, well, I believed him. If he had decided to tell Mr. Patterson, I am sure I would have been out of a job . . . or worse. I can tell you this because Bobby says your agency is sympathetic and can be trusted, Miss Smith, and, um, your associate Miss Walker. You won't mention this to anyone?"

Shyla shook her head. "No. We can be trusted," she assured him.

"Bobby . . . uh, Robert Charles says he owes you one. And I owe him. If something did happen to that man, Richard, all I can say is that I'm not surprised. He would have made himself a lot of enemies. I can't be the only one he did this to. Bobby knew about it, and when he asked me to tell you about it, I was happy to help. I heard what you all did for him."

"Thank you," Shyla said, wondering what it was exactly that her friend had done for Mr. Charles.

"Can I go now? I would like to. You won't need to contact me again, will you?"

Shyla shook her head. "I don't think so. Thank you," she repeated. "You have helped." She was sure Billie would find use for this information.

The man reached for his billfold and she allowed him to pay, unsure of what Billie would do in this situation. He stood, gave her a respectful nod, and left the refreshment room with his head down, as if wishing to disappear into his own collar.

That would not have been an easy exchange for him, she considered, though she still wasn't sure quite what the sensitive situation he'd alluded to entailed. The man Billie was looking for in London and Paris evidently wasn't well-liked. Blackmailers never were, and it seemed to Shyla they'd been proliferating like a virus in the cities since the war due to people's desperate circumstances.

Shyla left Central Station and made her way to the post office to send a telegram, intrigued by what it all meant. One thing was for certain: The man she'd spoken with was genuine. He'd meant what he said, and that meant Billie was looking for a blackmailer.

What an odd profession this was.

Fifteen

—m—

LONDON, ENGLAND, 1947

The stroll to Australia House from the hotel was just half a mile, and took Billie and Sam up the famous Strand, through London's scarred but still beating heart.

The German blitzkrieg—or "lightning war," as it was otherwise known—over London had taken a terrible toll, still evident years on in the many broken buildings and nearby flattened lots where historic establishments had once stood. Though no longer quite post-apocalyptic, the destruction of those infamous eight months of relentless bombing by the Luftwaffe was still very much visible. Sam was speechless, and Billie deep in thought as they walked. These streets of shattered brick and stone were perhaps not the London of Sam's childhood dreams, but it was something of an improvement on Billie's last experience of the famous city, when war reporting had brought her to these very streets, danger imminent.

They soon approached Australia House, a grand building erected on a triangular block of land on the corner of Aldwych and the

| 149 |

Strand—busy roads connecting the Parliament at Westminster and the City of London. The classical Edwardian building was fully intact and had a green roof and several circular and rectangular mansard windows, with a distinctive quadriga statue high above the eastern entrance. Titled *Phoebus Driving the Horses of the Sun*, the sculpture featured a nude man in bronze wearing a crown, his arms raised rather immodestly and a discarded cloak fluttering over one arm as the forequarters of four horses from his chariot reared on either side of him, caught in suspended animation. Indeed, why would you bother with clothes if you were the god of the sun, camped out in the Antipodes? Flanking the entrance below this statue were two more elaborate sculptures, each featuring scantily clad women with two men at their feet. The sculptures, once magnificent, appeared dusty and worn. These bare-chested women had weathered a war, after all.

Less than a mile past where they stood outside Australia House, Billie could see the great dome of St. Paul's Cathedral, still miraculously standing. Though the smoke had long since cleared from the bombings around the cathedral in 1940, the streets were gray, the buildings scarred and sooty, and locals still queued for food for hours.

The long shadow of war.

Back in Sydney, so far from the front lines, it had been easy to forget the true scale of the devastation, even though both Billie and Sam had been in the thick of it during the war. In time, the visions had faded or were relegated to unwanted dreams, but here they came back in full—the falling bombs and buildings, the cries, the air thick with the dust of shattered lives.

"London took a real hammering," Sam remarked, following Billie's gaze as she stared at the cathedral.

She took a breath and looked back at Australia House. "Let's head in and see what we can stir up, yes? Someone is bound to remember Montgomery, or at least their little delegation from the Bureau of Information." Would most of the staff have been there two years before? She would be grateful if she could make some connections in London with Montgomery's colleagues and the Caversham-Smithes, perhaps even his mother, before heading to where the real meat of the case was likely to be—Paris, his last-known location. Thankfully Billie was familiar with Australia House and the Australian High Commissioner's Office, even if she hadn't had occasion to spend a lot of time there during the war like other Australians had. She did have at least one contact she knew was still there—Mary Ethel Wood, private secretary to Mr. Beasley, the current high commissioner. Mary had worked there for almost thirty years and had seen many roles change hands over the decades.

They made their way through the main entrance with little fuss, and Billie observed that the once grand interior of Australia House looked somewhat shabby, much like the sculptures outside. The chandeliers were dusty, the marble dull; the furniture appeared worn. No doubt the under-resourced staff had other priorities beyond such tasks as dusting, mopping, and repainting. The staff seemed overworked and unexpectedly brusque. Doubtless none of this dissuaded immigrants eager to leave the wreckage of Europe to start a life on sunnier shores.

"Perhaps we should have tried just after lunch, instead," Billie said to Sam under her breath, observing the tired faces of the staff.

They'd opted to come after four in the afternoon, when the day was beginning to wrap up, to make their visit less formal and pressured, having already been busy gathering as much as they could on the Montgomerys and the Caversham-Smithes through the day—such as it was. Wealthy families did have an annoying habit of staying out of the news as a policy, but thankfully they showed up in more dignified and inevitable publications—births and deaths registries.

Searching for a telephone number for the Montgomery matriarch had not proved easy, however. As they hadn't a full address for her, the directory service had been unable to help, and Sam spent half the day traveling all the way to the post office in Surrey to get it. Billie only hoped that it hadn't been a mistake to head to Australia House last thing. She did rather need something to help lighten what had been a somewhat dreary day of groundwork.

Billie caught the arm of a harried-looking young woman traversing the hall. "Excuse me, I'm here to see Miss Mary Ethel Wood." She pressed her business card into the woman's hand. "I'm Ms. Billie Walker, and this is my assistant, Samuel Baker. I telegrammed ahead."

"Oh . . . yes. Welcome," she said, looking at the card. "She's quite busy, you understand. Perhaps you might like to wait in the Wool Room?"

The Wool Room was new, from what Billie had heard, but she had other ideas. "Thank you. If you don't mind, we'll wait in the Reading Room until she's ready."

The Reading Room had been a popular spot for Australian soldiers to catch up on news in their home country during the war. The shelves were lined with Australian books; newspapers were lined up along tables, the latest being editions they had read just before their departure six days before. They settled in and casually flicked through what was there.

AUSTRALIA HOUSE DISGUSTS CHIFLEY

DAILY TELEGRAPH SERVICE AND A.A.P.

LONDON, Monday—Australia House was dingy, dirty, and dreary, the Australian Prime Minister (Mr. Chifley) said in London today. "It is a bad advertisement for

Australia, and must be spruced up," he added. Mr. Chifley discussed with the Australian Resident Minister (Mr.
Beasley) pay and working conditions of Australia House
staff.

"Gosh. That's quite the headline," Samuel said, then fell silent
and hurriedly turned it over as a dignified older woman approached.
Billie saw that it was Mary.

"Ms. Walker!" the silver-haired woman called out with open
arms, and the two women embraced. "I got your telegram. I'm so
pleased you came."

"You're a sight for sore eyes, Miss Wood. May I introduce my assistant, Mr. Samuel Baker. Sam, this is Miss Mary Ethel Wood."

"Tell me, how are things?" Mary asked, apologizing that she
didn't have long. Billie explained her move back to Sydney and reopening her late father's agency, the disappearance of her husband,
and her current search for Vera Montgomery's husband. Mary led
them down a long hall toward her office, passing framed formal pictures all along the walls. The photographs interested Billie, even if
they gave her some concern about just how many staff members
currently working at Australia House might have met Richard
Montgomery and his party.

Stanley Bruce had been high commissioner when Richard disappeared, holding the position until October 1945. Bruce was replaced by Resident Minister Herbert Vere Evatt, who held the post
until January 1946, and then Jack Beasley took on the role of resident minister and had been high commissioner since last August.
Miss Mary Ethel Wood was the common thread between all of
them.

"It looks like there has been quite a changing of the guard, so to
speak," Billie commented, and Mary nodded. She welcomed them

into her office, which opened up into the high commissioner's office. Currently his door was closed.

"Australia must be a popular destination these days, as well as during the war," Sam said, looking around.

"Yes," Mary replied. "In 1938 we had no fewer than fifty thousand applications from people wanting to escape Europe and the rising threat here. Of course, the applications by far outweighed the available spots."

"How many spots were there?" Billie asked.

"Five thousand from memory. I still think of some of the families we turned away that year." Her eyes dropped for a moment. "You know, the exposition in '45 that your man Montgomery was involved in was a great success," she continued, perking up. "I have prepared some papers for you about it. There has been a lot of interest in emigrating to Australia since."

"I imagine so," Billie said. "Thank you." She accepted the folder. "Any chance we can track down the itinerary of the men who attended?"

"Oh yes. I'll get Alice to dig out what you're looking for. The gentlemen left here together. I remember it well, even if I don't recall anything very particular about this man you are looking for. I am frightfully sorry, but I don't have long today. The high commissioner has an event this evening," she explained. "And I'm sorry things aren't quite at their best here—they stripped back a lot of the staff, but they aren't *all* stuffy and overworked, I assure you. In fact, I think you should meet Charlie. He's from the Trade Commissioner's Office, and he'd *love you*. I think some of the boys are having a bit of a gathering downstairs tonight, in fact. They should be able to put the welcome mat out."

"Is that so? Do you think this Charlie might recall Richard Montgomery?" Billie asked.

"It's possible," she said, getting her handbag. "I am frightfully sorry, but I must dash now. Perhaps those papers will be helpful. Why don't you head back over to the Reading Room, and I'll send him your way? It's good to see you, Billie, and in these better times."

The two women exchanged a knowing look. When they'd last met, when Mary was working for the previous high commissioner, there happened to be a giant crater outside Australia House after a bomb attack. Only a short time before, nearby St. Mary's Church had been hit, leading many to believe Australia House itself was being targeted in the bomb raids. It had been a close one. Desks had been upended, glasses and plates shattered, and a number of casualties had been brought down to the Boomerang Club for medical care. Australia House had been in utter chaos.

Billie thanked Mary and headed for the Reading Room with Sam, the folder under his arm.

"I do hope we can get some essential information quickly here and then make our way to Paris this week. No sense in hanging around if Richard didn't return to London."

Sam perused the papers while they waited. "Here's one for us," he said, taking one from the top. "It looks like we may be safer here in London." He handed it to her.

"'Women Carry Their Own Weapons,'" she read aloud in a radio voice, theatrically brandishing the page. "'In an effort to break Sydney's present wave of crime, strong police patrols will be used . . . Women in one suburb are so frightened of being attacked that some are reported to be carrying weapons of their own device in their handbags, including black jacks, chisels, scissors and batons.'

"Seems rather sensible, really," she remarked, and patted her thigh, where the tiny Colt 1908 with its shining mother-of-pearl grips waited beneath her skirt. "Not everyone has one of these. But then a chisel might come in handy, also." She brought her hands to her lips. "Fighting Red, a few pounds, and a good chisel—all you need for a night out in Sydney."

A young man approached them. "Miss Walker?"

Billie whirled around to see a fellow of about thirty, far younger than Mary and much of the other staff. He was long and lean, and the pinstripes of his suit made him seem even more so, as did the way he wore his brown hair, long at the front, swept back and to the side. He possessed the air of someone who knew Australia House as well as he would his own home. Billie caught him looking her up and down as one might take in a painting at auction.

"I'm Ms. Walker," she said, taking a step forward. "I'm afraid I don't have the privilege of your name."

"I'm charmed, Miss Walker. Positively charmed. What a pleasure it is to make your acquaintance." He did a little old-fashioned bow, which was entirely unnecessary, and when he straightened again he smoothed his hair. "I'm Charlie Thompson. Mary sent me over to welcome you. I do think I owe her a debt of gratitude for that," he said flirtatiously, shaking her hand and seeming to stop just short of kissing it. He completely ignored Sam's presence. Sam, for his part, continued to peruse the Australian newspapers on the table, or pretend to.

"What brings you all the way to Australia House?" Mr. Thompson asked her.

"Well, the sights of London are always a delight, but for the moment I am here with my colleague, Mr. Baker," she said, pointedly referencing Sam. "On a more serious matter, I am hoping to find out about one of our fellow Australians abroad."

His eyes flicked to Sam, and back to her. "How fascinating," he said. "Well, you have come to the right place. Tell me, are you doing any sightseeing while you bless these shores?"

"I may do, but for now I am rather focused on the task at hand."

"Heavens, don't let work take up all your time. That would be a crying shame, Miss Walker, for a woman as lovely as you. Surely some young man should be showing you the town. London may not be quite on its feet yet, but it's still got its charms, I can assure you."

"And you have yours, I see. My name is Ms. Walker, actually," she added, continuing to smile.

Behind her, Sam coughed and flipped the page of a newspaper.

"Oh, I see," Mr. Thompson replied, taken quite off guard. "Ms. Please accept my apologies, Ms. Walker," he said, bowing his head again.

For her part Billie slightly bowed her head in return, a gesture of peace. "There is no need whatsoever to apologize to me. I spend most of my life being called 'Miss.' It is quite fine."

"But not correct," he pressed.

"But not correct," she confirmed. "You can call me Billie, if you like. I'm here from Sydney, perhaps Mary explained? We arrived just a couple of days ago."

"I'm Charlie, at your service. Did you travel by sea or by air?"

"The Qantas Lancastrian service," she explained, wondering what exactly he had in mind.

"Well, well," he replied, eyebrows raised. "A woman like you should be flying first-class. Still, I am impressed you took on one of those old bombers. Do you still have the headache?"

She laughed and nodded. Yes, she did. The altitude in the unpressurised planes caused it. "I'm afraid so, but it's clearing up. How delightful it is to meet you, Charlie. As I mentioned, we're looking for someone. His name is Mr. Richard Montgomery," she said, trying again. "I understand he was here in '45, with the contingent from the Bureau of Information who were here for the *Australia in Peace and War* exposition in Paris. Did you perhaps meet him, by any chance?"

Charlie shrugged, not seeming terribly interested in her query. "I can't be sure."

Sam had resumed his side-eye. Though he was carefully staying out of the conversation, she was quite certain his hearing had recovered fully. There was no way he found last week's newspapers that interesting.

Undeterred by Charlie's lack of interest, Billie took out the best of Vera's photographs of her husband and showed him.

"This is the chap, eh?" he said, giving a show of looking it over. "Well, he's lucky to have the likes of you looking for him, I can say that. I'm afraid I am not sure his face rings a bell, though. Pity. So, tell me about Ms.?" He moved a touch closer. "Are you married, Ms. Billie, or are you one of those fascinating women who avoids such institutions?" He tilted his head, and his mouth turned up in a coy grin. His long hair flopped over one glittering gray eye.

She put the photograph of Montgomery back in her handbag. "I'm a war widow," she answered with some reluctance. "One of far too many, I'm afraid . . . or at least it seems I am. Did you perhaps know Jack Rake? He was a photojournalist during the war and worked for a lot of the bigger publications. He hails from Sutton." She couldn't help but oscillate between speaking about him in the past tense and present, as if her husband were caught in a frustrating half-life—or perhaps it was she who was caught in that endless twilight.

At this, Charlie adopted a sympathetic expression. "I'm terribly sorry. I can't say I knew the chap. I hail from Victoria—an Aussie like yourself."

Billie had surmised this from his accent. Charlie had perhaps refined his accent to sound more British, but he was an Australian private-school boy through and through. "Frightfully sorry to hear about this fellow of yours. You say it *seems* so? So you are not sure if . . . ?"

"He went missing during the war and was last seen in Warsaw," Billie explained. Her throat was closing up, as if to prevent her from even saying the words, as if not saying he was missing would somehow make it less true. She didn't like the feeling of vulnerability that came over her at the mention of Jack. She looked around for a glass of water and spotted a jug across the room.

"Oh, let me get it for you," Charlie said, intuiting her need. In moments, he was back with a glass, but not before Sam gave Billie a look, eyebrow raised. Yes, Charlie was laying it on, but that wasn't a bad thing. Billie needed to make connections. It was no good talking among themselves.

"That really is rotten luck," Charlie said, handing her the glass and placing a hand on her shoulder.

"Thank you, Charlie," she said, moving gently away from the hand and noticing Samuel once again giving the man some terrific side-eye. She wanted to play nicely, she reminded herself. Mary wouldn't send this man over if he couldn't be of use, and they needed help if they were to get anywhere. "Thompson . . ." She steadied herself, turning on a touch of her own charm. "You wouldn't be related to the Australian grazing family in Victoria, perhaps?"

At this shift in tone, Sam excused himself to peruse another area of the Reading Room.

Charlie grinned at Billie. "Why, yes, I am. I haven't introduced myself properly," he said. "I am Charles Thompson, Esq., with the Trade Commission."

Naturally he came from a prominent family.

"I know everyone who is anyone here at Australia House," he added, puffing himself up. "Perhaps I can be of some help, introducing you to the right people, though I'm a touch confused. Are you looking for Mr. Rake, or . . . ?"

"Not precisely, though I would dearly love it if there were any records available. We're looking for Richard Montgomery, the chap in the photograph." She tried on one of her more professional smiles, which he seemed to like.

"I do wish I could be of more help. Some of my colleagues would probably have met him, though. Actually, we're having a little gathering tonight, downstairs at the Boomerang," he said. "Just an informal get-together. One of our number, Thomas Dunbabin, is just back in town. Interesting fellow. You'd like him."

Billie thought she recognized the name, though she couldn't quite place it.

"If you are up for it after all of your travels today, would you care to join me, Ms. Walker? Perhaps meet a few of the chaps here? See this place when it really shines? I promise you won't find us so stuffy as you might think. It might help you track down this Montgomery character."

"Why, I'm flattered. Thank you. Are you quite sure? I don't want to take anyone else's place at your side. You must have women throwing themselves at you." Billie anticipated he was the type to enjoy that kind of flattery, considering how he served it up.

"No one like you," he replied smoothly.

Clever Mary, giving her an entrance like this. "I would be delighted to join you," Billie agreed, knowing she could handle him. "Would my friend be able to come with me? We're working together," she explained.

"Ah yes. Your secretary, am I right? Regrettably, I can only bring one guest," Charlie said, without so much as a feigned trace of regret.

"I understand. What time shall I be ready? Is there a dress code?"

"You'll have no problem in whatever you wear," he said, taking the opportunity to look her up and down again, though doing it more politely than he had as he'd entered the Reading Room. "You look just marvelous as you are. It's informal, this gathering. The Boomerang Club isn't anything terribly special, as you may know, but it will be delightful company, I promise. I'll be in a dinner jacket, of course," he added. "Shall I pick you up at your hotel? Say eight? If that's not too late?"

"Not too late at all," she said. "I'm at the Strand Palace."

"Just down the road. Very good," he said. "Eight o'clock it is, then. I'll wait for you in the lobby. Let's see if we can't get rid of that headache of yours."

Farewelling her, Charlie left the Reading Room and Billie leaned back against the table, grinning.

After a few minutes, Sam reappeared with some papers.

"I have a date tonight, downstairs at the Boomerang Club."

"He works fast," Sam remarked.

"Why, yes, he does." *I do too*, she thought. "Hopefully I'll be able to meet a few of the men who knew Richard, or might know of his whereabouts. It's a start."

It seemed Sam might have had more to say on the matter, but he tactfully held his tongue. "You'll be okay on your own?" he asked.

"Oh, I can handle the likes of him," she said confidently. "And don't worry, dear Sam. Hopefully I'll get what we need, and perhaps I'll even have a message waiting at the hotel from the Caversham-Smithes, or Mrs. Montgomery. Let's see if we can make some visits in the next couple of days, yes? We'll soon find out what there is to know."

"I don't know how I feel about that," he said of her going alone. "While you were busy with . . . him, I read through the folder your friend Miss Wood was kind enough to give us, and I found another archival article on the exposition in Paris. It seems she was right—it was considered a real hit—certainly nothing that Richard

Montgomery would have felt embarrassed about and perhaps gone into a self-imposed exile somewhere in France for." He grinned and handed it over.

Billie chuckled softly and took the article. The exposition featured images of Australia's beautiful shores and wildlife, making a good advertisement for immigrants. It also seemed to feature some of that wildlife:

> Reuters correspondent in Paris says that the exhibition in vivid miniatures affords French people a fine opportunity of learning what Australia has accomplished, also of seeing something of the natural beauties of the country. A baby wallaby so far is one of the stars of the exposition . . .

She wondered who else might have been stars. Beautiful young mannequins Richard may have become interested in perhaps?

—m—

A night out in London was precisely what the doctor ordered and what the case demanded. And if a nice drop of something was involved, all the better to Billie Walker's mind. While the work sometimes involved searching through dusty archives, this was where she really shone.

By eight thirty in the evening of her first official day on the job in London, Billie was swathed in a figure-hugging ruby dress with diamanté-encrusted belt and matching tilt hat, standing in the basement of Australia House, sipping bubbly with Charlie Thompson of the Trade Commission. Much as Mary had anticipated, she had caught his eye and he seemed to think nothing of bringing her along to show off to his mates and colleagues. She could see this was an informal affair, as he'd warned her, but it was also a place to see and be seen for those wanting to climb the ladder at Australia House. Charlie was clearly such a creature.

The gathering was so far mostly made up of men from the staff, along with a couple of women who seemed paired up with them. It had a "boys club" feel, she noted, and as the high commissioner had an event on, the most important men on staff were likely absent. These would be the next tier, she surmised, the ambitious climbers and the long-standing gatekeepers of the institution.

"I don't know if you are aware of this, but most of the building materials used in the construction here were imported from Australia, as a way of representing everything the country has to offer," Charlie was explaining.

"Is that so? It must have been terribly expensive to ship it across," she said somewhat absently.

"Indeed, it was. The building is Portland stone on a base of Australian trachyte," he boasted, "and we have pale cream Buchan marble from Victoria, some Caleula marble in light and dark tones from New South Wales, and white Angaston marble from South Australia. The flooring timbers include varieties from all Australian states."

"How very fascinating. What are we standing on, precisely?" she asked, looking at their feet.

He hesitated. "You caught me there, Ms. Walker. I don't actually know. I just know the spiel," he admitted, laughing.

"Well, thank you for sharing it." She looked around the room and noticed a few couples sitting and chatting. "Actually, I heard this place is built on an old well of some kind, something from medieval days?" she added.

"That is true. It's hard to access, otherwise I'd show it to you right now."

"Well, I wouldn't want you to miss out on your gathering. Perhaps some other time," she said.

"Actually, while it's still quiet, I have to say I was a bit taken aback to hear that you're some kind of private detective," he said. "I'll admit I didn't realize your search was of a professional nature."

"Well, yes, it is," she said, turning to him. "I'm looking for Richard Montgomery for his wife, back in Australia. I believe I mentioned it? I'm sorry if the nature of my work concerns you in some way." She wasn't sorry. Not in the slightest.

Charlie shifted on his feet. "No, no. It's just that I had thought perhaps your reasons were personal."

"I see." *One can only have so many missing husbands of one's own,* she thought. "Montgomery was with the Australian Bureau of Information, as I said. They were here in '45. Miss Wood remembers them, so perhaps some of your friends do also?"

"I've not met a woman detective before."

"We are much like the male ones, apart from the lipstick," she said, pursing her Fighting Red lips.

"I do hope that's not all."

"Not in any ways that should affect the work. In Australia we're called private inquiry agents, actually. We're forbidden to use the term 'detective' in relation to our work." It was about the only piece of legislation particularly pertaining to the trade. Even those with criminal records could operate agencies, and often did, their special skills and contacts being of particular appeal to some. Her nemesis in the trade, Vincenzo Moretti, came to mind.

"Women are not allowed to call themselves detectives? How fascinating. I suppose it makes sense."

"No, not just women; no private inquiry agent, whether man or woman, is allowed to use the word, not being on the public purse. It's reserved for police detectives, public detectives if you will, of whatever sex they may be."

"Oh, I see. You are a fascinating woman, I must say. I haven't met someone quite like you before, Billie Walker."

She did the professional smile, the one with steel behind the ivory.

"Is this Montgomery character presumed dead, like . . . ?" He wisely stopped himself before mentioning her missing husband's name.

"Not necessarily, no. Unlike Jack, his work was not dangerous, as I understand it, though the bureau is not terribly open about their business, it seems. They were mostly involved with promoting Australia, from what I can tell, and having read a bit about the exposition, I can't imagine anything particularly controversial or dangerous about it. There's certainly no obvious reason it would have put him in the line of fire, as it were."

"And you have no other reason to be here?" Charlie asked.

Billie tilted her head. "Such as?"

"Well, I didn't realize we had such a famous investigator in our midst, that's all."

"I'm not sure I follow?"

Charlie shifted again. "Wasn't there some incident last year, in Sydney? After you left, I had it pointed out to me. Quite a story it was, too. There was a copy in the Reading Room."

Of course. She had seen stacks of *The Sydney Morning Herald*. It stood to reason that Billie's appearances in that paper had not gone unnoticed, along with the front-page drama of the high-ranking Nazi criminal found to be doing dirty business all the way over in New South Wales, so far from the sickening Ravensbrück concentration camp for women, where he'd made his name. "Yes. You know about that, do you?"

"Apparently I was the only who *didn't*. You must tell me

everything," he said, and grinned in his mischievous way. His hair again flopped over one eye, and he smoothed it back behind his ear. "It looked like quite the derring-do. When I read that, I thought perhaps you might be working on something larger," he suggested. "To come this far from your offices, I mean."

Billie placed a hand on her hip, tilting her head. "Charlie, I must confess you sound rather like you have something in mind."

"Charlie, my dear man," came a voice, and her host was slapped heartily on his shoulder. "Who is this lovely woman you've been hiding from us?"

"Oh look, here's Basil and Harold," Charlie said, standing a touch taller, their conversation instantly falling away. He flashed a broad smile to the pair of older men, one of whom was bald, and the other tall and thin, with a full head of silver hair.

"These old dogs have been here for a while and might have met your man Montgomery," Charlie explained, introducing her.

"What a charming woman," Basil Aldrich, the bald one, said, and she half suspected he wanted her to do a little spin for them. "What man is this we might have met? Is he the lucky fellow?" From the way he said it, it was clear he meant "love interest."

"Not so lucky, I'm afraid. He's missing presently, though I hope to change that. The name is Richard Montgomery. He came out here in '45 with the Bureau of Information."

"Oh, Montgomery, yes. It was for that Paris thing, wasn't it?" Basil said. "Richard was a good man. Very outgoing. What's happened to him, exactly?"

"That's what I hope to find out," Billie said. "He has been missing since just after the exposition in Paris."

"Curious thing, that is. I heard he decided to stay on." Basil frowned. "I wasn't aware that he went missing." He said the word as if it was terribly dramatic of her to reach such a conclusion, what with only two years having passed.

Billie's eyes lit up. "Do you remember where you heard that, about his choosing to stay on in Paris?" she asked.

"I think one of the gentlemen here told me that. I can't be sure. I think that was the understanding, though. I wasn't involved with the exposition, but certainly Montgomery was a solid man," Basil said. "Great success it was, too, I understand."

"Yes. I read a little about it."

"They had this wallaby—"

"How long did you know him for?" Billie asked, gently intervening.

"Not even a couple of weeks, but he was always working on something, was Richard, looking for an angle to get the promotion working, that sort of thing. A very entrepreneurial fellow, from what I recall. We could use more men like that, couldn't we, Charlie?" There was another back slap. "He was the kind of resourceful man you want on your team. I'm sorry to hear something may have happened to him."

Harold nodded in agreement.

"Yes. It's terribly difficult for his wife, Vera," Billie said, meeting his eyes and holding them. "She's a lovely woman. You'd like her, I think. She would be here herself, if she could, but sent me in her stead. If you would let me know if you do hear anything about Richard, or if you recall anything else, I would very much appreciate it, as would Mrs. Montgomery. I'm at the Strand Palace." She presented her business card.

"Certainly," Basil replied, and accepted the card. As he contemplated it, Harold bailed up her host.

"Charlie, what's this nonsense you were telling me about the government scrapping the dictation test?" He was clearly agitated about the possibility. "What rubbish!" he cried.

"Let's not get into politics again, Harry," Charlie said with a chuckle, flicking a glance at Billie as if to say, *Here we go.*

Ah, the dictation test. This could only be a reference to the part of the so-called White Australia policy legislation that favored whites and the British, and demanded immigrants to Australia pass a dictation test in a European language. This neatly excluded non-European immigrants, including those from countries closer to Australia.

"You did say there's talk about Chifley dismantling the legislation," Harold pressed, his jowls shaking. "Is this true? Most alarming, if it is. Most alarming."

Charlie shrugged in response, holding his drink close to his mouth. "Look, I don't know how I feel about it either," he said. "Australia's national character must be preserved. But tonight is perhaps not the time." He looked to Billie again and took another sip of his bubbly.

"Which aspects of Australia's national character, precisely?" Billie asked before she could stop herself.

Charlie turned back to her, perhaps not quite knowing how to take her question. She strategically blinked a couple of times, her lashes seeming to ease her inquiry somewhat. "Well, the character of the nation, of course," he answered. "Surely you do agree, Ms. Walker." It wasn't a question.

She opened her mouth to respond, but Basil interjected. "White jobs must be preserved," he declared. "Australia will see low-class Indians, Chinamen, and Japs swarming the country if the legislation is dismantled. Mark my words."

"And what of the considerable skills and contributions of those people wanting to join Australia from these nations?" Billie challenged. She wasn't there to rock the boat, she reminded herself, and certainly not in front of Basil and Harold, who had actually met Montgomery and were so far the only ones who seemed to much remember him. "What of the highly skilled workers and thinkers from different backgrou—"

"We must not unnecessarily offend the *educated* classes of those nations," her host, Charlie, interrupted. "But I agree, the legislation must remain in place for the preservation of the nation and economy." End of story. He clearly found it important to side with his colleagues over his rogue date.

Billie took a breath, her smile just holding on. There was much she could say about the problems with the test and its political uses, but she was moving into dangerous territory, and she knew it. A Czechoslovakian Jewish political activist, Egon Kisch, had arrived in Australia in 1934, escaping persecution by the Nazis and their growing powers, and the government of Joseph Lyons went to extraordinary lengths to exclude him using the test, as she well knew. Kisch was highly intelligent and was fluent in a number of European languages, and after completing passages for the test in several languages, he finally failed when they demanded he do it in Scottish Gaelic. *Scottish Gaelic.* The debacle had made the papers and brought the test into considerable disrepute. In the end, the courts had found it was not fair use of the legislation to require someone to complete the test in Scottish Gaelic to be eligible to immigrate to Australia. Quite. That strange affair certainly showed how the test could be, and sometimes was, manipulated. It seemed to Billie that there were better ways to judge a person's eligibility, character, or potential contributions. And here they were, on the other hand, advertising for new immigrants, just as Montgomery had been paid to do.

"Chifley is a levelheaded fellow. He's not going to scrap it, Harry," Basil chimed in.

"The Kisch affair made rather an impression," Billie said in a quiet voice, finding she could not quite bite her tongue tonight. "And how right Kisch was about Hitler . . ."

There was silence among the group now. Billie took a sip of her drink, feeling the bubbles go flat, along with the mood of the gathering.

"My uncle is quite active with the ANA. They have it in hand, trust me," Charlie said, trying his best to defuse the conversation.

"Thank heavens for that," Harold said, but Billie was now thinking about how Charlie's uncle was a member of the ANA—the Australian Natives' Association. That meant he was well-connected in his area. Membership to the influential men-only lobby was restricted to white men born in Australia, and they campaigned tirelessly against non-white immigration. How interesting, she thought, that these well-to-do men called themselves "natives," when it had not been a continent of white people at all—a fact Shyla could certainly attest to.

At last, the subject changed, which was a relief, and Harold went on his way to join another group, perhaps to complain about the same impending "threat" to Australia's national character with a solely sympathetic audience. As the evening continued, the guest of honor, Charlie's mate Thomas Dunbabin, still having not arrived, political discussions were thankfully avoided and Billie was able to gently ask around about Montgomery. Disappointingly, he was not particularly well remembered among those who had been working at Australia House at the time, perhaps thanks to his short time with them before heading to Paris, and many of the staff had changed since '45.

They gathered a small circle of male admirers, with Charlie dutifully introducing her to each in turn. As she had guessed, the only women she met were there because they had been invited by their male dates. As small talk took over, Billie reflected on how, under normal circumstances, she might have expected that the disappearance of Richard Montgomery would have been the talk of Australia House, but the high turnover of staff and even high commissioners for the past couple of years, along with the considerable aftermath of chaos from the war, perhaps explained why it didn't really seem to register with anyone as unusual. It seemed to Billie that if the man had died somehow, he might even have been left unidentified in a morgue, considering so few in Paris were likely to have known him. Was it as simple as Montgomery staying on for a fling with a Parisian woman—one of his "little adventures"—and then becoming the unknown victim of some type of accident? Perhaps he had not "abandoned" his wife, as she thought most likely, but had merely taken an ill-fated detour.

"Now, what's this I hear about you being the girl in the papers last year, mixed up in that case with the war criminal in Australia?"

The question pulled Billie back into the group with a start. "Pardon?" It was Basil, the bald one, who had spoken.

"The case with that Nazi?" one of the younger men remarked. "What are the chances of a man like that ending up in Sydney?" Despite speaking about Billie, he directed his question to Charlie.

"I was apparently the last to hear about it," Charlie answered. "We have a famous detective on our hands."

The group gawped at her, fascinated. Now one of the wives had joined the throng, hanging back dutifully to allow the men to speak.

"I wouldn't call it *mixed up*, per se," Billie piped up. "I suppose you could say that my colleagues and I did what the courts in Nuremberg were unable to—the man having been sentenced to death in absentia."

"Terribly sorry?" Basil said, confused.

"He was sentenced to death at Nuremberg," she explained. "But he died near my . . . office," she said in a low voice. She thought again of that oil drum she'd found hidden at his property, packed with gold fillings, and the wave of sickness swept back over her.

"What's this?" Basil asked.

"The Nazi bastard is dead," she said, clear that she had not a shred of regret about it.

Basil gasped audibly at her language, and Charlie laughed, trying to make light of her comment. "Fiery, isn't she? And a private detective, no less!"

"Not a detective. I'm a private inquiry agent. And I'm terribly sorry if I've shocked you," she shot back. "The man hurt some people dear to me, including a client, as if I needed any more reason to dislike a Nazi, let alone one with his track record." She wasn't sorry if she shocked them, not at all actually, though she suspected that when the dust settled and she woke in her hotel room she might regret having spoken quite so plainly when her plan had been to charm her way into their circle. She smiled, raised her glass to Hessmann's demise, then took a sip.

"My dear girl," Basil said, looking quite appalled. "You think this kind of work is appropriate for a woman?"

"Well, yes, Basil, I do. I grant it's not for everyone, but it's appropriate for plenty of women and men, given the chance," she said, left hand in a fist, trying not to let being called his "dear girl" grate too much. "In fact, I was rather hoping some of you gentlemen might know something of how he got to Australia. It would have been around the end of the war, or shortly after, and I'm quite sure he did not act alone. He would have got his papers somewhere."

"Still on the case, are we? The war is over, my dear." It was Harold now, returning, having overheard some of their awkward exchange. "I should say none of us would know a thing about it."

"I, for one, find this woman's plucky courage quite inspiring,"

Charlie said, intervening on her behalf. "Perhaps we ought to drink to that? And the war being over, certainly."

"To victory."

"To victory," the group said in unison.

Billie clinked glasses with the men, having felt the drink go sour in her stomach.

"Did you read they are even sentencing the *women* to death now?" Harold told the group. "Frightful business. Those women guards from one of the camps were executed a few days ago. How ghastly."

He was right on that score. Thirty-eight defendants of the Hamburg Ravensbrück trials were being tried in seven separate trials held by the British. Of the thirty-eight, twenty-one of the defendants were women. Ravensbrück had been a concentration camp almost entirely for women prisoners and their children, and female Nazi guards were trained up there. It seemed many of those guards had been keen to prove their dedication to the Nazi cause with unbridled brutality against their charges. The trials of sixteen defendants had just ended, all being found guilty and most sentenced to death for their crimes. Three of the female guards from Ravensbrück had just been hanged, according to the article Sam had shown her back in Sydney. Wardens, medical doctors, and a nurse from the notorious camp had also been hanged. This was where the postwar focus was—on the trials and the debate about them.

The camp commandant had escaped, his whereabouts unknown until Billie and Shyla had found him. Hessmann had escaped the trials, but not justice, of a sort, she thought, picturing his contorted face, his outreached hand as he fell.

"Are you quite well, Ms. Walker?" Charlie asked her quietly, obviously aware of how ill at ease she had become.

Billie nodded. "It's a sorry affair. All of it," she said softly.

"These are nothing more than show trials—high politics masquerading as law," Harold persisted, speaking over her. "You know Kesselring was just sentenced to death by firing squad . . . more honorable than hanging, I suppose. I'm not a lawyer but I do think it's terribly un-British to put people on trial for crimes that didn't exist when they committed them. Beastly people, no doubt, but is this kind of show really what we want? Hanging *women?*"

"Perhaps these acts should have explicitly been crimes in law before this, yes? You know the details, don't you? And if we can hang men for these war crimes, we can hang women for them," Billie reasoned in a low, deadly serious voice. "This is the Ravensbrück camp we're talking about. These people, women or not, weren't simply guarding the women and children in their care, they were torturing them, working them to death, starving them intentionally. Death as a punishment is a complex topic, I'll grant you, but as for the public trials, they seem quite necessary. How else would most people even know what had gone on? One could argue that without bringing these Nazis to some kind of justice for torturing and murdering innocent civilians, en masse no less, one sets a very poor precedent for what is considered acceptable in wartime—"

"The war is over, my dear," Basil said dismissively, "and that Nazi from back home is dead now."

"He didn't act alone," she declared angrily.

"Let me get you another drink," Charlie cut in, pulling her away from the group. "Excuse us for a moment."

The group stared at Billie as Charlie steered her away. She felt her cheeks burning at the intrusion into her space, the interruption of her view on something so passionately, righteously felt. She was angry, and at that moment not good at hiding it. Losing her cool was not something she often did, let alone in a professional context, but why should she have to hide this? Were they really in an argument about the seriousness of Nazi war crimes? At Ravensbrück of all places? Surely not. This was Australia House, not the German embassy.

Billie shook off Charlie's hand, which he'd placed on her elbow. "I had better go," she said, noticing her glass was empty, along with her patience for Harold and his colleagues. "Perhaps the travel is catching up with me."

"I'm sorry about those two. They're a bit set in their ways, is all. I'm sure it wasn't easy, what happened last year," he said, and she softened slightly.

"Nothing worth doing is easy," she said simply. "But I'll not listen to anyone play down what those people did in those evil camps." And there would be others, surely, who were living lives off the broken backs of the concentration camp victims they'd murdered. "Do you think anyone here might have seen Hessmann's paperwork? Surely it must have passed through these offices at some point."

"I admire your determination, Billie. Let me walk you back to your hotel," he suggested, ignoring her question.

"I'll catch a taxicab." Or perhaps she'd walk the Strand in the moonlight, let off some steam, she thought. "Thank you for tonight. Really. I do appreciate your help, Charlie. And I am sorry if my views . . . ruined the party."

"I'm only sorry more of them don't remember this man you're looking for. And they are rather too caught up in politics, especially old Harold, as you've noticed." He shook his head.

"It's quite fine," she said, and walked back to the group, who were all having their champagne glasses refilled. "It has been a long day. I have work to do early tomorrow, and so will bid you all good night. Thank you for your hospitality. Perhaps we'll meet again." She smiled graciously, shook a few hands, and explained that she would be at the Strand Palace for the next couple of days.

"Let me know if you remember anything else about Montgomery," Billie told Basil and Harold, managing one of her professional smiles.

She gathered her red coat from the coat check—it was cut to resemble Dior's New Look style, a home-sewn knock-off but still significantly more modern than what anyone else was wearing—and she departed the Boomerang Club with her head high, Charlie trailing behind to see her out onto the cool street. As far as she was concerned, the bubbly had gone flat hours ago.

Sixteen

—ᴍ—

Billie was uncharacteristically quiet over breakfast with Sam on Tuesday morning as she ate her toast and margarine over a strong cup of black tea. She had slept well enough, considering the earlier-than-usual wake-up, but was caught up in her thoughts, mulling over the telegram she'd received from Shyla that morning, and her discomfort about the conversation the evening before.

The war is over, my dear . . .

"You look especially wonderful today," Sam said.

"I'm dressed to impress," she said absently, talking into her cup. She'd chosen her carefully pressed navy silk trousers, and an off-white buttoned blouse, worn with a belt, and a scarf of gold, ruby, navy, and white, going for the effect of a country toff in springtime. On Billie, though, it was perhaps more reminiscent of Katharine Hepburn. She had packed a bag with supplies—a basket of food for two, some beer for Sam, and a pair of gumboots in case things got more physical—or wet.

"Aren't you always dressed to impress? By the way, did everything go okay last night?"

Billie took a breath and leaned back in her chair. "Yes and no, dear Sam," she said, frowning and taking another sip of her tea. "I did meet a couple of older gentlemen, Basil and Harold, who actually met and still recall Montgomery, but frankly I was disappointed by how little of an impression the man made at Australia House. So many people have moved on. Perhaps my hopes had been too high, considering the time that's elapsed. Basil remembered him being entrepreneurial, and they had heard that he'd decided to stay on in Paris for a while, but that was everything I got, really. I suppose it might have been assumed that Montgomery would head back home from there, perhaps after a short holiday. In any event, there were no alarm bells when he didn't return to London."

"I would have stayed on to see Paris," Sam offered.

"Indeed. Though Montgomery would have needed to travel through London to get the return flight to Australia. Unfortunately, a lot of the staff I met last night had only started at Australia House recently." She frowned again, her eyes drifting over the finely cracked marble wall next to her. "I'm not sure what I expected to learn, Sam, but I no longer hold high hopes of finding anyone there who knew him well. Certainly no one has been holding a vigil in his absence."

Sam looked like he didn't know whether to laugh or not.

"Also, I may have offended my hosts," she added.

"You?"

"Me," she confirmed.

In fact, she was left with the feeling that she had been off her game. Where she had hoped to draw them in and convince them to help her, she had instead been drawn into a combative discussion about politics. She stood by her words, yes, but usually knew better than to let that happen when she was on the job. Was it being here, being back in Europe, that was making her feel too strongly, with the ghosts of the past constantly plaguing her thoughts? Or was it the mention of Nazi war criminals and what they had done? At least she had resisted slapping Harold, whom she had found quite infuriating. That was a win, she supposed.

"It was not as successful an evening as I'd hoped," Billie confessed. "But never mind all of that." She waved a hand. "I told you I wanted to leave by nine this morning, and I do. The sun is out, dear Sam, and we have a full day ahead, and some interesting new information out of Australia as well. This does shed some . . . *interesting* . . . new light on our man, as a matter of fact." Billie put down her teacup and reached for the telegram in her handbag. She'd been mulling over the ramifications since it had arrived in the early hours.

"It seems Shyla has been busy on our behalf, and our respectable businessman Mr. Montgomery may have been working some not-so-respectable angles in Sydney." Shyla really was an inquiry agent at heart. Billie knew it. "She got some great information for us. Oh, Richard is a photographer all right, but he's not just a ladies' man using that eye of his to lure in pretty young mannequins for photographic sessions. No, it looks like he's also a bona fide blackmailer." She handed over the telegram for Sam to peruse.

"A blackmailer? Blackmailing whom? Do we know?"

"A man who he caught in a *situation*," she said. Billie thought she might know what kind of situation. "I don't doubt it is true, somehow, especially as this information came through an associate of Robert Charles, who seems genuinely grateful for our . . . *solution*. This kind of thing may well be how Montgomery supplemented his income until his disappearance and kept Vera in the lifestyle she was accustomed to—whether she knew it or not." Those mysterious deposit stubs. "A blackmailer."

"Golly. He seemed so successful, especially given his involvement in the exposition. I didn't pick him as a blackmailer."

"Indeed. But we must remember we've only really had his wife's view," Billie reminded him. It was quite possible Vera had been wearing rose-colored glasses when it came to Richard, and didn't know everything about his activities. That was all too common, as anyone in her trade quickly came to realize. "He was likely pretty good at keeping up appearances, especially considering his profession in the advertising world."

"Shyla got this information? I thought you said she'd refused you when you wanted her to become an investigator."

"She did. But maybe we're rubbing off on her." Billie smiled. "I couldn't be more pleased if that's the case. In any event, I'd say we might not have had this information until we returned to Sydney if she hadn't taken up the cause." It was unlikely Mr. Charles's associate, whoever he was, would have been happy to telegram Billie with such sensitive information.

"Oh, I tried Richard's mother, Mrs. Montgomery, this morning, early, and left a message with one of her staff. Who knows, perhaps she'll be less difficult than Vera imagines? One thing is for certain, though; the Caversham-Smithes *are* being difficult. Mr. Caversham-Smithe is already out for lunch, apparently." Billie looked again at the clock. "Heading out for lunch on a Tuesday, this early? Unlikely, unless he'll be supping at Balmoral," she quipped. "I tried over the weekend, and again yesterday, and I'm always told they'll pass on my message, and he's at some kind of meal. The man is constantly eating. With such an appetite there are only two explanations. I'm either unwelcome or he has a tapeworm."

Sam nearly spat out his tea.

"It's been four days since my first call to them from the hotel. I know Vera sent a telegram as well, so they are quite aware that we're here, and we won't be in town forever. I'm rapidly forming the opinion that I'm getting fobbed off, and I won't have it. I'd also like to know why."

"I'm beginning to understand your outfit."

"We'll be showing up at their country estate today, Sam," she confirmed. It had been easy enough to check the address Vera had given them, the estate having been established over centuries of family ownership. "They're in Malmesbury. It's about three hours each way to that part of the Cotswolds. I think we might want to catch Mrs. Caversham-Smithe alone, if her husband really is out. And if not, all the better, I suppose. I must say, it seems a fine day for it."

Indeed, the sun was even showing itself, which was not something London was famous for.

Sam's eyes lit up. "The Cotswolds! That sounds a dream, Ms. Walker. Though of course I know we'll be on the job," he hastened to add.

Billie thought again of those photographs of the Caversham-Smithe girl. She was beautiful, and there was something in the eyes. Something that seemed to be for the photographer alone, a kind of intimacy. It had given Billie a strange feeling.

"I organized a fine car for us, Sam. Are you up for a drive?"

—※—

Billie stepped out of the Strand Palace at nine sharp, looking stylish in her navy driving coat, the silk scarf tied over her hair, and chic round cheaters sitting over her eyes. Since breakfast she'd added a fine set of pearls to her outfit and repainted her Fighting Red, and she now looked like something out of a catalog or British *Vogue*. Sam was at Billie's side, in his best pressed suit, and would look the part nicely, she felt. Immediately she saw the motorcar that had been organized by the blushing young hotel concierge who had been most helpful. It was impossible to miss the beast. She'd ordered something special to catch the eye of the Caversham-Smithes—an estate car that would fit into the conservative and moneyed area of the Cotswolds they were visiting—and what she got was an Armstrong Siddeley Hurricane, named for the fighter plane.

"Well, isn't this just the tonic," Billie said under her breath as she walked toward the waiting automobile, grinning from ear to ear.

Black and glistening, it was a two-door, four-seater drophead coupe with a handsome front grille, suicide doors, and a canopy. As an inducement to attract tourists, they had been allowed extra petrol coupons. Billie fully intended to use them.

"This car suits you," Sam said. "You dressed especially for this visit."

Billie nodded. "Quite right, Sam. You must dress for the job you want, or in this case what the job needs. We have to slide into the Caversham-Smithes' world today."

"Am I dressed okay?" he asked.

She nodded, then thanked the porter, who automatically passed Sam the motorcar keys. Irritated by this predictable error, she nonetheless allowed herself to be helped into the driver's seat by Sam, who knew full well there was no question of who would be at the wheel. He handed her the keys to the motorcar and went around to the passenger side while the porter watched.

"Top down, shall we?" Billie suggested from behind the wheel.

"Of course." Sam signaled to the porter and the pair of them worked on rolling up and lowering the Hurricane's canopy.

With a little thrill, Billie pulled her driving gloves out of her handbag. A woman should never be without them, she felt. Though many left the driving up to others—including her own mother, who had nonetheless bought her daughter that glorious Willys Roadster—to Billie's mind being at the wheel of a fast motorcar was something every woman should experience, as often as she could. It was a rare thrill that was both legal and didn't leave a woman with hangovers, social embarrassment, unwanted pregnancies, or male attachments. Who could argue with virtues such as those? With a grin Billie felt the foreign automobile warm to her presence, and when the time was right and her passenger was ready, she pulled out into the traffic, leaving the gaping hotel staff in their stylish wake.

———※———

"I'm not sure I've ever seen so much green in one place," Sam re-marked as they stepped out of the Hurricane, and indeed it was a picture of English country perfection, floating clouds sailing across misty skies. As London had fallen away, rolling hills and fields tak-ing over, so, too, the war had seemed to fade into another time far away, leaving them instead in a tranquil place untouched since the time of Shakespeare.

Billie stretched from one side to the other, took off her driving coat, and much to Sam's surprise handed him the keys. "Happy to be the driver now?" she asked.

"The driver?" He was stunned, knowing her strong preference for being at the wheel.

"When I go in, I want you to wait with the motorcar, so we don't overwhelm them. Is that okay with you?" she explained.

He nodded, quickly getting her meaning. "Of course, Ms. Walker." She walked around and got into the back seat, and after closing the door for her, Sam climbed behind the wheel, grinning like a schoolboy.

"Steady now," she said, seeing that he was enjoying this. "Re-member, this is all perfectly routine."

"Perfectly routine."

Sam started up the elegant motorcar and followed Billie's directions as she looked at her borrowed map and navigated their way. Soon they pulled into the entrance of the Caversham-Smithe estate, moving through a magnificent iron gate surrounded by aged stone walls, and marveling at the manicured gardens as they made their way along a winding drive lined with tall trees. All was as one might expect in an English fairy-tale setting, and perhaps that was what this was. Spring flowers—daffodils, crocuses, and irises—were blooming, the sunlight glinting on freshly watered lawns. This was where those elusive greener pastures seemed to have been hiding. Nothing appeared out of place; not a blade of grass or tree had grown in a way that might disrupt the carefully constructed pastoral harmony. Had the war even come here?

As the drive opened up to the front of the stately home, there was a large clearing of pebbles bleached by hundreds of summers. Not only was there plenty of room for Sam to park the motorcar, but one might have pulled up twenty or more horse-drawn carriages with room to spare. Before them was a beautifully maintained double-story seventeenth-century home. To the right, farther back, was a carriage house, larger than many people's homes.

"Well," she heard Sam say, otherwise lost for words.

A uniformed member of staff came out to meet them, his face cautious and his bearing austere. Sam, sensing the moment, came around and opened Billie's door for her in a more formal manner than he was accustomed to. Billie stepped out and straightened her apparel.

"Good day. I am here to see Mrs. Caversham-Smithe. Ms. Billie Walker is my name."

"Is she expecting you?" the man said, as if to say he knew she was not.

"Oh, certainly. We telegrammed ahead from Australia."

This brought a suitably impressed eyebrow raise. "This way, please."

Sam stayed by the car, standing at attention, as Billie was led inside. To her left, above a wall of ancient-looking climbing vines, she saw movement in a window upstairs, a young face looking out, and a moment later she was ushered through the grand front entrance. Inside the house was a hall with ornate oak paneling, hung with hunting trophies and what appeared to be family portraits, through which she was taken into a grand room, a carved stone fireplace at one end.

"Please take a seat, Miss Walker."

"Thank you kindly," Billie said, pleased with herself. She was in.

A maid soon appeared from nowhere, bearing a tray of tea and biscuits, and she quickly retreated, averting her eyes. For a moment Billie was left alone. She gazed up at the molded Jacobean ceilings complete with pendant bosses, and after a beat she stood, mouth pulled to one side, ready to snoop. What was their story?

"I'm sorry, I wasn't expecting you," came a haughty voice, and Billie stayed in place, as if her standing up had been for the family matriarch, who now entered the vast room in riding boots, jodhpurs, and a blouse not unlike Billie's. Mrs. Caversham-Smithe looked barely older than Billie, at a glance, albeit considerably more moneyed and conservative, though on closer inspection, and knowing the age of her daughter, Billie could see that the woman was in her early forties.

"Thank you so much for your hospitality," Billie said, smiling, hands clasped neatly behind her back. "I'm sorry if I came at an inopportune time. It's a real pleasure to meet you."

Billie's strategic language placed the woman in an uncomfortable position.

"I . . . am sorry we weren't able to get back to you." Mrs. Caversham-Smithe took a seat with some reluctance, it seemed, and looked at the assembled teacups.

"Mrs. Montgomery gave me your details," Billie explained. "She spoke so highly of you and your family. I understand you knew Richard Montgomery well. I'm hoping you could tell me a bit about him, and when you last saw him."

The woman did not touch the tray. She looked over her shoulder at the empty doorway, as if she hoped to be rescued, then turned back.

"You are quite mistaken, Miss Walker," she said. "I'm terribly sorry you've come all this way, but we have nothing to say about Mr. Montgomery. We have nothing to say about him at all."

Billie raised an eyebrow. So she *had* been fobbed off. How interesting. "I see. I do admit this is surprising to hear. Mrs. Montgomery told me that you're family friends."

"As I said, we have nothing to say," Mrs. Caversham-Smithe said curtly. "I can't help you. I'm sorry you were led to believe otherwise." She paused, expecting Billie to respond, but Billie just looked at her expectantly, letting her keep talking to see what would come out. For someone with nothing to say, Billie suspected there was quite a bit she might, indeed, say. "I'm sorry if he is missing, but we can't help," Mrs. Caversham-Smithe added after a moment, not being able to stand the silence. "You've wasted your time coming all this way." She bit her lip, clearly uncomfortable with the situation.

Billie stalled, leaning forward and pouring herself some tea, black and strong. "Perhaps there has been a misunderstanding." She took a sip and let her words hang in the air for a moment. "Your friend Vera Montgomery is looking for her husband. I assure you, I am not with the police, or the press." Like many wealthy and conservative families, the Caversham-Smithes doubtless avoided the press—didn't want to risk being in the gossip columns. "I know your daughter traveled to Sydney and stayed with the Montgomerys a few years back—"

"We have nothing to say on the matter. I'm sorry if this disappoints you." Mrs. Caversham-Smithe stood, stone-faced. "Good day, miss."

Billie took a breath. Whatever it was, it was worse than she'd imagined. The door had been slammed now. How very awkward. But then awkward social situations were just what private investigators dealt in. Awkwardness was like the proverbial smoke to the fire. But what was it revealing? Just what was the nature of this particular fire?

"I do hope my visit hasn't upset you. Thank you for your time, Mrs. Caversham-Smithe," Billie said politely, bowing her head slightly. "Again, I am sorry if I was misled. Perhaps we will meet under different circumstances one day."

"Perhaps," the woman said, making clear the impossibility of this notion.

"If you do recall anything, or you just want to talk, you know where to reach me." Billie stepped forward and pressed a business card into the woman's hand. "I'm at the Strand Palace, and will be at the Ritz Paris next week. You can call me any time, day or night."

The woman said nothing but was staring intently at the delicate floral cups on the tray, as if they might shatter at any moment. Billie had been dismissed, and now the same butler was waiting for her, to escort her back to her motorcar. She could feel his cold stare from yards away.

"Thank you kindly for your time, Mrs. Caversham-Smithe," Billie said smoothly, and walked back toward the entry hall, where the butler walked ahead of her, eager to see her gone. She had upset his mistress. Billie imagined that uninvited guests did not often dare to venture here.

Seeing her emerge, Sam dutifully brought the motorcar around from where he had been waiting, and he opened the suicide door for her, helping her into the generous back seat. After returning to the driver's seat, he pulled away and waited until they were some way down the winding drive, out of view of the house, before he spoke.

"That was a lot faster than I expected, Billie."

"It was a bust, Sam," she said, and sighed. "A bust. They want nothing to do with Montgomery, or us. Stop here, will you?"

"Here?" They were only halfway down the long drive to the gate, a few minutes' walk to the grand house.

He stopped the motorcar and she leaped out of the back, wearing her pair of Wellingtons and holding an umbrella, despite the blue skies and white clouds. "I'm going back to find Jane, the daughter," she explained. "I think I saw her in the upstairs window."

Sam's blue eyes were wide, though nothing she did shocked him terribly much anymore. "Do you want me to come with you?" he asked.

"I might need you to give me a boost up."

His eyes widened farther.

The pair moved back toward the house, weaving in and out of the long line of oak trees alongside the drive. How handy that these had been planted centuries ago to aid their surreptitious way back. Once they were near enough to the house she could see that all was quiet. "Come," she said softly, and they went around to the left side, where statuary and trimmed hedges grew close to the climbing vines.

"You aren't going to actually climb that?" he asked, speaking of the side of the house.

"Perhaps," she said, refusing to rule out the possibility. It would make discovery awkward, though. She bent over, dropped her umbrella to the ground, and picked up one of the bleached pebbles. With excellent aim, Billie threw it straight at the window overhead, on the second story. As Billie had hoped, it did not take long before a pale face appeared, framed by long, wavy blond hair, worn loose over the shoulders of a checkered shirt.

Yes, this was the daughter, Jane, all right, the one who had come to Sydney. "Jane, my name is Billie." All of this was said quickly, in an elevated whisper. "I'd like to speak with you about Richard Montgomery, if you would. It's important."

There was no reply. The young woman, fair-haired and lithe, leaned against the window frame, looking off into the distance like Juliet waiting for her Romeo. The window was open a crack. Was she deciding what to do? Or could she not hear?

To hell with convention, Billie thought. What was the worst the Caversham-Smithes would do? Simply dismiss her again, or set the dogs on her and Sam? A flash of their hunting trophies and the guns they went with flashed across her mind but did not stop her. Billie eyed some of the thicker vines and reached up for them. She was just short. Without a word, Sam knelt on one knee and laced his hands together, creating a foothold, and Billie stepped up and hung on to the vines, bridging the distance to the window.

"Keep an eye out, will you, Sam?" she whispered.

Vera had said Jane adored Richard. Was that true? "Jane, I understand this may be difficult, but what you know could prove terribly important. I'm trying to track him down for his wife. He's been missing for so long and may need help, and Mrs. Montgomery is desperate now. This is why I've come to you." Billie hung on, muscles quivering, sure she now had Jane's undivided attention. "I hope you can hear me clearly, Jane. I dare not shout," she said.

The figure disappeared from the window without a word.

Blast!

Billie let go and dropped to the pebbled drive, just short of her umbrella. She brushed down her silk trousers, frowning, and just as she'd lost hope, the girl returned to the window, again without a word but now with eye contact. She opened the window farther and a small paper airplane sailed over the windowsill and down toward Billie and Sam.

Billie bent and gathered up the paper, pocketing it quickly. The girl in the window brought a delicate finger to her lips. *Shhh.*

"Miss Walker!"

They had been spotted.

"Miss Walker, how may I help you?" the butler said, breathless from running, and making clear that help was not what he had in mind. "I believe you were leaving."

"Yes, terribly sorry," Billie said. "It's so silly of me. We drove off and then I realized I'd dropped my umbrella. Gosh, I'd lose my head if it wasn't attached. But look, here it is," she said, bending down and picking it up. "Thank you ever so much. Good day." She smiled, waved good-bye, and turned.

"I don't think we'll be welcomed back," Sam said quietly as they walked back up the drive together.

"We were already quite unwelcome. The real question is why."

Billie waited until they were well out of view of the grand house before she unfolded the small paper airplane. It contained a scribbled note. "Well, I'll be," she murmured softly to herself, leaning against a tree trunk. "Race you to the car?" she said, laughing, and took off from where she was standing.

Sam, being rather stunned but certainly athletic, had unwittingly given her a good start in her gumboots, but with the advantage of his height he caught up with her just at the last moment. Billie flung herself into the driver's seat of the Hurricane, panting. "A tie, I'd say," she declared triumphantly.

There was the noise of hurried footsteps on the gravel, and she could see the butler running toward them, hopefully without a hunting rifle. She started up the car and pulled away, just as he appeared from behind the trees, frowning. As she drove off, he shut the majestic gates of the Caversham-Smithe estate, one after the other, ensuring there would be no more intruders.

This did not matter to Billie. The note in her hand had four hastily scrawled words on it: *SALLY LUNN'S. 1 HOUR.*

Seventeen

—∽∽∽—

By two o'clock sharp, Billie and Sam were settled into a creaking wooden corner table of Sally Lunn's in Bath, enveloped in the scent of freshly baked buns and scones. The ceiling and walls of the cozy tearoom were uneven with the settling of age, and painted in a charming soft pink and cream, feeling to Billie a touch off-balance, as if the Mad Hatter had been decorating. A kind but distracted waitress served them tea in willow-patterned china and served buns on embroidered damask table mats, and they waited.

And waited.

Though she had not had reason to visit, Billie had heard of the place—Jane Austen even wrote about Lunn's "bunns." It was famous enough that even a couple of Australians would find the place with no trouble, and Billie supposed it was far enough from Malmesbury that they were unlikely to run into the Caversham-Smithes or their immediate social circle. Yes, Jane had chosen the venue well, Billie thought. She just hoped the girl had not changed her mind.

Ten minutes later, having downed a full cup of tea, Billie was so absorbed in her ruminations about the awkward meeting with

Mrs. Caversham-Smithe, and its implications, that she missed Jane Caversham-Smithe's approach until the fresh-faced blond woman was almost at Sam's shoulder.

"Miss Walker?"

"Ah, yes. Jane, it is lovely to meet you properly." Billie motioned for her to sit, noting that she was dressed in the country uniform of jodhpurs and boots, much as her mother had been earlier. "Thank you for your note," she said gently. "Would you like anything? Coffee or tea, or a bite to eat?"

Jane shook her head and looked worriedly around the room. She was beautiful in the romantic way of Pre-Raphaelite paintings, with long, flowing hair and delicate, pale features, almost as if she might soon be calmly floating down a river like the Lady of Shalott, but right now her manner was skittish, hurried. Evidently she did not recognize any of the patrons, so she took her seat.

"This is my assistant, Sam," Billie said.

Jane nodded a greeting to him. "Sorry it took me longer to get away. I won't stay long. Mother thinks I'm taking one of my rides through the country, and she'd be furious if she knew I was speaking with you," Jane explained. "I overheard parts of your conversation with her and knew she wouldn't tell you anything, but considering how far you've come, I felt you should know."

Billie leaned forward. "You felt I should know what?"

"That Richard . . ." She shrugged, looking for the words. "He's not who he pretends to be, really. He's certainly not who his wife thinks he is. You'll get no help from my parents in your quest to find him, I can guarantee you that much. The fact that you came . . . well, you can't have known."

"I can't have known what? What is it, Jane?" Billie frowned, imagining the worst. "Did something happen . . . ?"

She looked around again. "Well, you know he was cut out of his father's will. His family wouldn't have anything to do with him, even for years before his father died."

The hairs on Billie's neck stood up. Cut off from the Montgomery fortune? Clearly he had hidden this information from his wife, or Vera would have mentioned it, and perhaps been even more concerned about the finances.

"And after my trip to the Antipodes . . ." Jane trailed off, caught in the memory. "That was the last straw, I think."

"When was that, exactly?"

"About nine years ago. It was over the Australian summer."

Late '38, then, when she must have been barely thirteen, Billie calculated. *So young.* "Jane, you must tell me. Did Richard make advances?"

Jane shook her head. "No, no. You have him all wrong." She closed her eyes.

"Do I? But he asked you to sit for him, is that right?"

"For photographs, yes," she explained. "He said I had a lovely look."

"And you do. Any artist would be lucky to have you sit for them, back then or today, and Richard is a good photographer, too. I've seen some of his work. He didn't use that photographic session to try to . . . initiate anything else?"

Sam frowned at this but wisely said nothing.

Billie tried to think back to when she was thirteen, how impressionable she'd been compared to the woman she was now, even as the daughter of a toughened ex-cop, even as the daughter of Ella von Hooft. Richard would have been a great deal older and more experienced than Jane, and he could have put her in a position where she felt she couldn't say no, felt she'd somehow given him assent by simply being alone in his presence. Some men had a real knack for this, especially with girls and women who were far younger, or had less power than them, as far too many did.

"Did he touch you, Jane?" Billie whispered.

Jane shook her head, waving a hand dismissively, and some tension broke. "You misunderstand." She laughed—certainly not the response Billie had expected. "No, Richard didn't touch me. He doesn't like girls," she added flatly.

"Pardon me? Did you say he *doesn't* like girls?"

Jane leaned her elbows on the table, their heads now close. "He's not romantically interested in women at all, Miss Walker," she said.

"But—" Billie began, about to protest that he was married to a woman, but that was foolish, of course. The penny dropped. Richard Montgomery knew the intimate secrets of the hidden homosexual men of Sydney because he was one of them, socialized with them. What had Shyla's telegram said? That Richard had caught someone in a situation and had blackmailed them with photographs? And this information was through a colleague of Mr. Charles's? It was all too obvious now. He'd been cut off from his family fortune years ago, probably because his parents had guessed his secret, and with his funds dwindling he'd turned to blackmail. Montgomery's comfort with a camera put him at a clear advantage, and if he knew the scene well, was able to gain some trust, he would know where the money was and whom to pressure. No one would dare go to the police about him, not when they stood to lose everything if he revealed their secrets.

"His parents couldn't accept his . . . nature," Jane said, and shrugged as if she couldn't understand the big deal. Hadn't Vera said that Richard's mother was terribly religious? "They sent Richard away, but he was still so desperate to please them . . . You know, by getting married, I think, and having the perfect, pretty wife," she added. "Vera is a very nice woman. But his father cut him out of the will anyway. I don't think Richard even knew about it until his father died."

"And Richard told you all of this when you were in Sydney?" Billie asked, gobsmacked.

"More or less," Jane said, tilting her head.

"Did his wife know?" She had to ask, because she'd taken her client at her word, and this went against the main assumption Billie had formed from that information—that Richard Montgomery had run off with another woman, as so many of the missing men Billie tracked had done.

"I very much doubt it, Miss Walker. I don't think she knew him well at all."

Billie was stunned. If this information was correct, it explained his knowledge of the Sydney homosexual, or "kamp," scene, but how would thirteen-year-old Jane Caversham-Smithe know all this when Montgomery's own wife did not? "And Richard trusted you not to tell? Why?" Billie pressed.

Jane nodded but she had begun blushing vigorously and did not say more. Richard must have had something on her to think she wouldn't talk.

"Tell me, Jane," Billie gently prompted.

"I just wanted to tell you that my parents won't help you, and Richard's mother probably won't either. She wasn't on good terms with her son. None of them will speak to you. They probably won't know where he is anyway. You came so far but you should not waste your time with them. If you want to help Vera, and I imagine this has been so hard on her, I'm sorry but you must find answers elsewhere."

"What did he do, Jane?" Billie urged, sure there was something else the young woman knew, something big enough to have caused the whole thing to come to a head. "Did he blackmail you? How?"

Jane tensed, her pale skin reddening.

"Please, Jane. You have my word I will not share it with anyone."

At this there was a sad shrug, and her head began to shake. "I don't know why I should even pretend it's a secret. My parents found out and . . ." She closed her eyes and when she opened them again they were glistening with tightly held tears. "He, um . . . that night he told me these things, we had been drinking. I'd never had anything like that before, and it went to my head. He was taking some pictures of me, and . . ." Her hands balled into fists.

That bastard. "I see," Billie said evenly.

"Just pictures, you understand, but not the kind I had planned on. I'm embarrassed to say I was a bit infatuated with him. I was a kid, really, and he presented himself as so worldly. But . . . it went too far."

"What you might have thought of him at the time doesn't make it right, Jane. It was wrong of him to take advantage."

"I know," she said, looking down. "It was just photographs, but I think he probably planned it. Yes, I'm sure of it now. A few days earlier, I had happened upon him with a man. Nothing too obvious, but it was clear to me that something was going on that they wanted to hide, and suddenly Richard was interested in me. At first I was flattered. I was excited that he wanted to photograph me."

At this Sam piped in. "What did you see that day, exactly?"

"It was a long time ago now, and I was so young, but let's just say he was talking with a man very closely, I thought, and when they realized I was there, they jumped apart, looking scared, guilty."

Jane settled down into her chair, as if to make herself smaller.

"He was smooth about it seconds later, of course," she went on. "But after that he was very focused on me. I realize that now, in hindsight. Like I said, I was flattered at the time. When I agreed to the shoot he was so nice, and I agreed to do it without telling my parents, and then when we were having the photographic session he just opened up—it was the drink, I believe, though I also remember thinking how it was flowing out of him, like a stopper had come out. That evening he got me to pose in ways I didn't really want to . . . shouldn't have. There just didn't seem to be any way to say no, and my head felt funny. Afterward, he said he wouldn't show my parents the photographs if I just passed on some of my allowance to him, so that's what I did that whole summer. He said he desperately needed the money, though he didn't say why, but I knew he'd been cut off by his family, so . . . yes, I knew. I felt sorry for him, I suppose, and I was terrified of what my parents would do if they found out about the photographs, if they saw. You think my mother is uptight, well, let me tell you . . . I tried to convince him to destroy the negatives, but he refused. He said . . . he said the photographs were beautiful."

A small tear escaped and rolled down her smooth cheek. "I'm sorry," she said in a small voice, embarrassed.

"Oh, Jane, that's terrible. He had no right to do that to you."

"I . . . I didn't mean to . . ." She shook her head, frustrated at her tears. "I just thought you should know. My mother found out what he did, of course. I can never keep anything from her—or at least I couldn't back then. She told my father, and they won't have anything to do with him now. Not since, and certainly not now. There hasn't been a word exchanged between them in all that time, I'd say. They won't help you, no matter what you do. And they blame Vera as well, because I was in their care, and . . ." She trailed off and wiped her cheek. "I don't think he meant to hurt me. He just . . .

Well, Richard was cut off by his family and . . . he made some mistakes."

Billie was not feeling quite so benevolent. The poor girl had only been thirteen and it had been a truly wretched thing to do to her. She now understood far better why Mrs. Caversham-Smithe had given her the cold shoulder. She had sent her daughter down under for a summer sojourn and a bit of cultural awakening, and the poor girl had ended up learning to trust no one. What a bastard Montgomery was, doing that to a child. And to Mr. Charles's friend, too, from what Shyla had uncovered for them.

The smiling photograph of Richard among the group of fellow ad men came to mind. Mr. Charles had been there, grinning alongside the group, she supposed before Richard had started to blackmail his friend, and perhaps even Mr. Charles himself? Another two men keeping secrets from their wives . . .

Jane pushed her chair out. "I must go now," she said, dabbing her eyes with a handkerchief and standing. She slid a pair of smoked glasses on, shielding her eyes. With the movement of an equestrian, she straightened and raised her head proudly.

Billie stood and shook her hand. "I truly thank you, Jane. This has been very helpful. You are a remarkable young woman." Sam stood up and shook her hand as well, adding a respectful little bow of his head.

Jane inhaled deeply and gathered herself. "I've never met a lady detective before." At this a little smile came over the pale face. "I . . . I wanted to meet you. Good luck, Miss Walker," she said, and strode out.

So Vera's respectable, successful husband had been a blackmailer, had preyed on a young girl who looked up to him, and had not told his wife that the money was drying up. And those had not been his only secrets . . . Perhaps now she was getting somewhere in this investigation.

—⁓—

"What a creep," Billie remarked, still fuming.

Billie and Sam sped back toward London in the Hurricane, top down, watching as the horizon shifted from clear blue to gray-streaked clouds, as if to underline the darker truths that Jane had revealed earlier that afternoon about the target of their investigation. It had been a long day, with miles to go, but the trip had proved more than worthwhile, even if what they'd learned about their quarry was disturbing.

"I wonder how much Vera knew about Richard's activities, if anything at all," Billie said, then looked in the rearview mirror, her heart catching in her chest. A dark Morris 8 saloon was coming up behind their Hurricane at a startling speed on the near-empty stretch of road. "That motorcar is going *awfully* fast."

Sam turned in the passenger seat to look at the automobile coming up behind them. "Late for dinner?" Sam suggested of the driver, sounding unconvinced even as the words left his lips.

Billie held fast and steady as the motorcar approached, her gloved hands on the wheel of the Hurricane, neither slowing nor speeding up just yet, her eyes flicking back to the rearview mirror to mark the progress of the Morris. The engine grew louder as it gained on them, and she saw that the motorcar was in disrepair and dirt streaked, though the engine for its make was handling well at speed. And that speed was far too fast, and the little woman in her gut, the little woman who knew things, knew perfectly well that it was not going to slow down.

"Hold on, Sam," she said, and in her periphery she saw him grasp the dashboard, as if anticipating impact.

It came seconds later.

The motorcar hit them with a jolt, propelling Billie out of her seat for a second, and they wove for a moment on the road before she deftly regained control of the wheel. She swung her head around to look. The impact had slowed the dented Morris 8, but it was coming back at them again.

Good goddess, they are trying to run us off the road, she realized with certainty. They were several lengths back but closing in again.

Billie bit her lip and prepared for impact. As the roar of the Morris 8 grew, she zeroed in on the sound and her instincts took over. She heard the gears changing, engine straining. Hers might be an estate car, but the elegant Hurricane drophead coupe was more than just a pretty build. It could outrun the inferior Morris by at least ten miles an hour if it came down to it, of that she was sure. But what was their game? There was a driver and a passenger in the rogue motorcar, she could now see, though their faces were not clear through the dirty windshield. Soon they would be out of the straight; a curve in the road was fast approaching, and they were traveling at well over fifty miles per hour.

This time the Morris came up alongside them on her right, and then she felt the impact as the Hurricane's aluminum paneling was crushed along her right flank, the Morris evidently trying to push them off the road. She automatically turned the wheel into the Morris, pushing right back, and the two motorcars made a sickening crunching sound as they continued at high speed toward the country bend, and the solid and deadly trees ahead.

With the Hurricane's top down, there was a strange intimacy between her and the road, and the stranger driving his motorcar into hers. Her silk scarf had loosened and now flew out backward, like a parachute, then floated up into the breeze. Her dark hair flew out wildly, coming unpinned, but her eyes did not waver, did not lose their focus, and though this was an unfamiliar car, she had to trust it, had to trust its build, its superiority to the Morris. The screeching and squealing of tires continued until just before the bend, and Billie pressed her foot down hard, front hydraulic brakes and rear mechanical brakes working superbly, and her assistant bracing himself against the dash.

With her sudden braking the Hurricane turned sideways and pushed to the left of the lane. The Morris 8's bumper caught along their side before sailing past, braking and sliding down the road, as the Hurricane came to a bumpy halt on the grassy verge in a plume of dirt.

"What in heaven's name was that about?" Sam cried as the air settled.

Billie pointed toward her handbag. "My gun is loaded," she told him, and then took the wheel firmly in both hands again, breathing deeply. He removed her small Colt from the handbag and awaited her instructions. "We don't want police trouble, but needs must." She didn't want to tangle with Scotland Yard if she could help it. Could that have been an accident just now? Someone who had spent too long at the pub before getting in their car?

"Should we . . . check on them?"

Billie thought on that. The Morris 8 had made it around the bend, though she didn't know how far. She was far less concerned about the driver's well-being than would normally be the case. "Keep that Colt handy." But when they started up again, and drove around the bend, there was no sign of the motorcar.

An hour later they pulled up to the Strand Palace, exhausted and still shaken after their ordeal. Mud splattered and dented, the stately rental car was not in the same pristine condition in which it had left the Strand hours before, though Billie was even more impressed with it, considering how well it had handled.

"Thank you. Here are the keys," Billie said to the astonished porter, and glided into the hotel with Sam at her side.

—⁓—

Half an hour later, Billie's heart was still beating more quickly than usual, adrenaline staving off a deep exhaustion she could already feel creeping into her bones.

She was stretched out across the settee in her hotel room overlooking the Thames, holding a small tumbler of the bracing whisky that Sam had just poured. He was sitting opposite her, shaking his head, a touch dazed after their automobile collision.

"Do you think it was intentional? I mean, do you think the Morris meant to hit us? Could it have been a drunk driver?" he asked.

Billie sipped at her drink, willing the tension to leave her body, and pondered his questions for a few moments before responding. "The first time might have been an accident if the driver was drunk or wasn't paying attention, but the second time? He turned the wheel into me. That's an awfully unusual error to make, even for the most errant motorcar driver, sober or otherwise, I should think. The fact that they'd already made off when we came around the bend tells me he couldn't have been too sauced to function. If they'd been quite out of control, I expect they would have hit the trees and still been there."

"I wonder if it's possible that the Caversham-Smithes sent along someone to warn us off—to make sure we didn't return again," Sam said.

She inhaled deeply. "I did rather make a nuisance of myself, I'll admit, but it would be a surprising move, especially for such a respectable family. They closed the gates to make sure we didn't return, but what could they be hiding that would make them go to such lengths as to send a motorcar after us? No, the information we got this afternoon from Jane, surprising though it was, doesn't fit with such a risky move."

Something still niggled at her, though. "You know, I'm searching my memory, and though it all happened terribly fast, I don't believe I recall seeing a plate on that Morris." Billie was trained to remember such things, even in the most extraordinary circumstances—*particularly* in the most extraordinary circumstances. "Did you see the number plate, by chance?"

Sam shook his head. "You think the plate had been removed?"

"No, there was something there. It was muddy, I think," she said, squinting as she focused her memory. She took another sip. "Yes, something was there but it was indecipherable." Billie's memory was hardly photographic, as she'd heard some people's were, but it was sharp nonetheless. There had been no numbers or letters to memorize. It was a blank.

"But if it was intentional," she continued, "what if they drove off not because of fright or shame but because they failed to finish the job? You'd cover your plates beforehand, wouldn't you? In case—"

"In case we survived the crash and remembered the plates."

She nodded, and the little woman in her gut seemed to confirm it as the most likely, albeit disturbing, conclusion. And that begged the question of just who would do such a thing, and why.

Eighteen

—◇—

"May I speak with the lady of the house, Mrs. Montgomery, please? This is Ms. Billie Walker. She should have received my message yesterday? I am here from Australia, on behalf of her son's wife, Vera."

The house staff on the other end of the line hesitated. "Yes, ma'am, she . . . did receive it. I'm afraid she is unavailable."

Billie frowned. "When might she become available? It is somewhat urgent."

There was another pause. "I will let her know that you called, Miss Walker."

A knock came just as she was hanging up the receiver, and Billie Walker crossed to the door of her hotel room, yawning and rubbing her tender hip and side. This would be Sam, more eager than usual for breakfast. She was rather in need of strong tea herself, to rouse her from the deep sleep that had followed their day in the Cotswolds, including that most surprising and bruising journey back to London. She was uncharacteristically sore, but she'd had worse. Tea would help. Tea always helped.

But when Billie opened her door, it was not her assistant but a uniformed bellboy handing her a piece of mail—one among many pieces of mail in his hands—before departing briskly to continue his rounds. The mail had a Paris postmark and was addressed to Billie at the hotel, using her full and correct name. Considering how rare it was for her title to be correctly attributed, she knew at once that it must be a friend or former colleague.

It was, in fact, both. At first with a smile and then a deep furrow in her brow, Billie began to read.

Dear Billie,

I was delighted to receive your recent telegram. It has been some years since our time together at Hearst but your departure was deeply felt, I must tell you, and we were all sorry to get news about your father's passing. I heard that you reopened his investigation agency in Sydney. I hope it is going well for you.

I have in fact been deliberating whether to write to you, Billie, and had begun a letter several times with the intention of sending it to Australia. When I received your telegram about coming to Paris it seemed the fates were intervening.

I write to you about our mutual acquaintance Jack Rake. Of course, for you he is much more than an acquaintance, I realize, and if I am not mistaken, you two may have married in France. Do forgive me if I have this wrong, but rumor had it that Jack did not make it out of Warsaw, so I was surprised to run into him at the Hôtel Lutetia in December. It was an odd and hurried encounter and stayed with me. I am writing to you because, although I may have it wrong about things, I thought you might wish

to know. I hope that in writing to you I have not
complicated matters further.

If you indeed make it to Paris I hope we will be able to
discuss this in person. Don't hesitate to contact me. Know
you are welcome anytime.

Yours in friendship,
Simone Chapelle

Billie's mouth had gone completely dry. She thought she might not be able to breathe. Carefully, as if it might be an explosive, she put the letter down on the bedside table of her room, took a step back, then returned to it and reread it. *Hôtel Lutetia in December.*

In December? How could that be?

There was another knock at her door, and she hastily folded the letter and put it back in its envelope, hands unsteady. She crossed the small room to open the door once more and found it was Sam, ready to accompany her to breakfast.

"Good morning . . . Why, Billie, are you okay?" he asked her.

"I'm fine," she replied, distracted. The blood in her head had run to her feet, leaving her faint. "Just some unexpected news, that's all. Or perhaps it's not actually news, just rumor?" But Simone said she had seen him herself. How, though? It could not be true. She had been convinced he hadn't survived Warsaw. Everyone had been convinced.

"I don't even know if . . . Never mind," Billie said, realizing how incoherent she must sound. What if Simone was mistaken, somehow? That could happen, couldn't it? Much had transpired during the war. Simone, who had always been as sharp as a tack, may have suffered in some way, so that perhaps her memory wasn't what it once was? If so, she would not be the only one to find their faculties faltering. But she had seemed quite sure, sure enough to write . . .

"I need some strong tea," Billie said, shaking off her rambling thoughts. She'd have to give the confounding letter her full attention later, but now was not the time.

—∞—

"London has been a bit of a washout," Billie said, frowning, after they'd finished their breakfast and were sitting in the elegant hotel lobby, discussing their plans for the day. "I'm going to look into our options for travel to Paris."

And Paris did beckon. True to Jane Caversham-Smithe's warning, and Vera's, the Montgomery matriarch had no interest in speaking with Billie. She well knew when she was being fobbed off. At least she was not surprised. The Caversham-Smithes' reaction she had not expected, however. No, it had not been the welcoming party Vera had primed them for.

Paris was next and would be more fruitful for the case, Billie hoped. And though she had not mentioned it to her assistant yet, she knew she could hardly stand another night in London, knowing that her friend Simone Chapelle was in Paris with new information about Jack—whether she was really right about seeing him or not. Billie would go mad, thinking on the possibilities, until they spoke.

Jack Rake, in Paris last year . . .

"As chance would have it, I heard from Basil Aldrich this morning," Billie said, steering herself back to the task at hand. "One of those two men I mentioned. I'll be meeting with him later today after I make our travel arrangements for Paris. Could you perhaps head to Australia House for those details on Richard's journey, while I see what I can get from him?"

"What, you don't wish to return to see your new friend, Thompson?" Sam teased.

Billie cringed. "Right. I'm off. Let's reconvene later this afternoon, shall we? Let's hope Montgomery's travel schedule will assist us."

Their favorite waitress passed their table as Billie rose to leave.

"Good luck," she said to Sam, and grinned as she watched the young woman give Sam an appreciative bat of her eyelashes.

—⁓—

The Winter Garden at the Strand was a beautifully appointed space set with tall palms beneath a dome that filled the space with light. Billie arrived ten minutes early and heavily stimulated by strong black tea and found a table next to a palm tree, her back to a marble wall. Here she could see the comings and goings of the place.

She sat and picked up a copy of an already well-read local paper. FRANCE DEMANDS JUSTICE FOR NAZI WAR CRIMES, it said in bold letters, a touch of powdered egg soiling the N in "Nazi." By the time she had reached the final paragraph, about a head of the French resistance, she saw movement near the entrance, and the bald head of Basil Aldrich appeared.

She stood to greet him. "I'm so pleased we could meet again before my departure. I fear that evening at the Boomerang Club I was not quite myself," Billie said smoothly, and shook his hand.

"Oh?" Basil replied, frowning. "You're leaving so soon? I did wonder."

He wondered? "Please, do join me." They sat. "I may return to London," she said, thinking particularly of showing up at the door of Richard's mother's unannounced—if all failed in France. "But we are headed to Paris to continue our search," she explained. "Richard Montgomery's last-known communications were from the Ritz Paris, as you may know."

"I see," he said. "You will stay there, will you? I wish you every luck with finding him. Good man, as I said. I'm sorry I haven't been more helpful."

"Thank you, Basil," she said graciously, hoping he would reveal the reason for suggesting their meeting. When he was not forthcoming, she ordered them some tea and scones to ease the conversation, though the scones turned out to be somewhat dry, and there was no cream available. Once, having to subsist on dry, moldy bread for three days, with only Jack and a torn picnic blanket to keep her warm, Billie had dreamed vividly of a future of butter and cream, like they would suddenly reappear once the Allies declared their victory. Years later, such luxuries were still not commonplace.

Jack . . .

"I, um, was pleased to hear from you," she said. "I wanted to ask if you might enlighten me on a certain matter."

"Oh?" Basil said, sounding intrigued.

"It does seem curious to me that Richard's absence after the Paris exposition was not more noted. I mean to say, there did not appear to be much concern around Australia House." She watched him, eager to read his response. "Why might that be, do you think?"

"Well, there shouldn't have been concern. He's a grown man, after all, and Paris is quite a jewel. The Third Reich were careful to preserve it." Basil downed his full cup of tea quickly, followed by most of a scone.

A grown man. A jewel. Paris had indeed been a jewel in Hitler's crown there for a moment, albeit a stolen one.

"You aren't going to go messing around with that other business, are you? It's terribly unladylike, not to mention dangerous," he said. "Not everyone wants to see those graves dug up again."

That other business. "Graves dug up?" She frowned. "I am not sure I catch your meaning. You mean unmarked graves from the war crimes?"

"*War crimes . . .*" He shook his head. "I mean from the *war*. The war has ended," he said with finality, as if it were so simple. "The papers called you a 'Nazi Hunter.' I mean, really," he said disapprovingly.

She shrugged. "There are worse things to be called, I would say. And you'd better believe I'll hunt down whoever helped Hessmann, if I can. What he did to those girls . . ." she said, thinking of Shyla's mob. "Not to mention the rest."

"Lives were lost on both sides, girl. Let the dead have peace and stay out of it."

Stay out of it. Girl. Was that a threat? Her eyes flicked to the headline on the article she'd been reading, and his gaze followed hers.

"Fanatics, those French," he commented. "But even they did what they had to, did they not?" he said, and Billie presumed he was referencing Vichy—the authoritarian, anti-Semitic regime that notoriously collaborated with the Nazis. "We all did."

We? Was he including the Germans in that statement? The Nazis? Billie realized she was getting hot under the collar again, and she put on her professional face. Serene. Smiling. Unthreatening. "Indeed the war has ended. Indeed," she agreed patiently, then paused and took a breath. "What did you wish to speak with me about, Basil? May I call you Basil?"

"Certainly. I must say, it's terribly poor luck that your parents saw fit to give you a man's name, don't you think?" he said. "And for such a pretty girl."

"It's short for Wilhelmina, but my name has always been Billie. I rather like it."

"Wilhelmina. Now, *that* is better. I shall call you that," he said.

"I'd rather you not. Billie is fine."

He tilted his head back and frowned deeply at this, his displeasure more than clear. In that pose Basil reminded her somewhat of a toad.

"Was there something you recalled about Richard, perhaps?" she pushed. "Was that the reason for your call? It was most welcome." Again the smile, and again, she felt the steel there, just under the surface. She would not allow her personal feelings to interfere this time, as they had at the Boomerang Club. That had been unhelpful, unprofessional.

"I simply wished to see if you had any new information on his whereabouts," Basil replied. "And to convey my pleasure that you are looking into his disappearance, and something is being done. Good man, Richard. Good man."

How odd. "I see," Billie replied, shielding her confusion with a sip of tea. She finished her cup. "Would you like anything else, Basil? A liqueur perhaps?"

"Thank you. I'll be on my way, in fact. Do let me know if you hear anything further."

She stood as he rose to leave. "I will," she lied.

He took her hand and shook it. It felt sweaty and stiff. "And do be careful, won't you?" he said.

She squinted. "Oh. Thank you."

"Good day, Wilhelmina," he said, and plodded out of the Winter Garden, leaving a rather poor taste in her mouth.

—⁓—

For Richard Montgomery in 1945, travel had been easy; the Australian Bureau of Information appeared to have spared few expenses for the men involved in the *L'Australie dans la paix et dans la guerre* exposition.

The travel schedule that Sam had secured from Australia House confirmed that the men had departed by way of Rolls-Royce Phantom limousine to Croydon Airport, before flying to Le Bourget Airport, Paris, in a Dakota C47. No mailboats or converted Lancasters for them. They were then met at Le Bourget by another Rolls-Royce from the Australian embassy, checked in at the Ritz Paris, and then were chauffeured to the nearby Australian exposition at Printemps— a large department store on Boulevard Haussmann. Billie felt rather envious at the ease of their journey two years before, but she did not see any return plans.

"This was all of Mr. Montgomery's available schedule? You are sure?"

"Yes, that's all they had," Sam said. "I did ask."

"I'm sure you did, Sam." He was thorough and reliable when put to any task, she found. "It's peculiar that there was no return schedule provided, though. Was there some reason for that?"

Sam shifted on his feet. "I asked about that as well. Some of the members wanted to stay on and see Paris, I was told. Not everyone elected to come back immediately, that's all they knew at Australia House. Budget was allocated for their return, to be used at their discretion, but there was no strict schedule."

Billie sighed. That did make things more difficult, and certainly would make it less likely that alarm bells would sound when Montgomery had not returned to London. This only confirmed Basil's account. They were grown men, cleared to do as they pleased, and without tabs kept on them once the exposition work was complete. "Did he return to Australia House at all after the exposition?"

"If he did, there's no record of it."

Billie shook her head. "Wasn't that considered odd?" she said, as much to herself as to him.

"Once the exposition was over, he was his own man, so to speak.

I was fortunate to speak with your friend Miss Wood, who sends her regards. She confirmed that was all she had for us."

Just as Vera had said, he wasn't working for the Bureau of Information or the advertising agency, either. He fell into a gap. Had he planned that? she wondered. Did he know that would aid his disappearance?

"I'm sorry I couldn't be more helpful," Sam said. "How did things go with Basil?""

"Don't ask," she said darkly. "I learned today that the scones are dry at the Winter Garden—not a patch on Sally Lunn's, for certain— that's about all. The sooner we get to Paris, the better. If it wasn't for young Jane Caversham-Smithe, I'm afraid we wouldn't have learned anything at all here on this leg of our trip. I gather Betty wasn't able to help?" Billie raised an eyebrow at the memory of the waitress who had seem so enamored of Sam at breakfast on Monday.

"Delightful young woman she is, but no. I've talked to her and she doesn't remember Montgomery or his group, though she has vague memories of them coming through. Nothing stood out. He didn't, um, proposition her, or anything like that."

"He wouldn't, would he?" Billie said.

"I suppose not, after what we've learned," Sam agreed. He had been as surprised as Billie that Vera had her husband so wrong.

"I would suggest the ladies' man routine may be an act to cover for his interests, or at the very least a convenient assumption made because of his photography. He obviously knew to blackmail Mr. Charles's associate because he is part of the same scene, or at least he was until he began behaving badly, and started making a few too many enemies. It's frightfully dangerous for men loving men, Sam. Faced with paying up or having their lives destroyed, or worse . . ." She trailed off, frowning. She'd always found blackmail distasteful, more than mere adultery. "I'm thinking those jewels his wife had were not bought with his pay from the Bureau of Information. How interesting that he was doing that sort of thing, making enemies, as Shyla called it, and then disappeared. Things must have really soured in Australia before his departure."

"But he wasn't in Australia when he went missing," Sam pointed out. "He was in Paris. If he got himself into trouble in Sydney, wouldn't he have been knocked off there?"

"I did have the same thought." She frowned, thinking of that note Vera showed her. *WE'LL FIND HIM.* Who had written it, and what was the meaning behind it? "It's not quite there yet, but the puzzle pieces are coming together, Sam, I can feel it. Paris will be more revealing."

The little woman in her gut knew it. But why exactly, she could not yet be sure.

Billie thought again about the letter from Simone Chapelle. She had to see her as soon as possible, and figure out just what was going on. Could it be possible that Jack really was alive? It was true that she was becoming distracted by her own personal quest, but it was also plain that Montgomery was unwanted in England, so much as his mother and the Caversham-Smithes were concerned, and so unless he had some other support, outside any opportunities at Australia House he clearly did not return to, it was unlikely that he'd have chosen to stay here.

No, the answers, she felt—hers and Vera's—had to be in Paris.

Nineteen

—⁓—

PARIS, FRANCE, 1947

On sera vite arrivé . . .

The taxicab sped along narrow streets and wide promenades, driving startlingly close to locals on bicycles and motorcycles, who weaved through the flowing traffic of Paris as if they were invincible. Perhaps they thought that if they'd survived a war, they could survive anything.

Billie leaned her head toward the window of the automobile, feeling the wind in her dark hair and watching with pleasure, and no small dose of nostalgia, as avenue upon avenue of the famed Paris stone buildings flew past, the windows of Parisian lives opening onto narrow balconies, one stacked upon the other, cafés spilling onto the streets below, with their large awnings and promises of fine pastries and good wine. The collective spirit of the liberated French capital was palpable, and it lifted Billie's heart. And surely the sight of Paris could lift nearly anyone's heart now that the Nazi swastika no longer flew above the Eiffel Tower.

The springtime sun was shining, and she caught glimpses of flowers blooming despite the years of deprivation and death, a testament to beauty and endurance. Billie knew that the strength of rebirth should never be underestimated. Yes, Paris was very much alive, and this was where she would find the truth; this was where the ghosts of the past would reveal themselves to her, would illuminate the path to much-needed answers, not only for her client, Vera Montgomery, but also for Billie herself. She could feel it even before setting a foot on the old cobblestones.

Jack? Are you out there, somewhere?

She leaned back against the seat again and closed her eyes. Airplane travel services not yet being regular enough to rely upon, they had taken the train to Dover, the passage taking more than three hours. There had been room available on the next mailboat to the continent, which was only a few hours' wait, and after that journey they'd been able to catch the train to Paris the next morning. Now, more than a day since departing the Strand Palace, they were en route to the hotel where Richard Montgomery had stayed before his disappearance, and where he had written his last letter to his wife.

The taxicab slowed and pulled into the magnificent Place Vendôme, a true throwback to another century. Billie smiled. Sam's head seemed to be on a swivel, taking in the sights with awe.

"Oh, this is beaut, Billie," he said. "I've never seen anything like it."

Indeed, if they'd thought the Caversham-Smithe estate was grand, this was something on another scale altogether. The famous square—in fact, it was more of an octagon—in Paris's 1st arrondissement had remained intact during the war, Billie was pleased to see, and showcased the late seventeenth-century designs of the architect Jules Hardouin-Mansart, who had also worked on the famous Château Versailles. Napoleon's grand and rather phallic Vendôme Column sat proudly at its center, surrounded on all sides by the kind of vast space that spoke to parades and gathered crowds. Now motor-cars passed through it as horse-drawn carriages had once done.

Much like the historic square, the Ritz Paris appeared un-changed by the war, to the naked eye at least. Certainly this was not a place that needed to recover from disuse. While other luxury ho-tels had vanished behind shutters during the war, Billie knew the grand suites had always been full at the Ritz Paris, the establishment ostensibly spared because Marie-Louise, the German-speaking widow of the founder, Cesar Ritz, was herself Swiss, and managed somehow to convince the Nazis to allow the Ritz to be designated as a kind of neutral territory, "a Switzerland in Paris," with French citizens and Nazis staying under the same five-star roof. It was even said that the air-raid shelters at the Ritz had been equipped with fine fur rugs and nothing less than silk Hermès sleeping bags, so at odds with the deprivations experienced by the average French citizen.

It was also true that this famous area of Paris had been preserved during the war in part by the Nazis themselves, who enjoyed what it could offer and who helped themselves to the fine goods, foods, and artworks of Paris—what was still there, in any event. Cleverly, in August of 1939 the Louvre had been closed for "repairs," when in fact Jacques Jaujard, the director of the French Musées Nationaux, had foreseen the fall of France and had arranged an evacuation of priceless artworks, initially to Château de Chambord, then moved from château to château to avoid falling into the hands of the Nazis. The Louvre had been all but empty by the time the Nazis marched in, though the rest of Paris had not been so lucky. Sacrifices were made, battles fought, and lives lost, but the famous face of Paris had been preserved, even after all she had endured. She was battle weary, yes, but still standing proud after all the trials the passing centuries had inflicted on her.

She was Hitler's jewel no more.

The bellhops of the Ritz soon appeared in their caps and finery, the taxicab having delivered them right outside the entrance, and with a few exchanged words in rusty French, their bags were gathered, and they were led under the famous arches and into the hotel lobby, with Sam content to let the porters do the work this time. Once inside, Billie could almost believe the war had been a figment of her imagination. The ceilings and walls were uncracked, tasteful statuary and furnishings in place. Vases were adorned with aromatic, freshly cut flowers.

"*Bonjour, monsieur.* We have reservations," Billie told one of the gentlemen behind the reception desk. "The names are Walker and Baker."

"*Mademoiselle, monsieur, bonjour,* welcome to the Ritz Paris," he said in heavily accented English, his gaze traveling up and down Billie and her companion, then back to her. Something did not sit right with him, she sensed. This would again be an issue of separate names, and a lack of wedding rings, she guessed. How boring it was to live in a world so obsessed with the marital status of women.

"*Merci.* The reservations should be for two rooms on the Cambon side, I believe," Billie specified. The rooms on the Vendôme side were grander, she knew, but her client, who was already funding quite an expedition in her quest to find her wayward husband, could not be expected to cover large rooms. More importantly for Billie, however, was the fact that her feelings about the Vendôme side were marred by their recent occupants—Nazi high brass. The pristine condition of the Ritz had not been without a price.

There was some discussion behind the desk, in lowered voices. Yes, something was amiss, she was sure. "Is there a problem?" Billie inquired. "Our rooms should be separate. We are work colleagues." *Not lovers,* she was close to adding, though the French were famously approving of lovers, were they not?

The man faced her and licked his lips awkwardly. "Mademoi-selle, I am deeply sorry, but the director does not allow women to wear trousers in the hotel."

Billie blinked.

"I do beg your pardon. Does not *allow?*" She looked down at her perfectly delightful navy silk trousers. True, they were a touch crushed after the travel, though not too badly thanks to the fine silk they were crafted from. No, it couldn't be that. There was no way she would be barred entry to a hotel, even one such as this, for so chic a silk garment.

"Monsieur Claude Auzello, the managing director. He does not allow it. It is a strict policy," the man explained.

"A policy against trousers?"

So, Nazis were fine, but not trousers on women.

"I do apologize, mademoiselle. It is illegal for a woman to wear trousers in Paris without a police permit, you see. The hotel policy applies even to Marlene Dietrich when she is at the Ritz."

Billie raised an eyebrow. Now, that was something, considering the movie star's deep appreciation of trousers and all manner of menswear. She had rather set off a trend for it. "Well, 'when at the Ritz,' I suppose," Billie said, relenting. "I can certainly change when I get to my room. Would that be acceptable?"

She looked down again at her silk trousers, marveling at their apparent power of subversion. She was distantly aware of the law, but it was never enforced, she thought. This pair was evidently cursed, it seemed. She'd only just got round to mending them after tearing them during a chase that had involved jumping several fences in pursuit of an adulterous man as part of a divorce case back in Sydney, and now she'd worn them twice on this trip and they were to be locked away for impropriety. Ah well. A woman had to pick her battles.

"Very good, Mademoiselle Walker." The unmarried "mademoi-selle."

"I prefer to be called Ms."

"Very good, Ms.," he said smoothly, and she warmed a touch. Yes, they would get on fine.

—⁂—

An hour after check-in, Billie made her way back down to the Le Grand Bar on the ground level of the hotel, feeling renewed by a refreshing bath in her very own room, complete with such a delight-ful soap that she did not need to use her own bar. Quite a luxury that was. She already looked forward to returning to that tub at her lei-sure, but for now she was dressed in more acceptably feminine garments—an attractive shirtwaist dress in a range of blue hues with dashes of cherry and a pair of fresh stockings. No doubt the manage-ment would approve, if not Marlene Dietrich, if they happened to cross paths.

She found Sam in the bar, waiting for her. It was a high-ceilinged space, beautifully appointed, and her assistant was difficult to miss, being somewhat larger than the average Frenchman. He, too, had freshened up and changed, and as usual he looked no worse for the travel, mailboat or otherwise. Trousers were just fine on him, natu-rally enough.

"*Bonjour.* You are glowing, good sir," Billie remarked as she joined him and sat, before he could gallantly pull out her chair. "Vera's friend Josephine will meet us here soon . . . Unless she gives us the brush-off like the Caversham-Smithes," she said and looked at the time. Yes, she would arrive soon. "Beautiful hotel, isn't it? Do you have a bath in your room?"

"I do, Billie." He looked about to call it "beaut," one of his pet phrases, but stopped himself. "It's quite a place. Like the war was never here at all. How peculiar about the trousers, though," he remarked. "I've never heard of such a thing!"

"I can hardly claim to be terribly inconvenienced, having only packed a single pair, but it is odd," she agreed. "I think it harks back to the eighteen hundreds and the *pantalons* fashionable with Parisian rebels during the French Revolution. Perhaps it could use an update?"

Was Billie a rebel? With a slight grin, she decided she wouldn't have minded being considered a rebel. But alas, trousers and the Ritz Paris did not go together.

"I thought Parisians were more . . . modern."

"Yes and no," Billie observed. "Frenchwomen only gained suffrage the year I left—the same year the Nazis left—which is very late when you remember that Australian women could vote in 1902. Except Shyla and her kin, of course."

Shyla Davis was not permitted to vote, nor run for office, because she was descended from the original inhabitants and owners of the land—a backward idea if ever there was one, and an idea no doubt clung to by Charlie Thompson's uncle at the Australian Natives' Association. "Authorities on all sides of the globe have some backward ideas," Billie concluded. "Some backward ideas, indeed."

Something or someone had caught Sam's eye, and evidently what he saw was pleasing. "Is this her, do you think?" he asked in a whisper.

Billie turned to see that a delightfully chic woman was looking around Le Grand Bar, searching faces for recognition. She seemed to be an older version of the woman Vera had showed her in her photographs. She was fashionable in that particularly Parisian way— quality clothes, understated and feminine.

Billie made eye contact, and the woman broke into a bright smile. If Billie had worried that the Montgomerys had also burned their bridges with Madame Josephine Laurent, her concerns quickly evaporated.

"*Bonjour*, Miss Walker. Welcome to Paris! I am sorry I couldn't be here to greet you," the woman exclaimed, joining them. Sam pulled out a chair for her and she sat and crossed her legs, looking each of them over in turn. "Monsieur, I am not sure of your name. My apologies. I was delighted when Vera let me know you were coming. I am Madame Laurent. You may call me Josephine."

"Thank you, Josephine. This is Samuel Baker. You are practically greeting us on arrival. We only just got in an hour ago, and trust me, you should be pleased we managed to bathe first," Billie said with a laugh.

"Separately, of course," Sam specified, awkwardly.

"Yes, in our separate rooms," Billie agreed.

"*Très bien*," Josephine said, looking from one to the other.

"You may call me Billie. Tell me, are you and Vera in touch often?" Billie jumped in before the conversation became more peculiar. Josephine was wearing Chanel No. 5, Billie could detect. The designer, Coco Chanel, kept a suite on the Cambon side, even throughout the war.

"Oh yes. We write to each other often, and I send her the latest on Paris fashions. She makes sure I send her Paris *Vogue* each month." She smiled and pulled a cigarette case from her handbag. Ever the gentleman, Sam removed his lighter, leaned forward, and lit her fag. Billie ordered them a round of drinks—a black tea for herself, a tea with cream for Sam, and a coffee for Josephine.

Billie got that familiar tingling feeling across her scalp and right ear, and when she turned, she could see they had attracted the attention of a stranger, a freckled man sitting in the far corner of the bar. He puffed on his cigar and looked away.

"She is a very fashionable woman, your friend Vera," Billie remarked, bringing herself back to the moment.

Over the years, Billie had carefully cultivated her powers of observation, as her father had before her, and naturally she was more adept than Barry had been at the finer points of fashion, owing to her personal interest in dressmaking. She had picked Vera's clothing as modern and surprisingly French for a woman who hadn't set foot out of the Antipodes. Josephine was clearly the reason for this.

"We met when we were both posing in Sydney. I was there for the summer and we grew close. I was a mannequin once," Josephine admitted with a shy smile. "I am—how do you say?—past my prime now, but I still get asked from time to time."

Billie could see why Josephine would be asked. She was a classic French beauty, with her large dark eyes, high cheekbones, even features, and a cascade of natural brunette hair. There was an effortlessly stylish way about her that was universally admired and recognizable as Parisian. And of course the French never wore too much makeup; it seemed to be some kind of unspoken national agreement. Billie felt almost overdone next to her, in her tailored shirtdress and her Fighting Red. Or perhaps it was that she felt clumsy somehow, or less feminine by comparison.

"I don't believe in the concept of being past your prime," Billie declared. If there were such a thing, this woman was not it. "Tell me, did you ever pose for Richard Montgomery? He had quite an eye."

"*Non!* Vera would have had my head." She laughed.

"Whatever for? Wasn't he working as a photographer at the time?"

"He was, but . . ." She waved her hand in the air. "He was a flirtatious man, you understand. I didn't want to pose for him once my friend was interested."

"I see." Billie again wondered if his flirtatiousness with women had been an act to secure his position within the advertising industry and to throw people off the scent regarding his true personal inclinations. "Did you see him when he came to Paris in '45?"

"Richard? *Oui.* My husband and I had dinner with him, and I tried my best to get him a good room while he was here. It wasn't a suite, but he had his own bath and was very pleased. After the exposition he just lost touch with us, though. *J'en fut surprise, je l'avoue.* Do you like your rooms?"

"Oh yes, Josephine. They are very fine. *Merci.*" Billie gave her a warm smile and noticed Sam nodding enthusiastically. "I meant to give these to you. It is a small token of our thanks." She pushed a neatly wrapped gift of English toffees across the table. "We are most grateful."

Josephine inspected the parcel and the pretty bow. "*Merci beaucoup,* Billie."

"When did Richard check out of the hotel, do you know?"

Josephine nodded. "Yes, I inquired about him, and they told me he'd already left. This was about one week after the exposition launch, maybe less. The others had gone back to London to fly home, I knew, and I didn't take it personally of course, but I had thought he might say good-bye before heading back to Australia."

"How interesting. And when he checked out, he took everything with him? There was nothing left behind?"

She shrugged. "*Non.* What sort of thing?"

"Anything, I suppose. And he checked out himself? Personally?"

Josephine straightened. "I did not think to ask. I did not know something could be wrong."

"Of course. And we don't know if anything was wrong at that time."

Richard may have chosen to disappear, but if he didn't—if he met with foul play—it was not until after checking out. Or, if he met with foul play before departing the hotel, whoever was involved took the trouble to clean out his room and cover up the nature of his disappearance.

Josephine shrugged again. "*C'est étrange*. Tell me, Miss Billie, how long has it been since you've been in Paris? Vera says you used to work here?"

"Three years," Billie said, raising the same number of fingers.

"When the Nazis left Paris."

Billie crossed one leg over the other, stockings swishing softly in the process. "The two facts were unrelated, I'm afraid, though I'd like to have been responsible for their departure."

Josephine laughed. Yes, Billie liked this woman.

"I had to leave Europe for personal reasons," she continued. "But I spent most of the war elsewhere. How did you hold up during the occupation? It must have been terribly difficult."

"*C'était horrible*," she said, and her face fell. "But that is the past. If you haven't been in Paris for a while, you need to get to know her again. I'd like to take you out on the town tonight, as a welcome to our city."

Billie sat up. "I'm afraid I have a prior commitment, with a former work colleague." Her stomach knotted a touch, simply at the mention. "It is rather urgent."

. . . rumor had it that Jack did not make it out of Warsaw, so I was surprised to run into him at the Hôtel Lutetia in December . . .

"Too bad," Josephine said, and turned to Sam, who watched her with wide blue eyes. "How about you, then, Monsieur Samuel?"

"Um . . ."

"*Très bien*. It is decided. My husband is out of town and you shall keep me company." She leaned over and linked her arm in his. "We'll have fun, *oui*?"

He swallowed. "*Oui*," he repeated.

Billie watched the exchange and grinned from ear to ear. "You'll have a fabulous time, Sam, and you could use a night off after all that travel. We'll meet up over breakfast, and you can tell me all about the sights of Paris."

"As long as it's not too early," Josephine said. "You need to see Paris at night. There's nothing like it," she told him with a flourish of her open hand in the air, as if to show him a glimpse of the nightlife.

Sam was in good hands.

Twenty

—◊◊◊—

Wrapped in her trench coat and wearing her trusty Oxfords, Billie Walker took the Métro Line 4 to Saint-Germain-des-Prés and walked to the fourth-floor flat of one Mademoiselle Simone Chapelle. Her heart was in her throat for the journey, but there was nothing for it. The sooner she saw Simone and discussed her surprising letter, the sooner she could resolve just what—or whom—Simone had seen.

The prospect of seeing Simone Chapelle again was a mixed bag. She was anxious about what her friend would say, but Billie didn't dare hope that it meant Jack was actually alive. It couldn't be, could it? It would be too crushing to hope again, and have those hopes dashed. She hardly dared to believe it was true, and yet she had not known Simone to be wrong very often. She was a woman Billie admired immensely, one of the finest war reporters she had ever met, and as it happened also one of the first. Billie had been quite enamored with her career back when they'd met in Paris in the late thirties and Simone had taken her under her wing when she worked at Hearst. Fluent in many languages, and a veteran of numerous battles, Simone held her own with the likes of Martha Gellhorn and Clare Hollingworth. Her work in the field had shaped her into a chain-smoking, razor-tongued, staunch socialist, and interestingly a pacifist. Seeing the ravages of war, up close and unedited, tended to do that to a person. Shortly after the liberation, she'd returned to Paris, where she kept her flat. This was where Billie would now meet her, and if there was anyone from her former life whom she hoped to visit in Paris, it was Simone. And the man she had written to Billie about, of course.

Billie buzzed at street level and soon heard loud footsteps.

Presently, Simone opened the door in a pair of wool trousers and a cream button-up blouse, a fag dangling from her lips. Billie took in her friend's trousers with a new level of respect, knowing now their subversive power, and reached out to embrace her.

Simone took her smoldering cigarette in one hand and smiled, her face breaking into deep lines. "Ma Chérie, you are a sight for sore eyes," she said warmly, hugging Billie's soft, lean curves against her sinewy muscle. "Come . . . come in," she beckoned.

Simone led the way up to the fourth floor, her leather-soled men's shoes slapping on the timber staircase. The door to her flat was ajar, and when she invited Billie inside Billie could see that not much had changed since her last visit some years before. Books were stacked on the floors and on makeshift shelves, some adorned with creeping plants and empty wine bottles that held candles, wax drip-ping down their stems. Old cameras and lenses were stacked on crates. Monochrome photographs were spread out over a desk. Large cushions, of the kind one found in places like Istanbul and Mar-rakesh, were spread out on the floor in lieu of a couch. Though far from grand, Simone's flat had an intensity about it, like the woman herself. It held the essence of long nights spent bent over negatives and photographic loupes, smoking and drinking wine, and for Billie was a glimpse into an alternate vision of fulfillment, something true and authentic that few women ever had the opportunity to choose for themselves.

"I must thank you for your letter, though of course it disturbed me somewhat when I read it," Billie said.

"I imagine so," Simone replied simply, and blew smoke out from between her lips. She offered Billie one from her pack and Billie shook her head. "A drink? I managed to acquire a bottle of Lillet Blanc, and I have a dash left. It's lovely over ice, if you don't find it too sweet?"

Billie nodded eagerly. "Thank you, Simone." The whisky she'd thrown back before hitting the Métro had worn off, and she felt she rather needed some liquid courage. After so much time without Jack, after grieving him and having to get on with her life, she realized she had not dared to quite believe that Simone's letter might be correct. But now, setting eyes on steady, sharp Simone, she had to concede that she was the same woman she'd been when they last met. She was not one to mix up Jack Rake with someone else, hurried meeting or otherwise.

What if Simone is right, and Jack was alive as recently as December? What could that mean? Billie wondered. *What does it mean for me now? For him? For us?*

Simone placed her smoldering cigarette between her lips again, walked over to her small kitchenette, took a block of ice out of the ice box, and stabbed it loudly with a chipper, breaking off a few pieces. "I did not much enjoy writing that letter, dear Billie. You must believe me on that score. I'm telling you the truth about seeing Jack, you understand," she said. She slipped chips of ice into a couple of clear tumblers and walked over with the bottle and glasses.

"Oh yes, and I believe you," Billie said sincerely, though her chest was tight at the admission. Her friend certainly would not make such a thing up, but believing that her recollection was correct, that it was really Jack, was an altogether different issue. "I can't account for just why or how he could have been there, however. It was December of last year, you say?"

She nodded. "I remember it as if it were yesterday. It's perplexing, is it not?" She sat on a cushion on the wooden floorboards and invited Billie to do the same. Slowly, to preserve each drop, Simone poured them each a small glass of Lillet Blanc, and they clinked glasses.

"*Santé.*"

"It is good to see you again."

Billie lay over a cushion on one hip. "You were right that we married in '44. He went off to Warsaw a few months later, and, well, as you know, the uprising was a terrible disaster. The Home Army had no help in the end. Jack was there, and . . ."

While Vera had received her husband's last letter from the Ritz Paris, the final letter from Billie's husband had been from a somewhat more dangerous place.

"Yes. It was disastrous, and I, too, had heard he didn't make it out," Simone said, and nodded gravely. "I did not know him so well as you, naturally, but I was sad to hear he had passed, like so many others. I grieved him, and I worried about you, Billie."

"Thank you, Simone." Billie reached out and placed a hand briefly on Simone's. "I hope you did not think I was in Warsaw with him."

"No," she said, and shook her head. "I knew you were not with him. But you can see why I was relieved to see him at the Hôtel Lutetia."

Billie licked her lips. "Tell me. What happened exactly, when you saw him?"

"I can't forget it. I'd been visiting a friend, and I walked out of the front lobby of the hotel and straight into our Jack."

Hearing her say it like that made Billie's heart jump. She was so matter-of-fact about it. There was no question of the memory being vague or elusive.

"So, you are quite sure—"

"Quite, Billie," Simone answered. "Quite. I told you I was. We nearly collided, and I called to him by name. He turned his head at the sound of it. He knew me, I am sure of it. Recognition passed over his face, and then a look that haunts me still: a kind of fear and panic. He shook his head and walked away briskly, like he was running from something, running away, or didn't want me to follow."

"Did you exchange words?"

Simone looked into the flame of the candle that illuminated their space on the floor. "No. I dearly wished we had. I still remember that look on his face."

This was, Billie realized, the first conversation she'd had with anyone since Jack's disappearance where it was assumed that her husband might still be alive. Everyone she spoke to danced around the possibility, trying to avoid saying the wrong thing, trying to avoid giving her false hope, and after so long without hearing from him, there were no good options to choose from. You either had to deduce that Jack Rake was dead or that he had abandoned Billie, his bride. There was no happy ending to hint at, to wish for. And now there was this conundrum of him, or his doppelgänger, at the Hôtel Lutetia, barely half a year before.

"I appreciate that it must have been an uncomfortable letter to write," Billie said, already pulling back from the possibility, despite Simone's insistence that who she had seen was Jack.

"It was, Billie. It was." Simone puffed on her cigarette, and the smoke drifted lazily out of her mouth. "I have thought on it often, and was troubled by self-doubt. Had it really been him? But I am sure."

This was what worried Billie. Simone wasn't the type to be mistaken, but it could happen to anyone, particularly after the trauma of that war.

"No matter how I turn it in my mind, I know it was him. He was changed, but it was him."

Billie cocked her head. "What do you mean by 'changed,' exactly?"

"He was skinny and drawn, Billie, and he had a significant scar across his neck, just visible above the collar. I notice such things, though I suppose he hoped to hide it. His movements were strained. Remember that ease with which he used to move? The lightness? That was our Jack. But the lightness was gone. Oh, it was him, though. It was him all right."

Billie felt a chill move up her spine and settle at the back of her neck. A significant scar? She could see Jack, his mannerisms, the way his lean form moved, as Simone said, with a kind of lightness and agility. There was a kinetic quality to him. He was always in motion, a spark in his eye and another adventure just around the corner. Then in a rush Jack was there, fresh in her memory, almost as if she could smell his scent, feel his hand in hers. Billie's eyes filled with tears, the room around her blurring. Her belly roiled, and she thought she might be sick. Quickly, she wiped her face and steadied herself. Simone did not comment and for a while the flat was silent.

"Do you think he might have been injured?" Billie asked tentatively, once she had her breath again. She brought her hand to her throat. It was a foolish question of course, but she wanted to hear more, needed to hear more.

"Undoubtedly, yes. That scar was something. Since I saw him last, with you, I believe he must have been injured, perhaps severely."

She stared into the flame again, and it danced and popped. "I wish I could tell you more, Billie. I really do . . . Oh, there was one more thing that struck me. He was wearing *a necktie*."

"Jack was wearing a necktie?"

Simone nodded. "Yes. It struck me as odd."

Indeed, anyone who knew Jack Rake knew that he was forever disheveled, as if he'd stepped out of the desert somewhere, or off an archeological site. He did not, as a rule, wear neckties. Perhaps he did have a doppelgänger in Paris somewhere, with a scar and a wardrobe full of neckwear. Perhaps she was opening up her heart to the possibility of his still being alive, and it was for naught, just another cruel twist.

But *could* he be alive?

"Tell me about Sydney," Simone said after a long pause, during which both women seemed to be lost in their respective memories. "I heard you opened a detective agency, and then I read about this case you broke with the war criminal, Hessmann. That was damn fine work, Billie. Damn fine."

"Thank you. I wasn't alone," Billie admitted, thinking of Shyla and her friends. "Do you know anything about Franz Hessmann? He was apparently camp administrator at Ravensbrück before he escaped to Australia."

Simone nodded. "Hmm. The women's camp," she said, face darkening. "Hessmann." She considered the name. "His name rings a bell. He had been sentenced to death in absentia, yes?"

Billie nodded. "Yes. He was a major in the Waffen-SS before working at the camp. He was sentenced to death in Hamburg in the British Zone but had already fled. He was well funded, too. He'd been a black marketeer in stolen Jewish treasures."

"Weren't they all," Simone remarked bitterly. "Remember Dr. Marcel Petiot?"

Billie squinted. "The bodies found in Rue Le Sueur?" She re-called the authorities being called to the doctor's home in Paris, re-sponding to complaints from neighbors about a foul stench. The doctor had promised Jewish families refuge during the Nazi occupa-tion, and had instead murdered them and stolen their property. The remains of nearly two dozen victims had been found in his base-ment, and Petiot had escaped, remaining on the run for months as the police and media pursued him.

"Petiot was finally recognized at a Paris Métro station. They found fifty sets of identity documents on him. *Fifty*. He was con-victed of twenty-six counts of murder by the court, and the guillo-tine was having some troubles, so he had to wait in suspense but it got him in the end." Simone drew her fingers across her throat in a sudden motion.

Billie imagined waiting for workmen to fix the machine designed to part you from your head.

"The reason I ask about Hessmann," Billie went on, getting back on track, "is that he would have been part of a network getting sto-len Jewish goods out of Europe, and perhaps he was even active in keeping the ratline going. He might even have been working with his former colleagues at Ravensbrück? I don't know. They'd have to get the goods out of a major port somewhere."

"But there are many ports in Europe. How to find out which one is the issue." Simone frowned and looked off, squinting so that her eyes creased in the corners, the lines shaped like spiders' webs. "I will keep my ear to the ground for you," she promised. "And you are here on a case, *oui*?"

"*Oui*."

"Come on, then. Can you tell me about it?"

Billie didn't see why not. There were many thousands of miles between Simone's Paris and Vera's Potts Point, and if anyone could be helpful to the case in Paris, it was likely Simone. "Actually, it's a missing husband," Billie explained. "And it's getting interesting because at first I believed him to be a ladies' man—perhaps a cheating husband who had slept with the wrong married woman and met an untimely end, or who had fallen in love in Paris and decided to stay—but now it seems likely he may have been a homosexual in secret, not interested in women at all, so I was wrong there. He may have needed to leave Sydney because of some of his dealings."

"Couldn't it be both?" Simone suggested.

"Pardon me?"

Simone watched Billie for a moment, deciding something. "Come, let's go out for a drink," she said after a moment. "You need a night off. Can you walk in your shoes?" she asked. "On the cobblestones?"

"On a tightrope if necessary," Billie replied.

—m—

Forty-five minutes later, after a pleasant stroll that reacquainted Billie with parts of the Paris she had once known well, they arrived in Rue Pigalle, at the lower end of Montmartre.

Billie was now within a stone's throw of Le Place Pigalle, she noted, a few blocks from the Moulin Rouge, but it seemed unlikely Simone was taking her to the famous burlesque show, or the dance club it had turned into during the war. Certainly Simone knew Paris well, and had been living here long before Billie met her, and long before she'd met Jack. If she had a favorite watering hole, Billie trusted it would be worth the walk. Along the Rue Pigalle, her friend slowed and smiled, indicating a doorway. *How peculiar.* If Billie was not mistaken, Simone seemed to be taking her into one of the *brasseries à femmes*, one of the many bars in the district for men seeking female company. But Billie was not in particular need of male company at the moment—putting aside the missing men who still frustratingly eluded her. Nor would she be particularly inclined to visit had she been in some kind of need.

Billie did not voice her concerns, and Simone took her through a discreet, darkened door into an establishment Billie would never have entered on her own. She found herself before a lush red curtain, behind which she could hear revelry. The secrecy of the red curtain, and what was beyond, made Billie stiffen. Had her friend really taken her to a *brasserie à femmes*?

"Don't be nervous," Simone said, and took Billie's hand in hers. She parted the heavy curtains, and they entered.

Immediately they were greeted by a haze of sweet smoke filling a small, lushly decorated bar with low ceilings. Patrons were seated at circular tables, drinking, sharing cigarettes and cigarillos, and enjoying little tête-à-têtes. Several looked up to see them enter, and Billie knew at once that she had only been half-mistaken in her impression. This was not where women came to seek the company of men, but to seek the company of other women. A sign by the bar indicated that this was La Coccinelle—the Ladybird—a bar Billie had heard of but had never had the occasion to enter.

Billie had long sensed Simone was not interested in men, or in any case did not enjoy the company of the opposite sex, except as a professional necessity, but she hadn't given it much thought over the years. For one, Simone had never married, which was a rare quality in a woman during an age where it seemed the powers that be were more enthusiastic than ever about pressuring the "fairer sex" into matrimony, and unlike Constable Primrose, who couldn't marry—at least not if she wanted to continue to work—Simone had no boss to enforce such rules on her personal life. She did not have to choose between a paycheck and marriage. Though Simone had kept this aspect of her life private from Billie until tonight, Paris had a long and rich history of lesbian culture, particularly in Montmartre and Pigalle, and it now seemed not in the least surprising that this scene would be part of Simone's life.

Billie followed her friend to an available spot, tucked in the corner, and they took their seats. Her long legs were barely able to fit beneath the table, but Simone straddled one of its legs without difficulty in her trousers and flat footwear.

"Cigarette?" Simone asked.

"*Oui. Merci*, Simone."

"You like it?" she asked, indicating the room with a sweep of her hand.

"Yes," Billie said. "Thank you for trusting me enough to invite me here."

"Don't worry, I know it isn't for you, but your secret's safe with me," Simone told her with a sly grin. "And if you find you change your mind, I feel confident you need not leave alone," she added, gesturing to the room of women.

Billie laughed under her breath. Indeed, several patrons had been looking her over with interest, though none would interrupt her tête-à-tête with Simone, not without a signal.

"I drink here once in a while with my friends. It's quite safe," Simone assured her. "There are a few bars. Some even survived the war and the Nazis with their crusade against us, and new places are popping up in St. Germain, nearer where I live, but this one I prefer. And so you see, this man . . . Montgomery, I think you said his name was? He may well have fallen in love in Paris—no, not here in this bar, but in a place like it for men of his kind, or even on the job. And he may have decided to leave his life in the Antipodes behind. He may even be interested in women and men, both. *Bisexuel*, as the

French say," she added. "Falling in love . . . It is a mystery, is it not? It is beyond one sex or another."

Billie watched as a slender woman slipped into the lap of another, the two talking intimately. Her friend was right, of course.

"Paris is one of the most libertine and modern cities, you see," Simone continued. "You can live the life you please—mostly—without the police interfering, and there are not many cities in the world where you can say that. Private lives are not criminalized in Paris, and so as long as men like your Montgomery do what they wish behind closed doors or even behind a curtain, no one cares. Even under the occupation, the streets may have been empty but the *pissotiéres* were full." *The urinals.*

Billie had known that the urinals in Paris had been important meeting places for the resistance—they were built into the streets with solid curved walls providing some privacy—but she had given little thought to other uses, beyond the obvious.

"That would have been terribly risky, under the Nazis," Billie commented.

Simone exhaled, a cloud of smoke forming in the air beyond her lips. "Human needs can be very strong," she said.

Billie knew it to be so. Her own needs were still there, she knew, and they were being tested dearly in Jack's absence—her desires simmering just below the surface, though she could do nothing about them. She pushed those needs aside for other priorities, despite her mother's frequent taunts about the nice young men she should respond to, but Billie knew a time would come when she could no longer deny herself, a time to let go. But what exactly was it that she needed to let go of to allow those desires to surface? Was it hopes of Jack? Thoughts of her vows? Social expectations? Her own mistrust in the world, barely given a chance to fade when case after case she worked on confirmed the worst about love?

"It is like with anyone—you make a human urge taboo, illegal, and it goes underground," Simone explained. "Many of these men are married because it is all society will accept—all that their churches, their parents will accept."

How true that appeared to be for Richard Montgomery, Billie thought.

"But who they are doesn't just go away because it's inconvenient," Simone concluded. "Here in Paris, at least, one does not need to pretend just for the sake of the law, even if other pressures remain. That isn't to say all of Paris approves, you understand," she qualified. "No. But they do not need to. It is not illegal for men to love men in Paris, or for the women here to live as they choose." She gestured again to the room.

"Of course," Billie said under her breath.

It fit together in a way she had not yet thought about, even after Jane Caversham-Smithe's recent insights. She had not set her mind on the matter of different laws. Mr. Charles would not have found himself in the same predicament in Paris as he had in Sydney. He might well have been rejected by his wife, yes, perhaps even his employer, but there would not be the threat of the authorities coming down on him for that kiss, and what it meant. "I have been too narrow in my thinking," Billie admitted. "First focusing on the possibility of a love affair with a woman, and then of his enemies in Sydney."

"Yes. Both may be true, you see. A love affair here during his stay, and with Paris beckoning, and his many other reasons not to return to the Antipodes . . ."

How fascinating that the Parisian authorities would quite sensibly allow consenting adults to love whom they chose, without the threat of jail. And yet they would not allow women to wear trousers? Not according to the books, anyway.

She looked around at the tables. Of course, many of the patrons here were flouting that outdated law. And doing it rather stylishly.

"Thank you," Billie said to her friend. "Thank you for sharing this with me this. And for opening my eyes."

Twenty-one

—⁂—

Billie Walker, a touch bleary-eyed after her night out, answered the knock at her hotel room door to find a neatly uniformed porter. She swayed on her feet and bid the boy good morning.

"*Bonjour. Un télégramme pour vous, mademoiselle,*" the young man said, and handed her an envelope.

Billie thanked him with a tip, closed the door, and pulled out the telegram, hoping for fresh information about Mr. Montgomery. Simone had opened her mind to possible reasons for Richard's disappearance. It had given her some ideas about how to search for him.

Billie fell onto the settee and looked over the page. She certainly was not expecting what she found.

YOUR FLAT BROKEN INTO. NO DAMAGE
OR THEFT. NOT TO WORRY. TOLD COOPER.
REGARDS, E

Billie sunk back on the cushions. The telegram was from her mother. Her flat at Cliffside had been broken into? Why in goddess's name would anyone do that? It must have seemed easy pickings with her being away, she supposed, but if there was no obvious theft, what had they been looking for?

Not to worry?

In all of the time she had lived there, her flat had only been broken into once before, and that had been someone trying to interfere with her case for the Brown family. It had been quite memorable and was certainly not a common occurrence in the building. Was it because of this Montgomery case that someone was rifling through her things?

Or perhaps the intruder was looking for the negatives of those photographs they'd taken of Mr. Charles? Would he arrange such a thing, just to ensure the negatives of his vulnerable moment in the alley were destroyed for good? She had given him her word, but was that enough with Australia's archaic laws hanging over his head? Simone had certainly reminded her of how troubling Australia's laws were by showing her the more civilized way France treated its citizens in matters relating to their sexual preferences.

And the next thought hit her like a slap.

The office.

If someone, Mr. Charles or otherwise, wanted something, they would break into the office as well, she realized. She would send a telegram to Shyla, to see if everything was in order.

Blast.

Billie did so hate feeling helpless, and so far away.

—⁓—

"Why, that's awful, Billie," Sam exclaimed, joining her in her hotel room. "Your mother must have been so shocked to find your apartment had been broken into."

She nodded. "I can be grateful she lives in the same building and was able to find out quickly. But I honestly wonder if I've ever felt so strangely disconnected and far from home, even compared to when I was last here, during the war. I guess I felt I had so little to lose then. Now I have built a home and something out of the agency, worked so hard for it, and I'm on the other side of the world and can't check on things. It's not ideal, I'll say that much."

Billie had not realized how much her little flat had come to mean to her, and her office, too. It was home—a sense of belonging and a connection to a place—and she had been so long without that while in Europe, until she'd built it for herself back in Sydney.

"The good news, at least, is that you're safe here," Sam said, giving her a supportive nod. "And don't forget, you're still building things, even while you're here," he said. "This case is a coup. You may be far away but it's not for nothing."

She closed her eyes for a moment. "I know. You're right, Sam, of course you are right. I'd just like to understand why someone is rifling through my personal things, if not to rob me. Or perhaps they did take things and it won't be clear until I get there. In any event, it's unsettling to know someone was in my bedroom, my space, and me so far away. I don't like to feel so powerless," she admitted. "Maybe if I'd been there, I could have done something about it."

"Or maybe you could have been hurt," he sensibly pointed out. "I'm glad you are over here, with me."

And there had been their drive back from the Cotswolds as well. Had that been the case throwing up danger for her again? Had Nettie Brown's recommendation of her services to Vera Montgomery been a curse, instead of the goddess-send she had believed?

Billie allowed herself to look at Sam, and their eyes met for a moment. *Sam. Steady Sam.* She was glad he was with her, and she was not alone. "I'm glad, too, Sam. They must have known the flat was empty. I fear it's something to do with a case."

She wasn't quite sure what she thought, except that she didn't believe in coincidences. She had so far come up against obstacles with this Montgomery case, mostly, it would seem, due to Richard's twin talents of keeping secrets from his wife and exploiting other people's secrets for money. Knowing a bit more about why he might have had reason to leave Sydney wasn't the same as knowing where he was now. Now it was time to find him, dead or alive.

WE'LL FIND HIM.

The note surfaced in her mind again. It bothered her. Could someone connected to Montgomery be behind the break-in, perhaps? Why? To find him or to make sure she didn't? Or was the break-in to do with another case, perhaps? The case that had made the papers and kept being brought up?

"I just don't know, Sam," Billie said, and shook her head. "How was last night, by the way?"

"Oh my," he said. "Vera's friend is sure lively. It was a nice evening, even if I couldn't understand her friends. It was . . . eye-opening."

"Is that so?" Billie imagined him dragged from place to place, Josephine's friends fascinated by the handsome Australian. "My night was also," she reflected. "Today may be something of a disappointment after that, I'm afraid. I have to head to the prefecture of police today and see if there is any record of Montgomery there. Perhaps, if you will, you could inquire at the department store Magasins du Printemps about the Australian exposition. It was set up in one of the upper floors there. Let's hope someone recalls him." She slid a copy of Richard's photo across to him. Vera did think he liked to live large. Perhaps there would be more evidence of that in Paris than there had been in London.

"I do wish my French was far better," Sam said with regret.

"Practice will help, but then a lot of the French do seem to speak some English. I know you can be a charmer, Sam. I have no doubt you'll come up with something." Particularly if the staff were female.

"I hope so, Ms. Walker. I don't want to let you down."

"I know you won't." She sat up from the settee and smoothed down her clothing. "In the end, I think we will likely end up at—"

"The death house?" he cut in, knowing her methods.

She nodded sadly. "Yes, Sam. It never bodes well when missing people had a habit of blackmailing for their coin." No, it did not bode well at all.

Twenty-two

———◊◊◊———

SYDNEY, AUSTRALIA, 1947

How is June?"

Like Billie Walker before her, Shyla Davis had struck up something of a friendship with John Wilson, the lift attendant at Daking House. He was a kind gentleman, always smiling and happy to see her, which was not a given among white folks, in Shyla's experience. They seemed always to be stuck between staring and trying not to stare at her, which she supposed was a feeling the disabled war veteran knew well. The first time he'd met her, she was with Billie. Now that Billie had gone to Paris, she was surprised by how quickly she and Wilson had bonded.

"She's well, thank you, Miss Davis," he said of his wife, June. "How are things going at the office?"

"It's stuffy," Shyla replied honestly, and he laughed at her bluntness, one side of his scarred face pulling up.

"You are refreshingly direct, Miss Davis. I like that." The lift rattled along to its destination, the floors passing them one after another. Wilson looked at his timepiece. "I'll be knocking off soon," he said. "You'll be okay getting down?"

She nodded. She often took the stairs, not liking the confinement of the lift. It harked back to something in her past, her youth, that she did not rightly wish to recall too closely.

"Well, here we are," he told her, arriving on the sixth level, straightening out the lift car in line with the floor after a couple of tries, letting go of the controls, and pulling open the folding grille for her with his strong left arm. He had lost his other in the war, the right arm of his jacket pinned to his side.

Shyla stepped quickly out, happy to be in the hall, and she bid the kindly man good night and made her way down the hallway. Reaching Billie's darkened office, she used her key to unlock the door, and switched on the lights inside, seeing the dust stirred up in the air by her presence. Again, she found a small, disordered pile of her friend's letters scattered at her feet. Shyla stepped over them, as one might a puddle, then reached back and shut the door with one hand. She bent easily on lithe legs, squatting on the carpet and gathering up the correspondence. The letter on top was addressed to a *Mr. B. Walker*, which made Shyla chuckle softly to herself. Billie had told her this happened. All those whitefellas just didn't see the woman coming.

Shyla walked over to the assistant's desk and spread the mail out. Sorting through it wouldn't be exciting work, but that was fine. Shyla had enough excitement in her life at the moment, trying to keep her brothers out of trouble, and now, having met the nervous whitefella at the Central Railway Refreshment Rooms, passing on his story about a Mr. Montgomery to Billie across the world. Among the mail was a telegram, she noticed. It grabbed her attention. Interested in any news that might be from her friend and wondering if her message about the blackmailer had been helpful for Billie's case, she absentmindedly threw open the communicating door to let some air into the stale reception area, and she stiffened.

Nunay . . . Something bad . . .

Shyla caught an odd scent in the air—something sharp and male. Someone was in Billie's office or had been recently. On instinct, Shyla took a step back and slipped the letter opener up her sleeve. Her friend dealt in some bad business sometimes. Shyla knew it. She knew to beware.

"Hello?" she said into the dark office, her heart quickening.

The answer came with a crash, someone—a man—charging out of the darkness to shove her to the side with force. She stumbled backward into the side of Sam's wooden desk, then lunged forward with the blade, using all her might. He had been quick, but she was quicker, and there was a cry and a grunt as the sharp blade of the letter opener made good on its promise, penetrating fabric and sinking into flesh. Shyla had stopped her attacker in his tracks. He was doubled over, a ball of suit fabric sinking to the floor, and behind him she could see Billie's office was in disarray, papers carelessly dumped on the carpet. She shook her head.

A bad business.

"You stuck me!" the man cried out, sounding baffled and pained. "You bitch! You stuck me!" He got up from his knees, and holding his stomach with one hand, he raised a weapon unsteadily with the other.

A pistol.

Now Shyla froze. She was quicker than this man, but she could not outrun a bullet.

As she watched, keeping very still, eyes on the business end of that gun, the man stumbled toward the closed door, doubled over and breathing heavily. She took in what she could from his appearance, his smell, his dark, silver-peppered hair. He threw the door open and fled, thundering down the hall. Shyla gave chase and saw that he had taken the stairs, as she so often did. He didn't want to be seen.

She brought a hand to her forehead, panting, then looked down at her gloves. The adrenaline was subsiding, a sick feeling taking over her belly.

Blood.

She had blood on her hands.

Twenty-three

—⁓—

The sun was setting as Billie and Sam met in the lavish reception area of the Ritz Paris.

The city outside was turning pink and red, and it was, truth be told, a most romantic sight. Despite this, they were solemn in anticipation of the task ahead as they headed out on foot through Place Vendôme toward the Métro, barely speaking. If this was a time for love for some, for Billie it was a time for lost love, for grief, and she did not know what lay ahead.

She dug her hands into her trench-coat pockets, ruminating on a frustrating day spent at the Préfecture de Police de Paris, where staff had been even more harried and under-resourced than she had been led to expect. Like the Red Cross and other agencies, they were overwhelmed after a war that had wrought chaos and death on a mass scale. The large, old Neo-Florentine-style building, close to the famous Notre-Dame Cathedral, bore distinguishable bullet holes, as if to further drive home the point.

"*Il n'y a rien dans les archives, mademoiselle*," she'd been told.

The Préfecture office had demanded a great deal of paperwork to even get close to checking records that seemed to Billie to be incomplete and certainly of no help in her case. There was no sign of a Richard Montgomery in police records, nor records she could access for corpses deposited at morgues. And no sign of a Jack Rake, either, which naturally was a relief. If the reports were complete and accurate, which she greatly doubted, neither man came to the attention of the police, posthumously or otherwise. But their records were not a guarantee of such a thing, according to the discontented receptionist.

"You think it's still worth heading to the death house?" Sam asked.

"Unfortunately, just because he isn't listed in *Les repertoires des cadavres déposés à la morgue de Paris*—the Paris morgue records—that doesn't mean he isn't on a slab in the city morgue, particularly if he's unidentified. If he met with foul play in the past couple of years, there's a chance he'll be there." And unidentified, being a foreigner.

Billie hopped around uneven cobblestones as they walked, nimble on her quiet Oxfords. "They don't even pretend their records are accurate, and that's hardly unique after the war."

"Records are a mess everywhere," Sam agreed, nodding.

"But even finding him in their records still presupposes he would have been correctly identified, and I'm increasingly of the view that that's unlikely. If he checked out of the Ritz but didn't have his return booked or any plans to meet at Australia House before his long flight home, and further, didn't let anyone know where he was going, not even his wife, perhaps he was keen to leave his identity behind. Simone gave me some ideas about just why that might have been . . ."

She paused, ruminating on the possibility. Would he have left so much behind? A house? She supposed he had access to other banking accounts, but tracking those down would be difficult. The Swiss were notorious for their discretion. And it occurred to her that perhaps, if he was in Paris and had access to the funds he needed, he might not need to resort to blackmail—nor would it likely be as effective in the kamp scene, considering what Simone had said. In the postwar chaos he might have got new papers, a new identity.

"But then again, he may have disappeared into anonymity a touch more effectively than he'd intended," she suggested darkly.

"A John Doe."

"It's one answer." She put her hands in her pockets.

Richard may have checked out of the hotel, not to head home, but to another location, under another name. "If he was separated from his papers, most likely there would be no one here in Paris to identify him if he was a victim of misadventure."

"I'd hate to be left somewhere, far from home, unidentified," Sam said.

Like so many soldiers.

Many men Sam had known personally would have lost their lives in battle for their country, only to be buried in unmarked graves in foreign soil, represented solely by the Tomb of the Unknown Warrior, like that in Westminster Abbey. The brutal violence of bombs and Mauser machine pistols stripped a man of his identity faster than few other things could.

They took Métro Line 5, and not long after got off at Quai de la Rapée, walking to their destination in the 12th arrondissement in silence. Billie was deep in thought, pondering her strategy for the evening. This wasn't her first rodeo, so to speak, trying to charm her way into places she might not be welcome, but this might prove to be one of her more difficult missions on this trip—to search for signs of Richard Montgomery, or perhaps even Richard himself, at the

Institut Médico-Légal de Paris. The Paris morgue. It was time to step around the frustrating bureaucracy and see what she could find.

She felt uncharacteristic trepidation about this visit to the death house, though not for the reasons one might expect. Bones and bodies bothered her even less now than they had nine years before, when she had wandered the ossuary beneath Paris with Jack, but looking for Mrs. Montgomery's husband at a morgue at which she had no connections would be no easy feat, especially two years after his disappearance. Perhaps, just perhaps, Billie could pick up a trail here, even now, if Montgomery had indeed met an untimely end. But she had to charm her way in first. This wasn't the Sydney city morgue, with Mr. Benny, the morgue attendant, accepting her smiles and the odd gift in exchange for free access. No, this would be a tougher entry. And worse, she had another reason for coming here, one that bothered her far more than the specter of rejection by morgue staff.

Jack Rake.

Billie had the habit of going to death houses hoping she would be unsuccessful in her search, and in his case that was certainly true. Without seeing for herself, she could not rule out the grim possibility of Jack ending up here, especially with the knowledge that he may have somehow been in Paris just the December before. She desperately hoped there would not be a single scrap of evidence to suggest he had ever been inside the brick walls of the Institut Médico-Légal de Paris. Likewise she hoped not to find Montgomery, but she had to admit her motivations were not solely professional on this occasion.

The sun had nearly slipped away as they reached their destination at the edge of the Seine. The Institut Médico-Légal was a large redbrick building, quite close to the Métro tracks. Billie paused to take it in as a train groaned and squealed over the nearby viaduct. She knew the facility was made up of two buildings joined together by an internal courtyard. One building housed the morgue and the other the forensic and educational institution. The portico in front of them was inscribed with the words MÉDICO-LÉGAL.

"This is the main entrance. Let's head around to where the bodies come in and see if we can enter that way," she suggested, and Sam nodded. Announcing their presence to any watchmen or night janitors at the forensic learning institute was not what she had in mind.

The sun was all but extinguished now, the Seine glittering darkly as they followed the path around the side of the building. Perhaps thanks to the open air there was no offensive odor coming up from the banks, but the rich flavors of Paris were on the wind—cigar smoke and a hint of cologne, something floral, jasmine perhaps, and of course the occasional stab of urine coming off the sidewalk, and the next moment taken away by the breeze.

At the corner closest to the river, Billie and Sam passed through a small arched doorway and made their way to the opposite end of the building, where the bodies were brought in motor vehicles. It was quiet, just as she'd hoped. The staff and students at the institute had gone home for the day, as had the doctors who performed autopsies on the deceased.

"This way," she whispered to Sam, walking purposefully inside. "Look for a staircase leading down, or a doorway. We need to get below street level."

"*Monsieur! Mademoiselle!*" a voice called out. "*Vous ne pouvez pas entrer!*"

A portly man with salt-and-pepper hair and a frown strode toward them, hands in the air. He was wearing a collared shirt and vest with trousers, over which was a white apron. Or at least his apron had once been white. Billie chose not to focus on the stains. A morgue attendant?

"*Pardon, monsieur.* I apologize. I have some French, but it is very rusty," she said with intentional clumsiness. "We need your help . . . *On a besoin de votre aide.*" She smiled with as much innocence as she could muster.

"I speak *anglais*," he replied in an accent, waving his hand as if it were nothing, or perhaps waving away her inelegant French. "You are lost?"

"*Non.*" Billie reached into her handbag and held up the two images, one of Richard Montgomery, one of Jack Rake. "We came all this way to look for these missing men. Have you seen them? We are worried for them."

The man leaned forward. "*Non.* I do not recognize," he said, courteously looking at each in turn. "But then, I might not by the time they find themselves here. You must go. They do not allow the public. This is not where to come."

Billie flicked her gaze from one side of the room to the other. They were still blessedly alone, and this man might be the only thing standing between them and the mortuary and its records, for now at least. She had picked their timing well. It might be a chance that would not come again.

"*S'il vous plaît, monsieur.* Please, for the sake of these men's families, can we look, to be sure? They have both left wives behind," she pleaded, laying it on.

"This is not for the tourists, *non*? Not now."

He was referring no doubt to the previous Paris morgue, which had still been a notorious tourist spot at the turn of the century, with bodies on display—even the corpses of children, which were apparently the source of some morbid public fascination. "If you want that excitement, you should visit the catacombs," the man added, perhaps having made such pronouncements before. Despite his words, he did not seem entirely unmoved by her pleas. Perhaps he was not above convincing, she thought.

"We are not here for sightseeing, I can assure you," Billie said. He had not walked off, nor taken her by the arm to lead her away, and these were good signs. "*S'il vous plaît, monsieur. S'il vous plaît . . . Nous devons trouver ces hommes.*" She tried to muster tears but found she was not quite that good an actress. She was no Ava Gardner. "These men may be here in your morgue, unidentified. *Please.* We must find them."

"Think of their children, sir," Sam, who had been silent throughout Billie's performance, added to the appeal. "They must know what happened to their beloved fathers."

Billie looked to him, impressed. He was getting the hang of this. She tried again to work up a tear. "We came all the way from Australia to find these men." She pushed her palms together, a prayer for the men and their families.

Something shifted then, somehow. There was a spark of recognition and the man's eyes lit up. "*Vous êtes australiens?*" he said with emphasis, perhaps having previously assumed they were British.

"*Oui, australiens.*" Recognizing an opening, Billie nodded and took the opportunity to slide some francs into the man's palm. The feel of the money seemed to ease the burden of his ethical or professional concerns somewhat, and he pocketed the notes, then swiped his hands on his apron and looked around to check if he had been seen. If Billie was not mistaken, he had done this before. This was common, especially with the deprivations of the war, and all of the death and uncertainty that came with it.

"*Australiens, non?*" he said again, pointing at the pictures.

"*Oui,*" she confirmed. "We flew here to find these men. If they are here, or there is a record of them, we can arrange to have them sent back home—"

To her astonishment, the man's face broke into a smile and he threw aside all ideas of convention and embraced them both in turn, cutting off Billie's words and very nearly her oxygen. "I am from Villers-Bretonneux," he exclaimed with emotion, now coming to tears himself. This was most unexpected. "I will never forget what your countrymen did for us."

Villers-Bretonneux. Yes, she knew about the place, as many Australians did. It was a village north of Paris, which had been taken by the Germans in the Great War, nearly thirty years before. Australian soldiers had saved the village from German occupation and imminent destruction, losing more than two thousand of their own men in the process. It was known as one of the most important victories of that war, though at a severe cost to the two Australian brigades that had surrounded the invading German soldiers and ultimately defeated them. If the Germans had achieved their goal of pushing on through to the French coast, splitting the French and British armies, it was believed the war might have been lost for the Allies. Villers-Bretonneux was a turning point.

"*Mon frère australien,*" he said to Sam, embracing him. "My brother." He then turned back to Billie, enthusiastically embracing her again. "What can I do? You are family of these men? Tell me." He reached into his apron and gave Billie her notes back, deciding he did not want the money.

"We are friends of the family and have traveled here from Australia to see if these men are in your morgue, or your records. Please help us."

"You have tried the Red Cross, *non? Tant de morts.* Oh, there are so many," he said, seeming to indicate the large number of missing men from the war. "But if I can help and you can claim some of these bodies, good luck to you. It would make my heart happy to help you, just like you helped us."

Billie imagined this was not an easy place to work, and his job was not well paid. Things can't have been easy once the Nazis came to the city, and so many Parisians died or changed addresses or even names to avoid the Gestapo.

"Registres de la Morgue is downstairs. But not now." He brought a finger to his lips. "I think it is not a good time. Come to the door, *dans une heure*. One hour, yes? You understand?" He held up one finger and pointed toward the way they had walked before. "By the river. You can do this?"

Billie and Sam looked at each other. "*Oui*. We can do that. Not the same way, then?"

He shook his head and pointed back toward the Seine and Pont d'Austerlitz. "At the river. I can let you in, but do not take or I will be in trouble."

Do not take. No, they were not intending to take any bodies out of this place, though she had her camera on hand, hopeful she could document what they found. "We promise we will not disturb anything," Billie confirmed.

The man's head turned at the sound of footsteps. "*Allez* . . . Go now, my friends," he said, making shooing movements with his hands. "See you soon. À *bientôt!*"

—⁂—

One hour later, they waited anxiously at the arched door they had passed on their walk along the edge of the Seine. As promised, their new friend soon opened it and let them in, holding a finger to his lips and looking over his shoulder periodically.

"Come quiet. Á *la cave*," he said, pointing at the floor. "We go."

To the basement.

"I will show," their new friend continued in his broken English, and he led them to a winding staircase that took them down wooden steps. "But I did not let you in. If you . . ." He made a comical gesture like fainting, or dying, eyes closed and tongue sticking out of his mouth. "It is not me. I did not let you in. I did not see."

Billie laughed softly. "*Merci*," she told him. He did not want to take responsibility if she fell dead away like some woman in an opera.

"*Alors . . .*"

In the basement of the morgue, he showed them to a room with shallow glass cabinets around the walls. The cabinets contained papers and photographs of people, pinned in place. The images were from the neck up, the faces slack.

The dead.

"*Les morts non-idenitifiés. Ici.*" The unidentified bodies. "Here *l'année dernière*," he said, extending a single finger and then gesturing to the cabinets.

"Unidentified dead from this past year? *Merci.*" Having images to check would be easier than viewing the actual bodies in the morgue, though she wasn't above doing that if necessary. "*Merci beaucoup.* We are grateful," she said.

The man waved his hand, again smiling—a facial expression that sat at odds with their somber surrounds. "I am grateful to you, my *australiens.* But it is not me. I did not see you," he said, still grinning. He was enjoying this, she thought. This was his rebellion, his way of helping his comrades.

"*Allez!* Go, go. Look," he said, flicking his hands toward the cabinets as he walked away, making his way back to the staircase, and pausing to listen for movement. After a moment he disappeared up the stairs.

Billie looked to Sam and threw her hands up, eyebrows raised. "We got lucky here, Sam. Right to the source." This was sometimes called an "exposition room," where photographs were kept for one year until positively identified by a relative or friend. Each image bore a sequence of numbers, the same as the corresponding morgue register. She grinned, rather pleased with herself, even if it was her nationality and not really her charms that had allowed them access this time.

"Look at dates," she instructed Sam, moving around the cabinets, absorbing one slack face after another. The dead did not reveal their secrets to her, nor did Montgomery. Not yet.

"His last communication was from Paris in the summer of '45, right?" Sam queried as he peered at the images.

She nodded.

They went quiet for a full ten minutes as they slowly circled the room, one from each end, checking face upon unidentified, lifeless face pinned behind the glass, each monochrome photographic specimen representing a life lost. They reminded Billie of a collector's butterflies or insects under that glass, but not quite so spectacularly or colorfully displayed. This was the collection nobody claimed.

"Billie," Sam said suddenly. The tone of his voice gave her a chill and she stopped in place.

"Richard?" she said.

He wordlessly pointed to one of the small black-and-white photographs pinned inside the cabinet before him. "No. Do you think it's possible that this could be . . . ?" He trailed off, not wanting to finish his sentence. "It looks a bit like the man in the photograph you keep on your desk, in the office," he managed, though his voice wavered.

Her heart sped up, and her breathing seemed to stop entirely. *Jack?*

Billie put a hand on Sam's arm to steady herself, and she leaned forward, squinting. "No, it's not Jack," she said with certainty. Then she paused, tilting her head. "Oh goddess, maybe it is? Maybe . . ."

Jack Rake, her husband, dead in Paris? Could it be?

I was surprised to run into him at the Hôtel Lutetia in December. It was an odd and hurried encounter and stayed with me, Simone's letter had read, those words etched into Billie's mind. Simone had sworn it was him. Could he have died that day Simone saw him, or shortly after? She had said he looked anxious. Had that been fear she saw? Had he been running from something, or someone?

"Sam, I need to be sure," she said in a guttural voice that was not her own.

Sam gently placed a large hand on her shoulder, blocking her view. "I can do it. Tell me what to do, Billie, and I will check for you. What do I check for?"

"No, I can do it," she insisted, shaking her head.

Sam looked her directly in the eyes, searching them, from one to the other. "Billie, I will do this for you. Just tell me how. How do you want me to do it?"

She stepped back from the cabinet, from the photograph he was shielding her from. "Match the number on the death photograph here in the cabinet to the record. That's first," she managed, pointing, her eyes cast down.

"Of course, Billie. Then what do you wish me to do?"

"Then we see if Jack—" She stopped and corrected herself. "Then we see if . . . *this person*, this man, is in the cold room."

Twenty-four

—ɯ—

Shyla, is that you?"

Alma McGuire was surprised to see Billie Walker's friend standing before her, looking haunted, at the door of the flat. The young woman was wrapped tightly in a dark blue wool coat, a scarf slung around her shoulders and over her hair, obscuring some of her face.

"Come in, come in. Are you okay? What's happened?" Alma ushered the young woman inside and locked the door behind them, before Shyla had even said a word in response. She'd only ever seen her with Billie, never on her own like this.

From her vantage point on the settee, Ella von Hooft took one look at their unexpected visitor and rose hurriedly from her usual position. "Shyla? Good goddess, what's happened? You look like you've seen a ghost."

Shyla's eyes were wide. She dropped the scarf, and they could see she had blood smeared on her forehead. "No ghost," she said. "A man was in Billie's office. I think he was stealing."

"Oh, how ghastly! A thief! And you've been hurt!" Alma declared.

Shyla shook her head. "Not my blood." Unsteadily, she took a letter opener from the pocket of her coat. It was bloodstained. Her navy gloves were stained as well, and her eyes were riveted to them. She had not even had time to take them off when the man rushed her. "I think it was the man Billie talks about. The detective. I stabbed him."

"Hank Cooper? You stabbed Hank Cooper? He was stealing from Billie's office?" Ella said, confused.

Shyla shook her head. "No, the *other* man," she explained. "The Italian detective."

"Vincenzo Moretti, the private investigator?" Alma asked.

"Well, that bastard!" Ella quickly covered her mouth on instinct. "Sorry for my language, my dear. If you stabbed him, I can assure you he deserved it."

"Billie warned me about him," Shyla said. "He was in there, in her office, and was looking for something. I surprised him and he came at me, right out of her office. He'd been in there and had a gun. I stabbed him with this and he ran away." She made the motion with the stained letter opener, while both women watched her, wide-eyed. "I defended myself."

"Good goddess, are you okay?"

Shyla nodded. "He didn't get me."

"Well, we need to tell the police. Hank Cooper will know what to do," Alma suggested reasonably.

"No gunjies!" Shyla said. "Billie promised me, no cops. They won't believe me when I say it was self-defense . . ."

Alma nodded, understanding. What a mess this was—and after Billie's flat had been broken into as well. Someone dangerous was at work, but Alma knew perfectly well what a shambles the local police had made of Billie's case the previous year. She could well understand this young woman's fear and distrust.

"I have an idea. You leave this with me, my dear," Ella announced imperiously, and without delay she picked up her shining telephone and dialed, as Alma blinked and Shyla stared.

"Hello, Detective Hank Cooper, please. This is Baroness Ella von Hooft."

Shyla shrank back against the wall, no doubt dreading what was to come. Alma put a hand on her shoulder to calm her, and proceeded to part her from the letter opener and her soiled gloves.

"Yes, Hank, it's Ella von Hooft. Billie Walker's mother." She stood with her head high, one hand on her hip, a mannerism Alma recognized in the baroness's daughter as well. "I'm calling because I've stabbed a man . . . That's right. Stabbed him. Vincenzo Moretti I think it was, though it was pretty dark. I'd do it again, too," she added dramatically, and Alma held back a chortle.

"That's right, Hank." There was a pause while Ella listened to him on the other end of the phone, her eyes gazing at the bay outside her window once more. Alma helped Shyla out of her coat, examining it for stains. There were some, but only near the cuffs.

"He's always causing us trouble," Ella declared. "He was in Billie's office and he attacked me. He had a gun. I stabbed him and he ran away like a coward . . . That's right."

Another pause.

"He's lucky I didn't stab him a second time. I could have finished the job."

Twenty-five

—⌇—

For a woman of action, Billie Walker was uncharacteristically motion-less in the basement of the Institut Médico-Légal de Paris.

The grim pinned photographs of unidentified dead and the morgue book filled with slack faces had shown no sign of someone like Richard Montgomery, the man she was in Paris to find, but these professional interests were far from her mind now. Since seeing that photograph, her thoughts were only of Jack.

Although she was wrapped in her coat with the collar up, goose-flesh still covered her as she held the keys for the cold room in one hand, having swiped them from the registry desk. She'd tried the lock, found it worked, and now she was bracing herself before enter-ing the icy domain of the cadavers inside—the remains of people who had met their end under the wheels of motorcars, at the pointed ends of knives and bullets, by way of poisonous mixtures, or in the murky waters of the Seine.

This was not Billie's first time in a morgue, but it was her first time in a morgue that might contain the decomposed remains of her husband.

As she waited, Sam searched for the corresponding record of unidentified body number 0003091946 in the morgue register, pulling open the wide pages of the bleak book on the desk and tracing his finger down the numbers. "Here," he said, and stepped back.

His voice reanimated Billie, and she realized her hand was gripped around the keys like a claw. She moved to the book and bent over it.

He had been found dead in December of 1946.

"What does it say?" Sam asked, looking over Billie's shoulder.

Billie's French was a touch rusty and the scrawl was not always clear, but she understood the morgue register well enough. This man, whoever he was, had been found drowned in the Seine, not far from Pont Neuf, a bridge she—and Jack—knew well. Gooseflesh again crept over her entire body, simply at the name. It seemed this unfortunate man was brought to the morgue without a large delay, owing to this central location in Paris, and thus decomposition was not as bad as it often was in drowning cases. Despite being found quickly, he had not been identified. The doctor who inspected the body was able to determine that bruises on the neck of the corpse indicated foul play. Cause of death was ruled as drowning, but under suspicious circumstances. It sounded like murder to Billie. Had Jack been . . . murdered? Perhaps he had met his death soon after Simone had spotted him?

"The man was strangled and drowned," she said flatly, her tight throat seeming to close up entirely after speaking those six words.

She bent farther and squinted to examine the black-and-white photograph, which was frustratingly small. A resemblance was there in the shape of the face, the hairline. It was a terrible resemblance, accompanied as it was with a look of torment in the features that might haunt Billie for some time to come, she suspected. This man was certainly no L'Inconnue de la Seine—the beautiful, unidentified young woman drowned in the same river some decades before, whose ethereally serene death mask became a popular fixture on the walls of artists' homes. This man had suffered and it showed in the fall of his mouth, which hung open as if caught in a scream. She imagined those cold waters. The drowning . . .

Billie straightened and stepped back from the book, rolling and squeezing the keys absently in her hand. She had paled and felt light-headed, and it doubtless showed.

"It's probably not him, Billie," her assistant tried to assure her, though she didn't know what the odds were exactly. Occam's razor and all that. The simplest explanation was usually the correct one, but just what could be simple about Jack disappearing and showing up two years later, seen by Simone with a new scar and an odd manner? *Jack goes missing in '44. Jack is seen by a mutual friend a couple of years later, in late '46, acting oddly. Jack is killed shortly after.* None of it made sense, unless Jack had terrible secrets he hid from her.

Did he? Did he have terrible secrets? How well had she really known the man she married after stolen weekends of passion during a war that took them from one scene of conflict and horror to another?

"I need to look at him myself," Billie said with cold certainty. "I need to know for sure." If she did not look, did not take this opportunity, she would be haunted by that photograph forever, she knew. She would be haunted by the possibility that Jack's body was in the Paris morgue and she could have identified him, sent him home to Sutton, to his relatives, and the lands where his ancestors had lived.

Sam sucked his lips in for a moment, doubtless realizing she could not be dissuaded. Their new friend was nowhere to be seen. He had left them to their own investigations, for the present. If he discovered them in the cool storage, would he be cross? Possibly. But then he had not specified that anything was off-limits—apart from taking records or corpses. They would talk themselves out of it if they had to.

"Should I use the camera?" Sam asked, and indicated her large handbag. That had been part of the plan, if they found Richard. Or *Jack*.

"Yes," she managed. They should have a record of what they saw, even if in this case it was not for their client. After they went into that room, who knew what would happen? Or if she would remember important details. She opened her handbag and handed the camera to Sam, and a flash to light the images. It would be necessary to use one in the low light.

Sam took it, expertly set up the flash bulb as swiftly as he had been able to load a weapon during the war, and carefully positioned the open morgue register and snapped. The flash was blinding in the low-lit space. Satisfied, he slipped the strap of the camera around his neck, removed the spent bulb and pocketed it for now, then readied another for what they'd find inside.

"Okay," she said, exhaling. It was time.

Billie turned and slid the key into the lock again. The door to the cool room gave way easily, welcoming them. It was colder than outside in the rest of the basement, but not by terribly much.

Billie moved toward the center of the room, then stood still, frozen in place. She was surrounded by metal doors, behind which were body upon dead body. Sam was kind enough to observe Billie's uncharacteristic behavior without comment, no doubt understanding the gravity of the moment well, having had to identify many of his fallen comrades a short few years before. Without a word he searched out the number from the files, moving around the cool space from door to door, checking against the scribbled numbers.

"Here," he said. He had found the corresponding digits on a small rectangular door with a handle.

"Do it," she said.

Sam opened the door on her command and pulled out the long tray. What emerged was a body wrapped in cloth. He covered his nose, impacted by the smell that hit Billie a beat later. "Do you want me to . . . ?" he asked.

"Open it up," Billie said in a small voice, a couple of yards away.

He did. Sam carefully unwrapped the head, then stood back and covered his mouth, reeling.

What was inside the sack of cloth was horrible, too horrible, and far worse than Billie had expected.

They were looking at a dead man from the crown of his head to his clavicle, but it wasn't right. Billie held her breath and forced her gaze to move over the face, the greasy hair, the neck, all of it a horror beyond any she had seen before, despite her frequent close proximity to death. The face of the man who could be Jack was swollen, and his eyes had sunk back into his head so that it was impossible to tell what their color might have been. His skin was tinged with an almost supernatural green—where it was still in place, at least—and much of it seemed to have sloughed off so that there was a strange, shiny substance where the skin might be expected to be. Something was coming out of the nose of the corpse—two white webs starting out of each nostril and fanning downward over the face. They covered the lower face and neck, disappearing into the sheet.

With a rush, Billie tasted the metal that usually came before vomiting, and turned away, fighting the impulse to retch. Sam grabbed her arm to help her and she shook it off and walked in a circle in the center of the cold room, shaking all over.

Quietly, he covered the corpse again.

"No," she managed, doubled over. She raised one hand to stop him. "Just wait," she said. It was a ghastly infestation of mold or fungus of some kind. It was nothing to fear. And if this was Jack, it was better that she knew.

Pull yourself together, Walker.

In time, she moved back toward the body, Sam watching her closely. She shut her eyes and took a breath through cupped hands. When she opened her eyes again, she could see past the webbing, past the horror of the misshapen features of death. The bruising around the neck was apparent, even if it was not so easy to identify now. She tried to take in the face. Those eyes. Those hazel eyes of Jack's. She could not tell if these were them, now darkened by the veil of death.

She was aware of Sam standing very close to her, silent and ready. "I don't know," she whispered, as if not wanting to wake the corpse they had disturbed. "This could be Jack." Her throat had closed again so his name was a croak. "I . . . don't know. I can't feel if it is or not. I don't feel anything at all," she said, aware that she was not making much sense. The little woman in her gut said nothing. That part of her had been shocked into silence. Or perhaps it was that she could not hear it with her blood pumping in her ears.

"Take your time. We've come all this way," Sam said kindly. "I'm here with you, Billie. You are okay. I'll stay here with you until they haul me away."

"Wait. Simone said something about a scar at the neck." She tried to find it, but beneath the sloughing skin and the webbing, and what was left of the bruising indicated in the files, she couldn't see it. "I'm not sure, Sam. It could be. Wait! I know a way," she said with a flash of clarity. She held her breath, hand across her mouth, and with the other hand opened the sheet yet farther.

A foul stench rose up, and Billie wondered what it would have been like to bring a man like this out of the river, strangled and drowned. The cool basement of the morgue had not stopped putrefaction, even if it had slowed it down. "Dear goddess, help me," she muttered to herself.

She was not religious but now might be a moment to reconsider.

With renewed determination she pulled the stained white coverings back until the dead man's sunken chest and stomach were fully exposed, but she realized she could not see the body clearly. It wasn't the light, it was her eyes; they were blurry. Tears, she realized. She wiped her cheeks distractedly with the heel of one palm and with the other hand, not quite touching the skin, traced a finger down to that spot she knew so well, that small mole below Jack's left nipple.

"It's not there," she declared, and exhaled. "Sam, it's not there!"

Her head began shaking side to side and she broke into a relieved smile, her shoulders dropping. "Good goddess. Sam, it's not him. I am sure of it. I don't know this poor departed man, rest his soul."

In a swift movement Sam stepped in, covered the sunken corpse, and pushed the drawer back in. He closed the cabinet door and came to her side. "It's cold in here. Come . . ." he said softly, an arm around her shoulders.

They stepped out, closed the door behind them, and found their host at the base of the staircase, looking more expectant than irritated by their adventuring. "*Vous etes ici!*" he exclaimed. "Here are you," he added, trying out his English.

"Thank you, friend," Sam said. "We did not find the men, but *merci*. You have helped us a lot. We know they are not here."

The man's face became solemn. "I am sorry, my Australian friends," he said, arms extended.

"*Merci*. Thank you," Sam replied, understanding he was wishing them well, and slid the key onto the desk. "The keys."

The man waved his hand. "Do not tell, eh?" He winked.

"*Non, non. Merci beaucoup,*" Billie managed in turn, though her heart was still pounding in her ears, her words seeming to come from some far-off, foreign place. She was aware that he might notice that she had succumbed to tears, and that thought was quite unacceptable. What a damn shame it was that it was not fashionable to wear smoked glasses at night. Her round cheaters would have been handy in such a moment.

"*Bonne chance*," the man said, and they wished him the same.

She sincerely hoped *chance*, luck, would be on their side. And that it had been on Jack's.

———

Billie and Sam sat near the banks of the Seine, watching a boat covered in fairy lights float peacefully downriver. It was a sight of such beauty that it could not come from the same reality as the corpse they had both encountered—let alone the fact that it had been fished out of the very same river, not even a year before.

Before them were two small glasses of brandy, a tablecloth, the incomparable view. They had a table to sit at, a waiter to call on, and even a wool blanket to hold back the night chill, presently placed over Billie's long legs. "I have everything I need right now, dear Sam. And, well, I don't think I shall eat again in some time." The menu, though it would have been tempting hours earlier, was not of interest after their morgue experience.

"What you need is more brandy," he told her. "Doctor's orders."

Billie laughed, then became serious. "Sam, you were . . ." She tried to find the words, at a loss for once. "Just thank you," she told him simply. "Truly. You've been a gentleman tonight."

"I hope I usually am?" he ventured.

"Oh yes. I think you know what I mean, though."

A vision of the corpse flashed into her mind—that webbing, the sunken eyes . . .

"There's no need to thank me, Ms. Walker," Sam said, reaching a hand across the table and bringing her focus back to the moment. "That is a hard thing to have to do."

"You've been there yourself, I take it," she said, looking at his hand on hers. It was his scarred but whole hand, and she found it warm and reassuring.

"Brandy. That's what they gave me. It helped. Is it helping?" he asked her.

She nodded. "I'm not sure how I'll feel tomorrow, but right now it's helping all right, as are you. It's been such a strange trip. Paris is changed. So much has changed," she said. "I didn't see it at first, but it's true. I thought at first it was like stepping back in time, but it's not. Nothing is the same."

She frowned as she watched the glittering water. The shifting reflections. The movement. Nothing was ever still. Time moved forward, seasons cycling through, the same and yet different. No moment could be preserved.

"Paris is still beautiful, Billie. Not down in that morgue, perhaps, but the rest of the city," he said, and smiled.

She turned to face him. "We were lucky to find him, the man who let us in. He liked you," she said.

"You also, I'd say," Sam replied. "Come, let's finish our drinks and walk back. Notre-Dame is close to here. I've always wanted to see it."

She nodded again. Thank goddess for Sam. She tried to imagine what it might have been like to sit there alone, staring at the dark water, as if into an abyss. "Yes, I know Notre-Dame well. It's beautiful at night." She'd spent countless hours there when she was living in Paris. It was a quiet, safe space, and that meant something for a young woman alone.

Billie found her eyes lingering on Sam's smile, his mouth. Yes, he was comforting to be around, she realized, and not just on this unusual Paris night. Even in the cramped conditions of their Lancaster plane, he had been a quiet, reassuring presence, bolstering her spirits in often unspoken ways, and then there were the countless times they had shared late-night shadows in Sydney, trailing targets or pretending to be a couple as they slid into bars and doss-houses, holding hands, having each other's backs.

"You know, my mother quite likes you," Billie confessed, and felt a horrifying warmth spread across her cheeks as soon as the words left her lips.

"Is that so. And what does her daughter think?" he asked.

Billie looked down at the tablecloth. "Her daughter thinks you are a fine gentleman, Sam. One in a million."

He grinned. "Then you are one in ten million, I'd say."

He did have a way with words. Billie straightened in her chair and adjusted the wool blanket, but it did little to sober her. That third glass of brandy had likely been a mistake. Why else would she be thinking of her assistant's lips?

Billie paled, and she instinctively sat back, retreating from him. "I know we are here for work, but I have to say it's a real pleasure to be here with you, Billie. Working with you is always a pleasure, but I'm grateful you chose to bring me on this journey."

"Well, it hasn't all been a pleasure, what with the automobile crashes and corpses," she pointed out.

"Yes, but with *you*."

His words hung in the air, her eyes again riveted to the lips they had come from, and somewhere in the distance someone was playing a violin. It was a cinematic moment and Billie considered everything she knew about Paris and its charms. "It's a romantic city, I'll give it that," she said carefully, catching herself.

"It's one of those cities you read so much about," he said. "I've always been keen to see the catacombs as well. Do you think we could take a look, just for an hour or so tomorrow, perhaps?"

The mention of the catacombs brought that day in 1938 vividly to the fore. Her first date with Jack, if "date" was the right word for it.

Jack.

Her husband.

Billie paled, her hand retreating from Sam's. "I . . . no. No, I don't think so."

When she looked up, just past his shoulder, she swore she could see the face of her husband across the river. Jack was there, just for a second, she could swear it, but she blinked and he was gone, the slim figure of some stranger turning and blending into the shadows once more. Billie blinked again and shook her head.

Sensing something wrong, Sam's expression changed in an instant. "I'm sorry, Ms. Walker, I know we are here on a job. And suggesting it so soon after . . . tonight's experience. I apologize for suggesting it. I should know better."

Now she was seeing Jack everywhere—in the morgue, on the banks of the Seine.

Billie shook her head again, this time in response to Sam, and noticing her glass was emptied of every last drop, she motioned for the waiter. "No, Sam, you didn't say anything wrong. It is a very famous attraction and you're allowed to sightsee, and to have the odd moment off even in this crazy trade," she said, and stood up, folding the wool blanket and indicating to the waiter she wanted *l'addition*, the check. A good night's rest and maybe she could shake the horrors of the evening off. "You are doing quite enough work at the moment. Why don't you see the catacombs for yourself tomorrow? I'll get in touch with Simone again and see if I can't narrow down some neighborhood hangouts to canvas for Montgomery." She knew best where he might be found, if her theory was correct.

Sam stood, looking concerned. "Did I say something to upset

you? If I did, I am awfully sorry, Billie." He helped her with the blanket and pushed their chairs back under the table neatly.

"No, it's not you, dear Sam," she said, looking out at the Seine. "Please do some sightseeing tomorrow. I'll catch you later and perhaps in the evening we can prowl Paris for Montgomery."

This town has ghosts, she wanted to say, feeling sobered by her memories of the catacombs. One ghost in particular would not stop haunting her.

Twenty-six

—◊◊◊—

Detective Inspector Cooper," Alma McGuire said. "Please do come in."

Cooper doffed his hat to Alma and entered Baroness von Hooft's flat at Cliffside, holding something in a small box. "Is the baroness in?" he inquired in a formal manner, doubtless knowing she was nearby. He seemed to instinctively know how to deal with Ella, which made Alma smile.

"Indeed I am, Inspector. Thank you for coming," Ella called out, and sauntered to the front door in shimmering emerald Schiaparelli beads to welcome her visitor from the constabulary. "What an honor," she said. "I gather you are not here to arrest me?"

He inclined his head. "No, ma'am. I am not here to arrest you." He took in her glamorous ensemble without comment.

"Then I guess we can still be friends," Ella said, sounding very much like her daughter. She placed one hand on her hip. "Please do come inside. What would you like to drink?"

"Nothing, thank you. I can't stay long," he said, looking around, holding his welt-edge fedora in large hands.

"Don't say that, Inspector. You'll have a tiny tipple," Ella declared, and took him by the elbow. "Alma, bring the man a drink," she called out as she led him to the settee. The man did not stand a chance.

Cooper seemed to realize there was no point in refusing, and he took a seat on the plush cushions opposite the baroness, as directed. "I thank you for your telephone call. You are unharmed, I hope, Baroness?"

"Quite," Ella said proudly, chin raised. "Not so the other fellow."

"I see," he said, resisting a smile. Alma presented him with a glass of sherry, which he courteously took and placed on the table with a thank-you. "I paid Mr. Vincenzo Moretti a visit. If you are willing to press charges, I do believe we may have something." He opened the box in his hand. "Do you recognize these?"

Ella gasped. Inside were a pair of glittering drop earrings, with ten little square sapphires set in a vertical line, surrounded by small diamonds. "Why, those are my sapphire earrings! They were taken from Billie's bedroom. They've been missing for months."

He nodded. "I thought so. They fit the description on file. These were found on a young woman at The Dancers and traced back to Vincenzo Moretti, who had given them to her to wear, according to her testimony. And they were found in his flat."

"That rat! How dare he!" Ella picked up one of them, holding it in her fingertips, admiring the way the light shone through the deep-blue stones. She had missed them dearly, Alma knew. Billie had said they might have been found.

"What was he doing with these? And what was he doing in Billie's office?" Ella demanded.

"I can't yet say," Cooper replied, his large hands clasped in front of him. Alma wondered what precisely that meant. He couldn't or *wouldn't* say? "Moretti has been arrested in connection with the theft of your earrings, Baroness von Hooft," he informed Ella. "He is thus far cagey about exactly how he received his stomach wound. He's in hospital presently, under police guard."

Ella gently placed the earring back in the box. "Did I, um, get him good?" she ventured.

"Perhaps you could walk me through exactly what happened, Baroness." Cooper stood up, encouraging her to do the same.

Alma watched this exchange with no small dose of concern, but Ella kept her cool. "Well," she said, standing up, "I was in the reception where that lovely young man she works with sits, and I opened the door to Billie's office and bam!" Her Marcel waves quivered as she made a stabbing motion. "*Stab!*"

"Where exactly did you stab him?"

Ella appeared puzzled, her thin brows pulling together. "By the door to the office. To my daughter Billie's office."

"I mean on his person," Cooper specified patiently.

Shyla hadn't furnished them with those details. "Stomach? I couldn't say, exactly," Ella replied cautiously. "It was dark and it all happened frightfully fast."

Cooper nodded. "I see," he said.

"Well, I couldn't," she shot back.

Alma watched the exchange silently, wondering if Moretti had admitted to being in Billie's office and had described the woman who stabbed him. Shyla and Ella had a few things in common, but appearance was not one of them.

"I couldn't see much of anything. My eyesight, you see," the baroness added dramatically, and shrugged. It must have pained her somewhat to admit this sign of age, but it was a good move.

Cooper remained poker-faced. "And you had a knife on you at the time, is that right?" he asked.

"The letter opener," Ella said, and Alma handed it to her, who then handed it to Cooper, quite neatly obscuring any remaining fingerprints, should there be reason to check.

Cooper, who had remained stoic and calm in the face of Ella's forceful personality, now raised his brows, accepting the item and noting the blood on it. "I had thought Shyla was helping out at the office," he pointed out, inspecting the blade.

Ella licked her lips. "Why, yes, she is. She was, uh, busy."

He looked up at her. "I see. Do you know where she is now?"

"No," Ella lied, and swallowed.

Cooper watched her. "And I understand that Billie's flat was broken into as well—is that correct?"

"Oh yes, it was. Yes. A ghastly thing," Ella lamented. "This is a respectable building!"

"I'm sure it is," he agreed, and sat back down. Ella took this cue to sit as well, but then he turned to look at her, still holding the blade in his hands. Cooper's hazel eyes were direct, drilling into hers, and Alma, observing this from across the room, imagined the uncomfortable sensation of succumbing to an X-ray, unable to break away. Could he see each of Ella's lies writ large? As plain as if they were painted on the wall? After a time, Cooper turned his head again, unlocking that intense gaze, and Ella's shoulders dropped.

Oh heavens.

Alma, unsure of how else to ease the situation, fetched the bottle of sherry to refill his glass, knowing full well he had not yet touched it. "Can we tempt you with some more, Inspector?" she pressed.

The inspector shook his head. "No, I'm afraid I must go, but I will be in touch again soon," he said, ceremoniously raising his glass, taking a quick swig, and replacing it on the table. "I do thank you for your hospitality. And for this weapon."

"We'll get it back?" Alma interjected, hoping to take his focus off her employer.

"Oh yes. Moretti is not pressing charges, and in fact seems content to pretend he did it to himself."

"Oh, I see," she said, relieved.

"An awkward angle for a self-inflicted wound. Still, I would like to keep this for a while, if I may?"

"Certainly," Ella said. "So, that horrible man will be in jail where he belongs? You know he caused my late husband quite a bit of trouble, and just last year . . . Well, my Billie believes he followed her, and caused her trouble, too. He's rather obsessed with her, I believe."

Or his clients were, Alma thought, wondering if it could be both.

"Your late husband, Barry, was a good cop, Baroness," Cooper was telling Ella. "I'm not sure if I ever told you, but he did arrest Vincenzo Moretti for bribery, back when he was in the force. I believe that was before you two met, but it might explain his . . . interest," he said delicately. "Don't fear, Moretti is in hospital for now, and he won't be out for a little while."

It seemed to Alma that he was holding something back, but then Billie had told her this was his way. He had a shell around him that she had tried unsuccessfully to crack, Alma knew. Ella knew it, too.

"Good," Ella declared. "I'm glad he's off the streets. Thank you for returning my earrings." She sipped her sherry and placed one manicured hand on the box. "I am very pleased to have them back after all this time. I'm not surprised it was that lowlife who was responsible."

"And I am pleased to see you don't seem very rattled by the encounter," he said, watching her closely. "You are more like your daughter than I thought," he observed aloud, which to Alma seemed to imply, among other things, that he knew well he was being deceived about her involvement in the altercation, and the likely reason for that. "Do pass on my regards, if you hear from Billie. Or Shyla," Cooper added, and shook Ella's hand courteously, while she tried to maintain a straight face under his shrewd gaze.

Twenty-seven

—— ∿ ——

He is familiar to you? *Vous le connaissez?*"

The man looked at her, his frown exaggerated, showing off full lips. "*Non.*" He was holding the best of Vera's photographs of Richard Montgomery, turning it in his fingers, as if the back of it might jog a memory. He wore high, pleated trousers, well cut, and a collared shirt that showed his slim, muscular build. In the pocket of those fine trousers were one hundred of Billie's francs, so his response was disappointing. Was he worth another ten?

"*Vous êtes sûr?*" She pressed some more francs into his hand. He was happy to accept.

While Sam was doing some enforced sightseeing, Billie had spent a long lunch with her friend Simone, reminiscing about old times with the aid of some red wine, and going over possible places for Billie to canvass for Montgomery, if the man was indeed living a new life in the more liberal and less risky scene in Paris. She'd needed that company, especially after the shock of having received news of yet another break-in—this one in her office, and involving Vincenzo Moretti, of all people. Shyla had been there, apparently, and was unharmed, but probably dearly wishing she hadn't agreed to help Billie.

Still buzzing slightly from the heavy-bodied wine she'd consumed with her friend, Billie had taken to the streets, visiting some of the kamp haunts Simone had mentioned. Though they did not advertise openly, there were many of these clubs for men, much like that which Simone had shown her for women, and now that Billie knew where they were located, the near-invisible kamp network of men became more transparent. One only needed to watch, discreetly, to see who came and went, and to observe the manner in which the men interacted.

Billie had hoped she might eyeball her target, not at the morgue, which she had now ruled out, but on the streets of Paris, in the cafés or parks. Thus far, however, she had not, nor had any of the men she was able to speak to. Or at least they weren't willing to say, which might not be surprising under the circumstances. However, this one—a well-put-together man of about twenty-five, dark-skinned and chic in appearance—was happy to string her along for a few francs, and Billie couldn't decide if that was progress or a sign that she ought to pack it in for the day.

"*Non*," he said, shaking his dark head, and handed the picture back. His voice was soft as he spoke, and though she had been hopeful at first, it seemed she was at a dead end.

"*Merci, monsieur*," Billie said, giving up on him and her francs.

True, Sam might get further, but his French was essentially nonexistent. They would come back that night, late, she decided. The darkness would make it harder to spot her target as he casually went about Parisian life, perhaps, but it also might loosen the lips of his friends—if he had any. And if he had former friends, men he had blackmailed, well, that might make her chances of getting information all the better. Getting into bars for homosexual men would be a challenge for Billie. She'd have to prime Sam for the task.

"*Attendez . . .*" the man said unexpectedly, turning, and Billie looked up from her handbag, where she had secreted Montgomery's photograph away. He swallowed, his Adam's apple moving up and down, and nodded toward an entrance Billie now knew led to a small bar for men looking for male company. "There is an Englishman some nights. He is, how do you say? *Similaire.*"

Billie stood a touch taller, her heart lifting. "*Merci.*" It seemed the man had been weighing up whether to tell her. "He is English?" she asked, hoping for a confirmation.

"*Oui.* The same, maybe." He shrugged, as if to indicate that he was not sure, and walked away, his head down.

The stranger left her several francs lighter but feeling encouraged. Yes, it was something to go on, a new path to pursue that was far from the grim possibilities of the morgue.

Billie was walking back to the Métro, buoyed by the possibilities of her new theory, when she became aware that she was not alone. The little woman in her gut clued her in to the presence of a set of eyes on her. As her senses sharpened after her long lunch, so did her certainty that she was being followed. Was it the man who had spoken with her? No. He would have no reason, would he?

Once she was back underground in the Métro, she was able to catch a glimpse of the man behind her—trench coat, fedora, slim to average build, slightly ruddy complexion, she quickly noted. This was definitely not the man she had spoken with, though he did seem distantly familiar . . . He had taken the same train, and got off at the same subway stop at Opéra, taking the same stairwell up to street level. Other people had, too—this was a popular area—but he was unaccompanied, a bit too neat, and those instincts of hers were rarely wrong. He was not her man, Montgomery, nor any of the men with whom she had broached conversations within Montmartre. He didn't seem Parisian, but he did not have the distinctive quality of a tourist. There was something off about him that put Billie on edge. But then, her instincts had been out of kilter lately, hinting at danger around every corner, especially since that unexplained motorcar clash outside London. It was as if there had been shadows following her since. Still, if there was one thing she had learned over the years, and in the course of her investigations, it was that her instincts were to be heeded.

On edge, but trying not to show it, Billie continued her casual progress toward the Ritz, deciding her next move. First, she made her way across the road to the opposite side of the street, easily negotiating the uneven cobblestones in her trusty stack-heeled Oxfords, with their quiet fabric soles. She stopped abruptly to look into the window of a patisserie, one hand at her forehead, and her heart sank. In the glass reflection, she could see the trench-coat-clad figure crossing to her side of the road. *Blast.* Trying not to let the tension show on her face, she began moving again and took a narrow road to her right, heading away from the hotel. It was more of an alley, really, she realized too late. Risky. She knew parts of Paris well, but not the area around Place Vendôme, having not had reason, or budget, to stay at the Ritz before. Realizing her error, she sprinted ahead a few yards, heart quick in her chest, and slid into a sunken doorway. She waited. *Please don't come this way, please don't . . .*

Footsteps.

Blast.

Yes, he was following her. There was no doubt about it. Barely breathing as the sound of the footsteps grew closer, Billie readied herself. She reached down, slid the Colt out of her garter, and flattened herself as best she could against the crumbling wall to the side of the old wooden door. *Why did I have to send Sam away?* she wondered. Her assistant would be currently walking through the Empire of the Dead under the city, and here she was, on street level, not two blocks from her hotel room, facing her own possible demise.

Now the footsteps slowed.

One, two, one, two, one, two . . .

He paused. Billie held her breath.

One, two, one, two . . .

There was another pause.

One . . .

Just ahead of her, the shoulder of a trench coat appeared beyond the wall. She had not a moment to waste. If she was wrong, it would be a bit of an embarrassment, but if she was right, this was life-or-death. Billie raised her right arm, pointed her weapon, which was cocked and loaded, and stepped forward.

"Looking for someone?" she said, her Colt in his side.

His mouth fell open. "I'm frightfully sorry. That's rather sloppy on my part, really," he said in a British accent, palms raised. "Don't kill me, will you?"

He looked and sounded like an Englishman, a smattering of freckles across his skin, and though he was older, he reminded her startlingly of Jack for a moment. It was the accent, she thought, or something in his bearing. She moved behind him now, her gun in the small of his back.

"And tell me, why shouldn't I? Do go on and convince me," she said into the back of his neck, with real menace, and jabbed the end of her gun at him for good measure. She'd had the feeling she was being pursued, and she did hate to be so very right.

In a heartbeat her right arm was shoved to the side, gun swinging out, and she was airborne, flipped over the man's shoulder in a neat and controlled move. Just before she hit the cold ground with full force, flat on her back, his arms were underneath her, catching her. Her tailbone smacked into the ground with a sharp jolt that made her gasp.

Billie found herself looking up, wide-eyed and furious, at the man as he bent over her. Already he had a hand around her little Colt, the two of them holding it as she pointed it skyward. She gritted her teeth, straining. His arm was stronger than hers, and he had a clear advantage from his position. They stayed there for a moment, in a stalemate, Billie struggling to hold fast.

"I do apologize, Ms. Walker. I had thought you might do me some damage there," the man apologized, still not letting go.

"What is this?" she demanded. "How is it that you know my name? Why are you following me?" She was breathless and a touch embarrassed by their tussle. Being on her back was no good. No good at all. With sudden force she tucked into a roll, swift and precise, his wrist twisting and his hand letting go. She came up on her knees on the ground, gun drawn on him once more, and only distantly aware of the damage she'd done to her stockings.

Blast. They were expensive.

"We have a mutual friend in Hank Cooper," the stranger explained, his palms up again. He lit up with a smile as he looked at her on her knees, staring at him fiercely over the barrel of her Colt. "I'm here to help you, not to hurt you. Though you do seem quite capable on your own."

He extended a hand to help her up. She didn't accept it.

Cooper?

"We shouldn't spend all day on our knees here. Someone might notice," he said.

"Hank Cooper sent you?" she asked finally, rising to stand on her own.

She watched as he did the same, slowly, palms up, careful not to move suddenly lest she loose a bullet. "He gave you my number, I do believe, though you haven't called it yet. I'm Lieutenant Archie Harrison."

Harrison?

Her shoulders dropped. She remembered the name from the card, though that's all Hank had written down for her. The thought of Hank, and their conversation in his office back in Sydney, made her ache. Why was it that here, in this alley, she found herself missing Sydney? Or was she missing Hank? He had been quite emphatic in his warnings about her poking around, trying to find out more about Hessmann, but so far she had been focusing on the Montgomery case. Yet here was his contact?

She dusted herself off with one hand, the other still on her nickel-plated weapon, eyes not leaving him.

"You can call me Archie, if you will," he said, but his wary eyes were on her gun.

"You're not planning on taking this from me, are you?" she said, gesturing to the Colt. "Because I have some strong ideas on that score."

"You're not still planning to use it, I hope? Because I have some strong ideas about not wanting to get shot."

"Well, that depends. Tell me your number," Billie demanded, though already she could feel her muscles beginning to relax.

"The one Hank gave you, do you mean?" He rattled off the numbers with ease. Billie had an excellent memory, and the number he gave fit with her recollections. This was either Archie or an excellent and well-prepared con man.

She lowered her Colt, and the two faced each other, each looking quickly over their shoulders to see if their exchange had been observed by anyone else in the alley.

"And how do you know Hank? You were in military intelligence together?" Billie guessed.

Harrison grinned in response, evading her question. "I must say, you're everything he and Tom, my man in Paris, said you'd be."

"Is that so? Who is your man in Paris, exactly?" She didn't know a Tom in France.

Archie didn't answer. "Avert your eyes for a moment, won't you?" she asked, and he did so willingly. In a practiced move, she lifted both her skirt and slip, and slid the Colt back into its hand-sewn holster. She smoothed her skirt back down. Her stockings were a mess, irreparable, she decided at a glance. A loose, dark curl had fallen over her eye and she pulled it back and secured it with a hairpin.

"You've made me ruin my stockings. Do you know how expensive these bloody things are?" she complained.

Harrison laughed.

"It's not funny," she said, and he turned around to face her again. "Now that I think of it, I believe I may have spotted you at the Ritz the day I arrived." He'd been smoking a cigar. "What say you tell me *why* you've been following me. Surely you don't give all of Hank's friends this kind of treatment," she said.

He laughed again. "No, ma'am, I do not treat all of Hank's friends this way, though in truth not many of them come to London and Paris." He took a small step forward. "You've caused quite a stir, you realize," he said. "Half of Odessa wants your head for what you did to Hessmann."

Her throat dried up. There was that word Hank had mentioned to her, had warned her to look out for. She opened her mouth to deliver another comeback, but found she had none. "Really?"

"Really. You need to watch your step while you're here."

Billie shook her head. "I mean I know it's a watch word, or a group of some kind, but I don't quite understand," she managed. "What happened with Hessmann was all the way back in Sydney." Of course, she realized her error as soon as the words left her lips.

"How do you think he got there? He had friends, and they'd been operating that ratline rather well until you came along and broke things up," he replied, then looked over his shoulder again.

"I did realize he had people helping him . . ." But all that had seemed so remote, with Richard Montgomery's case keeping her so busy, and Australia half a world away. Not to mention memories of Jack Rake flooding her brain.

"Perhaps you didn't realize just how many friends he had. These people don't mess around, Billie Walker. They look after their own, and they'd be well aware of your recent travels."

Hank had said the same.

"Right." She took a breath, heart in her stomach, then kicked the ground with her heel. The bothersome ladders in the knees of her nylons now seemed—almost—insignificant, in the face of this news. "Shall we go somewhere to discuss this or is the alley here our only option?"

"This isn't terribly civilized, is it?" he admitted.

"No. The way I see it, a friend of Hank's is a friend of mine," she said. "Or ought to be. Would you like to come to my room for a drink in an hour? Don't take that the wrong way . . ." she quickly added. "But it is somewhere private we can talk. Would I be right if I guessed you know where I'm staying, anyway?"

He nodded.

—ᴡ—

Lieutenant Archie Harrison arrived at Billie's hotel room at the agreed time.

"Please do come in, Archie. I suppose you know about my assistant, Samuel Baker," she said, indicating her tall companion, who was standing a few feet from the door, watching him. Billie had been pleased to find Sam in his room, back from his morning in the catacombs, when she returned. She wouldn't be insisting on his absence again any time soon.

If Archie was unhappy with Sam's presence, he didn't let on. He calmly removed his trench coat and folded it over his arm.

"Anything said in this room stays with us, and I assure you, Sam is to be trusted," Billie explained. She took his coat and placed it over a chair. Now that he was in her plush hotel room, instead of a back alley, she could again see he was well attired, if conservatively so. His shoes shone. His shave was close, hair neat.

Archie nodded good-naturedly. "It's quite all right. Hank had said so as well." He looked in Sam's direction. "Pleasure to make your acquaintance."

"Very good. Please have a seat. Now, what can I get you? I have whisky, but they are quite good at making anything you want magically appear at the Ritz," Billie said. "Choose your poison, sir."

Archie dutifully sat, first seeming to measure every angle of the room for possible escape routes, much like their mutual friend, Hank, would, and then he broke into a charming, crooked smile. "I do hope that isn't literal, Ms. Walker. Whisky would be a delight."

"I'm afraid I have no ice chips, though I could arrange them. No poison, either. You may call me Billie, if you like."

"Thank you, Billie. I'll take it neat."

"And we can thank my client, who is funding this particular trip," Billie said as she arranged three glasses and poured.

"Hank did explain, though he knew you were likely to dig around about Hessmann's colleagues as well." His gaze was still sweeping the room. Billie could almost hear him measuring up the distance to the exits, and to Sam. "This is not a bad room for the Cambon side," Archie said, sounding casual. "Some of the rooms are quite small."

"Indeed. I've done well. I felt the stench of Nazi on the Vendôme side would be too injurious to my senses," she replied. "And could ruin an otherwise fine stay."

At this, Archie laughed aloud. He was joined by Sam, who had finally broken character from the tough guy standing in the corner.

Billie handed Sam his drink as she passed, and presented her visitor with his. "I'd hate to sleep in the same bed that Göring did, though of course my client was unlikely to put me up in the Suite Impériale. Private inquiry work isn't quite so glamorous."

Hermann Göring, the man who established the Gestapo secret police and the notorious concentration camps, had been one of the Nazi high command that had infamously taken over one half of the Ritz during the German occupation of Paris, essentially dividing the hotel down the middle, with Nazis staying on the Vendôme side and French civilians permitted to stay on the Cambon side, where Billie's room was located. It had been, Billie believed, the only hotel in Paris with such an arrangement. The dining room had been mixed—French civilians and Nazi brass.

"Goebbels spent a fair bit of time here as well," Archie commented, sipping his drink. "Nice drop."

"Thank you. And Chanel lives upstairs. Or did?"

"Yes," he confirmed. "She did. I believe she may have decided to become better acquainted with Switzerland."

She'd heard some rumors about Coco's association with the Nazis during that time. Only rumors, of course, but there had been talk of a German aristocrat and Nazi propaganda officer. Certainly she had not lost her home, possessions, or business, as many French had. Her couture house was on the Rue Cambon outside, though it had closed through the war, as she had famously declared it was "not a time for fashion."

"I imagine her lover Baron Günther von Dincklage finds it less easy to stalk these corridors now his mates have been defeated, or blown their brains out in their bunkers," Harrison said. "Perhaps the baron joined her in Switzerland."

So, it had been true about the Nazi lover. Other Frenchwomen who had consorted with the Germans during the war had been imprisoned, many forced into humiliating displays, paraded through the streets with their hair shorn and clothes ripped off during the *épuration*—the wave of official trials that followed the French liberation and the fall of the Vichy regime—but not Gabrielle "Coco" Chanel. From the Antipodes Billie had not known fully what were rumors and what was fact. What a fascinating friend Cooper had.

"Well, this is all very interesting. I take it you are still intelligence, Archie?"

His smile gave her the answer. Of course, he would not say it aloud but it was clear enough. "We have a bond, I think, in our dislike of Nazis," Archie said. "Let me put it that way."

"We are no orphans there, I'd like to think."

He took another sip of whisky and made a satisfied face. "You'd be surprised. There are a fair few people who have rather taken their focus off the Nazis, in favor of worrying about the communists. Tell me, who exactly did you meet at Australia House?"

"At Australia House? Why do you ask?" Billie sat on the arm of the settee, and Sam stuck close to her.

"Well, you weren't in London very long, but you certainly made an impression."

"I did?"

He sat forward. "Oh yes." The way he said it made it sound like it should be obvious.

"We did have a strange car try to run us off the road outside London. Are you saying that someone at Australia House might be responsible for . . . ?"

"Not necessarily directly, but yes, it is possible that someone there alerted interested parties as to your presence here in Europe, and your possible intentions. Once they heard you intended to dig around, I'd say they took the news rather badly . . . considering your activities in Australia."

Billie stood up and paced back and forth for a few moments. "I do follow that, Archie," Billie said. "And I grant that the war-crime trials at the moment would stir things up, but I'm confused. I haven't actually been digging around, nor have I made ground with tracing Hessmann's colleagues here, as yet anyway. I've so far been too focused on my own case." *And on Jack*, she thought. "The investigation I'm being paid for is proving trickier than I'd anticipated, and I must earn my keep." She looked around. "No, I can't really see what threat they think I am," she concluded. It wasn't like she was breaking up Nazi smuggling rings all over the place, much as she might like to.

Archie leaned back and savored his drink. "Are you quite sure about that?" he asked.

"What do you mean?"

"Billie, you do realize you stirred things up almost from the day you landed, and you've been followed since you hit Paris. When I got word, I had to follow you all the way here from London."

She had wondered about being followed, but her instincts had been off. It was the proximity of her old stomping grounds with Jack Rake, that letter from Simone . . .

"But my flat was broken into, and my office. That's in Sydney," she protested. No, she could hardly believe it was related. "Moretti, who broke into the office, had a grudge against my father," she explained. "He's been on my radar for years."

"But what of your father's would he want in your office? Or your flat? Just what kind of a man is this Moretti? Is Hank aware of him?"

Her father had warned her about Vincenzo Moretti, and he had been a problem since she got back from Europe and reopened the agency—more than being a rival PI could account for. If something smelled off, he usually wasn't far away. It had been Hank who told her the reason for Moretti's gripe with her father—Barry Walker had arrested him once, while he was still working as a detective.

"Oh yes. Hank knows about him. Moretti and my family go way back . . ." *Moretti, who had been caught up in . . . the Hessmann affair.*

She blanched. He'd been working for a Nazi the year before—maybe he was working for one now? It figured that he'd back the fascists.

"Yes, Hank is aware of him," she confirmed again soberly, suddenly missing the detective inspector keenly. Hank had warned her. Could it really all be connected, somehow?

And now she recalled that odd meeting with Basil Aldrich; how he had not had more information about Richard, how he had made those disapproving remarks. She'd dismissed him as just another conservative man with backward ideas. There were plenty of those around, in her experience. Had it been more than that? Had those been veiled threats? Had he been keeping tabs, seeing what her next movements were likely to be, so he could pass on the information?

It's terribly unladylike, Basil had said of her work. *Not to mention dangerous.*

"So everything that's happening . . . this whole mess in Australia with the break-ins, isn't about the case I'm working on? It's about a dead Nazi?"

"I'd say so. I don't know who this chap is you're pursuing, but it's certainly possible you have bigger fish to fry. You're in quite a bit of danger," Archie told her.

"I can handle danger," she shot back.

He looked at her kindly, his eyes crinkling at the corners. "I like your spirit, I do. But Hank won't forgive me if you get yourself killed, and for that matter neither will my man in Paris. You have some admirers, Billie, I will say that, and so you see I'm afraid I have no choice but to help you, whether you want me to or not." He crossed one leg over the other. "I assume the fact that you did not call me means you do not want help? I do hope you won't make this too difficult."

Billie leaned against the wall, arms folded. "What are you proposing? And who is this man in Paris you keep mentioning?"

"Tom. A colleague of mine who was an acquaintance of yours, I believe . . . or perhaps I have that wrong," he said.

Billie sighed. "I realize you deal in cryptic messages, Archie, but must you be quite so . . . mysterious? An acquaintance of mine? I don't think I know a Tom."

He simply nodded, again evading her questions. "Just know I'll be keeping an eye on you, so try not to kill me for a start. Deal? Though I hope I won't make it quite so easy as it was today. That was sloppy work."

"It was," she said bluntly. Perhaps she wasn't the only one losing their touch.

"I did hate to throw you like that," he said, and Sam stiffened. He opened his mouth to say something, but Billie had the next word.

"I didn't hate to best you," she shot back at Archie, who laughed again.

"Yes, yes indeed. You are just as he described you. Extraordinary." He tipped his glass back. It was empty now. "I suppose Hank told you about the Port of Marseille?"

She shook her head. "It must have slipped his mind."

"The place you led Hank to—the property that burned down just outside Sydney? It didn't leave as many clues as we'd have liked, but there were remnants of crates with stamps showing they had passed through the Port of Marseille."

Her heart sped up. "So that's the route: Port of Marseille to the port near Botany?" She crossed the room to sit next to Harrison, now excited by the opportunity afforded by a well-informed ally.

"One of them, undoubtedly. We have a man in Marseille looking into it. In fact, we rather wondered if your coming to France might be related?"

She shrugged. "No, but what ratline did Hessmann travel through? Do we know? Did he travel through Spain or Italy, as so many seem to, or did he go a more direct route to Australia? Or did he possibly travel through France, with the goods?"

At this, Archie grew introspective. "I can't say, I'm afraid."

"You know, I have suspected at times that I've been followed; I mean, even before you tried to sneak up on me."

"Embarrassing work that was. I do hope you will forgive me." He rose from the settee, evidently having said his piece.

"And that incident with the car was very suspicious," Sam added, having thus far barely said a word throughout the meeting, content for his boss to run the questioning, as was her preference.

"Yes. I'm not sure I was aware of an incident with a car before you mentioned it," Archie said, frowning deeply and turning to Billie. "Was this after Australia House?"

"Everything was. I barely left the hotel for the first two days, after the air travel," Billie said.

"Good people there at Australia House. Good people, but underresourced. Though I dare say someone there has loose lips and questionable friends."

It only took one person. "Do you think Hessmann got his papers at Australia House?" she pressed. "There was one man, Basil Aldrich, who I can't say I trust." That meeting certainly had left a bad taste in her mouth. What had he said? *Lives were lost on both sides. Let them have peace and stay out of it . . .*

Archie thought on her question, bringing a hand to his closely shaved chin. "Aldrich? I'll check him out." He pulled a small notepad from his breast pocket and scribbled something down. "Who else did you speak with?" he asked, and she reeled off the names.

"Australia House was deluged with applicants after the war, and they still are," he said, closing his notepad. "The staff were terrifically underpaid and demoralized during the war years and immediately after, and there is some evidence that the verification procedures were hit-and-miss. I'd say it's possible he used falsified papers to get permission to travel to Australia, and I suspect that would not have been so hard. Did someone at Australia House knowingly allow a war criminal to travel? This Aldrich, for example? It's possible, but it's more likely he slipped through with fake documents and a new identity. Still, I wonder about the people you spoke to in London. It was like setting their networks aflame. You earned quite a reputation after that affair in Sydney, you understand."

He might just be right about that.

"I have to go, I'm afraid. You will heed my warnings, won't you?" He made his way to the door, his trench coat in hand.

"I do thank you for your visit, and the information, Archie. Some strange things have been happening, but I'd thought it must be to do with the case I'm on."

"It seems to me you're on more than one case," he pointed out. "I strongly suggest you watch your back. Here is my local telephone number. Do call me if anything else happens, anything at all. It doesn't have to be serious, just anything that seems amiss. Okay?" He looked at his watch. "Thank you again for the drink. I will see you around, I feel sure."

It seemed so.

Twenty-eight

—⁓—

Montmartre at night was dazzling and alive, even so soon after the war, Billie observed, watching the men spilling out of cafés and eateries. Areas where neon signs were glowing in the darkness made her think on Kings Cross, and the York Motors sign that had to be shut off at eight fifteen sharp. Here there would be no such rule to shut down the lights, nor the bars after anything like Sydney's frantic six o'clock swill. Even the Moulin Rouge, though not quite what it once was, was still humming, having successfully served as a large dance club during the war. Billie had always found it charming that this district of bartenders, cabaret performers, avant-garde painters, and sinners sat at the foot of Montmartre Hill, overlooked by the famous Sacre Coeur Basilica—two icons representing two very different passions.

Had Richard Montgomery's passions brought him here? she wondered, or was it simply another Englishman—perhaps one of many—who had frequented the area? It wasn't much to go on, but perhaps, just perhaps, the Englishman spotted here was the one they sought.

"Do you think it's safe to be here, after what Archie said?" Sam asked.

Billie frowned. "In Paris? I have to hope so, Sam. I can't let it put us off. We have a job to do." It would be no good to return to Vera empty-handed. A thing like that was not likely to go unnoticed, and would impact rather badly on Billie's track record.

"Of course," he said, and fell silent.

They meandered slowly, Sam attracting at least as much attention as his boss.

"That man there," Billie said suddenly, pointing discreetly to direct Sam's gaze. "Could that be him?" A heavyset man in a hat was walking on the opposite side of the cobblestone street, wearing a corduroy jacket and a blue scarf. He paused and looked both ways, then crossed, giving her a brief glimpse of his broad face.

She cocked her head.

"Sam, I think that could be our man, Montgomery," Billie said, heart speeding up. She had the photographs of him etched into her mind, and though she had not seen the man's hairline, his bearing was right, the arrangement of his features. Still, in the darkness she could not be sure, and this man looked very different without the omnipresent suit Montgomery seemed always to have worn.

"I'm going to go speak with him . . ."

With that Billie shot off down the street with Sam trailing behind, her Oxfords seeming to propel her like the winged sandals of Hermes. She could see his silhouette ahead as he moved with a slightly heavy, lumbering gait. The man looked over his shoulder—*Could that really be Montgomery?*—and decided quite suddenly to turn into an alley. Already he was a good pace ahead, moving faster than she thought possible, because when she arrived at the mouth of the alley, it was peopled by men, but he was gone. She licked her lips, frustrated, and made for the closest grouping. Men were gathered near a doorway, smoking and talking, and when she tried to walk through them, making for the dark doorway as if she belonged there, they wouldn't have it.

"*Que faites-vous? Ce n'est pas pour femmes.*"

This is not for women.

Blast. She was ushered away, politely but firmly, and walked back to the street to find Sam, cursing under her breath. "I need you to try the doors here, Sam. I think he went through one of them." She fished the photograph out of her handbag. "I can't get in, but you should be fine. Show this. I don't know if that was him, but my gut tells me we might be onto something. Go, quick . . ."

—⁂—

"Do you really think he's out there, living it up in Paris?" Sam asked.

Billie held her head in both hands and said nothing.

They sat side by side in a vibrating and screeching Métro carriage after a disappointing evening of canvassing the male hangouts in Paris. Sam had tried the places in the alley, as she suggested, and had come out looking somewhat shell-shocked and not much closer to finding their target. Having him with her had been helpful, but only when the men they spoke to could understand English, and perhaps unsurprisingly he'd thus far reported more propositions than leads. One man had been encouraging, saying he'd seen someone in Montmartre district who fit the description and who had a British accent, but it wasn't much to go on. Montparnasse, where Simone had also suggested they try, had been thoroughly unsuccessful—or perhaps they'd simply run out of gas.

"Perhaps, Sam. Honestly, I don't know yet. It could have been a real lead, seeing that man. And that's two men now who might have seen someone like Montgomery in Montmartre."

"Or just seen an Englishman."

There were plenty of those around, especially after the war. Wars had a way of rearranging populations. People met, fell in love . . .

Billie lowered her voice to hushed tones. "Whether in a shallow grave, or in a flat in Montparnasse, Richard Montgomery is here somewhere. My gut tells me that much. And it's telling me something else, too . . ."

Billie reached into her handbag and took out her mirrored compact and her stick of Fighting Red. Carefully she applied a fresh coat, and smacking her lips together gently she turned the mirror to look at the busy car behind her. "Sam, I believe we're being followed," she whispered, her head down.

"Again?" he whispered back.

"Yes." About a dozen travelers away, seated at an angle to them, was a man in thick glasses and a hat. He had a long, tanned face, and a turned-down mouth. She had caught a glimpse of those glasses glinting in the darkness in the streets of Montparnasse, and now in the Line 4 carriage, traveling north. He was fair and perhaps thirty, though it was difficult to tell his age beneath the heavy glasses and the tanned complexion of his face.

You're in quite a bit of danger, Archie had told her.

Sam shifted in his seat. "Archie?" he whispered hopefully, resisting the urge to look around in too obvious a way.

She stole another glance in her small mirror. It was definitely not her new intelligence ally. "No, unfortunately not." This was a blond man, tall and rangy, and he was wearing darker clothing than was fashionable in springtime. His coat was dark navy, and his shoes were black, trousers, too. He was obviously using her own strategy to blend into the shadows at night.

"One of his colleagues?"

"Perhaps," she admitted in a low voice. "But I doubt it. I'm guessing this fellow may not be here to help."

Sam swallowed.

Twice in one day she was being followed. Twice. She put her compact away and straightened her dark trench coat and dress. "You know Notre-Dame, where we walked last night? It's late, but there will be people there, I think. If he follows us off the train, we'll try to lose him." She hoped for crowds of tourists, but May might be too early for them. "Next stop, Saint-Michel–Notre-Dame, we'll get off and make for the cathedral as fast as we can, okay? There are often crowds out front. Take no chances, just bolt. After what Archie told us this afternoon, I am not going to bother with being embarrassed. If I'm wrong—and I don't think I am—I don't mind upsetting a few people on their evening journey home."

This was what she had learned again and again from the women who came to her office seeking her services: If your instincts told you something was wrong, it usually was. The risk of social embarrassment—relentlessly drilled into women as being the worst of evils—could be the most innocuous and deadly of barriers to survival. It was far better to listen to your instinct for survival and risk feeling foolish later than to ignore that primal warning and risk it being terrifyingly, fatally, correct.

"I'll be right by your side," Sam whispered, nodding.

The subway car screeched as it started to slow.

"Almost ready . . . Wait . . . Ready . . ." Billie said as the doors opened. "Now!"

The pair bolted up from their seats, pushing past shocked commuters and slipping out, causing grunted complaints and swearing with their rudeness. They ran down the platform and just before they turned up a staircase to make their way to the ground level, she spotted the darkly dressed man push through the train-car doors, forcing them open with gloved hands as they began to close. Again, the glasses glinted.

Blast! He was on the platform.

"He's on our tail, Sam," she said, and ran as fast as her Oxfords could take her. She saw the exit signs—SORTIE—and, knowing the way already, took the steps up to the street level two by two, barely noticing the scent of urine and sweat.

"He has a pistol," she heard Sam say at the top of the stairs, beneath the old Art Nouveau Métro sign, and she turned back in the direction of their pursuer. Billie felt her stomach freeze. He had drawn his weapon.

"You run. I'll meet you there, and try to . . ." Sam said, though his words faded on the wind that whipped past her ears on Quai Saint-Michel, as she sprinted along the footpath beside the Seine toward the inviting lights of the cathedral, turning heads as she ran over the Petit Pont. Sam was just a few paces behind. When they could get far enough ahead, they could lose him, or—she hoped—a crowd would surely scare him off.

A truck moved past on the bridge, giving her temporary shelter, and Billie pulled her Colt from her garter, holding it tightly at her side. When she looked behind again, she could no longer see Sam.

"Sam?" she cried out. "Sam?"

You run, he'd said, so she kept going toward the cathedral.

Even through Billie's panic, Our Lady Notre-Dame was a spectacular sight in the darkness, her gothic spires, statuary, and gargoyles illuminated from below, the stonework glowing gold, and the famous stained-glass "rose window" shining in blues and reds above the arched entryways. As she had hoped, the large square at the front of the cathedral was full of admiring sightseers—tourists and worshippers, believers and non-believers alike—despite the hour.

Trees and creeping vines flowed over the walls of the Seine at the eastern end. Far better that she slip into the crowds here than a lonely back alley in unfamiliar territory, as she had earlier in the day. She had been lucky enough to encounter a friend in Archie that time, and not a deadly foe. She could not be so lucky twice.

Bang.

Billie winced and crouched down, looking back the way she'd come. A shot had been fired. A couple strode right past her as she held this position, apparently oblivious to any danger. Had it been a motorcar backfiring along the bridge?

She stood up again slowly, warily. Billie could not see Sam nor the blond man on the bridge behind her. *I'll meet you there*, Sam had said, and that kept her moving. After a beat of indecision, she raised herself up fully and in a few steps she had joined the edge of a slowly moving group of male revelers. She took her coat off—she was warm from running—and tied it tightly around her waist, careful not to tangle up her right hand and the weapon it held. Farther on were other small groups—couples, tourist groups, and some men, perhaps having just come from the bars nearby. She moved past one group to the next, arousing the odd look or lascivious comment from leering men, until she was on the opposite side of the largest gathering.

There.

There he is.

It was the blond man with the glasses, coming off the Petit Pont and now striding across the flat square toward her, shifting and weaving like a snake as he passed the crowd and grew closer. *Oh, Sam.* Was he all right? This man would not fire on her in this open square, she wagered, but if he reached her they could end in a stalemate, pistol on pistol, near the glowing lights of the cathedral.

He means to kill you, Billie.

Billie moved into the middle of a small gathering of older

couples, shielding herself with their presence and ignoring their confused looks as they meandered closer to the front of Notre-Dame, the left side of which was covered in scaffolding from a great height. The group passed over the bronze circular marking in the pavement that declared this point to be the exact center of Paris, the Point Zéro des Routes de France. Glancing up again at the western façade of the great cathedral, Billie thought it looked like a giant, ornate letter H against the dark sky, the three entrances at its base currently closed to sinners. Was that H for heaven or hell? she wondered as she neared the structure, her mysterious pursuer gaining ground from the opposite direction.

The small assemblage of visitors she had inserted herself into turned their attention from the strange interloper as they stopped near the central arch, staring up at the statues of the twenty-eight Kings of Judah, which had been beheaded by guillotine during the French Revolution in this very same square because an angry mob had mistaken them for statues of French kings. Billie hoped there would be no losing heads tonight—or, at the very least, not her own. Troubling, however, was her impression that the blond man was not daunted by the presence of the people here, nor his possible exposure. Perhaps, if she could find a way to get inside the cathedral, she would find refuge. Those invaluable primal instincts of hers told her she would not be safe out here for long, and that wherever Sam was, he could not help her. She had found a nighttime crowd of sorts, but in truth was utterly alone.

She edged toward the front doors of the cathedral and tried them, but they were sealed and there was little time to decide her next move with the blond man hot on her heels. Instead, she found herself sprinting for a section of the building that was being restored, disappearing into the shadows of the structure, beyond the glare of the lights. Her Colt tucked into the coat wrapped tightly around her waist, Billie pulled herself up on the metal scaffolding, arms burning with the effort, and waited on top like a spider, stomach flattened against the platform, her arm outstretched, gun drawn. Had he sprinted after her, or opted to hang back so as not to arouse suspicion?

From her vantage point, swathed in darkness, Billie could see across the square to Petit Pont. There was still no sign of Sam.

Dammit. Where are you?

He had been hurt, she feared, or possibly worse. The thought of it stabbed her in the guts. If something had happened to him, it had happened because he was trying to protect her. *Sam. Steady Sam.* What had he said? *You run. I'll meet you there, and try to . . .* The rest of the words would not come. They had been taken by the wind. What had he tried to do?

Frowning, Billie dared to raise herself up to a standing position on the wooden platform. She licked her lips and looked around once more. The blond man could be out in the front of the cathedral or waiting directly beneath her. Or perhaps he had simply walked away, finally giving up? She took an unsteady breath, and then slowly, carefully, reached up and pulled herself to the next level, and waited again from her higher vantage point. Then beneath her, as if to answer her question, she heard the telltale sound of metal on metal. A buckle or cuff lightly tapping the metal scaffolding. *Or a gun.*

He's here.

Billie flattened herself again on the platform and pulled herself forward until she could peer over the edge at the level below her, the business end of her Colt ready. The platform was empty. She had almost begun to question her hearing when a dark-gloved hand silently appeared over the edge, gripping the platform directly below her.

"Come any further and I shoot," she told the hand.

There was silence, and the gloved hand retreated. Billie realized she was holding her breath.

Suddenly a blast tore through the platform below her and splintered the one she was now on. The bullet missed her ribs by inches, and without hesitation Billie shot back, her Colt firing a bullet blindly into the platform below. It hit wood and then metal. There was no cry. No sound. This was a poor game of chance, she decided, and, jumping up, began climbing the scaffolding again.

Two floors farther up, she was now nearly level with the beheaded kings, and could see that the next wooden platform above her was too far to reach, though the skeleton of the scaffolding continued practically to the top of this side of the cathedral. She could scramble up the skeleton of metal frames like a ladder of sorts until she reached that high platform, but she would be fully exposed from below. She feared the blond man could be too good a shot and would take her down.

Billie pulled herself farther up the network of scaffolding so she could try to climb above the cathedral's carved stone railing, and with effort, swung herself from the metal framework, leaving it shaking precariously, and landed on solid ground with a thud and a puff of dust. Her coat had untied itself in the process, and it dropped away to the dark ground the better part of one hundred feet below. She was on the Virgin's Balcony outside La Salle Haute, the Upper Room, just above the line of kings, and her Colt was in her hand, ready. Her pursuer had not yet appeared, and so she crept backward, eyes never leaving the scaffolding, until she reached a set of steps and two arched doors. Unceremoniously, she turned and began banging on them with clenched fists. Perhaps, if someone was inside, they would do her the courtesy of opening the door, unlike on the main level, where too many people congregated, too many tourists and merrymakers to warrant a response from any nuns or priests who might be inside.

One of the great arched doors creaked. The cathedral had become dangerously decrepit during the war, she noticed, the wooden door beginning to rot. The stray bullet holes across it had not been patched up. Even Notre-Dame had other things on her mind during the war years besides her appearance. Billie pressed against the door with her hip and felt it give slightly.

The hand.

The dark-gloved hand appeared, reaching up the metal scaffolding.

"Stay back!" she shouted, and loosed a bullet that ricocheted. She turned and shot again, this time into the old cathedral door at the level of its latch, and the wood splintered. With one kick she was inside.

Inside La Salle Haute, all was dark, and a dank, unpleasant smell permeated, a combination of rotting wood, dust, and pigeon droppings. She moved as quickly as she could through the darkness and decay, tripping over objects, but surefooted enough not to fall. The ceiling above her was high and arched, with trickles of light leaking through from the floodlights outside, though not enough to illuminate the uneven floor at her feet. Partially blinded by the heavy darkness, Billie made for the door, and once she was through it she knew her way. To her left was a winding stone staircase she had taken before, leading her to the familiar Galerie des Chimères, the collection of mythical guardians and gargoyles overlooking the Paris skyline, their mouths open as water drains carried rain away from the roof. Here there were plenty of places to hide, and to lie in wait if the blond man dared to continue his pursuit.

Paris.

The wind whistled through the stone chimera—the eternally bored demon known as Le Stryge, face in his hands in a pose of magnificent malaise, and the strange winged creatures and crouching half men. Some were crumbling into the void below, others standing stoically, their ribs showing as if to indicate a long wait between meals. The lights below caught only their outstretched necks and grotesque faces, part beast, part man. Billie's experience was that men were the most dangerous beasts—the one pursuing her right now being the most dangerous of all.

She heard a creak from the door she had emerged through. Then silence. Billie's breathing stopped as she focused on any sound, any shift in shadow and light. She extended her Colt.

"I told you to back off," she called into the darkness.

The answer was deafening, and blasted away a section of stone feathers from one of Le Stryge's companions. Billie shrunk lower against the stonework, eyeing the upper scaffolding to her left, the section she could not reach before. She knew she could not get back inside the cathedral without passing him. Could she make it to the scaffolding in time? Did she trust her hands enough to imagine sliding down safely, swathed in darkness?

Again, silence.

She peeked up over the low stone railing and saw a flash of movement. And then nothing. Somehow her pursuer was able to disappear into the shadows. Seconds passed with nothing but the sound of wind and the rush of adrenaline in her ears. Slowly, her eyes adjusted. There was the tiniest movement—a masked face emerging from the shadow like a ghoul. The man had donned a balaclava, she realized. Quickly, she raised her weapon and shot, aiming for his shining eyes, the only part of him that she could see clearly.

She heard the bullet hit stone. She'd missed and hit the cathedral. *Blast.*

"What do you want? Why are you after me?" she demanded. There was no response from the shadows, and she listened hard for movement. Was he creeping closer, or would he wait to let her reveal herself more clearly?

Time stretched out, as she had known in the war during times of danger—a soldier's minute. Her breathing marked the time. And then, barely having decided on her next move, Billie reached up with one hand, slipping hatpins out of her hair to allow her dark hat to slide off into her lap as she crouched in place. She made a wordless prayer to the bird of ill omen at her back, then sprang up and sprinted toward the scaffolding, throwing her hat toward the man in the same motion.

There was a blast and a whizzing past her ear, but she was there, at the platform, and she leaped onto it and crouched low, clinging to the wood as it shifted and swam with the motion. She could make out the man's silhouette running toward the scaffolding, ready to leap, and without another thought pulled the Colt's trigger, heard the blast, and saw a shoulder jerk back. A *hit*. There was a low, guttural sound and an exhale of shocked air as it made impact, but he kept coming, *dammit*, he kept coming.

How many bullets do I have left? she wondered fleetingly and realized she was down to one. This was it. This was her chance. She lined up her final shot, hoping for another moment of light, of clarity. Death felt close, and something else, too, as if the Blessed Lady of the cathedral were watching over her, perhaps overlooking her decidedly unladylike flaws. She could not tell which would win.

Billie squinted and pulled the trigger.

The scaffolding beneath her buckled and splintered, a shot from her assailant's gun having crashed through it. And there was a crash as the man's body propelled forward, hitting the edge of the scaffolding awkwardly, falling hard into it. She reached down and ripped the mask from the man's pale, shocked face.

"Who are you working for? Is it Odessa?" she demanded. "Or Montgomery?"

The flash of confusion in his blue eyes told her what she needed to know. He knew of no Montgomery. This could only be what Hank had warned her about, what Archie had warned her about. This was pure Odessa.

Suddenly a gloved hand shot up and gripped her throat with surprising strength. She dropped her Colt, barely noticing the sound of it falling, and she brought her hands together as if in prayer, but this was not for the Virgin Mary; this was for her own survival. She formed a steeple with her fingers and forced them skyward beneath his, separating his hands from her throat and pushing them apart. Gasping for air, she pushed out with the heels of her palms, hitting him in the chest with more force than she thought she could muster.

He fell backward and his body flipped over the low stone rail, just beyond the scaffolding. He remained silent as he fell, much as he had been in pursuit, his long arms reaching into space, gun sailing off. Billie watched this from the edge, the scene in slow motion, and she had a flash of Hessmann and his white face, his hand reaching for her as he fell from Daking House. There was a distant sound below, something sickening, and then a terrified scream from someone in the square. He had fallen on the newly erected railing. On the spikes.

There were cries of horror, and someone shouted, "*Policiers!*" The police were arriving.

Billie reached down for the swaying scaffolding and sat, willing her breathing to slow. That had been too close. The fantastical beasts along the Galerie des Chimères had nothing to say about the struggle. Le Stryge had not even turned his head. He still looked off, hands under his chin, bored.

Billie did not know how much time had passed before she heard Sam's voice just behind her, and another voice as well—Archie's.

"Billie, come away from the platform," Sam was saying. At first she did not look up, only kept her eyes fixed on the edge of the scaffolding and on the growing crowd around the grim figure of the impaled assassin.

Sam.

Sam was alive.

"Come off the scaffolding, Billie. It's not safe." It was Archie now, his reasonable, calm voice sounding uncomfortably like Jack's. That accent.

Archie was reaching out to her on the boards, his freckled hand in her peripheral vision. Without saying a word, she stood up carefully, first into a crouch, pulling herself up inch by inch, then walked toward him in careful steps, as one might on a frozen lake. "I'm fine," she said, finding her voice again, and realizing that she was cold without her coat, was shivering. She flicked her eyes back to the dark platform where she and the assassin had struggled, and saw that parts of it had fallen away, nothing but air beneath.

"We'll clean this up," Archie assured her as he took her hand and led her back through the door of the Galerie des Chimères and closed the portal behind them.

Billie blinked. "Clean it up? How on earth can you do that?" she asked him, thinking of the groups of people below, thinking of the tall man impaled on the iron spikes.

There was no answer to that.

The trio walked down the spiral stone staircase for several floors, round and round, and when they hit light, they stopped. She could now see that Sam had been injured.

"Oh, Sam. You were hurt!" He had a deep-red graze that ran from his chin to just below his ear, straight as a bullet's trajectory, dried blood covering part of his face.

"The bullet barely hit me. It just gave me pause, is all," he said, bringing a hand to his jaw. "I'm so sorry it slowed me down, Billie. And then I couldn't find you."

Archie was all business. "Go back to your hotel, and I'll speak with you tomorrow. You two weren't here," he said.

"Who was he, Archie?"

"Ah, of course you would not know," Archie said. "I recognized him, all right—a known associate of the Odessa network. Austrian chap. He's a serious operator, Billie. Sniper he was, injured in the war. He can't speak." Archie touched his throat as if to show an injury to his vocal chords. "Oh, and their network back in Australia has been busy again. You're obviously considered a threat—they're looking for how much you know."

Billie's stomach dropped. All this had not been someone protecting Montgomery for some reason or, say, the Caversham-Smithes, as she'd wondered after that incident on the road outside London. No, it had been Odessa all along. She'd known as much even before he was climbing that scaffolding. He was too determined. Too expert. This was all about the war still—a war that hadn't truly ended, not at the gallows of Nuremburg, not back in New South Wales, and not here at Notre-Dame.

Odessa was behind it, all of it, somewhere up the chain. Hank's warnings had proved all too correct.

"And you might want this back." Archie pressed her beloved Colt into her hand. She turned it over in her smooth hands, grateful to see its return. She could feel that the mother-of-pearl grip was cracked. It had fallen off the platform when she'd forced his hands off her throat. She'd learned that move from her father. *Hands in a steeple, and take it to the heavens.*

She hoped her gun, though battered, was still in working order. "Archie, do you think we'll be safe at the hotel?"

"For tonight, I should think so," he said. "But please understand, if they care this much about removing you, they will send someone else before long. You should look into moving to another location soon. And you should not refuse our help."

Twenty-nine

———≈———

Billie Walker's adrenaline was still buzzing through her like electricity. Once Sam had helped her to her room back at the Ritz, arm protectively around her shoulders, she had shut the door behind them with her foot and immediately poured them both a whisky, neat, slipping off her Oxfords in the process.

"Oh blast! My coat. It's still out there somewhere," she realized aloud.

Billie padded over to where Sam was standing, handed him his drink with a slightly unsteady hand.

Sam was watching her quietly. Sam, who she'd feared was dead.

"Don't make me drink alone, dear Sam. You know I don't drink alone."

Billie closed her eyes, tipped her glass, and felt the whisky go down, that marvelous burn, and after a moment, inexplicably, a laugh escaped her throat. "Great Hera, that was close," she said as the true gravity of what had happened dawned on her. "I didn't know if I would make it back here, if I would see you again . . ."

"You bested him, Billie," he said, and joined her in a silent toast.

A toast to making it through, to surviving the night. He took a long sip of his drink, and she finished hers.

In truth she'd been lucky, and she knew it. The blond man had been her match, and more. And sent from abroad to end her life. Agitated, she paced the room with her empty glass, overcome with nervous energy. *I could be dead right now. My body could be shattered for all to see in the floodlights of great Notre-Dame. Archie could be sending a telegram right now to Hank, telling him he had failed. And Sam. What of Sam?*

"We'll have to look into a new hotel in the morning. Perhaps we can stay one more night at the most, as we reorganize," she said. Perhaps Simone would have some ideas on where they could go.

Billie didn't want to leave the Ritz, but Archie was right. The man they'd encountered was a serious operator, and, having failed, he would be replaced. They would need to move to another area of Paris to continue their Montgomery investigations, and register under false names. Such precautions had not felt necessary before this. She had greatly underestimated how big a thorn she'd been in Odessa's side, or whatever Hessmann's colleagues called themselves.

Billie stopped pacing and leaned her forehead against the cool windowpane, the reality of the evening's events hitting her with full force. "I thought you'd died, Sam," she said, her breath fogging up the glass.

Slowly, inevitably, silence filled the room.

When Billie turned, she saw her assistant there, barely an arm's length away, standing and watching her. Instinctively, she put down her empty whisky glass and moved closer to him on legs that seemed to animate of their own accord. Sam had done the same, putting down his glass and taking a step toward her, and the space between their bodies—the space that was always there, safely, professionally there—was dangerously close to vanishing. A button of her dress brushed against his shirt, that last hair's breadth of separation between them betrayed by the small, hard circle of Bakelite.

She tilted her chin upward, heart thumping in her chest, and gazed at him. Her eyes were wet, she realized. A shadow of blond stubble had begun to show on his face, and she noticed for the first time, up close, the lines and faint scars on his skin. Not a fraction of an inch of what she saw displeased her, not even the fresh wound he had earned in her defense. It was little more than a graze, she realized now. But it had been close, so close.

He was near enough now that his whisky-mingled scent filled the space between them. This smell was somehow honeyed, and she knew she was in trouble. This was chemistry doing its work, their bodies speaking. The last time they had been so close they'd been on the crowded floor of The Dancers back in Sydney. There'd been so many reasons that time to hold back, to remain distracted. She was not distracted from him now.

"Sam," Billie began, hesitating, but words of sober authority and protest wouldn't come. Instead, her hand came up to his face and lovingly caressed that jaw she'd often admired, tracing the line of blood from his fresh wound. "Let me help you with that," she said, and stopped.

An uncertain pause, a breath, and then Sam bent and kissed Billie gently. He tasted pleasantly of whisky, warm and faintly caramelized, and his lips were firm and exciting. It had been so long since she'd been kissed, and her head swam a little at the enchanting sensation. She laughed softly at herself now, and leaned into him, breasts pressing into that broad, hard chest. Her shoulders dropped. She exhaled.

I nearly died.

Billie had survived falling shells, speeding car chases, an Austrian assassin, but she was nervous now, with dear, steady Samuel

Baker in her room. How ridiculous to be scared by such a thing, such a natural human thing, when she had been so close to dying little more than an hour before.

"I think I needed that," she said. "A kiss."

After a breath apart, another hesitation, Sam brought his hands gently up to her face—she felt the rough skin of his fingers, and the leather glove of his left hand on her cheek.

She did not speak, did not look away as their eyes met and held, faces inches apart, searching each other, or perhaps searching themselves. No laughter now. No distractions. Her eyes fell to Sam's mouth and their lips met again, tentatively at first, then passionately. The hotel room swam, and she closed her eyes, melting into the sensation and pulling him deeper into her. He bent at the waist to circle hers with both arms, and before long Billie found she had begun to cling to him with a hunger she had not acknowledged, her feet lifting right off the hotel rug. His shoulders were hard and tight under the fabric of his shirt as he supported her, and her only thought, if it was thinking at all, was of taking the fabric away that was separating them. She clasped her hands behind his neck and kissed the muscles of his throat in a neat line to his collar.

This man felt right under her hands, under her lips, her tongue. These were human desires she had suppressed for so long. Should she listen to them? Then, with an abruptness, they parted, coming up for air, she unlocking her hands and Sam quickly letting go of her waist in response.

"I'm so sorry," Sam apologized, and took a step back.

His brows were deeply knitted now, concerned that he'd crossed boundaries. But they both had. Restless, he seemed not to know where to look or where to put his hands.

Billie sat down on the settee, feeling pleasantly breathless. "Don't say you're sorry," she told him softly.

Sam knelt before her. He took both of her smaller hands in his, and Billie's fingers slid through his, around those leather-gloved wooden fingers on his left hand.

"Kiss me again, won't you? But only if you want to, Sam," she finally told him.

His eyes met hers, and then his lips met hers again, before pausing. "I'm sorry, Billie. I should have—"

She placed a finger at his lips. "I don't want to hear you say that again, okay? No more apologies—not from either of us. I'm not sorry, and I don't think you have any reason to be, do you? We are alive and we are here, right now. Having said that, I don't think—"

"Of course." He stood. "Do you want me to leave?"

She shook her head. "I don't mean that. No, I do not want you to leave, but I'll understand if you want to. I would like you to stay, Sam." She was not worried about appearances, and she trusted Sam with her life, now more than ever. But she had not prepared for such an eventuality as the one that was unfolding between them now, physically.

"Will you stay with me until morning?" Billie asked. "Can you do that?"

"I'll be here as long as you want me, in whatever way you want me, Billie."

He did have a way with words. "I want you to tell me everything, Sam. Tell me what happened to you, where you were. Tell me all of it. Remind me that I'm alive, Sam. I fear part of me has been dead for far too long."

Thirty

Are you awake?" she heard Sam ask from the en suite bathroom.

Billie stretched and yawned, rolling onto her side. She wasn't sure of the time, but from the light outside her window it seemed the sun had long since risen. She swung her legs out and sat on the edge of the bed, still in her silk slip, her dress having been carefully placed over a chair, along with her stockings. Sam's button-up shirt was on the floor, along with his trousers.

"*Bonjour*," she called back. "It seems I am still alive."

"And I am still here, just like I promised."

She spread her toes out, feeling the plush hotel carpet between them, and wiggled them, gazing at the floor, the wall, and then the ceiling of her room, recalling how only a few years before, when last she'd woken to the scent of a man in her bed, it had been her husband, Jack. Almost their entire courtship—even their brief time spent together as a married couple—had been during wartime, and frequently involved hiding, or being on the run or just beyond front lines. Often, there had been no running water, sometimes no sheets, let alone a tub and fine toiletries. Sometimes they'd been without food, or even a roof, and more often than not they hadn't known what they would encounter come morning. And here she was, sated and safe—relatively speaking—within the palatial four walls of the Ritz Paris, if only for another few hours. She was not tired, nor half-starved, and her body had been cocooned in the luxury of fine sheets, on which she had sought solace and protection in a young man's arms.

Sam.

As if on cue, her secretary-cum-assistant emerged from her bathroom, glistening from the shower, a white hotel robe tied neatly around his trim waist, but too small to quite contain his broad chest. His handsome jaw was adorned with a white bandage she had applied after gently cleaning his wound, before they had finally slipped into sleep. A fraction of an inch and the assassin's bullet would have penetrated his cheek, giving him more than a graze and a splitting headache.

Billie gazed at him, awash with a flood of conflicting feelings, but most overarchingly, she felt pleasure at the sight of him. The pale hairs on his broad chest. The shape of his muscles, his frame. And still his scent permeated the sheets on which she had reclined again.

Her vulnerability and confusion in that moment must have been plain, as Sam took one look at her—her lower lip between her teeth, her hair a mane of dark against the white linens—and stopped where he stood. "You are a vision, Ms. Walker." He then looked down at himself. "Sorry, I should—"

"Please don't," she said, sitting up, and holding the sheet over her crinkled slip. "And I think you can call me Billie now, surely."

They both laughed. It was one of Sam's peculiarities that he kept reverting to calling her Ms. Walker, even now.

They had spent the night together side by side, chaste, but deeply intimate. Whether it was the whisky or the closeness of death, she had not wanted him to leave, and he had stayed by her until morning, no questions asked, no more boundaries broken. Or at least none of her boundaries. Having a man who was not her husband in her room at all broke every convention where she came from, but to hell with conventions.

Sam came to the bedside, knelt in the robe. "Yes, Ms. Walker . . . I mean Billie. I hope you are okay this morning, with . . . everything. What can I get you? Tea? A café au lait? *Pain au chocolat?* I can head downstairs and rustle us up some—"

She looked down at his hand and he stiffened, standing up quickly, his left hand now behind his back.

"What is it?" Billie asked, the moment broken.

"No, no. It's nothing," he said. "Let me get us some breakfast."

He tried to turn away and she shot a hand out, placed it gently on his forearm, stopping him. "It's not nothing, Sam. Tell me."

He swallowed, eyes averted. "I don't want you to see it," he admitted, clearly embarrassed, his face reddening.

It finally dawned on her that Sam's left hand was without the glove and prosthetic fingers he always wore. He'd kept the glove on all night, even as they slept. It must have been terrifically uncomfortable for him, she thought. Naturally he had taken off his wooden prosthetic for his shower. She hadn't even given it a thought, the glove being so much a part of him.

Billie frowned. "If you think it would put me off, Sam, I have to wonder what kind of woman you think I am. We are closer than that, especially after Notre-Dame and . . ."

"I just . . . you don't need to see it," he said, shaking his head.

"Your hand does not bother me, dear Sam," she assured him. "No one worth their salt is without scars, not after that war."

He seemed to relax a touch, his shoulders dropping as her words sunk in, and he closed his eyes and let his arm and his injured hand fall to his side. In the light of day she could see that full fingers were missing from his left hand, his skin lined with deep grooves of purple and rose. She reached out and held it, stroking the injured hand tenderly, in case his scars were sensitive to the touch, as burns could be for some.

"You are beautiful, Billie," he said, opening his eyes.

"I hope you don't think any less of me, asking you to stay."

"Pardon?"

She looked down at herself. "I, uh, am unused to this."

Her mother's words came back to her: *As I've told you, darling, there isn't a thing wrong with the man, including being your employee. It worked just fine for me . . .*

"I respect you, Billie," Sam said. "Don't you worry about that, if that's what you mean. And I'm not going to go telling anyone anything. And besides, there is nothing to tell." *Except a kiss. Or ten. And the way their bodies felt, holding close.*

He pulled his hand behind his back again, hiding it. "Though I wouldn't mind shouting it from the rooftops, if you like . . ."

Billie chuckled. It had been years since she'd been kissed. Years. How depressing that realization was. There was no one to anger with this lovely man's presence, but it was awkward. He was her employee. They were here on a work assignment. It was confusing. And was she a married woman? She had not thought of herself that way for a while. *Ms.* Walker, not *Mrs.* She was in a strange limbo, made no stranger by the claims of her friend Simone, and that close call at the morgue, where she'd thought she might be facing Jack's corpse.

"You are a fine gentleman, dear Sam. I did not do anything I didn't wish to, and you were . . . most kind." She bit her lip, guilt still crashing in around her despite what her head tried to tell her about her circumstances, her right to live her life and be a free woman after so long waiting in her grief.

"Kind?"

"Let's go down to breakfast," she suggested, and wrapped the sheet around herself, over her slip. She stood, then looked at the clock. "Oh dear. *Lunch*, I should say." The Do Not Disturb sign had done its work rather well. NE PAS DÉRANGER . . .

"Perhaps I ought to get some fresh clothes," Sam suggested, looking at his crumpled shirt.

"Meet you back here when you are ready?" she said. "Perhaps in half an hour or so, if you can wait that long? We can have a bit of lunch, say?"

Before she disappeared into the bathroom to get herself together, she took his left hand in hers again and gently kissed it. "I'm so glad you're here, Sam," she told him, looking him right in the eye. "You are beautiful, also. Just as you are."

—⁓—

Twenty-five minutes later, there was a light rap on her door. A smile played on Billie's lips, and her heart sped up a touch.

She put out her cigarette and redid her Fighting Red lipstick. There would be time to feel guilty, perhaps, but the time was not now, not here during this brief, beautiful stay in Paris. She and Sam were honest with each other, and while perhaps those back at home wouldn't approve of a man having been in her bed—with the exception of her mother, who would be delighted—the French wouldn't care. Things had not gone so far, in any event. There would be time yet to decide if it had just been the adrenaline, the romance of Paris . . .

Steady, beautiful Sam.

She slipped on her shoes and picked up her handbag, grinning like a child. It could get tricky between them. Not that many men seemed to trouble themselves with such concerns when it came to *their* secretaries. No. She deserved a little happiness, didn't she? After the war, and everything she had been through. After her grief. This was Sam, after all. Had she any reason to fear him? To worry what he might do if she didn't want to pursue things? No, she felt safe with Sam. More than safe.

Most pressingly, after lunch they would have to talk seriously about where to move to. Somewhere smaller? Hôtel des Arts in Montmartre? Two men had seen someone who might be Montgomery frequenting the bars around there. Besides, it could be a terribly romantic area, she reflected. Beaming, Billie walked over to the door.

When she opened it, she dropped her handbag to the floor in shock.

"*Jack?*" Billie exclaimed, her husband's name hanging uncomfortably in the air, four letters full of hope and pain.

"Billie," Jack Rake said, looking down and then stealing a glance at his wife again, before returning his gaze to his polished shoes.

Billie backed away from the open door and tried to speak, but found that nothing further came out. All the air had been sucked out of her, as if she'd been struck in the belly at the sight of him.

She did her best to steady herself quickly and put on the best emotional armor she could muster without notice. "You *are* in Paris." *You are alive.* "I didn't . . . know if it could be true," she managed to say. *Why now? Why?* "I wasn't expecting you."

"I'm sorry to arrive unannounced," he apologized politely, his expression that of a man on the back foot, conflicted and uncertain. Her shock would be plain, despite her attempt at reserve, and he seemed to regret shaking her so. "May I come in for a moment?" he asked.

For a moment?

"Your sense of timing was always something," she replied. "Sure, you may come in for a moment."

Billie had fought back several instincts—to rush forward and embrace him, to slam the door in his face, to kiss him hard on the mouth, to slap him with fury. Now she couldn't move. She did nothing but work to calm her heart and think on what her missing husband might be doing here, alive.

After a pregnant pause, Billie stepped back from the door and motioned for Jack to enter her hotel room with a hand that was impressively steady. As he passed her to enter, she shook herself barely perceptibly and stood tall, chin raised, watching his back.

Sam would be back soon to accompany her to lunch. Sam, who had spent the night. He would have to wait, she supposed, and she would have to face this surreal moment on an empty stomach, and without tea, which seemed an extra measure of cruelty. She closed the door and placed her handbag on the side table.

Much as Simone Chapelle had warned her, Billie's estranged husband was changed. The clothes were different—new. Sharp. He wore a neat suit and necktie, and shiny leather shoes, like some kind of bureaucrat, or even an advertising man like the one she was hunting down. Despite these odd details, it really was him, even as he stood like an alien in her room, his eyes downcast. This was Jack Rake, returned from the grave or wherever he'd been since before the end of the war, before Billie's return to Australia, before she'd pulled herself up by her bootstraps and got on with her life alone, without her husband. Yes, it was him. This was really happening, one part of the mystery solved.

She was not a widow. She'd been abandoned and he was back for a visit.

Jack bloody Rake.

Jack was looking around, perhaps impressed by the well-appointed room, or even somehow sensing that she had not spent the night in it alone. She could still sense Sam in the room, his masculine scent lingering.

It seemed they weren't quite ready to talk yet, circling each other, silent and watchful. *Jack.* Those earnest hazel eyes of his were almost the same, almost the ones she knew, though the lines around them were much more pronounced, and when he looked up, actually dared to make eye contact with her, she saw something behind them she had never seen before. Something dark.

How odd to see him. How odd this all was. It occurred to her to be pleased she was fully dressed, her skirt suit and Fighting Red acting as a kind of armor against her vulnerability, and indeed pleased that he had not knocked when she and Sam were sleeping together in her hotel bed, having come dangerously close to intimacy of another kind.

"How could I not come?" she heard her husband mutter softly, as much to himself as to her. He tried unsuccessfully to smile as he looked at his wife, seeming as uncertain in her presence as she was in his.

"A drink?" she offered, on autopilot. Here she was, offering him hospitality. How utterly absurd.

"Yes, I think I will, despite the hour," he said.

"I gather you still enjoy a whisky." She poured and handed him a glass, which he instinctively sniffed. The bottle was getting low. At this rate she'd have to get another just to survive Paris.

"Well, I must say I am pleased to see you're alive," she said, aloud this time, finding the words surreal. "In truth, we all thought unlikely in the end, after news about Warsaw and the uprising, and no news about you."

Dangerously, a tear welled up in her eye at the memory of her distress, her concern for his well-being. She turned away and paced the room, letting the threat of tears settle back down and disappear. There had been quite enough tears spent on this man.

"I know," he said simply. "I . . . I knew you would be terribly worried."

A *drink. Now.* No matter that she had not eaten and had only just woken up an hour before. She poured herself a whisky, and no sooner did she recap the bottle than she wet her throat with the bracing drink. "You didn't write," she pointed out, the liquor fresh on her tongue. "I received one letter from Warsaw when you first arrived, and then nothing. But then I suppose you know that."

Jack did not answer, only stared at those new shoes of his, as if they held the answers. When he turned his head and looked out the window, she caught a glimpse of it—the raised scar above his collar, slashed straight across his neck and snaking up the side. Simone had been right about that, too. Billie fought an urge to ask him about it, or to move forward and cup that face with both hands as she had imagined doing so many times. He had lost weight since she'd seen him, and it seemed to her that there were deeper hollows below his cheekbones. Despite this, there was a kind of heaviness about him that was unfamiliar. A new weight and formality. Or perhaps that was the distance between them?

She didn't move, just waited for what he would do next, empty glass in her hand. She would get through this. She would. She'd been through worse. Hell, had last night not been worse?

"Mind if I smoke?" she finally said, breaking the tension. She walked over and pulled her cigarette case from her handbag. Jack stepped in to light her fag, her narrowed eyes watching his face. Again, the absurdity. She'd asked him if she could smoke, in her own hotel room. "Oh, of course you don't mind." She laughed cynically.

Her husband would be perfectly well aware that he had not written to her. Perhaps she had to make him confirm it, make him confirm that he had not tried to reach her, that it had not been some terrible mistake, some unfortunate turn of events that had prevented him from reuniting with her. In the intervening years she'd picked herself up, reopened her father's agency, and helped so many women find missing husbands or uncover the truth about cheating partners, and all that time she had still given Jack the benefit of the doubt, imagined him tragically killed in the Warsaw Uprising, imagined him a dead hero, only allowing for the slim possibility of his being alive, somehow separated from her due to circumstances beyond his control. He would be faultless in their separation.

And yet here he is in a new suit and shoes, scarred but fine. Just fine.

After three years without contacting her, what excuse could he possibly have? And why show up now, when she was finally finding some professional success in the new life she had built for herself, even some happiness of her own?

Jack was bent at the shoulders, as if an invisible weight pressed down on him. His was an expression she interpreted as guilt, and his silence seemed to be an admission—no, he had not written her, his wife. Despite their vows, despite their bond, he had not tried to contact her for all this time. Jack took a long breath and Billie continued to watch him, unflinchingly. She would do nothing to ease the moment for him. He had some explaining to do. Rage, relief, and frustration fought for supremacy inside her, but mostly it was the urge to ask if he was okay that overrode all else, and that fact was infuriating.

"Come, sit," she finally said.

He obeyed, finding a place on her settee. "You've come up in the world since you were last in Paris," he observed, and tried on a soft laugh, which sounded awkward and forced. "We certainly never stayed anywhere like this."

Jack, beneath her in the dark, the bombs falling in the distance.

Jack, bringing her a hunk of bread while she lay naked on a wool blanket.

Jack, kissing her passionately and murmuring her name, "Billie, Billie, Billie . . ."

"Well, some of us have held on okay, I suppose. I've been running an investigation agency in Sydney."

"I heard. That's good, Billie."

Funny, I hadn't heard a thing about you, she wanted to say.

A knock came at her hotel door, and Billie closed her eyes, readying herself. "I'll just be a minute," she said, and stood. She left her empty glass on the side table, noting that she would need to refill it presently, and strode across the room to open the door.

It was Sam. He was dressed in a fresh shirt and trousers, looking vulnerable and utterly wonderful. His eyes went from her pale face to the back of the male figure seated on the settee behind her, and his face dropped.

"I might need to take a rain check, Sam," she said. "I'm very sorry."

"Ms. Walker," he said stiffly. He shifted on his feet, studying her expression, and looking past her into the room again. "Are you okay?" he asked in a low voice, so that only she could hear.

"I am, Sam." She hesitated. "I believe I am."

"If you need anything at all, I'm going to be right outside this door, Billie," he told her.

"You don't have to do that. I'm okay."

"Are you sure?" His eyes searched hers for answers, for a clue.

"I know him." *Mostly. How much did she really know him?* She realized that Sam couldn't be expected to recognize her long since assumed-dead husband, sitting across the hotel room as he was, his head bent. There was no reason for Sam to guess who her visitor was. Who could?

"You go down and eat something. You must be starved." She knew Sam's appetite.

"I'll be here," he said. "I'm not leaving."

Billie couldn't explain right now, didn't even know what she would say. She placed a hand on his arm. "Please, for me? Eat something and I'll see you in your room in maybe an hour. Okay?"

Still clearly hesitant, he nonetheless nodded, and she closed the door softly, blocking Sam from view, and turned to face her visitor. He really was there. Her husband, Jack, sitting in her hotel room. Instead of the ecstasy and relief she had imagined in her dreams, it felt awful, like a weight was sitting on her chest, rather than being lifted. She could hardly breathe.

"Who was that?" he asked, as if he deserved to know.

"That was my assistant," she said evenly, and crossed the room to return to the settee. He didn't need explanations. She needed explanations.

"You have an assistant? You've done well," Jack remarked.

Three years of wondering if her husband was dead, only to find out he'd simply been . . . what? Avoiding her? She wasn't quite sure what he meant by "done well." This wasn't quite how doing well was supposed to feel.

"He mustn't tell anyone I'm here. Please."

Jack's plea was a surprise. "I see. Well, he doesn't know who you are yet, Jack. Besides, Sam doesn't have anyone to tell in Paris. He knows even fewer people here than I do now. Why can't anyone know you are here?"

"My work. I can't talk about it," he said cryptically. "You saw

Simone. I was pleased by that, though I suppose she told you about our encounter at the Hôtel Lutetia. That wasn't supposed to happen . . ."

"How did you know I saw her?"

"I know," he said. "This must all seem so strange to you," he added, staring off at the view as if he could see past the skyline of Paris all the way to where his mind was fixed, in some faraway place. "Paris held up okay, didn't it?" he said.

There'd been no Blitz here. No bombs had torn apart the very heart of Paris. The people of Paris, well, that was a different matter. And what of her heart, now? "Is this where you're spending your time now—Paris—or did you seek me out?" she demanded.

"Both. But yes, I am . . . in Paris these days."

Interesting. "You came here to tell me what happened, did you? To get that off your chest? Now that I know you're alive? Have you spoken to Simone? Is that how you knew where I was?"

Would she suggest he come, without warning Billie first? Surely not. But then, Billie had been sleeping in, with Sam, and a Do Not Disturb sign on her door.

Billie hadn't dared to believe Jack was alive, but she should have trusted that Simone would be right about seeing him. All Billie could do now was refill his glass, and then her glass, raise it to her mouth, and take a swig to partially replace the sting of grief in her throat with another, more immediate kind. It did nothing to obliterate the pain, though. Not really. And again her glass was empty. She looked at it, disappointed, and took her seat on the settee—the settee on which she had, only the night before, been kissing Samuel Baker, breaking years of romantic drought, tortured by the fate of this man she had married as the world was at war. The world was an ever-changing, always surprising thing, she concluded. Always surprising.

"What brings you all the way here? What's the case?" he asked, as if that was the topic of conversation. "I was pleased when I'd heard you'd reopened your father's private inquiry agency. Like I said."

Billie leaned back on the settee. "We're going to talk about me, are we? Okay, let's talk about me. I'm here on a missing person case," she said, and paused. "A missing husband. Ironic, isn't it? He went missing in '45."

Jack didn't answer, but removed a blue pack of Gauloises Caporal from the pocket of his suit, tapped a gasper and lit it. "I hear you're going by Ms."

"I am. And you're going by . . . What is it these days, anyway? John Doe, perhaps?"

"I deserve that," he said. He sunk down on the settee, one hand holding his cigarette, and sipped his whisky. Jack and his whisky. She would have to choose another drink from here on.

"Why are you here, Jack?" she asked him. "Be honest with me."

"To see you." He shrugged. "I didn't think I'd see you again."

"You say that as if you couldn't have just written."

There was a long silence. "I couldn't," he admitted with some reluctance.

"Why? What happened in Warsaw?"

Billie had found all the information she could, and every piece had supported the conclusion that her husband had been in the wrong place at the wrong time, his luck finally running out.

"I was almost killed, Billie. I should not even be here," he said, and went silent for a moment. "Warsaw was . . . brutal. Unlike anything I'd seen before. Himmler's orders were that it be completely destroyed and the civilian population exterminated."

As reporters, they'd covered Kristallnacht together, the deadly pogrom against the Jews in Austria in 1938. What they'd witnessed still haunted Billie. It was hard to imagine worse, though she did not doubt him.

"Tell me," Billie said. She wanted to know. She needed to know.

Jack inhaled deeply and let out a plume of smoke that drifted in the air. "The Polish were betrayed. The Brits sent some supply drops, but not enough and many didn't make it through and were dropped in Italy. The Americans sent one. *One*. And the Red Army did nothing to assist. There were mass executions, Billie. Himmler ordered the Nazis to kill Polish civilians," Jack explained. "They went from house to house, the SS and German police, shooting everyone they found and burning the bodies."

The Wola massacre. Billie knew of it.

"I was at the Warsaw Ghetto. The resistance had liberated the Gęsiówka concentration camp, freeing about three hundred and fifty Jews. There was hope there for a moment . . ."

"But what happened to you, Jack? What happened to us?" she pressed. "I'm not going to ask anything of you. Not anymore. But you owe me this, the truth . . . I think you know that, and that's why you're here."

He doubled over and held his head in his hands, seeming to diminish before her eyes. She fought the urge to comfort him. That was not her job. Not anymore. He'd seen to that.

"Yes, you deserve to know," he said.

Oh, here it comes. Out with it, she thought.

"There was a woman." The words came out forced, like they caused him pain.

Billie stood up straight and loosened her suit jacket, barely aware of what she was doing. A *woman*. The way he'd said the words, she was pretty sure she knew what was coming next, had all but concluded it, and now her stomach prepared itself for the inevitable, sinking lower, lower. This was not the first time she'd considered the possibility, but now here it was, the reality before her, whether she wanted to know or not. All of the conflicting emotions she'd felt at his presence vanished in an instant. She felt cold inside. Emptied.

She walked a few steps away, placed her jacket on the back of a chair, smoothed her blouse, and turned and looked at him, standing tall although she felt flattened.

She waited.

"It was unbelievable, Billie. What happened in Warsaw . . . The days as they wore on . . ." he said, stalling. The uprising had been a brutally drawn-out conflict, Billie knew—sixty-three long days of fighting and of waiting for help that never came.

"Tell me," she said simply, and leaned against the wall of her hotel room, just next to the window. The edge of the window frame stuck into her back and she kept herself there, feeling the corner dig into her like a dagger from an invisible foe. She could fight a dagger, or the Austrian and his pistol. But this fight was lost years ago, years before she'd even known she was in it.

"I don't know how much information you have about the uprising, but the Polish underground was encouraged to seize the moment, to rise up against the Nazi occupiers, and the USSR was to have been there for them, to help them rid the place of Germans." Jack had paled and his mouth contorted at the memory. He took another sip of his drink—more of a swig, really—and continued. "It was all planned in the lead-up. The Polish people had hope, real hope, that a coordinated uprising would finally liberate them. They really believed it would happen."

Billie knew some of what had transpired, mostly because of all the searching she'd done for her husband, realizing that his last-known whereabouts were right there, in the thick of the Warsaw conflict that he'd been documenting with his trusty Argus camera.

"Day after day it became clear that the Soviet liberators had no plan to help, and never had. They knew the underground resistance did not want to trade one occupier for another. They wanted Poland back for the Polish people. They wanted their freedom. So, the Soviets led them on—that's how many saw it—and then sat idly by as the Polish people were slaughtered, and I do mean slaughtered, Billie. They let the Nazis take care of their future political opposition for them, let the Nazis murder thousands of people. Those who weren't killed were dragged off to concentration camps, to be thrown into their fires or worked to death."

He had finished his drink. Silently, she refilled it and resumed her place against the window frame. Jack seemed to be almost in a trance, not looking at her, not focusing his eyes on anything really. He was caught fully in his terrifying memories, the ending of which, she knew, would likely break some part of her.

"I had not seen anything like it. Not since Kristallnacht. And yet this was worse. No distinction was made between insurrectionists and civilians, Billie. None at all. The Nazis aimed to exterminate the entire population, every man, woman, and child. Even babies. I was with a few of the underground who escaped, and I was lucky to survive."

"The woman?" she said.

He seemed to steel himself. "Her name was Natasza. She . . . when I first saw her, the Germans were holding her hostage. Billie, she . . . she was tied to a German tank, secured to the front of it by ropes."

A human shield.

"This was days into the Wola massacre. The Nazi tanks, having earlier been halted by heavy resistance fighting, were protected by the bodies of Polish women and children. They were alive, Billie, tied to these tanks. This wasn't war I was covering, I realized, not a battle—this was slaughter, torture. For two days the Nazis had run rampant through the city, raping and murdering at will. Most of those they killed were the elderly, frail and helpless, and women and children. Then as they approached positions where the Home Army still had a hold, they took those they had not already killed and tied them to the front of their tanks."

Billie felt ill.

"That's when I saw her . . . the Germans were using Natasza as a shield so the resistance wouldn't fire on them. Of course, I didn't know her name then. I broke from my position and intervened—it was foolish, I know, but I had no decision to make; I just couldn't do anything else. It was too much to bear. Her screams. But it was very nearly a fatal mistake. I'd exposed myself, and without the Armia Krajowa—the Polish underground—I would have been killed." He brought a shaking hand to his throat. "This is my souvenir. They . . . They . . ." He trailed off. "They tell you in my job not to intervene. I'm supposed to just record it all, document it, but how could I? How could I just stand by?" Tears spilled down his cheeks, and Billie felt her throat tighten.

He'd regretted not intervening at Kristallnacht, but they had been together then, hiding as a crowd beat a Jewish man to death, stomping his body into the street. If he'd run forward he would have died, and she well may have, too. What they'd witnessed had haunted them both ever since.

"I don't remember much after running forward and seizing the ropes that held her," he continued. "I know I was shot, but I don't remember feeling it, or feeling this," he said, and gestured to his throat. "It was my own camera strap, I'm told. I was caught by the throat, and I was dragged. I don't remember. It's all a blank. Natasza was Roma and because I saved her, her family helped me, cared for my wounds. I almost didn't make it."

Jack wiped his wet cheeks, and Billie watched as he became smaller, shrinking into himself. She had not seen him weep like this before, ever.

"Why aren't you saying anything?" he finally blurted, throwing his hands up.

"I just want to listen," she said. "She was Roma. Her family helped you. Go on." Her voice was cold.

"Billie, I'm so sorry. I can't tell you how sorry I am."

"Try."

For some time the hotel room was silent, and an electric vacuum came on somewhere down the hall, surreal in its banality. Billie watched her husband as he stared at a blank section of wall, his eyes unfocused, far away.

"Her family were performers, they all were. It was how she survived, I think. She used to perform in a circus, walking the rope and performing these amazing feats, and when the war came she did work for the underground as a courier. She was so agile that she could hide anywhere, even in the smallest places. Once she was captured and I rushed forward and freed her . . . I . . . From that moment on I was no longer a photojournalist. I put down my camera and joined the fight."

Jack's hand shook as he brought the glass of whisky to his lips and emptied it again. The air itself had become as tense as a tightrope under pressure, the stillness in the hotel room almost suffocating.

"So, you left me for this woman, Natasza," she managed, wanting to hear him say it, confirm it.

"It's not that simple. I had a responsibility. She became . . . with child."

She took a long, jagged breath. "Jesus, Jack."

"It was once, *once*, and it was a mistake. It was a terrible mistake.

I was barely myself, spending weeks on end in their caravan, hiding away, coming in and out of consciousness. Billie, I was close to death. I was grateful to Natasza and my feelings became . . . confused and I . . . we . . . Once I knew the consequences of that moment of weakness, I couldn't just leave her . . . leave them. I made a terrible mistake, and I've had to pay for that these past three years."

"*You* have had to pay?" Billie said, the rage welling up now. "You? I don't think *I* am quite ready to hear how much *you've* had to pay for breaking your vows to me. With respect, Jack, I thought you were dead. I thought your body lay lifeless in some ditch in Warsaw. I . . ." Her mind went back to that terrible corpse in the basement of the Institut Médico-Légal de Paris, thinking it was him, thinking that bloated, decomposing body was actually him. "You know, only a couple of nights ago I thought I might be looking at your corpse at the Paris morgue!" Angry tears were springing from her eyes now as she recalled the horror and sickness she'd felt. "I really thought I was looking at you, Jack. I thought you'd been fished out of the Seine."

"Oh, Billie," he said, and rushed to her side, enveloping her in those arms she had so longed for. There was solace to be found there, or there had been once. Finally, she was in his embrace, and yet nothing was as it should be; everything was wrong.

"Instead you had another family in Poland," she said quietly, and he pulled back.

"It's . . . It's not quite like that," Jack began to explain, but stopped himself, seeing her face twisted with pain. "It doesn't matter."

Doesn't matter?

"I never meant to betray you."

With great restraint, Billie slid away, away from that place in Jack's arms where she had sought comfort so many times before. She felt cold inside. "War is terrible, Jack. It is. But we all have to own what we do with it, what choices we make in the heat of the moment." Her voice had never sounded so icy.

"You must despise me, and I can't blame you," he said, looking wounded, his brow furrowed.

She closed her eyes, deep in thought. Somehow, she did not quite despise him.

"I wronged you, and I've never forgiven myself for it. Billie, I've brought you something. I should have given you this long ago. I am truly so sorry for what I did." He placed an envelope on the table, his eyes lingering on her. Those bright hazel eyes.

Jack.

While she stood against the cold window, feeling sick inside, he walked across the room, away from her, opened the door, and closed it softly behind him.

Jack was gone.

And just like that, her heart was shattered again.

Thirty-one

—∞—

Bang.

Someone was knocking on her hotel room door again.

Bang, bang, bang.

Billie did not want to answer. Only half-aware of what she was doing, still dressed in her blouse and skirt, she had only just co-cooned herself within the white, wrinkled linens of the bed and she wasn't sure she was keen to emerge.

The banging wouldn't stop.

"Billie?"

This wasn't Jack's voice. Jack had been there and then Jack had left. Jack was alive, had another family now, a child with another woman . . .

"Billie, it's Sam. Are you all right in there?"

Billie blinked. She realized again—for she had been in this fugue state for some uncertain length of time—that her fag was burning down and needed ashing. She dispassionately inspected it, noting the red lipstick stains on the end, turned in place where she was sitting, and crushed it in the overflowing ashtray on the bedside table. With a touch of disdain, she looked down at herself, her clothes crumpled and the white sheets twisted around her. Vaguely, she recalled being sick in the lavatory after her husband left, using the mouthwash to gargle, and then splashing her face with water before crawling under the sheets as if they would somehow shield her, just as she had sought comfort within them the night before.

"I'm not decent," she called out for lack of a better excuse. "Wait."

Time blurred, and the knocking resumed.

Bang.

Bang, bang.

"Billie, it's Sam. I'm worried about you. I'm with a porter. We have a key, and I'm coming in."

She opened her eyes. The sun was setting on Paris. She couldn't stay like this. And she couldn't let her assistant—her . . . what? Paris fling?—see her this way. She couldn't allow herself to be this way.

"Wait. Just wait!" she called out.

With a burst of determination, Billie threw off the covers, swung her legs out, and stood, then noted the unacceptable condition of her clothes and frowned. "I'll be just a minute," she called toward the door, hurriedly undressed, leaving her foundation garments on, threw the soft hotel robe around her body, and cinched it at the waist. Billie took several paces toward the door, realized how it might look, and thought again.

She didn't want to make it look to Sam—her assistant—like she'd been in bed with her husband—though of course he didn't know that her visitor was her long-lost husband. Not yet, anyway. What a confusing affair this all was, wanting to show her assistant that she had not been too intimate with her husband. *Forget it. Forget it all.* Billie completed her journey to the door, hauled it open, ushered Sam inside, and shut it behind him, thanking the porter without raising her eyes.

"You mustn't look at me," she said to Sam, covering her eyes with one hand. "I've been sick but I'm okay. Just give me a few minutes to—"

"I've been so worried. I could not raise you and eventually I . . . Why, Billie, you look—"

"*Don't*," she warned him, and disappeared to the lavatory, leaving him to sit on the settee from which her not-dead, long-lost husband had delivered his devastating news.

The reflection in the hotel mirror was not flattering. She took some time to remove the smudged mascara shadowing her bloodshot, red-rimmed eyes, within which her blue-green irises seemed to glow with the almost supernatural clarity of her pain. She splashed her face with cool water and started again. It was a new day. Well, not quite a new day, but it was the start of a new phase for Billie, whether she liked it or not. *The best thing to do is to get yourself together and move on*, she reminded herself under her breath. Her mother had taught her that. Perhaps she hadn't taught her quite well enough.

Darling, he's not coming back, Ella had said, and Billie should have listened. He was never going to come back to her. It was over, had been years ago.

"I think we need to go out, Sam," she said, once she'd emerged from the bathroom and small changing area with its modesty screen. "Tomorrow morning, we move."

Billie walked over to where Sam was sitting, arriving in a cloud of French perfume, a vision of smoky nighttime Parisian glamour in a beaded emerald dress that she'd previously shunned for being too revealing. "I'm terribly sorry about before," she said. "It's been quite a day."

Her eyes were still red, but no one would be examining them too closely, she suspected. Except Sam, perhaps. Billie hadn't been sure what she'd packed the dress for exactly, but now she knew. Everyone needed a dress like this when in Paris. It was where she'd bought it in early 1940, only a few months before the Nazis had goose-stepped their way into the city and changed everything. It was like it belonged here, in free Paris, on her, on a newly free woman.

The occupation was over.

Sam blinked and stood to greet her. His mouth parted, not quite falling open. "You look like . . ."

She raised a brow, daring him to say something about her bloodshot eyes.

". . . a goddess."

Billie smiled. She could still do that, it seemed—smile.

"Who was that, Billie? You seemed distressed. And you were sick?"

"That was my husband," she explained.

He blanched. "Your . . . ?"

"Apparently he is quite alive," she said flatly.

Sam's mouth fell open. "Billie . . . but I thought . . . ?" He tried to get words out but stopped. "Oh, I'm sorry if . . . last night . . . I mean, I didn't know."

"Of course you didn't know. *I* didn't know. How could you have known I was not, in fact, a widow and my husband would come waltzing into my hotel room after total silence for three long years? After all, we thought we might have been looking at his corpse two days ago at the morgue."

"Billie, I don't know what to say."

"Let's go out. I mean it," she said. "I can't be here right now. I really can't. I need to leave this room and get some fresh air. Or a drink. Yes, a drink." She glanced at the near-empty bottle of whisky. "Let's go to the bar, Sam. Please." She took a step toward him. "Please, Sam, take me to the bar. Now."

—m—

"Monsieur, may I have turndown service tonight?" Billie requested at the front desk of the Ritz Paris, and if the clerk there detected the slight desperation in her voice, he did not indicate it. "Better yet, would a full clean be possible? Yes, a clean. We check out tomorrow."

"Of course, mademoiselle. I will arrange it right away," he replied with utmost courtesy, despite the hour. It was already early evening. She'd lost untold hours smoking nearly her full supply of cigarettes and staring at the Paris skyline from her crumpled bed, barely aware of anything beyond the visitor who had just walked out on her.

Now Billie simply could not imagine reentering her hotel room. Not after Jack had been there. And just after being comforted by dear Sam! It figured somehow that Jack bloody Rake had to choose the same day to walk in and declare that he was alive and with someone else now, with his own family, for goddess's sake. Facing the tiniest lingering scent of the man would be too much.

Perhaps she would force Sam into a gaudy night in Pigalle. Even if it was too late to get tickets for the Grand Guignol, they could find their own real-life mayhem and terror if the past day was anything to go on, she thought darkly.

But first a drink.

Billie saw that Sam had questions on his tongue, but as usual he was too polite to voice them.

"I do rather need a drink," she said under her breath, and gestured to Le Grand Bar, saw the crowd, and turned around on the spot. Le Petit Bar was far smaller and more intimate, as the name suggested. She made for the entrance, holding on tightly to Sam, barely seeing through eyes that would not focus as they were led to a free table. Jack's words kept replaying in her ears.

There was a woman . . .

Sam called the waiter over. "The lady needs a drink." He leaned into her. "What do you want? Champagne cocktail?"

She shook her head. "Champagne is for celebrating."

"Madame, the Ritz Paris Champagne Cocktail is most agreeable," the waiter said in flawless, accented English, "but if the lady is looking for something stronger, may I recommend a cocktail I favor, of cognac, Pineau de Charentes, a drop of Grand Marnier . . ."

"*Oui. Merci.*" She nodded for good measure, wondering at his use of the term "madame," considering she was not wearing a wedding ring, and frankly felt she never could bear to consider such a thing, under the circumstances. Not now, not ever.

"And for your husband?" the waiter inquired.

Billie snapped her eyes upward, locking with his, and hoping her expression did not belie her shock and raw hurt. But of course he could not mean Jack, she realized. The barman, maintaining the kind of equanimity all of the staff at the Ritz seemed to possess, added in a conspiratorial voice, "Le Petit Bar is, of course, for ladies only . . . excepting their husbands if they wish." The way he spoke made it clear that they were in good hands. He was not about to move them on.

"Of course," she replied, recovering, and took Sam's right hand in hers. "He would like a planter's punch. Isn't that right, darling?" She gave his large hand a squeeze.

When they were alone again, he turned to her. She was still gripping his hand. "What hap—"

"Not yet, dear Sam," she said, raising a hand.

"Your hand is shaking. You need food. Let's get you a meal. I think we should stay in tonight and you should rest. I'll look after you, Billie. Anything you need. You've had a shock, I can tell."

This whole time he had another woman, another family. This whole

*time, while I searched for word of his whereabouts, stared at that horri-
ble, decayed body in the morgue, he'd already moved on, already decided
our vows meant nothing . . .*

Billie closed her eyes and leaned her heavy head against Sam's
broad chest. It was firm and warm under her cheek, his heart beating
quickly. She could not speak just yet. The whole thing had been a
shock, though she knew she would recover. She always recovered.
Billie might be many things, but she knew herself to be resilient.

Billie had opened the envelope Jack left her. It had contained an
application for a decree of annulment.

He was to argue their marriage was void. As if it had never
happened.

As if she had married him for nothing.

Waited for nothing.

Thirty-two

———∽———

When Billie was just a little girl, no more than six, her father had taken
her to Central Police Station in Sydney. Barry Walker still had many
friends there at the time, former colleagues who were bonded with
him in the way you only could be after facing death together. She
remembered the visit in flashes, vignettes through the eyes of a
child—men's voices, indistinct and low; the heavy herbal scent of
cigarette smoke and cigars; her father's trouser leg as she clung to it,
frightened by this place she didn't know, his hand reassuringly in her
hair, twirling her dark locks with his thick fingers. There was a particular scent that always took her back to that first time. It was her
Lucky Strikes. Her father's brand.

Billie took a drag of her cigarette, inhaled the distinctive scent
before it was whisked away in the breeze. She never liked the idea of
smoking every day, as a habit. But this? Well, this was a smoking day.

Yes, this was definitely a smoking day.

She had spent the morning packing, then taken a taxicab
with Sam to the Hôtel des Arts in Montmartre. The rooms in the
hotel were small, and not at all luxurious like the Ritz, but it was a

necessary change after what had happened at Notre-Dame. Archie was doubtless right—it was not safe. She had much to speak with him about. And she would have to take more precautions now. There would be no more handing out business cards and making herself easy to find—usually that was a necessary part of her trade. In any event, this was closer to where they had been canvassing for Montgomery, and it was possible that being here in the very district where he seemed to have been spotted would make the difference— if the two men they'd spoken to were indeed right about recognizing him, and Billie herself, if her eyes had not deceived her.

She was closing in.

Billie shut her eyes and took a deep breath, filling her lungs with fresh air before returning her cigarette to dangling from her lips. Her eyes hurt. Her stomach ached. She had not eaten breakfast, and now it was past lunchtime. Billie had taken this bracing walk to reorient herself to Montmartre, but most of all, to clear her head. She wasn't sure it was entirely working. Even with all she and Sam had been through, even with Notre-Dame and the assassin sent by Odessa, even with the case she was here for beckoning, she was focused on Jack.

He's alive and you have to try to forget him now.

Forget, Billie. Forget . . .

Another deep breath, and when she finally opened her eyes, Billie could see the world around her again. She had walked up to Sacre-Coeur and was outside the basilica, on the only hill in Paris, at the Panorama de la Butte de Montmartre. This was a peaceful place to witness the city from above, with its slanting white and gray rooftops and cobblestone streets spreading out in all directions. Here you could see for miles on a clear day, all the way to the only higher peak in Paris—the Eiffel Tower, sitting up in the far distance. And two and a half miles away, Notre-Dame.

This hill had been a place of worship since even before the construction of the famous basilica, and perhaps she was drawn not only to its vantage point but to something primordial there, she thought. It was overcast, and looking over the rooftops of Paris, the light seemed soft and somehow pink, a mist clinging to the city, and though it was not early, she fancied that perhaps it was a dawn of sorts, for her. A weight was lifted, even while her empty stomach ached, and her throat felt tight, and that bracing glass of morning whisky seemed not to be enough anesthetic for her circumstances. But a weight was lifted. Was this what freedom felt like? Billie valued freedom, had fought for freedom, but this?

Pull yourself together, Walker.

She was hardly the first woman to discover she had been abandoned. This was her bread and butter, her trade, after all, dealing with wives whose husbands had betrayed or abandoned them, so she knew better than most that she was not unique. What advice would she have for herself, if she walked into B. Walker Private Inquiries asking for help? Well, she'd say to move on. To know her own worth. To do what she needed for survival.

Billie straightened where she stood, the breeze pulling at the collar of her red coat—it was bright, not a good choice for blending in, but also stylish and now the only one with her, her other having finally seen its last case in that drop from Notre-Dame. She walked to the top of the stairs and paused, allowing her gaze to sweep across the uniquely Parisian scene around her—the narrow streets with identical rectangular windows, white shutters open, the seemingly chaotic lines of winding streets. Somewhere down there, Sam was shopping for supplies for them—a good bottle of wine, and some cheese and a baguette. Somewhere down there, the resolution of her case waited.

A pigeon swooped past, Billie following it with her gaze until it was silhouetted against the white sky, and after another breath, Billie Walker again did what her namesake suggested. She put one foot in front of the other, descending from the panoramic view and down white stone stairs, heading back to her new hotel. She had to keep going, no matter Jack, and no matter Odessa.

But first, a drink.

—⁓—

"Another, mademoiselle?"

"*Oui.*"

Billie looked at her watch. She was back at her hotel, had downed not one but two glasses of whisky, but Sam had not yet returned. By the time she finished this next drink he would be there, she thought. They had separate rooms, but he vowed to stay with her if she let him, offering to sleep on the floor. There wasn't much room on the floor, mind you. Not here. She did not like the idea of being coddled, but she had to admit she was still not herself. She didn't know if she wanted solitude or company now. But regardless of how she felt, the Montgomery case wasn't closed, she reminded herself. She had a client and a job to do, and the show had to go on, as performers were so fond of saying.

As Jack's woman, Natasza, probably said.

Her face was still caught in a frown, imagining this woman who had saved her husband's life and taken him from her, when a man suddenly appeared at her table, red-faced and angry. It was so confronting that she reeled back in her seat, the two front legs lifting off the ground. The face was familiar, and had she been sharper, as she usually was, if she hadn't been downing whisky again, like she was trying to forget herself, she'd have spotted him as he entered. As it was, he was only inches from her face.

"Montgomery? Is that you?" she asked, dumbfounded.

The man before her was dressed more casually than in the photographs Billie had seen—a light scarf around his neck, no tie—but his build was the same, the receding hairline only partially hidden now beneath a fedora. The features were the same as in those photographs Vera had given her, only Richard wasn't grinning now.

"Pay your bill. We need to talk alone. In your room. Now," he said gruffly, seeming every bit a man on the edge, veins pulsing in his forehead. "Nothing funny. I have a gun."

Her hand was already moving down her leg, to pull her dress upward and reach for her Colt. Even in this state, her survival instincts had not abandoned her.

Hell. Did it have to be now?

"Both hands on the table," he told her in a low voice, and her pale hand reappeared. He was no military man, no trained assassin. He was new at this. But why? What had made him come at her this way?

"I have a drink coming," she explained, stalling. "Shall I get you one?"

He shook his head.

"You know, Richard, I've been worried about you. I'm only trying to help. No one means you any harm," she said, shifting gears, her own personal concerns pushed aside, and those instincts of hers taking over, if a touch late.

"Up. Now." His voice was menacing and low.

Billie cast her gaze around her, and, spotting a familiar face by the entrance, her spirits lifted a touch. What a mess. She put some francs on the table and stood reluctantly, and the bartender watched her go, saying nothing. She wondered what, if anything, he would think of her walking away. Montgomery was not practiced like Archie, or that silent, terrifying blond man. He was just short of making a scene at the bar. He might not have killed anyone before, she hoped, but reading his body language, she guessed it was possible that he was just unstable enough to do it now.

The walk up the staircase and back to her small room felt like it took forever. Her mind, muddled from a sleepless night and whisky, was sharpening with each step. Yes, Montgomery was in Montmartre, perhaps even living here or close by, her gut told her. Or in any event, that *had* been him she'd seen with Sam, only he'd seen her, too. He'd probably seen her walking as well, that red coat of hers acting like a beacon. She'd found him a little too efficiently, homing right in on his turf. And she'd underestimated just how much this missing person did not want to be found.

The golden rule was simple. Never allow the man with the gun to get you into a private, isolated place. Never. Except he didn't know who he was dealing with.

"You aren't this person, Richard," she said quietly as they approached her room. "Vera loves you, wants the best for—"

"I'm not Richard anymore," he said, his teeth bared. "Open the door."

She inserted her key, hoping perhaps that Sam was already there, armed with a baguette and a fresh bottle he could smash over the man's head. Regrettably he was not. The room was neat and clean, her luggage near the door, not yet unpacked.

Richard . . . made some mistakes, Jane had said.

He was certainly still making them.

"Richard, think about this . . ."

"You don't understand," he spat. "Richard is dead now. I can't go back to Australia. I can't. You shouldn't have come after me. I finally found a life here. Why couldn't you leave me alone? Why did you have to go around asking about me?"

Billie closed the door behind them, leaving it unlatched. Her would-be captor seemed not to notice. "We can come to an arrangement," she said, and raised her hands again, wondering just how desperate he was.

Good goddess, he was crying now, she realized.

"Why did you come here?" he continued. "Why?" His face was round and red, and he wiped his face with his jacket sleeve. "There, stand there," he said, pointing.

He had her against the basin in her room now, and she kept her eye on that gun. Did he even have it cocked? With a sinking feeling she noticed that he did. And his finger was dangerously close to the trigger, the gun jerking as he spoke.

"I thought you might be dead," she said honestly, in a calm, soft voice. Blackmail was a dirty game. He was clearly in deeper than she'd thought.

She had thought she'd given enough francs away to get a tip-off about him, not to get sold out. But he must have seen her. That was the answer. She'd gotten too close, and underestimated how desperately he wanted not to be found. They should have stayed away, in another part of town. They'd caught his trail, had been close, but she just hadn't been sure enough about it, had been distracted.

"That's true in a way. There's no more Richard," he said, that trigger hand shaking. "They'll kill me if you drag me back there. They'll kill me."

"In Sydney? Who will kill you?" she asked. "The people you were blackmailing?"

She thought of the letter his wife had received: *WE'LL FIND HIM*. That was no letter of support; it had been a threat, though not one Vera had understood.

In response, tears strayed from his eyes, his hands shaking, gun wavering. It was all the response she needed. "You are okay. No one is going to drag you back. We can solve this together," she assured him. "Whatever you want your name to be, tell me. What do you want me to call you?" He did not answer. "I'm a resourceful woman," she continued. "You have no idea how resourceful. I can do something to release Vera for you, set up what we need so she can move on, and then no one will come looking for you. You don't have to go back. You don't need to speak to anyone from your past. Whoever you're running from in Australia, they won't track you down. You'll be free. I know what that means—how important it is."

As the words left her lips, she realized they were true.

Freedom.

"How?" Montgomery demanded. "They are powerful people. How can *you* do *that?*"

"Trust me. I can do it," she said, stalling, her hands still raised, the basin of her room pressed into the small of her back. Organized crime. That's who he was running from. He'd finally picked the wrong target. *Oh, Richard. You fool. You fool . . .*

She watched him as she sank down, lower and lower. The cold, hard basin moved up to her neck, her head, as she bent at the knees, squatting down in place.

The blast of the pistol filled the small room with such violence that Billie clapped her hands over her ears.

Montgomery dropped with a thud.

In seconds, Billie was on her knees beside him, bent over him and checking his pulse. "Montgomery, you fool, you damn fool," she told him. "He's breathing, thank goddess." He'd been shot in the shoulder. "It's nice of you to join us, Lieutenant Harrison," Billie said evenly, looking up at the figure in the doorway.

Archie Harrison had already kicked Montgomery's gun away, making sure it was out of reach. "You know this chap?" he said with surprise. "I thought he was trying to kill you. I thought it was another man sent by Odessa."

"Well, you were half-right. I do know this man, Archie, but he's not with the Nazis," Billie explained. "Though right now I can't say there's much more to recommend him. This is the man I've been trying to track down for his wife. It seems he's been on the run, and we got too close for comfort. He needs a doctor, quickly. You missed his heart, thank goddess."

"I told you I'd be looking out for you. I was glad you heeded my advice about moving."

"And look how well that's turned out," she said, pulling open Montgomery's jacket and undoing his shirt. She pulled a white pillowcase from the neatly made bed while Archie watched, and she pressed the balled-up fabric to Montgomery's wound, stanching the blood. He moaned. "Quickly now. He'll bleed out if we're not careful," Billie said.

Just then there was a knock at the door, four knocks to be precise. One with a pause, two in quick succession, then one more after the pause. Why would Sam knock in that pattern? It was not one of their codes.

Archie, however, crossed the room swiftly to open the door with the air of someone who knew exactly what that knock meant, and Billie realized he must be expecting one of his colleagues. She could not have been more surprised by the person he let in.

Jack.

Her Jack.

There really did not exist enough whisky in all of Paris to deal with this past forty-eight hours, she decided.

"Tom," Archie said to him.

"Archie," he said back.

"This man needs a doctor, right away. He's not . . . who I thought he was."

"*Tom?*" Billie said, astonished. "Tom? You've got to be kidding me."

"I guess you know my man in Paris," Archie said. "Tom . . . Jack mentioned you, uh, might have once known each other."

"I told you I couldn't explain about my work, exactly," Jack chimed in quickly, looking apologetic. "I'll get them to call for an ambulance, right away," he told his colleague, and disappeared again.

"*That* is your man in Paris? Well, yes, I know him, or I thought I did, once."

Richard Montgomery was still on the floor, now gaping at the exchange, looking from Billie to Archie and then back again. He appeared deeply confused.

"Shut up," Billie told him, though he hadn't said a word. "And try not to die on us, will you?" She pressed down to slow the bleeding and he groaned. "Can you get a towel?" she said to Archie. "This isn't thick enough. Lavatory is down the hall, I think."

"Of course," Archie said, watching her. "You really care about saving this man, even though he tried to kill you?"

"Is that what you were trying to do, you fool?" Billie said to Montgomery, shaking her head. "Your wife just wants a damn divorce. You men drive me round the bend; you really do."

Flinching, but without comment, Archie disappeared to find a towel, as requested.

—⁂—

Some time later, Billie watched as Montgomery was hauled away on a stretcher by an ambulance crew, now conscious enough to be muttering to himself. The hallway outside her room was filled with men now—Archie was there, and dear Sam holding a long baguette and that bottle of wine she'd asked for. Even the bartender was there, craning his neck to see what the commotion was about.

And Jack.

Jack Rake was there.

"I'll see you downstairs when you're ready, Tom," Archie said to him. He walked away, ushering the curious observers from the doorway of her room, including Sam, who appeared stricken as he looked back at her. "Let's give them a moment, shall we?" Archie suggested, pulling him away by the arm.

The door shut, and Billie and Jack were alone in the small hotel room now, Billie stained with blood and still holding the pillow slip in one hand. She threw it on the ground, near the small pool of blood by the basin. After that shot, the police would not be far behind.

"Billie, I'm sorry I couldn't tell you."

"Intelligence work, hmm. It figures."

"I couldn't tell you. I got involved after . . . well, after Natasza—"

"Yes, I can guess," she shot back, cutting him off. It figured for him. He was too passionate and political to simply take photographs. She'd known he was eventually going to put down his camera and get involved. Now he had—first with the Polish resistance and now with whatever it was exactly that he did for Archie. She'd only hoped that when the time came they would do it together. They'd been a team, she thought. A team. Billie turned to the basin, all business, and washed her hands. Her heart ached, dammit. It ached. She might vomit when the adrenaline finally subsided, but for now she washed her hands with her soap, the Savon de Marseille she had unpacked, the familiar scent calming her, and after a moment she found that almost eerie calm she possessed in emergencies, that practiced and steady focus.

Steady, Walker.

Billie turned, hands clean of the blood of her client's husband. She knew how many fresh bullets were in her cracked Colt, still strapped to her thigh; she knew the placement of every exit in the hotel, every possible weapon within arm's reach. Danger had been unavoidable, ever since Jack had walked into her life all those years ago in Paris. But the emergency had passed here. And the damage to her heart was already done.

"Tom, though?" Billie finally said, coolly, feeling more herself again. "I suppose you look like you could be a Tom."

"Tom Bell," Jack replied, looking mildly ashamed. He took a half step forward, in those oddly new, shiny shoes. "It has been necessary to take on another—"

"Identity. Of course," she said, as if it didn't matter. *Intelligence work.* Who knew how many identities her husband kept?

"Billie . . . at Notre-Dame . . . That was serious. I almost thought I'd lost you."

"Doesn't feel good, does it?" she shot back.

"No," he admitted, and bit his lip.

"You were there, were you?"

Jack, or Tom, shook his head. "Not at first, but I heard. I kicked myself for not sticking closer."

"Well," she said, at a loss for words. He really had been following her. She'd seen him outside the morgue, too, across the Seine. She hadn't been imagining it.

"You found your target," he said of Montgomery, though in truth her target had found her. That was a first. And she hoped it would be the only time. She'd let the shock of Jack's reappearance send her down the rabbit hole. Her father had always warned her not to drink alone. It was a slippery slope for private inquiry agents.

"I suppose you will fly back now?" he said.

"Soon, I imagine," Billie replied. "My client will be . . . Well, she'll be pleased perhaps. It's hard to say what she'll make of it all. Montgomery made a real mess of things here, though, and it may take a while to untangle him from the police, when they get here."

"Archie will be taking care of them now, I imagine."

Billie raised a brow. "I'd like to know how he does that."

The room was quiet for a moment. Billie had found both missing husbands she was searching for, all at once and not at all as she'd hoped. "Well, I guess you can go back to your work and your family now. I'll be gone from Paris, and you won't have to worry about me anymore."

He looked down at his shoes.

"Not quite. I didn't tell you. She . . . she didn't make it. She died in childbirth," he said in a tight voice, a tear straying from the inside corner of his right eye. Billie felt the revelation like a stab in her heart. "They both did," he added. "After that, well, you can imagine. Archie found me in Poland. We grew up together, did I tell you?"

She didn't know what to say.

"I did the wrong thing by you, Billie. Don't think I don't know that. I know. I do know . . ." He clenched his fists, unclenched them again. "I was ashamed of what I'd done to you. Too ashamed to face you. I just couldn't . . . I couldn't face living for a while there." His head shook, his eyes filled with dark memories. That new heaviness about him, the weight on him made sense now. It was grief.

"But now you are free," he said.

"And so are you," she replied, though in reality he always had been. Whether because of him, or the fates, he had never been hers. Not really. What they'd had was a dream of something that did not come to pass. It was a brief moment of joy in a terrible war. Had it been worth it? Perhaps. Perhaps every moment of joy was worth it.

"I have always loved you," Jack said. "That never stopped."

Billie closed her eyes. *I have always loved you.* There were so many things she wanted to say to that, so many ways to respond, but there was no sense in saying any of it now. It was too late.

"You know where to find me, Jack," Billie said simply. "Or Tom. Or whoever you'll be next. But then you always knew that. Be well."

With all the strength inside her, Billie held her head high and willed her feet to move, to walk to the hotel door and open it for her estranged husband, so he could leave her one last time on that surreal day in Paris.

—⁓—

Billie made her way down to the lobby of the Hôtel des Arts, where she found Lieutenant Archie Harrison waiting for her with Sam, both of them watching her anxiously.

"Are you all right?" Archie asked.

"Thank you. I am, I think. It's hardly my first rodeo."

At this, he laughed. "Yes, you are everything Hank said you'd be."

"I suppose you know Jack, uh, Tom was . . . well, he was my husband, once."

He looked down. "I'm terribly sorry to have brought him into this. I knew you two had some kind of history, but I didn't know that. Our man keeps his cards close to his chest."

She sighed. How true that was. Even when they'd married there had been few witnesses, no rings. Simone had not been sure about it, and Archie hadn't either. It was almost as if it never happened—except for the pain in her heart.

"I suppose that's why he's been looking out for you," Archie added. "He took a special interest when I mentioned you."

Had he? Had he been looking out for her?

"And you? Why have you been looking out for me?" she asked.

"I already told you. For Hank, of course." He laughed to himself. "I rather see his interest."

"His interest, eh? Did Hank know?" she asked. "About . . . Jack? My connection to Tom?"

"I had no reason to mention him. Tom . . . um, Jack and I knew each other before, when we were boys growing up in Sutton, and when our men spotted him in Poland with the underground there, I knew we had to get him out. He was in terrible shape, Billie. Terrible shape. Shell shock of some kind . . ." he said. "I've seen it before, but he was a bad case. He came back here to Paris eventually and started to work for us."

The Brits sticking together. Billie was glad someone had been there for Jack, even with everything he had done to betray her.

"I'm frightfully sorry Paris was not kinder to you, Billie. It can be a splendid town, though I suppose you know that already. I hope this won't be the last we see of you over here. You'd make a fine agent, and you could use the resources we can offer. I suppose you know that.

"Do say hello to Hank for me. You have my number, Billie," he added. "I do hope you'll use it one day."

Thirty-three

—◊—

He always did like his little adventures, I suppose," Vera Montgomery said, her perfectly painted fuchsia lips pulled into a frown.

"Indeed."

Billie sat with her legs crossed at her father's old, battered office desk, allowing her glamourous client to compose herself.

Vera had taken the news well—the best Billie had seen, in fact—but then, she'd had some time to get used to the revelations. After Richard's arrest in Paris for assaulting Billie, his wife had been informed of his whereabouts and at least some of what her errant husband had been up to. Once the police were done with him, he would doubtless stay in Europe, perhaps even heading back to England, where his papers were at least legitimate. But Billie and Sam had arrived home to find a letter from his mother waiting, disowning her "sinful" son in no uncertain terms, so he was unlikely to find refuge with her. In any event, Richard Montgomery was not about to come waltzing back into Vera's life, nor Billie's for that matter, not with some of Sydney's underworld having him on their hit list.

It seemed Richard had finally picked the wrong target and had taken his chance to flee Australia and find a new life—not that Billie knew exactly which underworld-connected man he had blackmailed. Some secrets one was best *not* knowing, but Billie knew one thing was for certain: Blackmail did tend to catch up with a person eventually. He was lucky not to have been found at the bottom of Sydney Harbor.

"I really never imagined it would be dangerous . . ." Vera said of the trip.

They never do, Billie thought. "Think nothing of it. It comes with the work," she assured her.

"Well," Vera said, impressed, and took a deep, steadying breath. "I knew you were the man for the job."

Billie reserved comment on how much of a man she was, and stood up, the two women shaking hands at the end of their meeting. She opened the communicating door for her client, smoothly letting her out of her office.

Samuel Baker and Shyla Davis were waiting on the other side. To her surprise, Sam gestured to a man who was seated in one of the walnut chairs in the waiting room, obviously having arrived while Billie was busy with Vera. Handsome, dark-haired, and about thirty-five, he wore a nicely cut suit and held a fedora in his hands. He beamed at Billie as if she should know him, though she didn't recognize his face.

"Ms. Walker, I'd like you to meet my fiancé, Mr. Pearson," Vera announced proudly.

"Well, it certainly is a pleasure to meet you. Congratulations to you both." Vera wouldn't be a Montgomery for much longer, now that her divorce could go through. That seemed rather for the best.

With her first husband facing time in Paris for assault and having apparently agreed to split the proceeds of the sale of the Potts Point house with his wife—perhaps out of a sense of guilt or hopefully a sense of fairness, and in return for their silence in Sydney circles about his whereabouts—Vera was now clearly wasting no time in using her newfound freedom to move on. Billie was almost impressed by her speed. She was already packing up the Potts Point house. It would sell swiftly, Billie felt sure; she only hoped Vera never left her financial matters to anyone else again—insomuch as any married woman had the option. Perhaps this man would let her be her own woman, and there was happiness for her yet.

Mr. Pearson stood up and stepped forward to shake Billie's hand. "Thank you for what you did."

"It's our job. Best of luck to you both," Billie said, and came to stand next to her assistant and her latest agent. Together they watched the pair walk down the hallway of the sixth floor of Daking House, arm in arm, clearly enamored, Vera's now-burgeoning belly leading the way to the lift—and to their future as a family. Sam clicked shut the door of B. Walker Private Inquiries behind them.

"Well. A happy customer," Billie said.

"And how about the inquiry agent? How is she feeling?" Sam asked gently.

Billie turned to beautiful Sam, giving him an affectionate look, and she thought on that. How was she feeling? Billie did have some things to be pleased about. Their latest job had indeed brought in a pretty penny, and now that she was back in town, she'd finally convinced Shyla to take on a more official role. (She was already "in up to her elbows," as she described it.) B. Walker Private Inquiries was expanding. And with Cooper having linked documents in Vincenzo Moretti's possession to the local Odessa network, the rival PI wasn't likely to be much trouble for Billie. Not for a while, anyway.

"You take the rest of the day off, dear Sam. You've gone above and beyond. Shyla, let's reconvene on Monday, shall we? And as for this particular agent?" Billie said, a wistful smile on her face. "Well, she feels like a drive, I think. A good, long, fast drive with the top down."

"Where are you going?" Shyla asked as she slid on her new gloves and picked up her handbag.

Billie took a deep breath. "I guess I'll find out."

ACKNOWLEDGMENTS

———∞———

The Ghosts of Paris is dedicated to my late mother, Janni Moss. At age four, at the end of WW2, she traveled across the seas with her parents, Teunis and Cornelia (my opa and oma, to whom *The War Widow* was dedicated), and her older brothers, Otto and Arie, and infant sister, Willie, their homeland in the Netherlands devastated. I grew up with stories of my opa's brave escape, and sabotaging bombs in the munitions factory in Berlin where he was forced into slave labor when Holland was occupied. There were painful experiences there, back in Europe, and Canada offered a better life. As the story goes, the ship leaving for Canada departed one day before the ship to Australia (it may have been longer, in reality), and so they eventually settled in my hometown of Victoria, BC. But for the sailing schedules, I may have been Australian born, one could say.

PI Billie Walker was born from a mix of real life and fantasy, of these family stories, my fascination with the 1940s and women's postwar history, my love of great noir and hardboiled fiction of the period, and the great women of the time—pioneers like Lee Miller,

ACKNOWLEDGMENTS

Virginia Hall, Nancy Wake, Josephine Baker, Clare Hollingworth, and more. This is a period of great impact on my family, and countless others, and is still in living memory of a fading few. I wish I had asked so many more questions while I still could.

It must be emphasized that no place in the world—including France—was a safe haven for LGBTQI people in 1947 (nor indeed today), but with the French Revolution, France did decriminalize homosexuality between consenting adults. That was in 1791. To understand the significance of this, many Western countries decriminalized same-sex sexual acts far later: Italy in 1890, Denmark in 1933, the United Kingdom in 1982, and the United States in 2003. As mentioned in this novel, Australia still had sodomy laws in place in the 1940s. Between 1975 and 1997, Australian states and territories finally repealed anti-homosexuality laws that dated back to the days of the British Empire and caused untold damage and lost or altered lives. These changes in legislation were far too late for the characters in this novel.

The characters in this book are fictional, though many are inspired by true accounts of real people from the period. And the places are all too real. For example, Ravensbrück concentration camp, which is mentioned multiple times, was a real place where an estimated 132,000 women and children were incarcerated under extreme conditions, including famine, slave labor, inhumane medical experimentation, and sterilizations performed without consent. Very few survived. As a disability advocate with CRPS (Complex Regional Pain Syndrome), I have peopled my novel with disabled veterans and other characters for the simple reason that they did, and do, exist. Disability—both visible and invisible—is present as a human experience, and always has been, and with recent events this is perhaps more important to face than ever.

ACKNOWLEDGMENTS

Telling these stories is a great privilege. My sincere thanks go to Lindsey Rose and the team at Dutton, and Jennifer Lambert and Harper Canada for their support for Billie Walker and my work, and Anna Valdinger and the team at HarperCollins Publishers Australia for twenty-three years of support through several genres since my first novel was published with them in 1999. Thanks also to the wonderful Chris Bucci at Aevitas in New York, Paige Sisley and the team at CookeMcDermid Literary Agency and Cooke International in Toronto, and Selwa Anthony in Sydney.

Thank you to Professor Dennis Altman for his invaluable feedback on the LGBTQI storylines in this novel; Melanie Seward, a descendant of the Bigambul and Wakka Wakka peoples, and Larissa Behrendt, professor of Indigenous research and director of research at the Jumbunna Institute for Indigenous Education and Research at the University of Technology Sydney (who launched the first Billie Walker tale, *The War Widow*, in Sydney), who both provided me with valuable insights into the history of Aboriginal women's experiences in Australia for this series; friend Chrys Stevenson for the research, Gretchen "Gertie" Hirsch for the launch in the US, and fashion historian Hilary Davidson for the hats and hair. Thanks also to Joël Clergiot and Miles Larbey for the French, and Tara June Winch for the Wiradjuri; Daking House YHA for access to Daking House and their historical and architectural plans; Joe Abboud for information about the historical block of flats I have renamed Cliffside for the purposes of this book; and Bob Waddilove for his hands-on knowledge of the Willys 77 roadster.

Thank you to my family for their love and support—most of all, Berndt and Sapphira, Jackie and Wayne, Annelies, Dad and Lou, Nik and Dorothy, and my dear friends who have been there through thick and thin, especially Auntie Linda (Miss J), Sharelyn, Kane,

Erica, and Martin. (Ugh, I miss you.) Thank you, Neil and Ellie, Amber, Charlayne, Janie, Claire, and Dawn. To my coven of girl-friends, you are amazing.

Here's to the thousands of brave rebellions of everyday people, and the healing of ancestral wounds.

ABOUT THE AUTHOR

A dual Canadian/Australian citizen, Tara Moss is the bestselling author of twelve books of fiction and nonfiction, published in nineteen countries and in thirteen languages. She is a journalist, doctoral candidate at the University of Sydney, public speaker, and outspoken advocate for children's rights and women's rights. She has earned her private investigator credentials from the Australian Security Academy and is UNICEF Australia's National Ambassador for Child Survival. In 2015 she received an Edna Ryan Award for making a feminist difference, inciting others to challenge the status quo.

Tara, with her husband and daughter, divides her time between New South Wales and Vancouver.

Visit her at taramoss.com.